Acclaim

"*Forsaken Oath*...is inform
and few can portray it better than V.S. Kemanis. Highly recommended.
— *San Francisco Review of Books*

"Besides being a well-written novel with interesting characters and strong narrative impetus, [*Homicide Chart*] is a law buff's delight, with intelligent discussions of unusual legal situations and excellent courtroom combat. Kemanis is an excellent writer." — *Mystery Scene Magazine*

"Riveting reading... V.S. Kemanis's compelling legal thriller *Deep Zero* distinguishes itself with its powerful blend of vivid writing, legal expertise and insight, and finely and compassionately drawn characters." — *Foreword Reviews*

Thursday's List is "engaging and thought-provoking... Well written, with a plot that...will keep you captivated..." — *The Kindle Book Review*

"Kemanis writes in a precise prose that elucidates the stakes of the cases while delving into the interior lives of her characters... [*Seven Shadows* is] a finely crafted legal thriller." — *Kirkus Reviews*

"*Power Blind* has everything a legal mystery should have: characters you care about, ethical conundrums, ripped-from-the-headlines legal issues, a compelling subplot, page-turning excitement, and an author who clearly knows her way around a courtroom... [A] well-crafted and timely novel." — *USA Today* and *WSJ* bestselling author Amy M. Reade

Homicide Chart is "a page-turner, expertly written and well crafted, deftly plotted with characters that portray real, human emotions... Kemanis is a writer of high caliber worth noting, and this is a novel well worth reading." — *The U.S. Review of Books*

Forsaken Oath "really shines. A powerful book..." — *Mystery Sequels*

Power Blind is "an engaging read, with plot twist after plot twist that will keep readers guessing... Cinematic in nature, the novel's complex plot lines will remind readers of some of television's greatest legal dramas."
— *The U.S. Review of Books*

In *Thursday's List*, "Kemanis draws on her experience as a prosecutor at the county and state levels and brings her personal knowledge of the investigation process into the story. Her overall attention to detail makes the work a true page-turner." — *Kirkus Reviews*

In *Seven Shadows,* "tension mounts and leads to a climactic confrontation that is surprisingly different from what one might expect. Kemanis has created an engaging plot on which to build her narrative—one chock full of technical legal expertise. Yet it is the emotional tributaries that flow from that plot that give this story a greater sense of literary weight." — *The U.S. Review of Books*

"In *Homicide Chart,* V.S. Kemanis weaves three separate plot lines into a compelling tale. Her characters are well defined, very authentic, painted with a deft hand. This is Ms. Kemanis' real talent. She makes us care for the characters." — *Online Book Club*

Forsaken Oath is "clever, immersive... Kemanis, a talented weaver of scene and exposition, keeps the reader engaged with each new twist and bit of evidence." — *Kirkus Reviews*

Power Blind "is a family saga, mystery, and legal tale all rolled into one... The author did a fantastic job drawing me into the story through compelling observations, descriptions, and dialogue... Frankly, there is a lot to like in this one." — *San Francisco Book Review*

"Kemanis writes in a style that adeptly dramatizes legal arguments while also finding moments of stark lyricism... [*Deep Zero*] is a well-drawn legal thriller." — *Kirkus Reviews*

In *Deep Zero,* Kemanis "vividly portrays the difficulties of balancing the intricacies of the practice of law with the intimacies of the practice of parenthood. Her principal players seem particularly real... This is a confident author as at home with courtrooms, legal briefs, and summary judgments as she is with bedrooms, term papers, and adolescent anxiety." — *The U.S. Review of Books*

"*Forsaken Oath* is a terrific legal thriller, written by a prosecutor who knows her way around the legal trenches. Kemanis's expertise brings wonderful authenticity to a twisting plot." — Allison Leotta, author of *The Last Good Girl*

Also by V.S. Kemanis

Dana Hargrove Legal Mysteries

Thursday's List
Homicide Chart
Forsaken Oath
Deep Zero
Seven Shadows

Story Collections

Dust of the Universe, tales of family
Everyone But Us, tales of women
Malocclusion, tales of misdemeanor
Love and Crime: Stories
Your Pick: Selected Stories

Anthology Contributor

The Crooked Road, Volume 3
The Best Laid Plans
Me Too Short Stories
Autumn Noir

Visit
www.vskemanis.com

Power Blind

a Dana Hargrove legal mystery

V.S. KEMANIS

Cover art by Roy Migabon
Paperback cover design by Valdas Miskinis

ISBN-13: 978-1-7378479-0-8
ISBN-10: 1737847906

Opus Nine Books
• New York •

"Writing laws is easy; governing is difficult."
— Leo Tolstoy, *War and Peace*

CONTENTS

	Calculus	1
1	Appeals	12
2	Tough	29
3	Weekend	42
4	Cold	53
5	Ides	68
6	Clues	87
7	Lockdown	106
8	Thesis	120
9	Threads	141
10	Blameless?	159
11	Security	179
12	Minor	185
13	Investigation	196
14	Recordings	212
15	Power Blind	219
16	Heart	228
17	Brothers	235
18	Link	251
19	Pursuit	258
20	Motives	278
	Life	301
	Dear Reader	309
	For Law Buffs	311

CALCULUS

Monday, January 3, 2022

LET HER SLEEP. Peaceful, dreamless, deep. No fear, no pain.

That's the hope, but Bianca has her doubts. Fever can arouse hallucinations, induce terrors.

Checking on her niece from the open doorway, Bianca detects signs of distress. Wet strands of black hair tangle in a gothic pattern against the sallow skin of Josefina's face. Her skeletal frame, ravaged by weight loss, still possesses a fierce determination to resist confinement. Her legs are kicked free of the down comforter strangling her torso in a twisted mass of happy colors—hot pink and aquamarine. Atop that cheerfulness, a single spindly arm clutches Monito tight to her chest. The sock monkey's soft head is clamped under her chin. In this intimate embrace, Bianca sees Josefina's desperate grasp on life.

Two months ago, after the diagnosis, Josie reverted to these childhood behaviors. The bedroom door must remain open at night, offering an illusory escape from the body that imprisons her. She rescued Monito from the top shelf of her closet to resume his role as her nighttime companion. The homemade toy's red grin is a comfort, a reminder of her mother's handiwork and the happy times they shared before everything went bad. Six years on, the acute pain of losing her mother has dulled, replaced by Josie's own physical suffering. Now she needs her mother in a new way, as a daily reference point and spiritual presence to be consulted and honored. Monito helps.

Should Bianca go to the bed, towel off Josie's sweat, and readjust the comforter? She decides against it and turns away from the door, trusting in the healing power of sleep. Josie has taken all prescribed medications for her symptoms, and there's nothing to be done about a cure, except to let the body do its own best work. God has equipped His children with a miraculous immune system, the ability to self-heal. Josie *will* be cured if it's part of His plan. She's a valiant fighter, her daily battles often rewarded with good days after the bad. But if the tables are turned and the fight is lost? To dwell on that thought is to embrace it, something Bianca won't allow.

I love you so much, *mija*.

Bianca takes a few steps down the hall to her square box of a kitchen where she pours a cup of coffee, picks up her aging cell phone, and sits at the dinette. 10:43 AM on the digital display. She'll give Josie at least another hour of sleep. Their appointment is for two o'clock.

Thankfully, Bianca's employment contract provides family leave so she can care for her niece. She hasn't been to work now for a month and misses the maternity ward, the challenge and delight of guiding new mothers in caring for their infants. But she'll be back when Josie is better, and with good luck, it will be before her paid leave runs out.

Positive thought and faith have long been Bianca's guiding lights, carrying her through trying times. The pandemic. Long hours, reassignment to the Covid ward, exhaustion. Yet she never caught that plague. Even worse, six years ago: the heartrending ordeal. She refused to succumb to despair and helplessness. Who can deny the healing power of love? The sisters, Bianca and Dolores, felt its unspoken benefits. Not a cure, but a supreme comfort, an analgesic to soften the acute edges of pain, emotional and physical. Before the end, Dolores gave Bianca the greatest gift of all: guardianship of her daughter. Bianca later adopted Josefina, then a girl of eleven.

A woman of weaker character might wallow in the unfairness of being tested a second time. First, her younger sister. Now, her much too young niece. Dolores was only twenty-nine when she died of ovarian cancer. A rare disease for someone so young—and why? The senselessness nearly extinguished Bianca's faith, but her relationship with Josie restored it. They grieved together and grew closer. The girl amazed Bianca with her intuitive understanding and love of the world. A truly exceptional child, intelligent, mature, and compassionate. A scholar in math, with aspirations to attend a top university.

Josie has the drive and the smarts to accomplish what her mother could not. Dolores, pregnant at eighteen, was abandoned by the child's father, never went to college, and struggled to support them with hourly-wage service jobs. The sisters teamed up, sharing childcare responsibilities. Bianca finished her degree in nursing and built a career as a postnatal care specialist. Spent all her free hours with her sister and niece, no time for men or her own nuclear family. No regrets. The full package is meant for the next generation. Josie will have it all, a college degree, career, *and* family.

Just one thing first. They will have to get through *this*.

At the start of Josie's senior year in high school, she developed a "cold." Oddly, the strong, energetic teen couldn't seem to shake the symptoms. Swollen glands, malaise, fatigue, fevers, lack of appetite, sudden weight loss, and before long, Josefina and Bianca were reeling from a shocking diagnosis: Hodgkin's lymphoma.

Brutally unfair, but they don't have time to cast blame. This is a test, a battle to be fought and won, trusting in the reward to come. Bianca is committed to the fight and supports Josie's plan for handling it. They've carefully considered and weighed the options. Three oncologists, three opinions about chemotherapy, all the same, or nearly the same with slight numerical variations. On Josie's stronger days, they discuss it endlessly.

"I'm not a percentage," Josie says, "or a probability. These abstractions have nothing to do with me. The doctors like to talk this way because it always makes them right."

"How can they always be right?"

"It's like the weather report. Ten percent chance of rain. If it rains, the weatherman is right. If it doesn't rain, he's also right. Even *more* right because it proves the ninety-percent chance of clear skies."

"*Mija*, I've never thought of it that way." But Bianca's heart stalls on the words "ninety percent," bringing to mind a number attached to a certain prognosis if Josie does nothing.

"It's probability theory, Auntie."

"I see what you mean. You're not a probable person. You're a real person." Josie smiles at that, showing a real person's beautiful smile, lifting the sunken cheeks, lips stretched over large, bright teeth. Bianca wants to believe that the numbers mean hope. "What about the chances it will work? Sixty percent. One doctor even said seventy-five."

"They're talking about data from big groups of people. Numbers on paper. I love numbers, I play with numbers, I think about numbers all the time, but they aren't me. They don't say what *I* will go through before anyone knows if I'm in the sixty or forty. Either way, the doctors are always right, you see. They're right, even if you die after going through...all *that!*" She breaks down, tears and mucus streaming, emotion clouding her intellectual pleasure in mathematical theory.

Bianca doesn't try to talk her out of the emotion. Its truth is rooted in fact, experience, physical pain. Josie's emotion strengthens her decision. Who can blame her? No one would want the girl to suffer the way her mother suffered from the chemo. It was unforgiving. Savage. Merciless. Dolores experienced unbearable pain. Incapacitating nausea and weakness, hair loss, swelling and tenderness in odd places. Yellow skin and dizziness. Bianca helped her sister as best she could with warmth, prayer, and touch. Presence. Words of support, the analgesia of love. Still, Dolores suffered immeasurably from a treatment that ultimately didn't work.

Bianca tried to protect Josie from the worst of it, but the girl knew. She beat on every closed door, demanded entry, and ran to her mother's side. She saw everything, felt the pain viscerally, cried out from her soul. No wonder Josie doesn't want that for herself. Possibly, as Bianca recalls, Dolores was given lower odds than her daughter, but either way, as Josie says, the doctors are "right" whether she ends up in the sixty percent or the forty percent or whatever other number they come up with. Her place on the doctors' graph won't be known until she's been made to suffer.

Torture with no guarantee. They won't allow it. Bianca respects Josie's wishes, to fight the disease with her inner strength and spiritual guidance. They've told all the doctors "no" but promised to give it more thought, and they have, but the answer is still "no."

Today they will see the doctor they'll be keeping. Financial need dictates their choice of Dr. Jeremy Stanz, who has admitting privileges at the hospital where Bianca works and belongs to the network in her insurance plan. He comes with an impressive CV and seems to listen and care. Two or three times already, they've heard his gently persistent case for chemotherapy, and they've responded with their questions and their story and their resistance. The sessions always end with his kindly nod and warm smile of acceptance. Josie has agreed to take the medications he recommends for her symptoms, any palliatives he prescribes. But chemo? A poison meant to sicken her, to kill half the healthy cells in her body on the slender hope of killing all the diseased ones as well. No. They've done what he asked and have given it more careful thought, and today, at two o'clock, they will deliver their final verdict. Again.

At a minute to eleven, Bianca takes the final lukewarm sip of coffee and gazes blankly into the distance, her mind wandering. Inside her fog, she remains on call, always alert to any sign, any summons, like the shuffling of feet in the hallway and a word at the door. "Auntie."

Hot pink and aquamarine assault Bianca's eyes. Josie seems bigger than herself, wrapped inside that puffy, brightly colored comforter. She jumps up and puts an arm around Josie's shoulder. "Come and sit." She guides her to a chair, and they take opposite sides of the tiny table. "How do you feel?"

"Incredible!" Does she mean it? Her posture slumps into the frailty hidden under the covering, but her eyes shine with life. "I just finished that calculus problem."

"Just now?"

"Yes!"

Only two days after the new year, when other kids lament the end of the holiday break, Josie thrills at the prospect of tackling calculus! Schoolwork is a welcome distraction from her illness, a vital connection to her life's ambition. Having missed so many days of school, with more to come, Josie seizes every clear-headed moment in every good day to keep on track for graduation.

"And guess what?" The shine grows brighter.

"I can't guess."

"The answer was in my head when I woke up! I was dreaming it!"

"Well, wonders never cease." No nightmares, hallucinations, or terrors. The fever, the sweat, the tussle with bedclothes: all that energy was directed into the solving of a calculus problem. An indication that the girl is healing.

At two thirty, Bianca pulls out her cell phone and scrolls through *People* magazine online to pass the time until Josie emerges from the examining room. Looking for fantasy or escape, Bianca sees only absurdities in stark contrast to the value of Josefina's life. What could be more important than health? Such trivial nonsense here. The messy divorce of a cheating Hollywood couple. An embarrassing *faux pas,* two actresses wearing identical red ruffled gowns to an awards ceremony. *Who wore it better?* Bianca votes for the woman on the right. In the next article, a health exposé? A young heartthrob tells his inspirational tale of rehab from alcohol abuse. His doctor reminds readers that alcoholism is an illness that can only be controlled, not cured.

Hardly the same, Bianca thinks.

Time creeps, too long, longer than usual. Focused on her phone, Bianca avoids eye contact with the half dozen people in the waiting room, ill patients and distraught family members. If she wanted, they could exchange sympathetic looks in recognition of their common plight. But Bianca can't connect with them today. In the back of her mind, she replays the conversation in the doctor's office only a few minutes ago.

Bianca let Josie do most of the talking. It's her body, her health, her decision, but Dr. Stanz virtually ignored the patient, his eyes on Bianca much of the time, and not in a nice way. Almost a glare. He's different today, slightly off. Even doctors have bad days, she supposes, but shouldn't he strive for an uplifting mood around a patient suffering from cancer?

"We can admit you right now and get you started," he said, almost angrily, supposedly talking to Josie but looking straight at Bianca. The hospital, next door to the doctor's office, has an open bed, ready and waiting.

"No, thank you," Josie said politely. "We thought about it again, like you asked, but we've decided not to—"

"Both of you?"

"*I've* decided."

"Yes, Josefina has decided, and I support her in this," Bianca said.

"My mother… I've seen what it does—"

"Everyone's different."

"I can fight it. I'm feeling better. The medicines you gave me are helping." Josie added the last thought with a hopeful lilt, as if she wanted the doctor to feel better: *You've done well. You've given me medicines that help.* But her voice, once so strong, is weakened from the disease and sounds even more tenuous in contrast to the doctor's arrogant authority.

"All right," he said gruffly. "I'll see what I can do." That's when he sent Josie to the examining room and Bianca to the waiting room.

Is he in there now, bearing down on Josie, pressuring her in the absence of that annoying, hovering aunt? Is he hoping to break her down? A nurse accompanied Josefina into the examining room, but who knows if she's still there. Bianca has seen male doctors who dismiss the nurses when a young female patient doesn't know any better to protest.

A droplet of water splashes onto the vast lawn of a Beverly Hills mansion. Bianca swipes at the screen, pushing the image away. How many heartbroken mothers and fathers have sat in this waiting room, trying to forget the impossible odds? Is Bianca doing the right thing? Why should she, a health care professional, reject the advice of a doctor? Has she seen too many emergencies when attentive nurses, not doctors, saved lives? Is that a kind of arrogance of its own? And what about her role as parent? Should Bianca stand up to Josie, a girl who's almost an adult, and make her accept the treatment that works best for most people in her situation? *Everyone's different,* Dr. Stanz says so easily without knowing any details about Josie, who she is and how she's different from everyone else, the pool of test subjects who provide the data for numbers and percentages and probabilities.

At ten minutes to three, Bianca has managed to control her emotions while resuming her scroll through *People*. A few times she turned her head, discreetly, to dab at her eyes with a tissue. She feels the presence of struggling life in this room but doesn't see the people sitting here. No one has been called into the inner sanctum for a very long time, and the waiting room twitches with nervous energy.

A door opens, and a surge of movement forces Bianca to look up. Two people are walking straight toward her with deliberation and purpose. She doesn't know them, has never seen them before, but they seem to know *her* perfectly well. The young man wears a dark uniform with official instruments dangling and clattering from a utility belt. NYPD. The middle-aged woman half a step behind him wears an ill-fitting gray pantsuit. She's slightly disheveled, as if the pressures of her workday allow only a finger-combing of her graying hair.

They come up to Bianca and stand uncomfortably close, towering above her. "Bianca Merced?" the officer asks.

"Yes." She slips her phone into a pocket.

The man pauses, glances behind him and all around, reconsidering how he'll accomplish what he wants to do. "Would you come with us please? Just outside."

"I...I can't. I'm waiting for my niece. What's this all about?" She notices the raised heads, all eyes on her. "Who are you?"

"I'm a police officer, ma'am." His shaky declaration of the obvious betrays his inexperience. He doesn't look much older than Josie. "Scott Knudsen, NYPD." He gestures toward the woman at his side. "And this is..." He doesn't even know the woman's name?

She jumps in. "Amy Shapiro, MSW, CPS." Her voice drops on the last acronym. "I have this for you." She hands Bianca a piece of paper, folded in three parts, covering what's printed inside.

Bianca takes it, not understanding a thing. MCP… What did she say?

"We'll explain, out in the hallway," Officer Knudsen says.

Clutching the paper, not daring to open it, Bianca says, "Let me talk to Josefina first and let her know I'm still here." She tries to get up, wobbling a little. The room gently spins, the edges blurred.

Officer Knudsen takes her arm. "That's not possible, ma'am. Please, come this way." He leads her toward the exit.

"But no! I have to wait for Josie!"

Shapiro nods to the paper in Bianca's hand. "Don't make this difficult for yourself. Let's go have a talk about Josefina." What could this untidy woman know about Josie?

"We'll talk about Josie when she comes out. No, don't!" Knudsen is pushing her to the door. "We have to wait!" Bianca is frantic now, resisting, the policeman exerting force, his hand tighter on her arm.

Around them, the energy in the room is toxic. Everyone judging her. Bianca shouts her objections. Shapiro raises her voice to drown her out. "Don't fight this! Come with us and we'll explain. We're doing what's best for your niece."

"What could you be doing? *I'm* doing what's best. No!" Officer Knudsen has pushed her to the door and Shapiro holds it open.

"Come outside and read the order on that paper I gave you."

Bianca struggles against Knudsen as he pushes her through the exit into the hallway. "What is this?" The paper is crumpled and feels dirty in her hand.

The door slams shut.

At once, Bianca gives in. She stops struggling and drops the paper on the institutional gray carpet, knowing in her heart what Shapiro is about to say.

Officer Knudsen's hand feels warm but forgiving on her upper arm. Shapiro gives her a weary look and picks up the paper. "This is an order of the Family Court, an emergency removal of Josefina from your home. Your niece has been taken to the hospital where they will administer lifesaving treatment."

1 » *APPEALS*

Friday, January 7, 2022

ON THE STROKE of ten, the door opens. "All rise!" Black robes entering. Associate Justice Dana Hargrove steps out first, three others follow.

Head of the line, *not* because she's the star. Quite the opposite. Dana ranks next to lowest in seniority among the eighteen justices of this appellate court. The calendaring system shuffles them like a pack of cards into ever-changing panels of four to hear oral argument. On today's panel, Dana is most junior. Protocol dictates that they enter the courtroom in backward order of seniority.

At times, Dana misses the autonomy and authority she enjoyed not so long ago. As a trial judge on New York's Supreme Court, she was master of her own courtroom, sole decisionmaker. A year ago, she was appointed to the Appellate Division, the venue for civil and criminal appeals from trial courts in Manhattan and the Bronx. Collegiality and compromise are valued in this institution steeped in hallowed tradition. From Dana's first day, matters of rank were evident in the subtle and not-so-subtle behaviors of her fellow jurists. The pecking order is tolerable as long as her voice isn't censored. Honest debate is one thing, but quite another when a senior justice equates lengthy tenure with superior intellect. Egos abound here, at times unrelated to the ego-holder's level of legal prowess.

But most of Dana's colleagues respect her strengths in areas of expertise. She expects as much today. The first appeal on the calendar, *Matter of Citizens for Open Government versus New York State Attorney General*, raises familiar issues from her years as a district attorney.

"Hear ye, hear ye," a court officer intones as the justices enter. "All persons having business before the Appellate Division of the Supreme Court, draw near, give attendance, and you shall be heard." The justices head for their assigned spots at the bench: Dana Hargrove far right, Ahmed Khouri near left, Jerome Morgenstern near right, and Maria Navarro center. On a silent cue, they sit. The array is lopsided, the far-left chair empty. In quieter days, the court sat in panels of five, now cut to four to handle the burgeoning caseload. A fifth is added as a tie breaker in rare cases of split decision.

"Be seated and come to order," bellows the court officer. Business-attired backsides discreetly nestle into the leather upholstery. Aging wooden chairs creak at the joints. Nervous anticipation suffuses the air. This morning, when these attorneys and spectators arrived at the courthouse, were they too anxious about their cases to appreciate the grandeur of this historic edifice?

At the dawn of a new century, January 1900, the justices of the Appellate Division, then numbering only seven, moved into the new courthouse on the corner of 25th Street and Madison Avenue. Renowned sculptors contributed the statuary gracing the white marble Beaux-Arts façade. On the front steps, flanked by the figures of Wisdom and Force, visitors pass between Corinthian pillars under a triangular pediment holding the five-figured Triumph of Law. Ancient lawgivers Manu, Justinian, and others loom at the edge of the roof, looking down on those who ascend the steps to seek justice within.

Security measures, today's reality, couldn't have been foreseen by the painters and artisans of 1900 whose works adorn the lobby. Uniformed guards, beeping scanners, and security wands distract from the rich surroundings: mosaic floors, Sienna marble walls, the gilded coffered ceiling, a bronze and glass chandelier, carved oak furniture. A 62-foot mural, Transmission of the Law, runs above a branching staircase. Opposing walls display artistic visions of Justice, with figures representing Transgression, Law, Equity, Peace, Prosperity, Protection, and Mercy.

After passing security, did today's attendees pause to enjoy the art and contemplate its meaning? Not likely, as they wrestled with briefcases and winter clothing. Coats, scarves, hats, and boots are removed in the cloakroom, a long, narrow space that preserves quaint features from the past: hooks for top hats, slots for walking sticks, dark wood cubbies decorated with carved winged mermaids, symbols of eloquence to inspire the attorneys on their way to oral argument.

Plush carpeting in cloakroom and courtroom dampens the noise of human existence. Inside, rows of high-backed oak and leather chairs are arranged in sections for the public and the attorneys, who pause to consider seat choice. Aisle seats are taken first. When an attorney is called to the podium, the gymnastics of squeezing past one's fellows can be unsettling, throwing off concentration.

This room is an artistic masterpiece. As tension mounts before calendar call, who has the luxury of admiring its splendor? The lawyers are reviewing their arguments, not gazing at the sumptuous surroundings. Intricate stained-glass windows are set in veined marble walls. On the coffered ceiling, shimmering gold patterns frame an enormous stained-glass dome at center. Natural light filters through radiating panels of floral and fruit designs, bearing the names of past justices. Painted murals depicting legal themes border the ceiling on three walls. Behind the justices' bench, a wall of intricately carved wood bears the gold lettering "In God We Trust" at top center, and above that, a painted scroll reminds us that "Law Reigns."

Decades ago, when young attorney Dana Hargrove sat in this audience waiting to make her argument, she didn't have the presence of mind to admire the art surrounding her. That appreciation came later. But she remembers and holds dear her first impression, a lofty feeling that arose without conscious awareness of physical details. The majestic aura of this courtroom seeps into every pore through the senses—sight, touch, sound, and even the musty smell of antiquity—rendering an intangible certainty. If true justice exists anywhere, surely it is achieved and dispensed here.

Now, sitting at the bench, Justice Hargrove smiles inwardly as she regards The Triptych on the far wall behind the audience. Three large paintings depict The Justice of the Law, Wisdom, and The Power of the Law. In 1900, when the world of men scoffed at the idea of women lawyers and judges, male artists chose female subjects to depict their ideals of law and justice. Classical traditions in art may explain it, but Dana enjoys her own thoughts. Ignorant of today's fifty-fifty composition of the court, were they, nevertheless, unconsciously prescient? Subliminally apologetic? Precociously woke? Perhaps all the above. The paintings betray recognition, even admiration, of female intellect, wisdom, compassion, and intrinsic understanding of the human condition.

Justice Maria Navarro launches into her opening spiel with the usual scare tactic. "Welcome to the Appellate Division. We have *eight* hours of argument time requested today. When I call your case, please ask for the number of minutes you *actually* need. Remember, we've read your briefs and records." Case by case, the attorneys stand and modify their time requests. Magically, eight hours turns into four. Still, it's a long time until lunch.

First case up, *Matter of Citizens for Open Government versus*

New York State Attorney General. The nonprofit group COG is appealing the denial of its petition for public release of grand jury evidence. A high-profile case. Spectators perk up as the attorneys approach the bench. Reporters, concerned citizens, family members and friends of Lonnie Douglas are in the audience and outside the courthouse. Despite the icy, thirty-degree weather, protestors are gathered on the sidewalk with signs reading "No Justice, No Peace," and "Justice for Lonnie," the Bronx teenager fatally shot by Police Officer Michael Welton on July 4, 2021. In August, the grand jury voted "no true bill," declining to charge Officer Welton with any crime under New York state law.

Is it any wonder that *COG v AG* is the first case on today's calendar? Court officers want to clear the courtroom and sidewalks of extra people as soon as possible.

COG's stated mission is to publicly reveal the closed proceedings in every branch of government. Their legal weapons: Freedom of Information Act requests and lawsuits. Illegal weapons? Rumors of COG's complicity in computer hacking and planted spies have never been substantiated.

A year ago, Dana wrote her first opinion for this court in *Matter of COG v District Attorney of New York County*. Same legal issues, different facts—a murder case handled by her former colleague, DA Jared Browne. Having left the Manhattan DA's Office almost twenty years ago, Dana had no reason to recuse from deciding that appeal. Still, thoughts of the underlying criminal investigation, the way it ensnared people Dana admires, can stir gut-wrenching emotion. Something she tries to avoid.

Today, she needn't go there. Today, the court considers the circumstances of Officer Welton's fatal shooting of Lonnie Douglas. To do their job, the justices have access to the full grand jury record. COG's attorney would grumble that *in camera* review by this appellate court is just another example of government secrecy.

Justice Hargrove is all for transparency and accountability, but not when confidentiality will actually serve the greater good.

Today's case is the latest in COG's assault on the grand jury, a closed chamber of twenty-three citizens and a popular political football. On one team, an enraged public, knowing a fraction of the facts, demands retribution for police use of excessive force. On the other team, prosecutors hide behind the shield of the grand jury in politically charged cases. When there's no evidence of police misconduct, they dodge responsibility for declining to prosecute: "Not me. The grand jury exonerated the cops." Handy, but secret, adding fuel to the fire.

And then there are cases like Officer Welton's. Not a slam-dunk either way. Conflicting evidence and close issues of fact. Who should wield the power to indict? A single judge or a group of twenty-three citizens? Dana would say that factfinding is best left to a jury.

So, the state Attorney General did the right thing in the Welton case by empaneling a grand jury, but she expected a different outcome, an indictment for manslaughter, or even murder. Her public statements implied as much before she sent her Assistant AG into the closed chamber with marching orders. The plan backfired. The grand jury found that Welton was justified in using lethal force.

The AG isn't happy. She's been critical of the NYPD and supports legislation for the unsealing of grand jury evidence upon a mere showing of "significant public interest in disclosure." In 2021, a bill in the state legislature with that relaxed standard failed to pass before end of session. A problem for COG. For disclosure in this case, COG must satisfy the "compelling and particularized need" standard set by the court's longstanding precedent, a nearly impossible hurdle. In this odd limbo between old and new law, the AG is taking an atypical approach. She doesn't oppose disclosure of a redacted record, removing names of witnesses and jurors. *Not my fault*. She'd like the world to know how hard she tried to get an indictment. In the order appealed from, the Supreme Court denied COG's petition and rejected the AG's compromise.

Affirm, is Dana's silent inclination as the attorneys take their places, but an exceptional oral argument might send her in another direction. Julian Aird, for the appellant, sets his notes on the podium as Assistant Attorney General Patricia Trentino takes a seat at the respondent's table.

Wiry and energetic, Aird bounces in his loose suit jacket and gapping button-down shirt collar. His ardor is rough and tumble, his voice a notch lower than soprano. "May it please the Court. We've shown the need for full disclosure of this grand jury proceeding. New Yorkers are demanding answers. Twenty-three people behind a closed door were misled into making the wrong decision."

Assistant AG Trentino shifts uncomfortably in her seat. *Misled*. Is this the thanks the AG gets for supporting COG's petition?

Aird rushes past his little jab. "If they weren't misled, these twenty-three people were either biased or *blind* to the facts in front of them. We all saw what happened. Lonnie Douglas. A kid. Eighteen. Unarmed. Murdered in cold blood by a trigger-happy NYPD rookie. The grand jury ignored this evidence. People are crying for justice and deserve an explanation. The answer, we submit, will be found in the system itself. A broken system."

Dana is not swayed by Aird's disingenuous reference to "facts." Clearly, he's talking about the ten-second video clip played relentlessly on news outlets and social media. Click bait, good for ratings. The camera is at street level, angled diagonally behind Douglas's right side, his left side hidden from view. On a dark street against a background of shouting and July 4th firecrackers, Officer Welton yells, "Freeze!" Douglas's right arm seems to cross his torso and he lurches forward. Three shots ring out. Douglas collapses. All in the space of a few seconds.

The problems with that video are obvious. The full encounter lasted three minutes, not ten seconds, and the vantage point is skewed, cutting off most of what Officer Welton saw. Less popular videos cropped up on social media, a half dozen cell phone recordings with similar problems, fuzzy, dark, incomplete, slanted angles. But there were two longer videos, not released to the press, taken from open windows by people inside their apartments. Together, they show the full story. The two witnesses reluctantly came forward with the evidence on condition of anonymity. They did *not* want to testify and were compelled by subpoena. Every witness in the grand jury, whether subpoenaed or not, is assured the cloak of confidentiality. And these two have special reasons to want that promise fulfilled.

Eager to engage with Aird, Justice Hargrove nevertheless defers to the senior justice, Navarro, who leans forward, ready to strike. "Counselor, as you're aware, mere public interest is not the legal standard. You're required to demonstrate a 'compelling and particularized need.' Our cases consistently hold that public curiosity, or even public unrest, does *not* rise to that level."

"Your Honor, the interest in disclosure goes *way* beyond public curiosity. The huge public outcry indicates a complete lack of faith in the police department and government officials." He throws an oblique look at AAG Trentino. "Public distrust is at an all-time low, at crisis level."

Navarro is not having it. "Crisis? Perhaps you didn't use that word last year in the McBride case, but you made the same argument and we rejected it. Why isn't *Matter of COG against Manhattan DA* controlling here?"

Yes. This is one question Dana can cross off her list. She wrote the opinion in *COG v DA*. Navarro uses the conventional "we" to remind Aird that Dana spoke for the full court.

Aird responds, "It's distinguishable, Your Honor. In that case, we sought to uncover nepotism in the handling of a cop-on-cop killing." His eyes dart away from Navarro and land, momentarily, on Justice Hargrove. Despite herself, Dana is annoyed. He continues, "Here, the public interest in exposing police brutality against unarmed citizens is more compelling."

On Dana's left, Justice Morgenstern interjects, "In other words, this case points to the urgency for the legislative action amending the grand jury statutes. Isn't that what you mean, Mr. Aird?"

"Exactly, Justice Morgenstern!" Aird can't believe his good luck. It's like the smart kid in class just whispered the exam answer in his ear. "As the Court knows, Citizens for Open Government has been at the forefront of the legislative reform."

"And that relates to your factual burden in this appeal, does it not?"

What? Morgenstern is making Aird's argument for him!

"It establishes our burden completely, Your Honor. This Court held, in the case of…," Aird stutters and draws a blank, "…in many cases, that a compelling interest is shown when disclosure will advance the goals of legislative investigation and reform."

Dana can wait no longer. "But Mr. Aird, what about the key words 'particularized' and 'need' in our legal standard? How have you shown that you *need* this *particular* transcript to inform legislative debate at this advanced stage, beyond the facts and arguments already in the public discourse?"

"Because the evidence the public has seen against Officer Welton is at odds with the grand jury's vote, causing huge distrust in the system. There's been an outcry like no other, hordes of people demonstrating…"

"Like other cases in recent years. Some have led to indictments and some have not, an indication that grand juries carefully weigh the evidence put to them. Isn't the public outcry always aimed at a desire for justice?"

"Yes, of course—"

"And a desire to find the truth?"

Truth may not be high on Aird's list. "Uh, yes, the truth, but..."

Dana holds out an open palm. "How is truth found and justice achieved if we renege on our promises?" She makes a fist and yanks it back. "How are these ideals served in the next case, perhaps a case of egregious police misconduct? Why would reluctant witnesses trust us to give them the protections they're owed under the law?"

"But this was a public encounter on a public street..."

"With many people in the vicinity who didn't ask to find themselves in the middle of it, some of whom had to be compelled by process to testify. And many citizens who didn't ask to be picked for a grand jury. If we break a legal promise of confidentiality to them, who's to say we'll have witnesses and grand jurors the next time we seek truth and justice?"

"Yes, well, it's their duty to come forward, as witnesses and grand jurors..."

"Is it their duty to bear public scrutiny and criticism and maybe even physical threat from the 'hordes of people' who, as you say, don't agree with their final decision?"

Aird opens his mouth, but nothing comes out. He fidgets nervously, dropping his gaze to his notes on the lectern.

A supernatural silence falls. Two hundred people hold a collective breath and wait.

Conference is over at three thirty. Around the big table, the justices ate lunch, debated, and voted on the day's calendar, twenty cases. Felons appeal their convictions of rape, robbery, and assault. Prosecutors appeal pretrial orders suppressing evidence. Ex husbands and wives appeal spousal support and child custody orders. Doctors and hospitals appeal medical malpractice judgments. Injured motorists appeal damages verdicts. Corporations appeal judgments in contract disputes and employment discrimination claims.

For each appeal, one of the four justices will write the court's order, anything from a single paragraph to several pages in length, depending on the case. Dana steps out of the conference room with her assignments: criminal appeal, med mal, products liability, matrimonial, and *COG v AG*.

Before oral argument, she predicted that they would affirm Supreme Court's denial of COG's petition in a single paragraph, citing *COG v DA Browne*. But she was reminded today of how much she still has to learn about her fellow jurists. Morgenstern's bias in favor of COG came bursting forth. When Aird botched his answers to Dana's questions, Morgenstern seemed to retreat and became interested in the respondent's argument. AAG Patricia Trentino, a persuasive advocate, made a credible pitch for the compromise position.

At conference, debate was heated. Outnumbered, Jerry Morgenstern stressed the benefits of appeasing an angry public. The others didn't go for it. Navarro, Khouri, and Hargrove voted to affirm, Morgenstern reserved decision. Going forward, Dana will try to win him over. If she fails and he writes a dissent, she's in for more work, writing a longer opinion to rebut his arguments. Worst case scenario, his dissent could convince the other justices to change their votes. It's been known to happen.

Walking back to her office, Dana ponders her best approach. Let the dust settle over the weekend, gather her arguments, and meet with Jerry privately on Monday. She doesn't like the AG's compromise. Merely redacting names and addresses isn't adequate protection. She's seen it happen before. Nosy people can easily find out who's involved. In this case, releasing the videos is just as good as releasing the witnesses' names. Their apartments can be determined from the camera angle. And they have reason to fear retribution from family members and supporters of the late Lonnie Douglas.

Hard cases make bad law. Funny, but does Julian Aird have any idea of Justice Hargrove's internal struggle? As a tenacious truth-seeker herself, Dana feels the temptation to disclose the facts. If it were only that simple! Details mean everything.

July 4th. Revelry, chaos, firecrackers on a city street. A 911 call. A bulletin goes out: "Man acting erratically, possibly armed." Officers Welton and Perez are first to respond. A young man is out of control, high on something, crazed and volatile, yelling obscenities at strangers. Welton recognizes him. A week ago, he arrested Lonnie Douglas for punching his girlfriend and shoving her down a flight of stairs. The court issued an order of protection and released him on his own recognizance under the new bail reform law. Welton yells, "Freeze!" Douglas ignores him. Spectators move back but are stubbornly curious, aiming their cell phones. Douglas staggers away and circles back. He reaches for something sticking out of his left pants pocket. An abrupt lurch at Welton. Gunshots. Douglas falls.

On the pavement, next to his right hand, lies a shiny object. An aluminum-topped homemade rocket.

Intentional murder, reckless manslaughter, or justified lethal force? All the details, everything Welton saw and knew, added up to this reasonable belief: armed and dangerous. A flash of silver, a split-second decision. Welton was justified in defending himself, the jury concluded.

This case is about trust in people. Ordinary people who participate in the process. But to Aird it's a thing called system. Who's really at fault when people protest and riot? Selective reporting, sensationalism, click bait, viral videos. Ubiquitous screens recycle snippets and memes that foment division.

And the two witnesses who provided the clearest video evidence? The ex-girlfriend's current boyfriend who fueled Douglas's rage on the day he assaulted her. And the 911 caller on July 4th who mistakenly told the police that Douglas had a gun. As yet, the identities of these witnesses are unknown to the world.

By the time she's back at her office, Dana is done with these mental gyrations, the internal debate that always plagues her in tough cases. Endless if she doesn't shut it down.

In the anteroom to her chambers, her law clerk, Nia Glover, looks up from the computer. "Good afternoon, Judge." Her eyes dart to the stack of papers Dana carries.

"Hi, Nia." Dana lifts the bundle in the air. "No worries! All straightforward today. You'll knock them out in no time." Nia writes most of the first drafts on the shorter decisions. Her work is so good that Dana usually does little editing.

"Even the first case on the calendar?"

"Were you watching?" Computers in chambers can access live feed from the courtroom.

"Yes, and I sense a problem."

"Care to guess the vote?"

Nia smiles. She likes these guessing games. "Three to affirm, Justice Morgenstern dissenting. Either that, or he's thinking about it."

"Hit the nail on the head! He reserved decision. Let's hope he comes around. For now, just draft a short memorandum decision, citing *COG v Browne*. If he circulates a dissent, we'll beef it up later, if need be."

"We'll hope for the best."

"Come on in and I'll give you what you need." Dana goes into her office and pulls out the case summaries with her notes. Nia follows and accepts the papers in exchange for another set of papers in her hand. "This just came in," Nia says. "An expedited case, special calendar, a week from today. Briefs are due the day before oral argument."

They settle into chairs on opposite sides of the desk. "*Matter of Josefina M. (Bianca M.).*" Dana reads the caption out loud as she scans the first page, a Family Court order. With secrecy and anonymity so recently on her mind, the caption strikes her now as another example of ineffective compromise. By court rule, captions in cases involving minors identify the parties by first name and initial only—a protection that isn't foolproof. Anyone who tries hard enough can figure out identities from the information revealed in published decisions. On appeal, the justices don't have to guess; they have access to the full record. "Have you taken a look at this?"

"Yes. The full record is e-filed. Family Court sustained an emergency removal of the child from the home. She's a teenager actually. Seventeen years old. The legal guardian, the child's aunt, is appealing."

"Seventeen?"

"Nearly eighteen."

"What's the alleged abuse or neglect? Have you looked at the testimony and fact-findings?" The order in Dana's hand merely recites the disposition.

"I have. The aunt refused lifesaving medical treatment for her niece. She has stage IV lymphoma."

"Oh, my goodness. Did the aunt move for a stay?" Dana flips to the next page, a printout from the Appellate Division's case tracking system.

"She did, and—"

"Okay. I see it here." One of Dana's senior colleagues, Justice Nathan Shields, denied the aunt's motion to stay the Family Court's order pending appeal. "So, Josefina is now in the custody of ACS." The Administration for Children's Services. "Any other history of removals?"

"No, and actually, from what I've read so far…" Nia seems momentarily at a loss for words, her smooth, wide brow contracting into that single line over the bridge of her nose. Her compassion runs deep, a quality somehow enhanced by her changing appearance. Nia's complexion and features radiate with the fullness of pregnancy, her sixth month.

"Mm-hmm…" Dana waits for Nia's opinion. It's bound to come.

"Sorry. This case just hits me here." Nia's free hand, the one not holding the papers in her shrinking lap, makes a fist and places it over her heart. Dana appreciates her emotional engagement as an asset to their team, whether she acts as complement or foil to the judge. In professional circles, people who don't know Justice Hargrove well can find her staid and reserved. Dana would be the first to recognize her own skill at hiding the roiling waters. External calm and a modulated, velvet voice don't always tell the full story. As a judge, Dana seeks out and listens to every viewpoint, especially that of her trusted law clerk, a woman of thirty-three with a vastly different experience of America, about to have her first baby.

"Hmm. A tough one. Did Family Court get it right?"

"I'm not sure. There's no clear path here. The aunt and the niece are very close. You can almost hear it in the cold transcript, reading Bianca's testimony. The attorney for the child was passionate, arguing against separation. It's the worst possible time to rip them apart. Without chemotherapy, Josefina has only a few months left, but her chances of survival, even *with* the treatment, aren't great. It's…it's just heartbreaking."

"Why is the aunt refusing treatment? Is there a religious objection?"

"No. I believe they're Catholic, but the objection isn't based on religion. It's more like Bianca wants to honor Josefina's decision. The girl's mother was Bianca's sister. She went through months of horrendous suffering and died of ovarian cancer when Josefina was eleven. They both think the chemo made her suffering worse."

Dana shakes her head, and they lapse into silence for a moment. "So," Dana says with a little smile, "what you're trying to say is, 'good luck deciding this one'!"

Nia returns the smile and stands up. "With you on the panel, Judge, it'll be the right decision. I'm just glad *I* don't have to call it."

"You'll be in the same spot one day." Dana can see a career path to the judiciary for Nia. "Believe me, that day will come."

Nia pats her baby bump. "Sure will. Can't stop it!" They laugh, and Nia says, "I'll get cracking on these." She nods at the papers in her hand and turns to go.

Dana's eyes follow her briefly on her way out the door. Those were the days. Young and pregnant, juggling home and career. Dana's firstborn, Travis, is now thirty and expecting a child of his own. Where has the time gone?

Thoughts of Travis redirect her focus to the AD case tracking report in her hand. The court clerk wouldn't have put her on the panel if she has reason to recuse, but better check… No problem. The attorney representing ACS is Noriko Takeda, head of appeals in Family Court cases for the NYC Corporation Counsel. Two other attorneys are listed, one each for Josefina and Bianca. Dana recognizes the names. Excellent appellate counsel. If nothing else, the arguments in this case will be clearly and masterfully presented.

It's more like Bianca wants to honor Josefina's decision. Seventeen, almost eighteen, a "child" under the law, represented by "the attorney for the child," a legal term of art. What were Travis and Natalie like at age seventeen and a half? *If* she can remember… Dana's children are now solidly adult, no longer questionably on the cusp. Looking back at their respective senior years in high school, Dana remembers a distinct difference in their levels of maturity. From birth, Travis has always been Evan and Dana's little adult.

The desk phone rings, and caller ID displays her husband's name. A little after four o'clock. He couldn't be home yet. Must have just finished. "Evan! How'd it go?"

"Just peachy. The room shook with laughter."

"So, you told them your best jokes?"

"I thought so, but they almost gave me the hook."

"Why would anyone ever do that, darling?"

2 » *TOUGH*

WELL WHAT DO you know?

The door to the conference room opens, and Professor Amelia Durst walks out. Interesting, the people you meet while waiting to be interviewed by the Commission on Judicial Nomination.

Amelia's gait is loose, her features calm. Not a hair out of place or a glimmer of perspiration. The Commission is done with her, Evan is next.

Their eyes meet, they exchange smiles. Easygoing Evan is an open book behind his frameless glasses, an honest face and bald head offering an unimpeded look into his soul. His cheerful, devil-may-care personality is not, however, immune to a quickened pulse at the thought of facing twelve inquisitors. Perhaps Amelia can detect those butterflies, perhaps not. For nearly a decade, they've been friendly colleagues at NYU Law. As she walks toward him, Evan is reminded that years of courteous, professional interactions are not always a true indication of character.

A month ago, over bag lunch in the teachers' lounge, Evan told Amelia he had applied for the opening on the Court of Appeals. Since then, they've spoken about it a few times, Amelia throwing out names, speculating on Evan's competition. Never did she mention her own aspiration to sit on New York State's highest appellate tribunal. If she'd told him, he would have wished her the best and really meant it. Maybe she doesn't know Evan as well as she thinks.

Awkward. A back door would have been the thing. *Thanks for coming in. Step this way, please,* guiding the applicant into an empty hallway, avoiding the next candidate who waits in the front room.

"Hello, Evan." A big smile, too relaxed to suggest any underlying regret about her omission. More like pride at having aced the interview.

Evan returns the pleasantry. "Hello, Amelia." Best to ignore the whole thing. "How'd it go in there?"

"Quite well, thank you. You have nothing to worry about. They're very polite."

"Good to know."

"Best of luck to you."

"Thanks. See you at school."

She walks out, and Evan glances at the wall clock. Three thirty-one. In the next instant, another woman opens the conference room door. "Professor Goodhue? The Commission is ready for you."

A single empty chair. The woman gestures. Evan takes three steps into the room and places a hand on the hot seat.

"Good afternoon," he says with a glace around the long rectangular table, giving a nod here and there. No time for introductions. Evan has studied the names and knows a few people on this bipartisan commission of jurists, lawyers, and business leaders. On the opposite long side of the table, facing the hot seat, sits Honorable Anthony Vespasiano, former Chief Judge of the Court of Appeals. As Commission Chair, he's hosting these interviews in the conference room of his midtown law firm,

Vespasiano, Glicksman, & Rudolph, LLP. Evan met him three years ago when he came to the law school to judge the moot court competition.

Evan's greeting is met with murmured responses all around, the strongest voice rising from the Chair. "Welcome, Professor Goodhue! Have a seat and settle in. I assure you, we don't bite."

My God, do I look that bad?

Just then, the earth turns. A dazzling ray of low winter sun shoots between city skyscrapers through a picture window, slicing the middle of the conference table. Brilliant.

Evan, ever the optimist, takes it as a good sign. "Thank you, Judge," he says, resisting the corny jokes that pop into his head. *I'll try not to bite too*. Or maybe, *Glad I wore my muzzle*. Why does his mind work like this? He dons imaginary rose-hued lenses and sits down as if among friends. A pleasant squeeze, three commissioners on his right, two on his left, and seven opposite him, Vespasiano in the middle. Eye to eye they are.

"Can we get you anything? Soda? Coffee?"

"No, thank you. This'll be fine." Evan's place at the table has a clean glass and a small pitcher of ice water. If he gets desperate, he'll pour a glass, trying not to spill.

Although this is the tenth interview of the day, Vespasiano looks like he's ready to run a marathon. In his mid-eighties, the former jurist exudes the vigor of an active mind and athletic body. He glances down at a summary sheet on top of Evan's multi-page application. "You've had quite a long career in the law, wide-ranging and distinguished."

The word "long" rings loudest in Evan's ears. No doubt, he's one of the older candidates for this position. "Thank you," he says in the breath Vespasiano grants him before rushing on to list Evan's qualifications.

The Chair is well prepared, on a mission to shake the eleven muddled memories around the table, sifting out the highlights of

Evan's curriculum vitae. Time is short, a mere half hour allotted to each candidate. Cut and paste: Amelia Durst out, Evan Goodhue in. "Started your career prosecuting street crime and complex financial crimes for the Manhattan DA, went on to civil litigation and class actions at Belknap & Rose, P.C., promoted to partner and added to the masthead of your firm, currently a tenured professor of civil and criminal procedure at NYU Law School." A longer breath, as he picks up and tap-taps the bottom edges of the papers on the table. "So..."

Evan smiles. Here it comes.

"...you've been the captain of your own ship for much of your career, wouldn't you say? Independent. Running your own cases, and now, writing your own lesson plans?"

The intent behind the question screams at Evan. Although lack of judicial experience is not disqualifying, perhaps even attractive in some ways, he is untested as a judge. Will he be open to the opposing viewpoints of his colleagues or closed off, unwilling to compromise? Seven judges sit on the Court of Appeals. A repeat dissenter among them would be extremely unpleasant, a destabilizing influence on the institution.

Evan considers himself principled but also openminded. Whether the commissioners get this impression during their half hour together will be a matter of intuition. How does a person judge the character of another? Superficialities, words, demeanor, facial expressions, eye contact. A professional life recorded on paper. "Much of my career, yes," Evan answers, "but plenty of teamwork as well, collaboration with colleagues on the larger criminal investigations." A fleeting neural connection is triggered. *Dana*. Teamwork on the cartel investigation is how they met. Evan blinks and continues. "Plenty of strategy sessions with co-counsel in big lawsuits, class actions and," his mouth twists upward, "academia is not without the pressures of collaboration and compromise."

Oops. "Pressures." Bad word choice. One of the commissioners here is an academic, and Evan may have found her. Across the table at the far end, a smiling woman levels a direct gaze. Is that Professor Georgina Sparrow from Albany Law? She's an older version of the headshot on the school's website, a photo taken twenty years ago, Evan would guess. They've never met. He quickly adds, "Not to mention the rewards of collaboration, like co-authoring the civil procedure treatise with Professor Bendig. At the law school, I'm surrounded by incisive legal minds, absorbing their wisdom." Evan taps his temple.

Chairman Vespasiano smiles cordially. "Not to mention the incisive legal mind in your own home. How is Justice Hargrove enjoying her life at the Appellate Division?"

"Very much, thank you."

"On the theme of teamwork," a pensive nod, "I'm reminded of the difficult adjustment a trial judge makes, switching to appeals."

"It seems to suit her," Evan says, ignoring the tiniest voice reminding him of Dana's occasional complaints. "What can I say? I'm married to a brilliant woman."

"Who happens to sit on one of the courts reviewed by the Court of Appeals."

"That too."

"What are your thoughts on that? Any tension on the home front?" The twinkle in his eye and levity in his voice encourage a few muted chuckles around the table.

Hmm, is this really an issue for them? The Chair's tone is tongue-in-cheek, and Evan goes with that. "No tension at all. I always get the final word at home—*except* when she tells me to take out the garbage."

Radio silence. A few polite smiles. Evan's boyish grin fades, and he clears his throat. "Seriously though, I would, of course, recuse if my wife participated in deciding a case under review..."

"Indeed, yes."

"...on those few occasions it occurs." Evan could go on, but he holds back. Not a good look to rattle off statistics he compiled from his exhaustive study. The four Appellate Divisions are the courts of last resort for nearly all cases in New York. In Dana's Appellate Division, she decides only a small percentage of the cases, and only a few of those will ever be heard in the Court of Appeals.

The Chair helps him out. "The need to recuse would be rare, I imagine."

"Yes, statistically rare, by my estimation."

"Well then," Vespasiano pauses and looks around the table. "I yield the floor. I know some of our members have questions." He turns to the man on his right. "Bruce?" The name resolves Evan's doubts about the man's identity. Bruce Ling is a successful civil litigator specializing in insurance defense. Twenty years have passed since Evan faced off against Ling in court. The man is much changed, completely gray now and a little jowly.

"Professor Goodhue, welcome." A powerful voice. In his mind's eye, Evan sees Ling addressing the jury, impressing them with his eloquence, almost winning that case they were on. Almost.

"Thank you."

"I read, with interest, your recent law review article entitled...," Ling glances down, "'Suspension Bridge Ahead: Pay Toll.'" He looks up again, his face impassive. "A creative play on words."

Yes, Evan is proud of that. He notices a few smiles around the table, people who get it. But his enjoyment won't last long. This will soon get serious. There has to be at least *one* hardball zinger in this interview, doesn't there?

"I'm sure you're aware," Ling goes on, "the Court of Appeals is about to hear arguments in *Broadhurst v Care Med Hospitals*.

The case hangs on the issue you discuss in your article, and it looks like you've already made up your mind. Care to comment?"

The reason for Ling's interest is obvious. Pending cases against his clients are now in the Appellate Divisions, awaiting the outcome of *Broadhurst*. Ling claims the actions are "time-barred"—filed too late. The plaintiffs say they're timely because the governor granted a nine-month reprieve from statutory filing deadlines during the coronavirus pandemic. But the governor's order is ambiguous, using a mishmash of language about "tolling" and "suspension" of statutes of limitation. In Ling's view, the plaintiffs should have filed their lawsuits the day after the executive order expired because, under normal circumstances, they were required to serve their complaints during the nine-month "suspension" period. In Evan's view, the executive order "tolled" all statutes of limitation, stopping them from running, effectively tacking on an extra nine months to effect service.

"In my article, I pointed out conflicting interpretations of the executive order and gave my opinion as to the stronger argument. That's not to say that my mind is made up."

"Your view is forcefully presented."

"Thank you," Evan says, as if Ling intended a compliment. "The concept of 'tolling' has been around for a while. The clock stops running and starts again at the end of the toll."

"But the word 'suspended' implies a grace period for complying with the law, *only* for the duration of the suspension."

"True, but we're faced with an ambiguity; both words are used. One way to look at it," [interpret: *my way*], "favors the well-established concept of tolling in the context of a health emergency. The policy to protect public health takes temporary precedence over the policy behind statutes of limitation. Ordinarily, you forfeit your rights if you don't assert them within a reasonable period, but what's reasonable in normal times may be unreasonable during a shutdown. Litigants don't have access to the resources they need for preparing their cases."

"An excuse for procrastinators, is it not? Remember, we're talking about limitations periods that were almost expired when the lockdown started. The plaintiffs already had plenty of time to 'prepare,' as you say. On top of that, they're given the boon of a nine-month grace period."

Ling is pumped and enlivened. No longer the poker face. Baiting Evan? Testing his judicial temperament? Evan focuses on his inquisitor, nodding to indicate serious contemplation as he feels the heat of twelve pairs of eyes on him. The commissioners understand both sides of the coin. No need to belabor the finer legal points. No need to abandon his well-supported position. Plenty of need to finesse his response to the attack! "As a former litigator, I hear you. I'm all in favor of diligence. Some plaintiffs drag their heels. But the pandemic was a unique situation with uneven consequences. The lockdown hindered some in preparing their cases, and others were dealing with physical illness or caring for families. This is the context that will guide the Court in resolving the ambiguity in the executive order."

Ling nods but doesn't look satisfied. Evan isn't sure if anything he said helps or hurts his chances here. In a way, it doesn't matter. He's been true to himself, whether they like it or not. Most faces around the table are cordially pleasant and noncommittal. Maybe they're sleeping with their eyes open. It's twelve minutes to four. The clock ticks, and Ling must yield. "Thank you for your views on this issue, Professor." He turns to Vespasiano.

The Chair nods at Ling and turns away, to his left. With a smile, he says, "Professor Sparrow. Care to sell our colleague here on the high points of Albany?" More tongue-in-cheek? The upstate capital city, home to the Court of Appeals, isn't known as an exciting or attractive metropolis. Sleepy compared to Manhattan. Depending on traffic, a three- to four-hour drive separates the cities.

Professor Sparrow, a resident of the city where she teaches law, doesn't seem to mind the implication. To Vespasiano, she says, "It's especially lovely in wintertime." She turns to Evan, her intelligent eyes settling on his. "Reports that we got two feet of snow yesterday are *greatly* exaggerated. It was only eighteen inches." Laughter around the table. "Professor, I believe your career has brought you to Albany on occasion."

"Yes. I argued a few cases at the Court of Appeals, many years ago."

"How do you feel about trekking north for extended stays?"

"I always have a blast when I'm in Albany. And I've got an excellent pair of boots."

"Wonderful. I'll be happy to show you around, then." Evan is reminded of the Chair's question, *Any tension on the home front?* The Court hears oral arguments in one-week sessions, nine or ten times a year. Only a few judges reside close enough to commute, others live in Manhattan or outlying regions and maintain home offices near their residences. The out-of-towners stay over in Albany a week or two at a time. Evan's appointment would require these regular separations from Dana.

More interested in changing the subject, Professor Sparrow picks up a paper on the table and says, "I found an article about you, written by your former student Alison Yearling, published in the *ABA Journal*."

"Alison, brilliant student, now with the Justice Department, I believe."

"Yes. She writes," Sparrow looks down and reads, "'The mentor with the greatest positive influence on my education and career is Professor Evan Goodhue. He has a gift for clarifying complex legal concepts with his unique teaching style, a combination of modified Socratic method and standup comedy. The students love him. I'll never forget the day I was in the hot seat, fielding hypotheticals about postconviction motions, as Elvis Pressley gyrated to the 'Jailhouse Rock' on the wall behind the Professor's head.'"

Big smiles all around the table. Evan says, "I detect a typo in there. Alison actually wrote '*bad* standup comedy.' Most of my jokes fall flat."

"Nevertheless, a glowing testament to your skill as a teacher."

"It's a good day if the class stays awake."

"My question: Why trade in your life as a beloved professor in exchange for a one-seventh slice of an appellate bench?"

"Quite simply, I love the law and the Court of Appeals is at the cutting edge. I'm proud to have given young lawyers a good start in their profession, and I would be happy to carry on, but change is good, especially since the twenty-four-year-olds are starting to look younger every year."

"I know what you mean."

"As a judge, I can contribute in another way. I have the experience to give something to the Court."

Professor Sparrow smiles at Evan, turns to the Chair and nods, indicating she has nothing further. Vespasiano doesn't hesitate to follow up. "Something to give. That takes us to a question I like to ask every candidate. Can you tell us what you would bring to the Court, something *unique* that distinguishes you from the other fine candidates who've applied?"

The final kicker. In the next three seconds, possible answers flash, burn, and crash, falling victim to a key lack. Uniqueness. *I'll bring a fresh perspective to the Court, having never served as a judge*. Although most applicants are trial or appellate judges, Evan isn't the only nonjudicial candidate. Case in point: Professor Amelia Durst. *I have wide-ranging experience, civil and criminal, litigation and academia*. Other candidates might boast the same, and the Chair already recapped Evan's background. A reminder would be pure repetition. *I work like a dog and leave no stone unturned*. What lawyer doesn't, except the shysters who give the profession a bad name? *I'll bring my video clips to the Court, Elvis included*. Ha ha. Alison has already instilled this fear with her mention of his unique teaching style.

Evan Goodhue, nobody special. A beloved professor, excellent lawyer, some would say brilliant, a hard worker, no slacker. Nothing to distinguish him from the other shining stars on the Commission's list.

So, at the end of his three seconds, this is what comes out: "I'm a tough grader."

A moment of silence, the words settling in. Facing Evan, the Chair and surrounding commissioners are mildly stunned, their expressions an odd mixture of perplexity and awe.

Evan goes on. "We live in a world that increasingly seeks to impress with gloss, glibness, and packaging. Law students and lawyers aren't immune to it. I see through slickness, superficiality, and filler and look for clarity, completeness, knowledge, reason, ethics, impeccable logic, and fealty to principle in their work. Critical thinking wherever logic and reason break down. In other words, substance over splash."

Uncharacteristically, Vespasiano looks like he's struggling for words. Evan adds, "This is what I would bring to the Court, in every argument I hear, every brief I read, every decision I write."

Vespasiano says, "Interesting, and well said. So, not many students get a 100 in your class, eh Professor?"

Ling says, "Only Alison Yearling."

"Very bright," Evan says. "I might have given her an 85."

"Both wrong," Professor Sparrow pipes in. She reads, "'The 83 Professor Goodhue gave me was my lowest grade in law school but the highest in his criminal procedure class. I treasure that grade, so hard won, an indication that I'd learned a lot and had performed very well on the exam but that I always have more to learn and strides to make in becoming the best lawyer I can be.'"

Only thirty blocks. Why not walk it?

Anyone else might think it crazy, walking thirty blocks in thirty-degree weather, a frosty wind, the sun fallen to the horizon behind concrete, stone, and steel. But there's no precipitation in the air or on the sidewalks. Manhattan missed the weather pattern that dumped eighteen inches of snow on Albany yesterday. More proof of the distance between the two cities.

Evan is overheated from the inquisition, and the cold air feels good on his face and bald head. He fingers the knit cap in the pocket of his winter coat. When the afterglow fades, he'll pull it on. Better word: aftershock. Afterglow sounds like something good, like sex, and his current state isn't exactly relaxed and rosy.

Friday rush hour always starts early. People jam the pavement, heads down or focused ahead, some talking into the air on Bluetooth, weaving, dashing, bumping shoulders. Evan could turn around and head downtown instead, to his office at the law school, but it's too late in the day. At home, he can do another hour or two on his lesson plan for the upcoming semester. Two weeks remain in the winter break. After Martin Luther King Day, Professor Goodhue will, no doubt, be back at school. After an interview like that, why would the Commission ever recommend his appointment to the Court of Appeals? *A tough grader*. Could it get any worse?

Well, maybe it wasn't so bad. At the end of the day, neither Evan nor the Commission could doubt that he's well qualified for a judgeship that the legal community regards as a plum in a distinguished career. But he isn't so invested in the dream that he forgets the fullness of his life as it is, and will remain so, no matter how this turns out.

Five blocks uptown, he ducks out of the wind into the

vestibule of a skyscraper and pulls out his cell phone. Can't wait until he gets home to talk. Is this a weakness? Evan considers it a strength, the closeness of their relationship.

Any tension on the home front? Instead of his crack about taking out the garbage, Evan could have listed the possible reasons Dana enthusiastically supports his application: (1) She loves him, wants what he wants, thinks he's brilliant and right for the job; (2) She loves him, wants to show her support, but knows he's a longshot for the Court, possibly the longest shot in the history of the world; (3) Doesn't matter if she thinks he's brilliant or merely competent, she hopes he succeeds so she can get him out of her hair for long stretches at a time.

He likes to rib her about number (3), and now, as her phone rings in his ear, he's ready to do it again. Dana's hopes of regular long breaks from her live-in partner are about to be dashed.

"So, you told them your best jokes?" she asks.

"I thought so, but they almost gave me the hook."

"Why would anyone ever do that, darling?"

"Because, I'm sorry to report, I totally blew the interview."

"Now, there's a joke I can see right through. You couldn't possibly have blown it. You're too lovable and smart."

"Oh, they tried hard to love me. But then the Chair led them in a chorus of 'Little Boxes.'"

"What on earth…?"

"It seemed fitting for someone like me, just one of many little boxes on their list of candidates, insufficiently unique."

3 » *WEEKEND*

GINGER BUSTLES AROUND the kitchen in last-minute preparations. She hums, she's happy, she's protected and protecting, a man, a child. Travis hovers and heels, a little awestruck, baffled and helpless. It's Saturday night, and they've invited his sister and her boyfriend over for dinner.

Now solidly in her second trimester, Ginger is enjoying a euphoric freedom from nausea. Her effervescence and spunk have returned full force, her outlook ready for social engagement. Travis isn't so sure, but the idea for company was Ginger's, and the newlyweds, in their third year of marital bliss, are still attached at the hip.

Ginger opens the oven to check on the roast and gets a blast of hot air, rich with the aroma of juicy red meat. Potholder on one hand, baster in the other, she bends into the heat.

"Let me do that," Travis insists.

"It's okay!" She suctions up the drippings, squeezes, and asks the roast, "Did you put the salt and pepper on the table?"

"On it." Travis hustles off to complete the fine-tuning on the dinner table. His job.

Refills all around, wine for Travis, Natalie, and Max, lemon water for Ginger. Plates are empty, would have been licked clean if not for Emily Post. Homemade bread sopped up the moist crumbs. Dinner, a success.

Travis sits across from Max. Ginger, across from Natalie. The female side of the table is in full tilt, at high volume. Max got them started with, "An amazing meal, Ginger. Delicious!" The hostess thanked him, and the women launched into lively conversation about cooking and recipes.

Travis puzzles over his sister's new boyfriend. This is the first opportunity he's had to get to know him. Max is conventionally handsome without distinction, square and scrubbed, three years older than Natalie, the same age as Travis. Quietly attentive, Max cautiously chooses his lines and delivers them theatrically, as if aware of his audience. Not the type for down-to-earth Natalie, but what does an older brother know?

Troubling, though, that Nats is living with her new boyfriend, or so Travis suspects from clues he's picked up. The two have been together only a few months. They met in September at a party Aunt Cheryl hosted at her Westchester home—the former Goodhue-Hargrove family home where Travis and Natalie did most of their growing up. Cheryl's additions to the structure have made it a grand place for social gatherings. She kept this one modest, a healthy mix of family, close friends, and "industry" professionals from the cast and crew of her latest movie, *Swamp Wars*. Max had a supporting role in the Netflix feature film.

Travis didn't speak to Max at the party but noticed, from a distance, when Cheryl pulled Natalie over to make the introduction. Could Cheryl's stamp of approval be a reason for Natalie's fascination with Max? She's close to Aunt Cheryl, loves her to the point of idolization. Cheryl's matchmaking signifies her belief that Max and Natalie are right for each other. Therein lies the implicit message.

The pleasant chatter and laughter of the women at the dinner table provide cover for the men, who smile and listen. Travis steals glances at Max. He seems genuinely interested and focused, paying keen attention with a light in his eyes. Not a bad guy. *Don't be so harsh*. Graduated college with a B.A. in theater. After that, was the proverbial starving actor, working as a waiter, before getting his first break in film a few years ago. All this according to Nats.

But what is it with that name, "Maximilian Hastings"? It has the sound of British royalty or colonial invader, although nothing about him looks British. More East European. Must be a stage name. Travis makes a mental note to ask Natalie about it when he can get her alone. His sister is a cognitive scientist, a budding expert on detecting truth and falsity. Although her relationship with Max is new, she should have a good sense of her boyfriend by now. That's not to say that Natalie has outgrown her gullible side, the trusting nature that, sometimes, puts her at risk of falling victim to misdirection and illusion.

The subject changes from food to baby. Ginger says, "I'm feeling tip-top. All my energy is back, and we're getting excited about our new human." She pats her belly.

"That's wonderful," Natalie says. "You two are going to be great parents." She glances at Travis with a teasing wink. "My brother gets plenty of on-the-job training in parenting techniques at his office."

"Very funny," Travis says. He's an appellate attorney for the New York City Corporation Counsel, representing the Administration for Children's Services. Many of his cases involve child abuse and neglect.

Natalie feigns embarrassment. "Oh, so sorry! I meant that you get plenty of tips on what *not* to do as a parent."

"More than enough."

Natalie turns to Max. "Travis decided on his future line of work at the age of two when his nanny was arrested for murdering a child."

Max's eyes widen, his toothy smile crumbles. "Is that so?"

"She's just kidding," Travis says.

"Not really. It's family lore. I'll tell you the whole story later."

"Yeah, save that one for later," Travis says. "It's not dinner hour conversation."

"Actually, Max," Natalie's tone changes from teasing to respectful, "my brother has a really tough job, saving kids from abusive parents." She turns to Travis. "I don't know how you do it. Doesn't the work get to you?"

"It didn't at first, but it's starting to wear me down. I see a lot of depressing stuff. We do what we can to protect children, but solutions are never perfect. I'm thinking of asking for a transfer to another bureau after I finish a brief I'm working on now. I got a new assignment, an important precedent-setting case."

"Awesome," Natalie says. "Are you going to argue it in court?"

"Yup."

"Can I come watch you in action?"

"Of course." A warm surge fills his chest at this expression of his sister's esteem. Natalie always puts family first.

"So cool. Let me know when it is. Are you going too, Gingie? Wait a minute… Talk about *depressing*. How's *your* job going?"

"All good. I don't find it depressing at all. There's always a chance to have an impact on someone's life. It makes the effort worthwhile."

"When are you going to start your maternity leave?"

"Oh, as long as I have the energy I'll wait till the last minute before I switch to the new set of needles and bottles!" She laughs, her eyes darting from face to face. "You know what I mean. Inoculations and feedings."

Travis eyes his wife with admiration. And worry. Ginger spends her days with drug addicts and alcoholics. As a substance abuse counselor, she works magic with her clients at RealYou, a residential rehab clinic in lower Manhattan. Been there eight years, loves it, has no desire to quit.

"That would be interesting," Natalie says. "Maybe you'll go into labor when you're leading a group therapy session. They can all gather around with a stopwatch and time your contractions."

"Eight people yelling 'breathe'!" She laughs. "Too traumatizing for them. They could relapse." She turns to Travis, who might have a horrified look on his face. "Don't worry—"

"I'm not worried really, but…the very last minute? Doesn't it depend on what the doctor says?"

"I remember stories your mom told about you. Didn't she practically give birth in the courtroom, in the middle of a murder trial?"

"Highly exaggerated," Travis assures her.

"That was me, I think," Natalie says.

"Both of us," Travis corrects her. "But she was only seven months pregnant with me on that really grisly murder trial against that doctor."

"Yeah, that's it. Daddy made her stop work a couple of weeks before Travis came. For the firstborn, he was overprotective. For me, who cared? She worked up to the last minute."

"Like father, like son," Ginger says, placing her hand on her husband's. She gives him a loving look, and in that moment, he's taken aback by the recent, dramatic changes in her appearance: the new distinction in the spray of freckles on her nose, the fullness of her cheeks and lips, the shine in her thick auburn hair. His beauty speaks: "Every morning, he makes sure I'm safely in the door at RealYou before he goes to work."

Max nods in approval, a celebrity smile splashed on his face.

"It's not the best neighborhood," Travis explains.

Ginger pouts in mock dismissal. "A perfectly fine part of town."

"Things have happened there with some of your clients."

"Things happen everywhere. The only really bad thing that ever happened in that neighborhood had nothing to do with my clients." Ginger turns to their guests, regarding them one at a time. "Natalie, you told Max that whole story, right?"

Max's brow knits in dramatic concern. "There's another story here?" he asks.

"More family lore," Natalie says. "We have stories galore. Hey, that rhymes!" This isn't the time to reminisce about the nut case who was stalking and threatening Judge Dana Hargrove and her family. One of Ginger's clients was briefly suspected.

"See, Max? This is what you get in our family," Travis says. "Crime stories from all sides." In order, he rattles off the careers of his mother and father, mother- and father-in-law, aunt, and sister: "We've got former prosecutors, defense attorneys, an actress who appears in crime thrillers, and a cognitive scientist fascinated with crime."

"Am not," Natalie says. "I'm fascinated by perception, cognition, and the ways our memories become inaccurate."

"When testifying at criminal trials."

"That's one application, but the research applies to everything we observe. Every memory we try to describe. Ask ten people who saw the same thing and they describe it ten different ways. What's true, what's false? How can you rely on anything anyone says? How can we trust our own memories? From the minute you see something, the images in your head are attacked and distorted." As she speaks, Natalie "attacks" her head, throwing invisible objects toward it with her right hand, then left and right. "Any traumatic bits are repeated and reinforced, skewing and limiting what you remember."

Travis gives Max a wry look. "You're duly warned. Don't get in her way. She'll catch you in a lie."

"So far so good," Max replies.

"But I'll bet…"

"Oh, go away, Tug." Natalie swipes her hand at Travis, who isn't fond of his childhood nickname, an acronym of his initials. In faux ignorance of his displeasure, she picks up the wine bottle, turns to Max, and offers, "More?" Without waiting for an answer, she fills Max's glass, then hers. "Don't worry," she says to Ginger, "this is my last."

"As I was saying before being so rudely interrupted," Travis continues in jocular fashion, "I'll bet my sister, by now, has subjected you to one of her relentless inquiries. We've all been through them. Luckily, she found enough test subjects for her research, so we're off the hook. Thank you, Nats, we're very grateful." Travis enjoys getting back at his sister with her own less-than-favorite nickname.

"Ha ha."

"Relentless inquiries. Is that what those are?" Max teases his girlfriend. "Sorry to disappoint you, Natalie, but I never tell a lie." They all smile at his stilted delivery, while Travis muses about the grain of truth to be found in every joke.

Could the same be said about Travis and Natalie? Sibling rivalry is a fact of life, but these two are particularly close, and their style of playful sarcasm is born of deep love for each other. Travis swells with pride for his little sis, who's working toward her PhD in cognitive science on the research team led by Professor Emmett Louden. The world-renowned theorist on perception and memory often testifies as an expert in criminal trials on variables affecting the accuracy of eyewitness identifications. Where such testimony is permitted, Louden is sought by every trial attorney who can pay his fee.

Natalie turns to Max and says, "Sweet. You never tell a lie, *except* when you're under oath!" That sparkle in her eye reveals… what? Love for Max or mere infatuation with his promising screen career? Travis feels a tinge of embarrassment for Nats, but maybe that will resolve once he gets to liking this guy more. He's trying hard.

Natalie's mention of Max's latest role, the biggest to date, brings out a cake-eating grin on his face. "Yes, well, what can we say about Cheryl Hargrove?" He clears his throat. "The term 'relentless' doesn't come close to describing her scathing interrogation!" This one gets a good laugh. They've all seen *Swamp Wars* and especially enjoyed the drama during a congressional hearing of the Committee on Homeland Security. Senator Traci Greggs ripped into FBI Special Agent Justin Fleet, backing him into a perjury trap.

"Cheryl gave you a good drubbing, didn't she?" Ginger says.

"She's an amazing actress."

"And you're not so bad yourself," Natalie says. "That scene was the best in the movie."

"She caught you, all right," Travis says. "The minute before you reached the point of no return, we were all yelling at the TV screen, 'Don't do it! Don't say it!'"

"Special Agent Fleet thought he could outsmart the good senator, but it backfired. He wasn't the brightest lightbulb in the FBI. That's how I played him, anyway. So, it's for the best they threw him in jail."

Yeah, all for the best, but here he sits at the dinner table, sentence served.

Not a bad guy, Travis tells himself. Keep trying.

Ginger and Max surrender to forceful persuasion and remain seated while Travis and Natalie clear the dishes. "Sit, sit, sit!" Travis insists. Nats and I will get these dishes under control and brew the coffee."

"You can warm the pie too while you're at it," Ginger calls after him. "Twenty minutes at three hundred."

"On it."

In the kitchen, as Natalie fills the dishwasher and Travis turns on the oven, she says, sotto voce, "How do you like Max? Isn't he wonderful?"

Travis turns away from the oven to the counter where the apple pie awaits. With his back to his sister, he says, "Yeah. Great guy," raising his enthusiasm level a notch above lukewarm.

"He's really a lot of fun."

"I can see that."

Keeping busy, avoiding her eyes, Travis glances at Natalie's hands before putting the pie in the oven. "Ginger doesn't like to put those wine glasses in the dishwasher."

"Okay." Natalie removes a glass. "But you like him, don't you?"

She's not giving up.

Obviously, he hasn't convinced her, or maybe, she hasn't convinced herself. They stop what they're doing and face each other. Natalie really does care what her big brother thinks. He needs to assure her and postpone any deeper thoughts for another day. The walls in this small apartment aren't soundproof, and Ginger and Max are in the next room. Travis takes hold of Natalie's shoulders, looks her in the eye, and speaks in a low, but sincere, voice. "If he's good to you and good for you, I'm all in. I love the guy." She breaks into a luminous smile. He squeezes her shoulders and lets go. On to the coffeemaker.

"I haven't spoken to Daddy yet, have you?" Natalie asks. "Do you know how it went yesterday?"

"No, but I'm sure he aced it. He's a good pick for the court. There's a lot of competition though."

"I think he really wants it. Won't that be amazing? Two judges in the family."

"Yeah. They'll just have to adjust to Dad being away."

Natalie puts a dinner plate in the dishwasher, straightens up, and turns to him. "What do you mean, 'being away'?"

"In Albany."

"But he interviewed in Manhattan. Isn't the court in Man..." It dawns on her. "Of course. I knew that. I just didn't really think about it." She shuffles the dirty utensils with a nervous clatter. "You mean, he has to move to *Albany*?"

"No, he won't move there. He has to go up several times a year for a week or two at a time, when the court is in session."

"A week or *two*?"

"It's no big deal. It'll be worth it for that job if he gets it. He'll be hearing the most important cases in the state."

Natalie freezes, holding a large serving fork in front of her like *American Gothic*.

"Hey, it's nothing," Travis says.

"They're not having problems, are they?"

"No way!"

"Remember when Mommy was appointed to the Appellate Division? That night, we were kidding Daddy about how she's leaving him behind in the dust, or something like that. I forget the exact words."

"We were all happy and laughing. Dad likes to joke. He started it."

"That could be a reason he applied for this job—"

"Nats!"

"He took it as a personal cut!" She throws her arms wide, fork raised. "He has to prove something to himself."

"You really think our father is that insecure? No way. Not like him at all. Not even close!"

From the other room, Ginger yells, "Hey, what's going on in there? Do I have to break you two apart? I'm sending Max in."

Travis yells back, "All okay! Not too many bruises yet! We're just having fun."

In a lower voice, he says to Natalie, "Look. The opening on the court is a great opportunity, and Dad's going for it, that's all.

His whole career has been leading up to this."

But she doesn't look convinced, her face etched in worry. "I wish we hadn't said those ridiculous things."

"It was five minutes. Everyone was joking, and Dad's the biggest kidder of them all."

Kidding around. But isn't it so? Every joke contains a grain of truth.

4 » COLD

NEEDLES OF FREEZING RAIN on the window and the aroma of freshly brewed Colombian coffee are good reasons to stay inside on a Sunday morning in January. For Dana and Evan, nine o'clock is late, pure luxury to be snuggled in bathrobes, lounging on the living room sofa sipping coffee, newspaper sections strewn over the table.

By the second cup, they are fully awake and ready to think about adding food and conversation. Evan disappears for a few minutes and returns to the living room with two plates, a toasted and buttered muffin on each, dollop of strawberry jam and butter knife on the side.

"Your Honor," he says, setting her plate atop the "Living" section on the coffee table.

"Who's going to prepare my muffin and jam on a Sunday morning when you're up in Albany?"

"Oh, I'll always be home on the weekends."

"I don't know about that," she teases. "During those two-week calendars, you'll be holed up with your colleagues on the weekend, hammering out your opinions."

"Dana! I'm shocked." He sits down in the easy chair, plate on lap, and applies jam to his muffin. Head down, focusing on the task, he keeps the banter going. "I can only *guess* what you're suggesting."

"About the muffin? You make it the way I like it."

"And what about Albany, where I'll be pounding away, as you put it?"

"Hammering." She laughs and takes a delicate bite. He stuffs half the muffin into his mouth and gazes at her with mirth in his eyes. There was a time when he would use that gleeful glibness as a mask for an underlying insecurity. But by now, they understand certain things about each other. Evan's openness and need to connect. Dana's tendency to disguise her innermost feelings—a challenge to Evan's powers of discernment.

She avoids any deeper meaning and keeps it light. "We're well beyond such nonsense, darling." If not well beyond it, well on their way. Although young at heart and comfortable in their strong attachment to one another, they can't say that the sixties compare equally to the forties in every significant way.

He swallows and says, "Thanks for the green light on the *Big Chill* weekends."

"So funny. At the court, you won't have time for anything but the majesty of the law."

"Ooo, you're giving me the shivers. One thing's for sure. The night life in Albany isn't a distraction. Such an exciting place."

"You can keep pretending, but I know you can't wait to get there."

"*If* I get there. The competition is fierce."

"They'd be fools not to pick you. It'll be a happy day when you're appointed."

A happy day for them both, but she doesn't say it like that out loud. No need to stir up the remnants of his old proclivity to misinterpret *her* happiness as a rejection of sorts. He's been joking about her wanting to get rid of him, but nothing is further from the truth.

Here's the crux of it. She'll be happy for Evan to achieve the position he wants and deserves. Happy for herself because she has already achieved what she wants and doesn't feel a jot of jealousy or sense of incompletion. She doesn't yearn for a spot on the higher court. For Evan, if he gets it, the trips upstate are an integral part of the job. Dana has no doubt they'll both enjoy the brief periods of physical separation, without any harm to their relationship. Likely the opposite. They'll grow stronger.

It doesn't mean she won't miss him. She adds, "Of course, I was kidding about the weekends. No *Big Chill* for you. I expect you to come home. I need you here." She mimics a bang of the gavel. "So ordered!"

He shudders to attention, sitting taller in his seat. "Yes, ma'am." He's looking happier but not quite euphoric.

"I can't live without you." She gets up off the sofa, steps to the easy chair, and plants a big kiss on top of his smooth head, not minding that the sides of her bathrobe loosen and open partway.

He grabs her hand. "More please."

She kisses the top of his ear.

"Okay," he says, letting her hand go. "That's better."

She goes back to the couch, and they resume the business of eating. A minute later, she picks up the thought again. "You know how I need your counsel on weekends for the week in review. I can't possibly cover everything on weeknights."

"What's the latest legal disaster at the Appellate Division?"

Dana launches into a detailed summary of the facts and procedure in *Josefina M*. She's curious to know Evan's opinion of the legal issues. "The aunt, Bianca, is appealing the emergency removal order. She has two main arguments. First, she says Josefina is mature enough to make her own healthcare decisions. She wants us to adopt the "mature minor exception" to the statutory age of majority. Alternatively, Bianca claims it isn't abuse or neglect to support Josefina's decision to reject chemotherapy. She's acting in the girl's best interests under the circumstances. What do you think?"

"Seems to me this one is easy," Evan says.

"You're calling this an easy case?"

"I don't mean on the facts. It's incredibly sad. Tragic. I'm talking about the legal issues. The girl isn't eighteen. She's still a minor under the law. Crafting judicial exceptions to statutes is always problematic. If you start playing with who's mature and who isn't, that's a slippery slope."

"I know someone who was more mature than most adults at age sixteen."

Evan doesn't have to guess who she's talking about. "If we'd been in the same situation, I seriously doubt we would have allowed Travis to make the ultimate decision whether to undergo chemotherapy. You're into this mature minor doctrine?"

Dana raises her eyebrows. "I haven't decided yet. All I can say is, this young woman definitely fits the bill from what I've read about her. Only six months shy of eighteen. She's very smart, a national scholar. And the reasons for her decision are rational, based on personal experience."

"This doesn't strike me as a rational situation at all. The girl is terminally ill. How can you make a rational decision when you feel so unwell? Same goes for the aunt. She must be out of her mind with worry and grief. Not an ideal mindset for analyzing her options. Why isn't she doing everything she can to save the child?"

Dana nods, pensively. "A question relevant to the issue of abuse and neglect."

"Exactly. I'd say that depriving a child of potentially life-saving therapy fits *that* bill."

"Even if it causes intense physical suffering and is unlikely to succeed?"

"Even so. The aunt is squandering the only chance to save a young life. It shows disregard for her role as a parent. Abnegation of her duty. That's abuse and neglect under the law."

"I'm not so sure." A moment ago, Dana was sure of the exact opposite, but Evan is, and always has been, a convincing debater. A keen mind. And now, she's not so sure which way she will rule on the case. But that's why they go at it like this, using each other as sounding boards, exploring every argument. "I'll know more when the briefs come in this week. But there's one thing I *am* sure about. You're right, this isn't a situation guided by reason. Statistics and likely medical outcomes aren't the only consideration. It goes deeper into the irrational, the emotional. The bond between parent and child. The support and comfort of family at a crucial time. The relationship between these people, their feelings and beliefs about life itself."

"Are they arguing a religious reason to refuse treatment?"

"No, but it's clear they're very close. They only have each other. The aunt knows Josefina better than anyone, and she's guided by what's best for her—"

"There you go. You just said it. The aunt and the niece are like this," crossing his fingers. "The situation is emotionally charged. They're too close to it. *Exactly* why they need an objective outsider to make the rational decisions. The child is better off in ACS custody so she can get proper treatment."

"The omniscient, all-powerful state, stepping in to save us from our bad decisions."

"You make it sound like a tyranny."

"Isn't that what it is? The state asserts total control. Pulls a teenager out of her home, forces her to live with strangers when she needs the emotional support of family more than ever. Dictates her medical treatment. Sticks the needle in her arm against her will, pumping drugs that can make her feel sicker—"

"Treatment that can save her life!"

"We don't know that for sure."

"But if it works, if she's saved, won't they be grateful? Won't they regret that they ever rejected a chance at life?"

Abruptly, their back-and-forth stops. Dana sighs into their impasse. A bit of cold muffin remains uneaten on her plate. Although their heated argument leaves them at loggerheads, the clash isn't about them personally. They feel and express no rancor. They're energized by debate and thrive on discussions like this. Encapsulated in the realm of the intellect, it's possible to put aside the human impact, the real people who will be affected by the final judicial intervention.

Temporarily. For now.

Bianca and Josefina. Who are these people, their thoughts, fears, beliefs? Is Dana idealizing them? When the time comes to decide the case, her angst over judicial interference into private lives will keep her awake at night. As that day approaches, the litigants come into focus, their existence growing in immediacy. The words in their briefs or their presence in the courtroom will trigger Dana's imagination and deepest compassion. Will Bianca accompany her lawyer to court for the oral argument? Will Josefina be in the audience? Is she strong enough to sit through the proceedings? If she's there, will ACS allow her to sit with her aunt? Dana wants to see them together, to lift the veil between bureaucratic authority and vulnerable subject, to read their thoughts and emotions from their demeanor and facial expressions. To understand the reality and consequence of judicial power.

Impossible.

As Evan's final questions resonate, Dana's eyes wander the room. Evan bends toward the coffee table and deposits his plate, empty but for a few crumbs and a smear of red. He catches her eye on the way up and they exchange smiles. Dialing down from their raised voices of a moment ago, Evan says, in a softer tone, "What's next? I can tell we're not stopping at child abuse."

"Mind reader," she accuses.

"You've got that look."

Another case *is* bugging her, and unlike *Josefina M.*, it isn't about strangers. She knows the people involved and cares about them deeply. To open the subject, she skirts the edges, like testing the water with her big toe. "Citizens for Open Government."

Evan points to the "Week in Review" section. "Today's paper. You weren't fond of that little op-ed about *COG versus AG*?" The columnist, in lofty prose, likened the grand jury to a star chamber and called for its abolishment, beyond the reforms already underway. A complete revamp of New York's criminal justice system. "Opinions like that always come out when passions are running high. You've never allowed the media to get to you."

"Oh, I'm not worried about the press. And my mind is made up on the case. We're bound by the law as it stood when COG filed its petition."

"Your opinion last year in *COG v DA Browne* controls. COG loses. End of story. So, what's the deal?"

She smiles and avoids the real "deal" with a change of subject. "Lucky you. At the Court of Appeals, you won't have to rehash the same issues repeatedly." Dana's court is obligated to hear every direct appeal from the trial courts, including COG's endless lawsuits raising the same issues. But the highest appellate tribunal has the luxury of picking and choosing most of its cases, rejecting requests for a hearing where the law is settled.

Evan says, "I'd never vote to hear a case like this. Why would I? You're already handling it so well."

"Gee, thanks."

"Unless your court issues inconsistent opinions."

"Could happen. We have a potential dissenter. He could take the other judges with him."

"Anything's possible."

"Right about that. To be honest, I don't know how I'd vote if I thought the grand jury got it wrong. But I reviewed all the evidence, and they got it right. There's no basis to charge Officer Welton."

She falls silent again and picks up her coffee. Down to the dregs, the last sip is cold.

Evan waits a moment, expecting more. She hasn't mentioned what's *really* bothering her. "Reminds me of another case the grand jury decided correctly," he says, finally. A hint.

"You know where my head's at."

"Corey McBride and Marlon Stokes. You're not so worried about grand jury procedure as you are about a particular murder case. Why didn't you say so from the get-go?"

Dana twists her mouth into an apologetic grimace. "Maybe it's too painful." She recalls Julian Aird's argument as he tried to distinguish *COG v Browne*: *In that case, we sought to uncover nepotism in the handling of a cop-on-cop killing*. The victim was Officer Marlon Stokes. The grand jury declined to charge Officer Corey McBride with any crime. The "nepotism"? A stretch of the term. Aird was referring to former DA Patrick McBride, Corey's uncle. The current DA, Jared Browne, was alleged to have mishandled the murder case because of his close relationship with Patrick.

"I feel I've let Patrick down," Dana confesses. She still thinks of him in the present tense, as if she's still a rookie, sitting in his office at Trial Bureau 90, spilling her problems and absorbing his sage advice. Her affection and veneration for her former boss and mentor run deep. Patrick is larger than life.

"Just what you need. Irrational self-flagellation."

"Right-o," she laughs. "Guilty as charged."

"Have you heard anything new about the investigation?"

"I have no idea what's going on. I'm worried it's gone cold. Last year, with COG's appeal in our court, I couldn't talk to Jared, and I've let it drag on. We haven't spoken for more than a year, since before my appointment to the AD." She looks at Evan with pleading eyes. "Do you think…?"

"You want to ask Jared about the Stokes case?"

"I've waited long enough."

"More than long enough. I don't see any breach of judicial ethics. And there's nothing to stop you from calling Harriet or Corey either."

Dana rolls her eyes guiltily. She hasn't spoken to Patrick's widow or nephew since the memorial service in late 2020. "I sent them each a brief note when they wrote to me with congratulations on my opinion in the COG appeal. I didn't want to ignore them. Just a short acknowledgment, best wishes and all that. Would've been improper to comment on my opinion. You remember."

"Yeah, they were nice about it."

"I feel for them."

"And this new appeal in your court brought it all back for you."

"Mm-hmm. There've been other times too, whenever it pops up in the news. Jared's political enemies dredge it up and scream favoritism whenever it suits them. They like to imply that Corey got away with murder. Maybe it would've been better for the McBrides if I'd thrown my principles out the window and ordered disclosure of the grand jury materials."

"I don't think so." A loud buzzer interrupts Evan. He gets up and says, "Hold that thought."

But as he walks away, Dana's thoughts shift. An unpleasant idea, buried under the layers, rises to the surface. What makes her so damned sure about her views of the case? People at a distance may see more clearly. Outsiders with the intuition to spot political favoritism. Patrick, her mentor. Jared, her close friend. Men who had and have the power to make decisions that change lives. What makes her so sure that Jared pursued all avenues and Corey is innocent? She doesn't know Corey well, has met him only a few times…

Absorbed in these doubts, Dana picks up and takes their plates and cups into the kitchen. In the background, she hears Evan at the intercom in the foyer. "Thanks, Bashir. Send her up!"

"Natalie?" Dana asks when he walks into the kitchen. Their daughter mentioned she might drop by.

Evan nods. "Yup. I left the door open for her." It will take a few minutes for Natalie to call the elevator in the lobby and ride up seventeen floors to their apartment. "More?" he asks Dana, coffeepot in hand.

"Why not?"

Evan pours. "Where was I? Oh. It wouldn't have made any difference to the McBrides, however you ruled on that case. Politics is always nasty. If you'd opened the evidence to public view, Jared's opponents would have found something in there. The way he questioned the witnesses or his legal instructions to the grand jury. Anything they can twist to make him look bad, if it fits their agenda."

"I know, I know." There's more, but she holds tight to the thoughts she shouldn't be having, her desire to get involved, boots on the ground. In a throwback to her early career, she's reliving an urge to join the investigative team, to interview witnesses, open new channels of evidence, and help Jared in his quest for the truth. Because her heart says that Corey *is* innocent and the killer hasn't been found. But should the heart rule in matters of evidence? Did she merely convince herself that she applied pure reason, untarnished by personal prejudice, when she reviewed the case? Thanks to Associate Justice Dana Hargrove, the evidence heard by the grand jury is now kept under wraps.

"Hello, dear parents!" The front door slams, entirely too loudly. All that youthful exuberance.

Natalie bursts into the kitchen and throws her arms around Evan's neck. "Congratulations, Daddy! But I miss you so *much* already."

"I'm not going anywhere, kiddo!" He sets his coffee cup on the counter. Her assault has nearly caused a spill.

"Travis says you'll be spending *weeks* at a time up in Albany."

"No need to jump the gun. I may not get the job."

"But I heard you *aced* the interview. We were talking about you last night."

"Oh, were you?"

Dana, still distracted, looks on with a gentle smile. Her two rays of sunshine. Natalie inherited all that cheeriness from her father and a face more like his than her mother's. If Evan still had his hair, that would be the same too, dark blonde.

"How about a hug for your mother?" Evan suggests.

"Mommy!"

"Hello, sweetie."

A gentler hug, two-armed from Natalie but one-armed from Dana as she keeps her full coffee cup in hand. Dana is proud of her daughter, now twenty-seven, mature, intelligent, and reasonable, while retaining a few vestiges of childlike behavior. The energy. The tendency to veer off on tangents, head in the clouds. The deep attachment to her parents. Dana loves being Natalie's "Mommy" and always encouraged her to use that endearment. But it never stuck with Travis. She's "Mom" to her son.

Natalie backs up and says, "Look at you two, still in your bathrobes."

"It *is* Sunday," Evan says.

"What time is it?" Dana asks. She hasn't stepped out of her thoughts yet.

"Ten thirty. Practically lunchtime." Natalie takes a longer look at her mother and scrunches her brow. "What's going on here? I'm interrupting something."

"Not at all," Dana says. "We were just talking about a case

that got some press this week."

"In your court?"

"Yup."

"What's the case about?"

"Citizens for Open Government wants to see the evidence in a grand jury investigation."

"Oh, you mean... Wait! I thought that was last year. Isn't that the case Professor Louden was interested in?"

"Mm, no. This is a different case." Cat out of the bag, too late. Dana doesn't like the reminder of Professor Emmett Louden's interference in the Stokes murder investigation. She'd rather not talk about it. "Grab some coffee, and let's go into the living room." Dana gives Evan a look and they head out of the kitchen.

Natalie says, "No thanks, already had my coffee." She follows them but won't drop the subject. After all, her life is currently dominated by her thesis advisor at the university, now that she's winding down her research and starting to write her dissertation. "I never found out if Dr. Louden got to see the recordings in that case," Natalie says. "You know, when the police first interviewed the witnesses on Skype. We're starting to see how the virtual setup skews witness memory and testimonial accuracy."

Dana doesn't comment as they settle in the living room, parents on sofa, daughter in the easy chair. Natalie goes on. "I suppose I could ask Zachary. He's the student who's collecting data from *real* cases. It's just so maddening. I've been cut out of this part of the research."

"I can see how frustrating that would be," Evan says. "But Professor Louden is taking your advantage into account, your firsthand knowledge of the criminal justice system. You grew up in a family of lawyers, not to mention that time you were a witness in a case—"

"Daddy! You don't know how hard I tried, but Zach grabbed

that part of the research. The courts were limiting how many people could get into the courtroom to watch the preliminary hearings. Zach went to a few on his own and some with the Prof."

Exactly what led to Louden's inexcusable interference, Dana is reminded. During the pandemic, investigations and court proceedings went virtual. Police interviewed witnesses on Skype, and preliminary hearings were held via Skype. Only the judge and a few staffers were masked up in court, everyone else on screen, participating remotely, the attorneys, witnesses, and defendant. Dr. Louden, renowned expert in cognitive science, got special permission to attend in person with a student of his choice. Months later, when the grand jury opened again and heard the case against Corey McBride, well, Louden and his big ego just couldn't shut up...

Dana cools herself down. Focus on Natalie, the important work she's doing. Steer this away. "I wouldn't minimize your end of it," Dana says. "Your simulation is an excellent way to test the effects of the virtual set up on cognition and memory."

"Thanks, Mommy, but *real* cases are just that. *Real*. What could be better for our objectives? Zach is comparing real witness interviews and recorded testimony with real outcomes, in the grand jury and after trial."

"But it seems to me your data might be more useful. I'm no scientist, but I think your fellow doctoral candidate is going to have real problems with his data. A lot will be missing. He won't have the entire investigative file, and he has no way of knowing what the witnesses actually saw. Your subjects were questioned about a simulation. You know what they saw and how their recollections are distorted."

"You're right, in a way," Natalie concedes. "But..."

Dana knows she's right. How can Zach possibly get much "real" data to work with? So much is protected from public view by law and evidentiary privilege.

Natalie's attraction to "real" criminal investigation stems from her obsession to understand the vagaries of the human mind. But Dana also knows *this* about her daughter: The drama and tragedy of crime can frighten and overwhelm her. Natalie's direction in life, into academia, keeps her a step removed. She would have been a great detective, but a career in law enforcement would have brought her too close to emotions she can't handle.

Meanwhile, Natalie's face brightens with a new thought. "Can't a witness get a copy of their own testimony in the grand jury?"

Where is she going with this?

"Nothing in the law prohibits it," Evan says.

Thanks, Evan. Dana adds, "You'd still have to petition the court, but the burden isn't as high as an outsider who wants it. Why? You want to see your testimony from 2009?"

"No way, Mommy. I'm talking about the witnesses in that case you decided a year ago. The one where Dr. Louden saw the prelim. I wonder if Zach asked for their testimony?"

Time to stop this! "That case is sealed. When a grand jury declines to indict, the file is under seal to protect the wrongly accused." Dana isn't going to mention that she, in her official capacity, has authority to access those records. She saw the entire file, *in camera*, during COG's appeal, and it still exists in the Appellate Division's electronic files, with a big fat "SEALED" warning in red. "I'd leave it alone, Natalie. The witnesses have a right to their privacy, and your professor…" She holds back the vitriol for Natalie's sake. Dana has held her tongue for a long time, not wanting to put a wedge between herself and her daughter, who so admires the great work of the esteemed Emmett Louden.

"My professor what?"

Dana chooses her words carefully. "I don't think it was appropriate for him to give an interview on TV about the case."

But too late. Her tone is sharp, her displeasure evident. Seeing the hurt and shock on her daughter's face, Dana wishes she could take back what she just said.

5 » *IDES*

Sunday, March 15, 2020, 11:52 p.m.

ALMOST MIDNIGHT, AND Corey was waiting for Marlon.

Everyone on 8-to-12, McBride and Stokes included, would be heading to The Book and Brew, favorite watering hole of the Fifth Precinct. Tough luck for officers on graveyard. They'd miss out on the last chance to go pubbing before Manhattan restaurants and bars were shuttered by executive order. Luck of the Irish—two days before St. Paddy's Day! The beer would be green, but no parade this year. "Two weeks to flatten the curve," was the mantra.

When Marlon entered the locker room, Corey was in blue jeans and bare chested, hanging up his uniform. "Jah has come," Corey intoned gravely with a glance over his shoulder at his friend.

"And alive in everything, Mick." Marlon raised a hand, shielding his eyes from Corey's bare back. "Turn off the glare! Need my shades."

"Hah!" Corey pulled a white polo shirt over his head. "Guttersnipes don't need shades." His head emerged. "You're already coated in scum." He nodded at the Rasta cap on Marlon's head. "And you *look* like scum. I'm getting another date for tonight." Around the room, a few colleagues snickered.

Marlon answered in a high-pitched lover's tone. "Anything

for you, Royce." The classy anagram was Corey's preferred nickname, although he really didn't mind Marlon's ironic version of "Mick." Marlon unpinned and removed the filthy prop from his head, realistically stuffed to create the illusion of copious hair. He hadn't been working undercover long enough to achieve more than short, incipient dreads. "Let me put a comb through this, baby." He scooped a fingerful of his favorite apricot-scented pomade out of a jar, spread it, and raked his scalp with long fingernails.

"Better." Corey, the neatnik, was tucking in his shirt. "But that perfume don't cover the stink."

There was little actual stink in Marlon's ragged clothes, but he played along with a half-lidded euphoric grin. "Wuz a mighty good spliff, mahn."

"Wicked X or Atomic?" But Corey didn't wait for an answer. He grabbed his navy-blue windbreaker, the kind that half the force had bought from the PBA to support the Widows' and Children's Fund. "I'll be in the squad room. If you're not out in five minutes, I'll assume that shit killed you."

Corey hoped to God that "Chug" hadn't actually smoked Wicked X or any other lethal variant of synthetic marijuana that evening, just to maintain his cover. Marlon's assignment was to gather intel that could lead to the identification of manufacturers of synthetic products and additives that had sent many ganja aficionados to the hospital, killing two.

Throughout the stationhouse, boisterous chatter about the impending lockdown heightened the usual ruckus at shift-change time. To fill the roster, some officers had put in overtime. The precinct was down a few members who had caught Covid-19, including the captain. In police work, avoiding human exhalation and spittle was next to impossible. The deadly virus was a new danger, adding to the many risks these public servants already faced.

"Coming?" someone yelled at Corey.

"I'll catch up with you." People were leaving for the pub, but many were still working or starting the next shift. In a corner, detective first grade Aurelina Vargas conferred with two second grades, Rodman and Schutte. Odd to see them here at this time of night, but Corey supposed they were working a lead on a recent unsolved murder that had stymied them.

Glancing around, Corey was satisfied that his partner, Fred Winchell, had already left. Good. Corey had learned to tolerate Fred without having to like him very much. Ten years Corey's senior, Fred had stalled in his ascent up the career ladder, even though—or because—he was the authority on everything. He also liked to make the occasional crack about former District Attorney Patrick McBride, just to get Corey's goat. Fred began his career when Corey's uncle was the Manhattan DA, and he didn't agree with the prosecutor's handling of a few notorious cases. Not that Fred had been personally involved in any of them or had any firsthand knowledge, but everyone is entitled to an opinion, right?

Off duty, Corey preferred to hang out with Marlon, a fellow classmate from the academy. Both twenty-nine, seven years on the job, they'd shared a lot in that time. Different as night and day. Corey was destined for a career in law enforcement from the moment he was born into a family of cops and prosecutors. The brawnier McBrides entered the police academy, the brainier ones went to law school. Corey was midway between the extremes and initially unsure of his path but opted for the NYPD, figuring he'd learned enough law from his uncles, aunts, and cousins. Hours and hours with books did not appeal to him.

Marlon could have pursued any calling. He had the wherewithal, smarts, brawn, *and* sensitivity. Most of all, compassion. Raised in a single-parent household in the Bronx, Marlon came to his career out of gratitude and respect for a beat cop who mentored him through Big Brothers of America. Inquisitive and excited by life, Marlon developed his wide-ranging interests and talents, from playing classical guitar to appreciating the poetry of Langston Hughes and studying the writings of Thomas Sowell. Hell, he could have been an actor raking in millions, Corey liked to say. Marlon understood human nature and dynamics better than anyone. A natural for undercover work. He played the part so well.

Corey excelled at police work but was otherwise uncomplicated and less layered than Marlon. He supposed that stubborn loyalty was the main asset he offered their friendship besides the obvious contrasts in their backgrounds, which kept the relationship interesting. Corey's light didn't shine as brightly as Marlon's, and if the conversation turned intellectual or concerned a subject outside his knowledge, he'd find himself lost. Marlon could infuse enigmatic statements with a daunting power, triggering Corey's bewilderment and frustration. There'd been a few hurt feelings, nothing serious. When alcohol was involved, Corey might not remember the gravity of his reaction.

A few minutes after Corey stepped out of the locker room, Marlon emerged with a scrubbed face, wearing a clean yellow T-shirt. The transformation in appearance was dramatic, enabling him to disavow any relation to Chug, the Rastafarian who gulped bottles of all natural, organic green tea. In a city where a few blocks make a world of difference, his UC identity in the northernmost neighborhood of the precinct was lightyears from The Book and Brew, just inside the territory of the bordering precinct to the south. Marlon didn't worry about being recognized while socializing at the pub, enjoying shots of good whisky. Corey usually drank beer but consumed enough of it to keep up with his friend, and then some.

They donned their jackets and strode out into the cool night. "I can use a couple," Marlon said.

"Bad night?"

"Not the best. Ready to knock back something other than tea."

"Any new leads?"

Marlon glanced right and left and over his shoulder. "We'll talk later. How about you?"

"Just bullshit. Broke up a fight on Mott. Domestic call on Elizabeth."

"Streets are quieter this week."

"Yeah." Corey laughed. "People getting nervous about catching the Chinese bat plague."

"It's no joke, man." Marlon shook his head. "One of my mamma's friends has it. Rushed to the hospital. She couldn't breathe."

Marlon's tenor was dark, enough to suggest that he'd understated tonight's drama on the street when he described his shift as "not the best." Corey was surprised to have touched on a sore point. Sure, the virus was no laughing matter, but the illness itself wasn't personal for him. Of more concern were the doomsday predictions and unprecedented government directives. Ordering businesses to close and people to stay home? Unheard of. Next, they'd be closing the courts and other arms of criminal justice. Corey felt a perfect storm brewing, police work hampered, maybe even shut down by bureaucratic tampering. The department had already undergone years of stress, clashing with a mayor who had no love for cops, and this year, dealing with more offenders on the street after the new bail reform law went into effect.

In front of the pub, a spillover group of drinkers congregated on the sidewalk. The familiar façade displayed a dark wood sign, stretching over the door and windows. In gold lettering, "The Book and Brew" was framed by sets of fat tomes in 3-D, as if propped upright with bookends on a library desk. The owners, a husband-and-wife team, once fancied their pub as a destination for intellectuals, but the clientele had gradually shifted to the law enforcement community. Not that a solid wall divided the two types of customers. There were plenty of jokes and mock indignation about inaccurate profiling. Other patrons suggested that the owners should remove the philosophy books on the sign and install huge sets of handcuffs, in honor of the proper definition of "book."

Corey and Marlon bypassed the sidewalk loiterers and squeezed inside. The dark walls and mirror behind the bar were decorated in green, an overabundance of shamrocks and leprechauns. After some effort, they got the barkeep's attention and scored their first round. A group of four colleagues, two men and two women, drew them in for shouted conversation above the din of voices and music. Politics was the topic underway, a discussion peppered with colorful terms of the crudest sort. In this presidential election year, opinions were heated.

Corey stayed out of it, enjoying his green beer. Steeped in politics from a young age, he'd lived through the ups and downs of many campaigns for public office, the lawyers in his family who'd run for judgeships, district attorneys, and state senate. He admired the liberal traditions of the McBrides and how they'd held fast to a defining line of reason against the erosion of public trust in law enforcement. Evenhanded policing, service and protection, respect for the rights of accuser and accused alike—but law and justice, nonetheless. These had always been the solid values of Uncle Patrick and others in his family.

But Corey had no real interest in politics, the nastiness and games. He kept his distance, didn't like to talk about it. Just wanted to do his job, protect people, keep public order.

With one ear open to the conversation, Corey spotted a server and waved to her. In front of him, the two male cops in the group were suddenly in each other's faces, hurling barbs in a macho contest teetering between good-natured sarcasm and mortal combat. Meanwhile, Corey turned away and leaned into the server, rasping out his drink order. He didn't mind the closeness, his lips nearly touching her ear. She looked and smelled good. People in front of him were arguing? He hardly noticed.

Abruptly, Marlon jostled Corey from behind and pushed past him into the middle of the debate. "You buy that bullshit?" he roared. His powerful voice obliterated the din, stopped them short, jolted their tight circle into stunned silence.

But that was it. Marlon said no more. He turned away, and Corey followed.

They didn't get far into the crush of bodies, jammed together like commuters at rush hour. Corey assumed that a full head of reasoning had triggered Marlon's outburst of "bullshit." He always had the knowledge and insight to support his opinions. In a different setting, he might have expounded, but what was the point in a noisy bar with people who were already half drunk and irrational?

Corey grabbed his shoulder. "Hey, man, what was that all about?"

Marlon turned to him. "Nothing. Forget it."

"Those two are assholes."

"No, they're not."

A surprising statement. Corey wasn't sure he'd heard it right. "They were about to kill each other over some fucking politicians."

Marlon leaned closer and spoke distinctly, resignation in his voice, with a touch of anger. "They're not bad people. They're like half the world. Manipulated. Gaslighted. Fed lines of bullshit on their screens till they believe it."

"I hear you, but—"

"Smiling liars sowing division. When a politician says, 'Let me help you,' he really means, 'Let me help *me*'."

"They were just shooting the shit. Those guys really don't care—"

"That's what I mean, Royce!" Marlon was on fire about this. "Nobody gives a good goddamn. Nobody digs for the truth. Nobody wants to think. They'd rather be hypnotized by a narrative."

Corey shook his head. "Not me. I stay away from politics."

Marlon thrust a fist between their chests and stared at him hard, their noses inches apart. "More than politics, man. It's everywhere," he seethed, "this mind fuck for dominance and control! Power, feeding itself! Obsessed with getting it, keeping it, lording it over you with sweet lies, making you think they're entitled. And no one calls them out on it!"

Had Marlon gone off the deep end? The words spilled out rat-a-tat, his eyes shining in a look akin to despair. Corey couldn't help thinking this was about something else. His friend was pissed as hell about something else. "What's with you, Mar—?"

"Here comes your bae," he interrupted, indicating with a nod.

The server came up behind Corey, balancing several drinks on her tray, among them, another draft beer and a double shot of whiskey. The men exchanged their empties for the fresh drinks, and Corey, with a wink, put a twenty and a ten on her tray, cost plus fifty percent.

"Being mighty generous," Marlon said as she walked away. "'s why the girl likes you. And you like her."

"Yeah, she's a looker."

"Play your cards right, you'll get lucky." Marlon laughed, more relaxed, more himself. He teased Corey about his dry spell, and Corey ribbed Marlon about his fiancée roping him into a proposal.

Somehow, this sudden transformation and change of subject angered Corey. Talk about mind fuck. Marlon was deflecting. What was all that mystifying crap about power a minute ago? Corey gulped half his beer as the surrounding voices grew louder with jokes, shouts, and laughter. He caught Marlon's eye and gave him a sharp look as he tried to formulate a sharp comment to go with it, a rebuke about sending him on a rollercoaster of nonsense. What was really going on here? If Marlon was interested in digging for the "truth," then why wasn't he speaking the truth?

But before Corey could lash out, Marlon's eyes softened under his friend's glare in a silent plea for tolerance. When he spoke, his voice was genuine and dramatic, full of subtext. "Don't be surprised if you hear something about me."

"Hear what?"

"I can't tell you now. You'll know soon enough. But it isn't good. I'll need you to have my back." He quickly turned away from Corey's bewilderment and raised a hand in greeting. "My man!" A friend came up and slapped his palm; they laced fingers and locked hands. Big smiles. This was the Marlon everybody loved. A person who connected with folks on a level that felt like kinship, knowing and historical, without intrusion. His insight into the human condition ran so deep that, at times, it overwhelmed him or carried him away, like it had a moment ago.

In the next hour, as they mingled, sparred, and laughed, Corey couldn't forget where Marlon had left him. The bait had been dangled but the prize withheld. Perhaps it was Marlon's way of smoothing over their rough exchange by explaining his edginess, but it only annoyed Corey and planted the thought permanently. Why hint at a secret just to hold it back? Corey would find out.

By the fourth round of drinks, the spark of curiosity, fueled by alcohol, had burst into flame.

About twelve thirty, Wesley Guerrier and Janjak Bernard squeezed into The Book and Brew. Janjak had convinced Wesley to come. The young man's enthusiasm was hard to walk away from, even if Wesley would rather go home to his sleeping wife and three kids, tucked away in their apartment at the Farragut Houses in Brooklyn.

Janjak and Wesley had just finished their shifts in the financial district, where they worked as security officers for an investment bank on Broad Street. Wesley, a more senior member of the security team, manned the desk in the lobby while Janjak circulated on higher floors. Although the building was busier during regular weekday hours, the crazy workaholics at the bank came and went every day of the week, at all hours. Financial managers, analysts, brokers, and traders. At any moment, somewhere in the world, a financial market was open for trading, or a big deal was in the offing.

Near quitting time, the men spoke by handheld radio. "It's my one-year anniversary," Janjak said. "Let me buy you a drink!"

"Thanks, but I should get home." Wesley, a family man of forty-three, rarely went out drinking after work. Janjak, twenty-two and single, belonged to a different generation and was always ready to party. Although Wesley wasn't a likely companion for late-night carousing, this night was different. A full year on the job, and Janjak's last chance to celebrate before businesses closed. Wesley understood the young man's desire to show his gratitude to the countryman who had gotten him a foot in the door last year, days after he stepped off the plane from Port-au-Prince.

Janjak insisted. "It's the last night we can do this. I know a good place. You'll like it. A lot of police and detectives go there, and security too."

When Jan described the bar and its location, Wes agreed. He figured, what could it hurt? One drink at a pub that wasn't so out of the way, on the route home. Afterward, he'd skip the subway and walk home over the Brooklyn Bridge. The fresh air would do him good.

But when they got there, Wesley wasn't thrilled with the

place. So many people! And so loud! But he smiled and let his young companion lead the way, snaking through the bodies. It took forever to order their drinks, and Wesley was shocked to see what Jan paid for them. Twenty dollars for two beers! Four dollars of that was just the tip. Wesley supposed that a young man without a family could occasionally afford to be so extravagant, but it didn't seem wise. Janjak had just gotten started in his career and earned far less than Wesley.

"Thank you," Wesley shouted, as Janjak handed him the glass. The liquid looked rather strange in the dim light. Green? But he took a sip, and it *did* taste powerfully good. The house draft, whatever brand, cold and frothy.

"You're welcome and thank *you*!" Jan shouted back, a little spray coming out of his mouth. "Isn't this a great place!"

Wesley nodded.

"Maybe my friend is here. The cop who told me about it. We came here last week."

They inched through the crowd, looking around. Wesley saw two familiar faces and stopped short, turning his back to them in embarrassment. Financial analysts, so young, but they already made ten times more than Wesley. In their late twenties, they were well on their way up the ladder into the top one percent. Wesley had signed them in and out of the building countless times, with a "good morning" ("afternoon," "evening," or "night," depending). Why had they come to The Book and Brew when they could afford The Mark? For that matter, how had Wesley ended up here, a duck out of water for the opposite reason? Maybe this bar was convenient for the young analysts too, on their way home to luxury high rises in uptown Manhattan—*not* to public subsidized housing in Brooklyn.

Janjak didn't seem to notice Wesley's discomfort and became excited when he saw his friend talking with another man who might have been a colleague, a fellow officer. Janjak pushed through the crowd, Wesley close behind. The friend smiled but didn't seem particularly happy to see Janjak. Names were shouted and they spoke briefly in Creole before changing back to English. Wesley smiled and nodded but was having trouble hearing anything. The men flagged down a server and ordered more drinks. Wesley refused a second drink with gestures and sign language, shaking his head and lifting his half-full glass to demonstrate lack of need.

An hour or more of this went on. Additional "friends" were found. Wesley did a lot of nodding and smiling and one-word rejoinders, trying to think of a polite way to leave, but then he accepted a second beer when Janjak was on his third. Not accustomed to drinking, he started to feel the buzz and couldn't help enjoying it. The noise and crush of human bodies was now a step better than tolerable, almost otherworldly, floating and magical.

"Hey, Wes. How's it go, man?" Jan yelled this good-natured greeting as if he'd just discovered Wesley by his side. He was obviously feeling a nice buzz too.

"Good brew," Wesley said, taking a big gulp, the last one. The first glass had been sipped, this one he slugged. "I'll find the men's room," he said as loud as he could, and maybe Janjak understood. He nodded.

Wesley zigzagged to the back, leaving his empty glass on the bar as he went. He was surprised to feel the effects so strongly. In a dark hallway, he propped up against the wall next to three people, waiting in line for one of the single rooms, unisex or no sex or whatever they meant with signs on each that said, "Anyone." Wesley's rest stop, from start to finish, seemed to take forever or no time at all, he didn't know. He'd lost any sense of the clock, and the cell phone in his pocket had gone dead. When he returned to the barroom, he resolved to get out of this place, to go home to Fabienne. He'd left her a voicemail at midnight and hoped that she'd listened to it, but he doubted she was awake or even aware of the time. If she woke up now and found him still gone at this hour, she would be worried. Maybe shocked. He felt a bit of shame. He liked that boy Jan and was glad to see him enjoying himself, but there were more important things in life.

The crowd had thinned somewhat while maintaining the same decibel level. Fewer voices, more heavily fueled. Wesley formulated the words he planned to say to make his escape as he searched the barroom. It would be nice to walk out of here together, to have some company on the street this late at night, but Wesley had no real worries. He would go solo if need be.

Janjak saw him and raised a hand. He'd shifted spots and stood closer to the front door. Good. That would make his exit easier. Jan lifted his glass and pointed to it, nodded his head enthusiastically, and pointed at Wes, all of which seemed intended as an invitation for another round. Wesley, now a few steps away, sliced the air with his hands and shook his head, "no."

"Thank you for the drinks, but I best make it home."

"You sure?" Janjak started to introduce him to a new friend but couldn't remember his name. The man filled in the blank with something like "Bob" or "Rob." They were standing next to the end of the bar where it curved around, connecting to the wall. Every barstool was filled, the two closest to them taken by men having a heated conversation, radiating aggressive vibes.

"Nice to meet you," Wesley said to "Rob," not sure if he could hear. To Jan he said, "Thanks again, I'll just—" When suddenly, he was jostled, a sharp elbow in his side. Startled, he turned to the bar, to the man closest, who must have twisted away from his companion abruptly, sending his elbow into Wesley's ribs.

"Sorry! You okay?" The man touched Wesley's arm and gave him a direct look full of real concern.

Everything seemed like a dream. "Okay, okay," Wes sputtered, more than ever ready to get out of there.

The man who'd elbowed him turned away again and had another tense exchange with his companion that ended with something like, "Let's take it out of here." They got up and walked away. Wesley's eyes followed them to the coat rack near the door, where they grabbed their jackets and walked out.

Janjak touched Wesley's shoulder, leaned in, and asked, "Did that guy hurt you? I didn't really see..."

"No, no, it's okay."

Janjak smiled, but his eyes had changed, watery and sleepy with drink but not smeary enough to hide the worry under his furled brow. Like a son for his father. He gulped the rest of his brew and said, "Let's get out of here. I'm ready." He placed his empty on the bar and nodded at his new friend, making no further effort to nail down his exact identity. With a motion of his head—a tilt to Wesley and a toss to the front door—he indicated an immediate intention to leave.

Wesley was flooded with relief. That Janjak. He really was a good kid.

Marlon regretted saying anything about it. He should have gone straight home after work and avoided this crowd scene. His mind wasn't in the right place, a burden weighing so heavily that he couldn't shake the mood. It showed. Corey saw it. And Marlon's attempt to diffuse the bad feelings had backfired.

What an idiotic slip. He knew better and should have foreseen that Corey wouldn't let it go. The bar environment was no help. Marlon's estimate was roughly fifty-fifty: the good times and problematic times he'd had with his friend while out drinking. Corey and alcohol were not always a good mix. Not crisis level. Marlon had never seen Corey out of control or under the table, but there'd been times, like tonight, when the alcohol made him indignant and combative.

Marlon had said something about it a few times, all in jest, while meaning to make a stronger point one day, suggesting that Corey avoid alcohol. Marlon would lend support and encouragement. But not now. This wasn't the night. Another time, when they were both lucid and rational.

The pub scene was still going strong when they walked out, almost two hours remaining until closing at 4:00 a.m. Marlon was well past his threshold and anxious to leave. The squabble with Corey at the bar was the last straw.

"Let's take it outside."

Marlon stepped out at a good pace, the fresh air slapping him alert. Corey stumbled and fell back a few paces, adding to his unhappiness. He caught up and they walked together in stony silence. After a while he grabbed Marlon's arm and said, "Hold it! We've taken it outside. So let's have it."

Marlon halted and jerked away, like he'd done at the bar a few minutes ago when he accidentally jabbed that fellow standing next to him. As a precaution, he glanced around at the nearly deserted street. They were a block away from the pub, and only a few pedestrians were around, walking with purpose, noses to the ground. He took a conciliatory tone. "Chill, man. I didn't want to raise a whole thing about it."

"You want me to have your back, then you tell me who it is."

"Who *what* is?"

"Don't give me that! You think I'm blind and deaf? It's obvious. You have a problem with someone. Who is it?"

"The less you know, the better for you. It's dangerous." Marlon started walking again. But, damn, he'd just made it worse! Corey took his comment as a personal cut.

"Dangerous! You think you have the corner on danger? What do you think I *do* every day? I'm on the streets like you."

Is that what this is? A competition about who's job was more dangerous? Corey had no taste for undercover work and had never expressed a desire to do it. He knew he'd be no good at it, stick out like Mr. Clean. But there'd always been a hint of insecurity and admiration for Marlon, and now, the beer was talking. How many had he drunk? Four or five at least.

Marlon picked up the pace. "Sorry, man. My bad. My mistake. I shouldn't have said anything."

"I'm talking about trust here!" Corey beat his chest with a fist. "Where's the trust?"

They were nearing the spot where they would part, City Hall Park on the left, the pedestrian ramp to the Brooklyn Bridge on the right. Corey would be taking the subway to his apartment on the West Side of Manhattan while Marlon walked over the bridge to Brooklyn.

Marlon didn't need the extra burden of his friend's resentment hanging over everything else he was dealing with. But he recognized his part in causing it. He grabbed his friend's shoulders, looked him straight on, and gave him a genuine promise to include him when the time came, to enlist Corey's strength, friendship, and trusted support when the moment was right. And Marlon spoke many more words in all sincerity, using his talent for crafting language in a way that could draw in another soul, heart to heart.

Did Corey go for it? Did he understand and accept it?

They embraced and parted.

Wesley was glad for the company home. He wasn't sure if Janjak was just humoring him by claiming that he also wanted to walk home instead of taking the subway. They both lived in Brooklyn, only a few buildings away from each other on the other side of the bridge.

Wesley attempted a joke about it. "Nice of you to walk this

old man home!"

"Ah!" Jan swiped a hand through the air and teetered a bit, rebounding from the motion. "I was ready to get out of there too. But you liked it, didn't you? Had a good time?"

"Oh, yes, of course. A good way to celebrate."

The air was crisp, and Wesley felt better to be outside, walking. The world was more sharply defined, even though he still felt like he was floating. In half an hour he'd be home, and if Fabienne was awake, he'd explain everything. There'd be no problem. She'd understand. She liked this kid Janjak as much as he did. In the morning, she'd let Wesley sleep in while she got the kids ready for school. That was always her way even when he got home at his usual time after a late shift, between twelve thirty and one. Fabienne and the children would all wake up at six or six thirty, and sometimes, in a half-wakeful state, he'd hear her scolding them in a raspy whisper, "Hush, children. Your father needs his sleep."

But… How had he forgotten? The schools were also closing! The children would be staying home. Six, nine, and eleven years old they were, his two girls and the youngest, a boy. Well, maybe they'd all sleep in, and later, as a family, they'd figure out how to get through these next weeks. The mayor had said there would be "remote learning," whatever that was, starting March 23, and the schools would reopen in a month, April 20. Wesley and Fabienne had only one laptop at home, and it wasn't in the best shape. Nothing like the amazing computer system at the lobby desk in the building where he worked.

The sidewalks were quiet, only a few people out walking. Within minutes of leaving the pub, they reached the pedestrian ramp to the Brooklyn Bridge. About fifty meters ahead, two men were pressed together in a tight embrace. Wesley was embarrassed by the public display. He slowed his pace and quickly looked away.

But then he heard Janjak say, "What's going on there?" Wesley looked again, and the men weren't doing what he'd imagined. It looked like one of them embraced the other tightly with both arms and slowly descended with him to the ground. The other was apparently sick, trying to hang on with an arm hooked around the hugger's neck. Janjak and Wesley approached slowly but kept their distance. Who knew? Maybe the man was coming down with this new plague.

As they started to pass, keeping a wide berth, the sick man was sitting on the ground without much of him visible under the back and arms of the man holding him. "Everything okay?" Wesley asked tentatively.

The crouched man gave them a fleeting glance over his shoulder, then quickly looked down again at his companion. "No problem here!" He laughed loudly. "My friend just had a few too many!"

Janjak said, "Okay, okay," and tugged at Wesley's sleeve. They kept walking. A short distance on, Wesley had a new thought. "If he's that drunk, maybe he needs a doctor."

Jan shook his head, staggered a bit, and said, "He's okay." He chuckled, not a care in the world, clearly still feeling his own buzz. "His friend is helping! Looks like those two made up. You remember them, don't you?"

"What do you mean?"

"From the bar. The two men arguing."

"That was them?"

Janjak stopped dead and swayed a bit. "Yeah. The one who said, 'no problem,' was with the guy who hit you at the pub."

"It was an accident. He didn't mean it."

They turned around. Behind them, in the distance, the sick man was a dark lump on the ground. Alone. His friend was nowhere to be seen.

Janjak said, "Falling down drunk!"

"But where's the other guy? We should call an ambulance."

In a confused minute, they realized they didn't have a way to call. Wesley's cell phone was dead, and Janjak, in his foggy state, couldn't find his phone in any of his pockets. Had he left it at work or the pub?

Just then, a stranger appeared next to them, on his way into Manhattan. "Excuse me," the man said, wanting to pass. Wesley and Janjak had been pacing around aimlessly as they talked, monopolizing the walkway.

"Sorry," Jan said, scooting aside.

"Wait! That man needs help," Wesley said, pointing. "Do you have a phone?"

The man jumped aside in alarm, but when he saw what Wesley indicated, he pulled a phone out of his pocket. "What happened to him?"

"We think he's drunk, but maybe it's something else."

The man dialed, and as he spoke to the operator, he started walking slowly toward the fallen figure.

They watched for a few seconds until Jan turned Wes around by the elbow. "He'll take care of it."

"Yes, but…"

"Don't you want to get home?"

Wesley thought of Fabienne. Yes, he *did* want to get home. He'd like to be home *right this minute* if he could. "I suppose he'll be all right. That man will get help."

They walked on.

6 » CLUES

Monday, January 10, 2022

DANA'S REAWAKENED OBSESSION with the Marlon Stokes murder investigation won't leave her alone. Before starting her workday, she'll give Jared Browne a call. She's dying to know if he's made any progress.

At her desk, before dialing, she considers the optics. This is not an official call to the DA. She picks up her cell phone and taps her contact entry for his, both numbers reserved for family and close friends. Dana is one of his closest. So much so that she's surprised to realize how much time has elapsed since their last conversation. Sure, they're busy people, and yes, ethics rules erect a wall around certain topics. But Dana and Jared have never allowed their careers to interfere with their friendship. She's reminded of her priorities, on guard, anew, against losing perspective and skewing the balance toward all work and no play.

On guard, also, against slipping through the transparent wall between personal and professional, worming her way into a place she has no right to be. A year ago, she turned away from the heartbreak. Now, she wants back in. Her latest case at the court reminds her of the Stokes murder and reignites the flame. A resurgence of emotion drives her to become fully embroiled, just as a faint voice tells her to hold back, to show restraint.

The prospect of a comfortable conversation between friends

who know each other well should be enough of a reason to call. They can laugh over old times and catch up on the news. But she's guiltily aware of the true impetus for her call: a criminal investigation that concerns her deeply on a personal level. She has no official authority to work the case. She isn't a prosecutor or an investigator. She shouldn't intrude. But she wants to help, to brainstorm, to make suggestions. Nothing wrong with that, is there? Especially when close friends are involved.

Dana and Jared go way back. Fresh out of law school in 1987, they were rookie recruits at the Manhattan District Attorney's Office, two of the littlest fish in a pool of nearly 500 assistant district attorneys. They became best buddies, the closest of comrades under fire in a communal office they shared with two other ADAs. In their noisy, confusing, tumultuous environment, each handled a caseload of two-hundred-plus misdemeanors under the supervision of bureau chief Patrick McBride. In 1994, their wise and revered mentor Patrick was elected District Attorney, reelected three times, and served until 2009, when he "retired," only to get even busier as a board member, consultant, or policy advisor for every criminal justice commission and agency under the sun.

A lot can change in thirty-five years. Half the cases assigned to the rookies in 1987 wouldn't be sneezed at today. Farebeat, loitering for prostitution, jostling, unlawful gambling, disorderly conduct, public marijuana smoking. They learned the ropes on cases that were considered the throwaways, the lowest street crime and quality of life infractions. If they made mistakes along the way, who would be hurt? Plenty of people, Jared and Dana realized, guided by conscience. Even the "little" cases sow big consequences for the defendants and their families, witnesses, and victims. The young ADAs vowed never to lose sight of their duty to strive for the truth, never to abuse the power they possessed to prosecute their fellow human beings. The goal:

justice. *Not* the same as lock 'em up.

Have they been true to their ideals, faithful to their oaths? In these thirty-five years they've ascended the ladder of position, prestige, and power. From their start as rookies handling misdemeanors, they went on to become experienced trial attorneys prosecuting felonies, to senior trial counsel on homicide chart, to supervisors of junior prosecutors. After that, their paths diverged. Jared was an executive assistant DA before being elected the Manhattan DA when Patrick retired. Dana was elected DA of a suburban county before entering the judiciary, first as a trial judge, now as an appellate judge. Through the years of growing friendship and mutual admiration, they've shared their challenges and helped each other through the storms.

Now, as Dana taps Jared's personal number to start the connection, she plans only to arrange a social meeting, knowing they'll both be interested in talking about Corey McBride and Marlon Stokes. A sensitive topic they shouldn't discuss on the phone. And when they're together, they won't be able to avoid what's right in front of them, the heart of the matter, their love and reverence for Patrick. May he rest in peace.

Jared is an early bird, so she expects he's already in his office. It's just past eight thirty. Will he pick up?

"Hey, stranger!" Jared sounds happy to get her call.

"Hey, stranger, yourself. I think it's time we get together, don't you?"

"Couldn't agree more."

Their day is full, and neither one thinks it a good idea to meet at the other's office or in a public place. Lunch or dinner on the town with bodyguards? They're both public figures, and as a consequence, they make tradeoffs in their lives to maintain privacy. Jared is always more concerned about this than Dana. Judges tend to make headline news far less than the DA of the largest prosecutor's office in the country.

Jared offers to host. They will meet this evening, after work, after dinner, at his apartment.

Drinks in hand, comfortably settled in Jared's den, they catch up on the essentials. Jared's wife Delia has joined them, encouraging Dana to have a glass of wine with her. Jared sips at two inches of cognac in a wide-bowled snifter.

What do parents always talk about? Their children. The bragging rights don't expire when the "kids" are in their twenties and thirties. Jared and Delia's three are all out of college or grad school and well on their way in the world. Dana shares the latest in Travis's law career, Natalie's progress toward her PhD, and Evan's aspirations for the Court of Appeals.

Delia glances heavenward and sighs deeply, her face a vision of serene radiance. "We can all be thankful our families made it through these very hard years."

"Yes," Dana says, "and *you* get the biggest share of everyone's thanks." Delia, an internist at one of the city's largest hospitals, was in the front lines at the height of the pandemic, working long hours.

"I just wish Patrick had made it. I know how you miss him."

Jared and Dana nod somberly.

"I miss him too. Greatly admired the man." Delia pauses, allowing silence to fall for just a moment before she pats the armrests of the easy chair and stands up. "I know you two have things to discuss. Just holler if you want anything." She steps delicately through the carpeted room and closes the door behind her on the way out.

"I still can't believe Patrick's gone," Jared says, pausing for a sip of warmth from the snifter. "He was my go-to advisor whenever I was between a rock and a hard place. Saved me a hundred times. I still have conversations with him in my head."

"Me too. Remember how he almost ran everywhere he went? Used to stride into our office with all that energy. He seemed so healthy. He was the last person you'd think the virus would take down."

"He was seventy-six…"

"And we're sixty."

"Speak for yourself," Jared says with faux indignation.

"Oh, that's right. I'd say you're holding up admirably well for fifty-nine. Just wait till sixty hits." Their shining eyes meet and hold, Jared's all-inclusive smile drawing her in. She's reminded of the nickname she coined for him when they were rookies. Denzel. Use of the nickname has fallen off over the years while the resemblance has not.

"Happy belated birthday, by the way," Denzel says. "A milestone. And you haven't changed a bit from the day I met you."

"You're *so* kind." The crow's feet and looseness under the chin weren't there the day they met, but he's right about a few things. Dana's tall frame is still slender and lithesome. Her hair is still thick, shiny, and dark as mink (with help from a bottle of "cover the gray"). More important, she still holds fast to the ideals of truth and justice, even when reminded of their elusiveness. "I never used to think about age, especially with seventy-six-year-olds like Patrick running around. Now, maybe I'm more aware of numbers."

"He did radiate that patina of youth."

"You're a poet."

"My next calling." He smiles. "Patrick was so driven, it may have affected his health. Always working, even in retirement." Jared puts finger quotes around the last word. "Every politician and criminal justice advocate wanted his opinion. And he never missed a step, kept up to speed and then some. Studied the trends and could see the future."

Is Jared suggesting that Patrick worked himself to death?

Dana wouldn't agree. "He loved to think and talk about the law. Couldn't keep still. Thrived on stress, if you could call it that. To him, it wasn't stress."

"You're right about that."

"But…," she has to be careful about this, "above all, he was a family man."

"Unavoidable when your clan populates half the state. All those McBrides."

"And one of them, a favorite nephew. Corey's situation weighed heavily on Patrick, don't you think?"

Dana recalls her last conversation with Patrick, the month before he got sick. He kept up a good front and glossed over Corey's "situation" with an optimistic forecast, but she could detect the underlying anguish. His distress ran deep and wore on him, not to mention the bad press and political problems surrounding the case.

A physically strong and fit man, so he appeared. But emotional stress, in anyone, can batter the immune system, weaken a person to the point of vulnerability, susceptibility. The illusion of invincibility dissolves rapidly, replaced by an awakening. Life is fragile. A razor thin line separates this existence and the next. Dana grasps at this explanation because she needs one, because her powers of logic and intellect are no help. The disease kills some and spares others. Evan, a social animal, came down with the virus but recovered in a week. Dana never caught it, or so she thinks. For all she knows. She could have been asymptomatic.

Ironically, Patrick's ordeal arose during a respite in the pandemic. In the summer of 2020, infection and hospitalization rates dropped dramatically and the second wave was still months away. Restrictions on gatherings were eased. Cause to celebrate. The Long Island arm of the McBride clan hosted a barbeque on Saturday, July 25. It was the last time many in the family saw Patrick alive. Corey did not attend. He was still in the middle of his nightmare. But he was a topic of conversation that afternoon, discussed and worried about, dampening the smiles of many on that sunny summer day.

After the family party, everyone carried on with their lives except Patrick. He woke up one morning gasping for air and was rushed to the hospital where, two weeks later, his life ended. No one was blamed. Possible exposures were theorized. Two college-age McBride cousins at the barbeque had recently returned from an out-of-state trip to a Covid-19 "hot spot." But Patrick had also been exposed a day earlier during a meeting with members of the DA's Association, one of whom later developed symptoms.

Of one thing, Dana is sure. On his death bed, Patrick would've had no regrets about working through the summer, meeting with other legal experts and brainstorming. He wasn't about to sit back. The criminal justice system was in crisis mode. There'd been anti-police riots, and big swaths of the system were shut down or struggling to keep pace via computer screen. Patrick and others were developing recommendations for these immediate emergencies and long-term reforms. Ways to uphold constitutional rights of inmates in a system brought to its knees during lockdown. Measures to ease the growing backlog in the courts. Changes in policing to address widespread public criticism. Revisions to the criminal procedure statutes to promote transparency and accountability.

As for the Stokes murder investigation, Patrick died before the charges were dropped against his nephew. In early August 2020, the grand jury voted "no true bill," declining to indict Corey. But this outcome offered only partial closure. The Stokes and McBride families still need the full story. Who killed Marlon? Dare they think that the grand jury might have gotten it wrong? Doubts about Corey's guilt still linger. Dana isn't sure how prevalent those doubts run within the two families, the law enforcement community, and the public in general. Insinuations are dragged out in the media from time to time. Corey hasn't returned to his career with the NYPD, and as far as Dana knows, he may still be struggling to find his new purpose in life.

And so, it's a touchy subject when Dana asks Jared, "Corey's situation weighed heavily on Patrick, don't you think?" The question hovers between them. She doesn't fault Jared for any of the pain Patrick might have felt about Corey's ordeal, but she suspects that, deep down, Jared might blame himself. He answers her question with a silent nod but changes the subject. Almost. "Delia and I saw Harriet about a month ago. She's hanging in there. Have you spoken to her?"

"Not since the memorial. But we did exchange brief notes after my opinion in COG against you-know-who." She grins, trying to make it light.

"Your Honor. Let me remind you it wasn't personal. The defendant was 'Jared Browne, in his *official* capacity as DA of New York County.' By the way, I think Patrick would have approved of your opinion in that case, even though he recommended changes to the grand jury statutes before he died. What a hellish summer that was."

"He never would have been okay with wholesale disclosure just to please the mob."

"No, you're right about that. But he felt it was possible to have a middle ground. Limited disclosure to promote transparency but with procedural safeguards to protect witnesses, jurors, and the wrongly accused."

"That's what the AG argued last week in the Lonnie Douglas shooting. A compromise position while we're in this statutory limbo. Of course, COG wants the whole shebang." Dana holds back from revealing her debate with Judge Morgenstern. In a pending case, she shouldn't comment on the inner workings of the court, even to a trusted friend. But the parties' arguments in open court are public record. "Guess how the appellant's attorney distinguished *COG v Browne*."

"Who was arguing?"

"Julian Aird."

"Let me guess. Aird said something like, 'Who the hell cares anymore about DA Browne's official decisions?'"

"Close but not quite. He argued that the public interest in uncovering 'nepotism' in the handling of a cop-on-cop killing is not as compelling as the need to reveal unlawful police action in shooting an unarmed man."

"Nepotism. That's a good one. I'm not related to anyone involved. And Corey wasn't applying for a job."

"Kind of a cute analogy though, don't you think?"

"Ha ha. But just so you know, I have *no* complaints that the governor took these cases off my plate."

Dana and Jared don't need to rehash the political scene that ignited new procedures, shifting the responsibility for investigating police brutality from local to state authorities. At the time of the Stokes murder in March 2020, the New York State Attorney General, by executive order, had authority to investigate the killing of any "unarmed civilian" at the hands of the police. But the AG deferred the Stokes case to Jared because it didn't seem to fit. Although Corey was a person of interest, he wasn't initially a suspect, and even so, the killing of an off-duty cop didn't easily fall under the definition of "civilian." Had the crime occurred a few months later, the AG would have handled it. In June 2020, new legislation broadened the AG's authority, removing any ambiguity in the earlier directive.

"Let the AG handle those cases," Jared goes on. "I have plenty of other ways to get bad press. Soaring crime rate, more gun crimes and murders, a huge backlog, felons released without bail committing more crimes."

"Speaking of bad press," Dana says, "you still haven't gotten a free pass when it comes to the Stokes case. The media smear against you and Patrick gets recycled on slow news days, or whenever it suits them." *No thanks to Natalie's dear Professor Louden*. Dana tamps down this thought, in keeping with her habit of avoiding any reminder of her dislike for that man, big ego, stellar reputation, and all. Over the years, she's seen Louden enough times in court, on the news, and at conferences to form a strong opinion of his personality. As for his unwanted involvement in the Stokes case, Dana doesn't need to remind Jared of the details. He knows perfectly well what happened.

"Media smears. All part of the job," Jared says.

"Not a very nice part of the job. Not a fair part of the job, but then again—"

"Whoever said life was fair? Especially in the public arena. You've had your own boxing matches, Dana. We get bruised and build a thick skin."

Jared's bruises were many. He was the punching bag for everything that went wrong in the case. The first news articles reported that off-duty Police Officer Marlon Stokes was found at two thirty in the morning, unconscious, in a pool of blood on the pedestrian walkway of the Brooklyn Bridge. He was pronounced dead at the scene. A day later, more details hit the internet. Police Officer Corey McBride, nephew of the former Manhattan DA Patrick McBride, was the last person to see the victim alive. Stokes and McBride had been drinking at The Book and Brew. Yet, DA Jared Browne, a protégé of the former DA, did not see fit to arrest McBride.

"I have no regrets about how I handled it, from the minute Lina called me in the middle of the night." Jared is thinking back, looking into a near distance as he declares his lack of regret. He takes another sip, his snifter nearly empty.

Jared was personally involved from the start, choosing not to delegate the inquiry to an ADA in his office. Not immediately. Soon after Marlon's death, before dawn, he got the call from

Detective Aurelina Vargas, lead investigator. Hours earlier, at midnight, Lina had seen Corey and Marlon heading out to The Book and Brew. She suggested they call Corey in for questioning before news of the murder hit the outlets.

Early morning, in a private room at the DA's office, Jared and Lina videorecorded a Q&A with Corey, who was clueless as to why they'd called him in. They broke the news of Marlon's death. "How?" Corey was shocked and confused. "He was fine when I left him." Lina tested him with a few open-ended questions, giving nothing away, looking for a slipup that didn't happen. Finally, Jared revealed, "Marlon was murdered." But he kept quiet about the pre-autopsy cause of death: a deep stab wound mid-chest between the ribs, angled up into the heart.

Corey was devastated. He kept asking, "But how did he die? Who did this?" His ignorance seemed genuine. Jared found no reason to arrest him. Why would he stab his best friend? The murder weapon was not at the scene, never found. Later that day, Corey turned in the clothes (he said) he'd been wearing the night before. No evidence of blood spatter.

Days later, the lead detective ran into troubles of her own. Lina's husband came down with a life-threatening case of Covid-19. Before taking a personal leave of absence, she assigned the investigation to Detective Kyle Rodman, the most senior member of her team. The case went nowhere until an eyewitness magically came forward in April, claiming to have seen McBride and Stokes at the pub, and later, on the Brooklyn Bridge. The witness convinced his drinking buddy to come forward too, and Detective Rodman interviewed them individually via Skype. They identified Corey from a photo on the screen.

After watching the interviews, Jared was skeptical. More than a few things seemed off or unexplained. Why did they delay in coming forward? How much did they drink that night? Was there enough light in the pub and on the bridge? Couldn't have been very well lit. Nor was a photo identification via Skype reliable. Had they seen Corey's image in the newspapers or online? Entirely possible. In this and every case, Jared's angst was starting to grow about the impact of social distancing on solid police work, the switch to virtual platforms. All things considered, there was a real chance of misidentification.

Jared decided the evidence against Corey was insufficient to charge him. In a system that was getting more backlogged by the minute, how could he subject Corey, a police officer, to the dangers of jail on such a thin case?

The police interviews of the eyewitnesses were confidential, but as things happen, word got out. Who leaked the story? Jared hadn't a clue as the headlines started to appear, worsening into a scandal as time went on.

Mystery Witnesses Name Former DA's Nephew in Cop's Murder

Pressure Mounts for Arrest of McBride

DA Browne Fails to Act in Stokes Murder Case

Is Nephew of Former DA McBride Getting Away with Murder?

As pressure mounted, Jared became convinced his judgment was clouded. He resolved to put the evidence before a neutral arbiter. But the normal route—the grand jury—was closed due to the pandemic. The governor, by executive order, had suspended all procedural time limits, and the system was jammed. The only option was a preliminary hearing on Skype. Demand was high, and hearings were available only for jailed arrestees who might languish in Rikers even longer than the usual ridiculously long waits. Pretrial detainees accused of misdemeanors and low-level felonies were released on their own recognizance, but the same wouldn't happen in a murder case.

At a preliminary hearing, the judge decides only whether there's reasonable cause to hold the case for grand jury action. In normal times, busy prosecutor's offices rarely take this extra step. They go immediately into the grand jury. But these were unusual times. A prelim offered Corey his only chance to beat the charge at the outset. The only chance for Jared to prove, publicly, his fairness and good judgment.

Before making an arrest, Jared arranged everything in advance. Filed a felony complaint, got a hearing date. A questionable move? Was he using his position to pull strings in a high-profile case? Jared didn't let skeptics worry him. Any prosecution against an alleged cop killer was the kind of case, even objectively, that should be prioritized. And now that they were going to court, Jared delegated the prosecution to ADA Ernest "Ricky" Chin, a career prosecutor and top litigator, formerly Dana's deputy when she was chief of a trial bureau, early in the century.

Jared kept the drama to a minimum. There was no surprise arrest at dawn with a perp walk. Corey cooperated, got a lawyer, surrendered voluntarily and discreetly, out of public view. He was arraigned via Skype and remanded. Spent two days at Rikers, segregated from gen pop, awaiting his prelim.

The only aspect completely beyond Jared's control was the courtroom assignment. Judge shopping is not allowed. A spin of the wheel in the court's random assignment system got them Seth Kaplan, Justice of the New York County Supreme Court.

Responding to Jared's comment that he had "no regrets," Dana quips, "I'll bet you and Ricky had a few regrets when you drew Seth's name."

"We had a brief panic attack." Jared winks at her. "But our old friend didn't do so badly." Former Legal Aid attorney Seth Kaplan squared off against Jared and Dana many times in their early careers. He was a gifted and successful champion of the underdog, fought like hell for every client. Didn't like or trust any police officer and was no fan of DA McBride. How would Seth's preconceptions and sympathies lie in this case, an alleged cop-on-cop killing, the defendant related to the former DA? Corey was no underdog or victim of the system, not a person to stir the judge's inborn sympathies.

"Say it," Dana taunts. "You were hoping *I'd* get the assignment! All of this could have been avoided." She was a trial judge at the time, on the roster for preliminary hearings.

"Would've been nice, but you would've come out the same way, Dana, and you know it."

"You're saying I'm not up to throwing a case?"

Jared picks up the wine bottle, leans forward, and hovers over her glass. "Here. I don't think you had enough."

They break out laughing as Dana waves the wine bottle away.

Settling down, Jared says, "But think about it. I have. I was deluding myself that it might go away at the prelim stage."

"Witness IDs. Not one, but two. Against the testimony of a self-interested defendant."

"You got it. Judge Kaplan didn't need proof beyond a reasonable doubt. Just reasonable cause. Barely enough to hold it for the grand jury. I thought those two witnesses were mistaken, but was my judgment compromised? Was I just hoping they were wrong because I believed Corey and couldn't figure him as a killer? Kaplan got it right. Credibility issues are better left to a jury. Not a single person. Not me. Not him."

"You're right," she says. "Seth gave you the best you could hope for."

"Surprised me, actually. Besides making the right decision on reasonable cause, the good judge gave his heart and soul to the case. Showed true compassion." Remand was expected. Judge Kaplan could have held Corey in jail to await the reopening of the grand jury. But he knew Corey wasn't going to run away from this. So, the judge entertained a bail application and set a high bond, 750K. He figured, correctly, that the extended McBride family would pull their resources together to bail out a favorite son and nephew. Allowing Corey's release was an act of compassion in the face of a stark reality. No one knew how long it would be before the grand jury convened again. It turned out to be months. Corey would have faced a double risk in jail: exposure to an outbreak of coronavirus, and exposure to inmates he'd arrested or who simply had it in for cops. A target on his back.

"Seth handled it well, and I'm grateful for that much," Dana agrees.

"Yes, and grateful for the grand jury's vote." Although deliberations were private, the outcome suggested that the jury believed Corey's testimony and rejected the eyewitness identifications as mistaken. Meaning: The killer is still on the loose.

All this talk in the past tense brings Dana into the present, in the clutches of a needling curiosity. Does Jared consider this case over and done? Has he abandoned the investigation? "One thing is clear," she says emphatically, as if to convince herself. "Corey is innocent." In her heart, she *does* believe this, although the full truth has not been uncovered.

"No doubt in my mind," Jared says.

"But the two families won't have full closure until the killer is found." She hopes Jared picks up her suggestion, without having to ask him directly.

He does.

"We've had a number of dead ends," he says, "but we haven't packed this one away. It's been a process of elimination. The killer couldn't be a stranger, some nutjob or a junkie. The man the witnesses saw was dressed neatly and spoke coherently. We doubt it was a random robbery attempt. The clumsiest thief could've easily grabbed Marlon's wallet and cell phone from his jacket pockets, even after the witnesses saw him. They passed by and kept walking. And the most promising clue led nowhere. The DNA. We got no hits in the CODIS database."

"It's remarkable you even have a DNA sample in a case like this."

"Yup." Jared nods his agreement. This bit of evidence was made possible by Marlon's special talent. He played classical guitar and kept the fingernails of his right hand long enough to pluck the strings. Long enough to scrape up some skin cells of his assailant. The eyewitnesses saw the men "hugging" before the victim slumped and began his descent, hanging onto the killer with an arm hooked around his neck. Marlon must have dug his fingernails into skin above the killer's collar as he slid to the ground.

Dana can guess the next step Jared took after searching the law enforcement index system, CODIS. "How about the database for those ancestry sites? GEDMatch. No leads there?"

"We tried. Twice." Jared thinks a moment as he takes his final sip of cognac and sets the empty snifter on a side table. "It's been a couple of months, though, since our last subpoena. Wouldn't hurt to try again. People keep sending their toothbrushes off to those genealogy sites."

"Surprise, surprise. You happen to be related to a cop killer!"

Jared smiles. "Some of those genealogy buffs don't appreciate a call like that."

"Any lawsuits?"

"We're playing it safe. We don't look at genetic data unless the donor signed off on law enforcement use. Informed consent. I'll have Ricky draft a new subpoena and get Lina on the task."

"Good. What about the things Marlon told Corey that night? Any new developments?"

"We've studied every angle and gotten nowhere. Maddening, 'cause we think it's the key to finding Marlon's killer."

"He was scared of something or someone."

"The killer could have been a player in the synthetic dope ring he was trying to crack. Someone who knew he was a police officer. We've followed up on every lead and haven't seen that his cover was ever blown."

"Until his photo appeared on every news site."

"After he was murdered."

"So, the person he feared could've had something against 'Chug,' not Marlon."

"Could be, but then, why not confide in Corey or someone else at the precinct? No reason to keep quiet about a development in the investigation, to get advice and support from his colleagues about something going down on the street."

Dana thinks a moment. "Didn't Marlon tell Corey that he would be hearing something about him? Words to that effect."

"Close to that."

"And he hoped Corey would have his back when it finally came to light. Doesn't that suggest that *Marlon* did something wrong? Or, rather, Chug did something wrong, committed a crime in the course of his work. He went too far. Opened himself to internal investigation or criminal charges."

"Then who's the killer?"

"Right. Doesn't make sense. More like, he crossed someone dangerous when he did this bad thing. Someone who now carries a grudge."

"Possible. We wish Corey knew more but he was stumped. And when we broke the news about the murder, he was really down on himself for arguing with Marlon about it."

"They'd been drinking. Alcohol can turn any discussion into an argument."

"My two cents? Corey took umbrage at being left out of the loop."

Dana and Jared exchange telling looks. Although they don't know Corey well, they gleaned a sense of his character from things Patrick said over the years. He encouraged his nephew to study law and was surprised when he entered the police academy. Did Corey feel pressure to carry on the McBride tradition? He didn't seem right for police work, soft in some ways, maybe insecure, but he was a boy with a big heart and a desire to serve others, and that made Patrick love him all the more.

"As Corey interpreted it," Jared goes on, "Marlon had a problem with someone, whether on the street or at the precinct. He kept pressing Marlon to say who it was. In his somewhat inebriated state—"

"How inebriated?"

"He said about four or five beers."

"One glass of wine is my limit."

"Well, that's you, Dana. We really don't know how well Corey handles his beer. But he did admit that he took it as a slight. Marlon wouldn't entrust him with his secret, and even worse, he implied that the situation was too 'dangerous' for Corey. Well, you can figure…"

"Corey took it personally. It was a dis. Can't handle the danger."

"You got it. Anyway, we've explored this idea that Marlon had a 'problem' with someone. Seems he had no enemies or rivals at work, was well liked, highly regarded. Same goes for his personal life. He was going to be married. Had friends everywhere who loved him. We ended up thinking there were only two possibilities."

"One, an officer on the take from the crime ring. Marlon discovered him and was going to expose him."

"That's the first possibility. But no leads. Second possibility we already talked about. Someone in the neighborhood with a vendetta against 'Chug.' But, like I said, no indication his cover was blown. So how could this person know where to ambush Marlon the cop?"

"How did the local residents handle the news he was undercover? I bet the shock of that revelation tightened a few lips."

"It was a problem. The undercover operation had to be abandoned without any arrests as they investigated the murder.

The locals haven't been much of a help."

Dana gazes down at the empty wineglass. Stem in hand, she's been twirling it right and left, watching the light play on the surface. "I can't stand this."

"I know what you mean. Push the limits, girl. You're not driving home. Have another glass."

She looks at him askance and says, "Thanks for the offer, but I'll self-medicate another time, thank you." They smile and sit in silence for a moment.

Dana's mind, never idle, plots her options. Despite the red "SEALED" warning, there's nothing unethical in taking another look at the file, is there? She already saw the entire record when she was working on *COG v Browne* and has authority to open it in the court's e-files. Dana also knows that Corey, the person protected by the sealing law, welcomes all efforts to search for clues to the real killer. Maybe she'll find something she missed in the witness interviews or testimony at the preliminary hearing and grand jury.

No need to let Jared know the extent of her obsession. She doesn't mention it. Finally, she says, "You don't mind if I talk to Lina about this, do you?" They haven't met in person since before the death of her husband in 2020. A tough year for Lina.

"Not at all. You two were the dynamic duo back in the day. Who knows? Maybe you'll come up with a bright idea for a new angle."

7 » *LOCKDOWN*

March 16 - April 7, 2020

JANJAK AWOKE AT NOON on Monday with a colossal headache, only a couple of hours to recover. He was on swing shift again. Same schedule as last week, for now.

When the news first hit about the governor's emergency order, Janjak's boss made no changes to the security roster. Business as usual at the building on Broad Street. The governor's mandate covered government employees, schools, restaurants, and bars. Employees of "nonessential" businesses were only "advised" to work from home. Did investment bankers put themselves in that category? Hell no. Financial markets made the world go 'round. The offices remained up and running as usual, and security was needed.

But the whole thing was strange, unheard of, and Janjak was worried. They were talking about two weeks to slow the spread of the virus, but would it go beyond that? Would they cut back his hours? He resolved to cooperate if the boss wanted to switch him to graveyard duty. He would take it without complaint if that's what was given him.

In a daze, he searched his pockets again and still couldn't find his phone. He went out for coffee but found his usual diner closed. A storefront was selling coffee to go from a window. Apparently, that was allowed.

Janjak settled on a park bench to drink his coffee and picked up a discarded morning edition of the *New York Post*. The news was all about the emergency order, nothing he didn't already know. He scanned other headlines without reading the stories: Two hundred new Covid-19 cases yesterday and a murdered off-duty cop. He finished his coffee and returned home to take a couple of aspirin.

Later, on the way to work, subway ridership was lighter than usual, holiday level. Soon after arriving, Janjak found his cell phone in the break room where he'd left it the day before. The battery was dead. His shift was easy, quieter than usual for a Monday, as many people were taking advantage of this "emergency" as an excuse to stay home. The talk in the hallways was all about the virus. Seriously? In a city of millions, all this fuss over two hundred new cases yesterday? After the earthquake in 2010, Janjak saw more sick people than that every day, wandering any single square block of Port-au-Prince.

The whole evening had a dreamlike quality, a little creepy. At the back of his mind, Janjak couldn't shake the worry about his job. At every chance, he took the elevator down to the lobby to chat with Wesley at the front desk. Their conversations reassured him. Wes had no worries about losing his job. At his level of seniority, why would he be concerned? "I just have to get through these two weeks," he said. "With the kids home, they're gonna drive me and Fabienne crazy."

The next day, St. Patrick's Day, was the life changer.

Over morning coffee, scrolling through his fully juiced smartphone, Janjak checked the "recommended news of the day." The top story was the murdered off-duty cop, much expanded from the brief paragraph he'd seen on Monday. But it wasn't the headline that got him. Two photos jumped out from the little screen and nearly knocked him over.

He knew those faces. No question about it.

He called Wesley and urged him to read the story about the dead cop and his friend. "The man we saw on the bridge was murdered, Wes! The police are asking for witnesses."

"I don't know what you mean," Wesley said. "We didn't see any murder."

"Just look at the story. It's on every news site. With pictures of those two guys."

Wesley seemed reluctant, and Janjak couldn't figure why.

Later that day they spoke again, in the lobby at work. Janjak opened the news story with the photos and put his cell phone under Wesley's nose. "Those are the two guys we saw." His words echoed through the cavernous space of gleaming marble and chrome. He glanced around and lowered his voice. "They were the ones arguing at the bar. The murdered one, Officer Stokes, jabbed you in the ribs. Then we saw them on the bridge. This Officer McBride must have stabbed him."

"Maybe it looks a little like them." Wesley frowned and turned away with a shrug. "It might be them, but I don't know for sure. We saw a drunk man fall down, that's all."

"Read the story. All the details fit. They were at The Book and Brew, then the man is found dead on the ground at two thirty, on the Manhattan side of the bridge."

"Could be a different guy, Jan. They said two thirty? How do you know that's when we were there? You'd had a bit to drink."

Janjak hadn't been so drunk he couldn't figure this out. The timing made perfect sense. Wesley was being evasive. Avoidance was in his eyes and behavior. No question he recognized the men. He just didn't want to get involved. Jan liked Wesley and was grateful for his help, but now he fully realized just how different they were. The prospect of getting involved in a murder investigation excited the younger man but repelled the older one. Reserved, quiet, and staid at his age, mid-forties, Wesley was already settled in his ways, every other word out of his mouth about his wife and children.

"Come on, Wes. You know it's them."

"It looks a little like the men at the bar, but how can I say they were on the bridge? I didn't see their faces."

"But you agreed with me when I said we'd just seen them at the bar."

"Maybe. But if that's so, I still didn't see anything to help the police. I didn't see a murder."

"Doesn't matter. We have to report what we saw. It's our duty."

Wesley thought a moment, then waved him off. "Go ahead. You can go without me if you're so sure. I'm not going to say something I'm not sure of."

And so it went for days, Janjak raising the subject anew, many times. And why didn't he go to the police on his own, as Wesley suggested? Every time Wesley cast doubt on what they'd seen, Janjak's insecurity grew, just a little. Going to the police was a big step, and he'd like to feel sure of himself. Hell, he *was* sure! But would the police believe him? This was a first for him, volunteering information about a crime. He'd be walking into the unknown, even though he fancied himself a member of their brotherhood. As a security officer, dutybound to serve and protect, he shared the same goals of law enforcement, but for a private employer.

Janjak felt an affinity for most police officers he met and sought their company, as he had that night, at The Book and Brew. He'd even thought about applying to the academy. One day, he might become one of their own, with a personal stake in the NYPD's integrity. Any dirty police officer should be called out, prosecuted, removed from the ranks, and this McBride was the worst. A murderer. Janjak kept his eye on the news. The district attorney was under fire to make an arrest, but so far, had failed to act.

With every resurgence of conscience, Janjak resolved to come forward, on his own if need be. It would be easier if they went together, a thought that generated another line of persuasion. "When I go to the police about this, you won't be able to stay out of it. I can't lie about who I was drinking with. They'll call you in."

Wesley reluctantly acknowledged his point. He was inching closer but continued to resist.

In the second week of the emergency measures, Janjak's fears were realized. Even a skeptic could see that the numbers of ill and dead were mounting. The building on Broad Street had the feel of a mausoleum in its immaculate stony emptiness. More and more people were staying home, working remotely. Security was cut to a skeleton crew. Wesley's job wasn't affected, but Janjak's hours were reduced to half and would have been cut completely if Wes hadn't put in a good word for him.

In his idle hours, heavy with boredom and worry, Janjak kept abreast of the story and thought about it constantly, the excitement helping to fill the void. Obituaries and human-interest stories about Marlon Stokes cropped up, giving Janjak another idea. "Everyone loved this guy who was murdered. We'd be heroes if we tell them what we saw."

"Not if we don't know anything for sure."

"Doesn't matter whether we're sure this McBride was the killer. We saw details that could help them. And maybe there's a reward for information." Cash was even better than a fleeting moment of fame.

"I haven't seen any announcement of a reward," Wesley said, hinting at the fact that he too had been following the news.

"Well, even if it isn't official, I'm sure the family of that dead man would show us their gratitude…" The minute this slipped from his mouth, Janjak felt ashamed. His decision to come forward shouldn't be about money. Wesley cast a disappointed look, making him feel even lower. He added, "But, of course, I would never ask."

Finally, the day arrived when they could delay no longer. April Fool's Day, an empty Wednesday, a day for Janjak's new hobby, his habitual scrolling through the news and social sites. He jumped with alarm at the sight of this headline: "Mystery Witnesses Sought in the Stokes Murder Case." He read the short blurb about the 911 caller, the man who discovered Stokes on the pavement, bleeding to death. The man's name was Rincón. Janjak clicked an arrow to start a video that went with the story.

In shaky footage, Rincón emerged from his apartment building on the Lower East Side and walked into a group of waiting reporters. They accosted him, yelling and shoving cell phones in his face. So much for the warnings to maintain "social distance" that had been prevalent recently. A few words came through their garbled mess: "Mr. Rincón!" and "Did you see the killer!" and "Was Officer Corey McBride on the bridge?" Rincón kept his head down, trying to push through. But it was useless, and he gave up, stopping dead in his tracks. He bellowed: "Stop bugging me! I saw nothing. That man was alone on the ground, dying. I called 911. I stayed until the ambulance came. That's it! Go look for the other witnesses. Two guys on the bridge pointed to the man. Maybe they saw something. Maybe they even did it. That's all I gotta say."

Maybe they even did it? Where did that come from?

And what had taken Rincón so long to mention their existence? Maybe he'd told the police, but this detail had been kept out of the news, intentionally or through pure luck. Maybe Rincón hadn't told anyone, but the reporters kept hounding him and he couldn't take it anymore. This was the last straw for Rincón, and quick thinking produced this ploy to get the reporters off his back.

Well, it worked.

Janjak and Wesley discussed it, again. Wes agreed they

should come forward. Together. But he left it to Janjak to make the first contact on their behalf.

With a fluttering heart high in his chest, Janjak called the NYPD crime tip hotline and asked to speak to an investigator on the Marlon Stokes murder. The operator asked, "What is the purpose of your call?"

The purpose? Wasn't it obvious? He hesitated, one thought tumbling over the next, fretting over how much he should say to this nameless person.

"Sir?" the operator asked. "Do you have information about that case?"

I'm one of the mystery witnesses, flew through his mind, *and I did nothing wrong!* Into the phone he said, "Yes. I saw some things. On the bridge. That night."

"Your name please."

"Janjak Bernard."

"And the number you're calling from is…" She recited it from caller ID.

"Yes."

"Please hold. I'll connect you."

He waited forever. Minutes of silence, nothing in the background. Had they hung up on him? Finally, a gruff male voice came over so loud it made him jump. "Fifth Precinct, Detective Rodman."

Janjak sputtered a few syllables and froze.

"You called crime tips?" The man sounded angry, not the way Janjak had imagined. He didn't answer fast enough, and the man said, "Is this Mr. Bernard?"

"Y-yes. Are…are you investigating the murder on the Brooklyn Bridge?"

"I'm your man. Whatcha got?"

With that, the floodgates opened. Janjak got started and couldn't stop. The words he'd bottled up over many anxious days came rushing out over Detective Rodman's attempts to stop him. "Whoa, there… Back up… Hold on!"

The detective's words finally got through. "Sorry! So sorry…" With a sense of relief, Janjak submitted. The detective took charge, nailing down the basics first. Names, dates of birth, occupations, addresses, phone numbers. He explained the restrictions, that interviews were being conducted remotely on Skype, and said it was okay to use a cell phone (as Janjak silently wondered if Wesley would let him use his computer instead). By the end of the call, Rodman had arranged separate times for Janjak and Wesley to give their formal statements.

Her fourth day as a widow, Aurelina was numb. The first day had been an electric white shock. The second day, an earthquake of choking sobs. The third day, a logroll on a hazy river, her body and mind depleted, catatonic.

Time and again, reminiscence and imagery renewed the swell of emotion in her chest. It hadn't been a long marriage. Six years. Mateo and Lina tied the knot in their mid-forties, well beyond her childbearing years, and they looked forward to the decades ahead, just the two of them, together. Their common thread was an abiding first love: hard work and the sense of purpose it gave them. Inseparable as they were, there was no jealousy. Never would they demand of each other an abandonment of that first love. Their union only added another layer of meaning and dedication to their careers in criminal justice. Lina, detective first grade with the NYPD. Mateo, director of the NYC alternatives to incarceration program.

The city had lost a great man. Lina's loss was heavier. Hardest of all had been their involuntary separation during his illness and last moments on earth. Little did she know on the day she rushed him to the ER that, a few days later, the hospital would ban all visits from family members. A heartless precaution. She pleaded with them, but they rejected her offer to don multiple layers of plastic armor before entering.

Alone in her apartment, Lina felt her isolation more acutely as the days of lockdown progressed, the restrictions growing tighter. No visits, no hugs and kisses from extended family and friends. No gathering for a funeral. With the help of her closest sister, by phone and computer, Lina managed to make arrangements for Mateo.

Now what? On the fourth day, she called her commanding officer. "Take your time," he said. "You have months of leave coming to you." She could count on one hand the number of personal days she'd taken in her three-decade career. "Don't worry about us," her CO went on. "We've got your cases covered."

At the back of her mind lurked the biggest case she'd been working. The Stokes murder. God, what a thing. The call came at three in the morning. On the Brooklyn Bridge, in the glow of flashing red lights, she squatted next to his body, still warm, curled up in a fetal position, lying in a pool of blood. Never nice to see a good man down, but Marlon was someone special. Extraordinary.

Lina oversaw the evidence collection at the scene, then called DA Browne. They interviewed Corey McBride about six-thirty that morning and had no reason to doubt him. Later that day and into the next, she interviewed officers who'd been at The Book and Brew. Then, in the middle of a Q&A on St. Paddy's Day, Mateo called her, gasping for breath. She rushed out of the precinct and hadn't been back since. When it became clear she'd be out for an extended time, she assigned the Stokes investigation to Kyle Rodman. From that day on, she hadn't thought about the case, hadn't asked Rodman or anyone else for the status, hadn't even watched the news.

And now, on the fourth day after Mateo's departure from this world, Lina went to her apartment door and thought about stepping outside for the first time. Had it been that long? She'd been holed up inside since that phone call, the nurse telling her that Mateo was gone. She could go down to the lobby of her building, if nothing else, and from there, if her legs carried her, a walk to the corner. One step at a time.

Opening the door, she nearly stumbled over a little pile of four newspapers rolled up in their plastic sleeves. The small surprise took a bite out of her numbness. From the start of her leave of absence, March 18, she'd been tossing the plastic-sleeved papers into a corner of her kitchen where they would remain until the day, if it ever came, when she'd be motivated to unwrap and stack them for recycling. What day was it now? April something. These four in the hallway marked the days since Mateo's death.

Lina and Mateo had been devotees of the old ways, trading off newspaper sections at the breakfast table every morning instead of scrolling through their cell phones. They loved this early morning ritual, the wakeup call of coffee and newsprint, an enticing mix of aromas. Tears stung her eyes at this reminder, coaxing her out of her retreat from a world that had continued to turn without her. The heartbeat of the city was recorded on these pages, crimes and events that defined her professional existence.

Guiltily, she admitted that her first love had not died with her second. She felt the attraction again, the suction and pull. Mateo wouldn't mind. He would expect as much from her.

Lina scooped up the papers, brought them inside, and plopped them on the kitchen table. She would start with the day's news and move backward if need be. She pulled all the plastic sleeves off and found the most recent. Tuesday, April 7, 2020. Front page of the Metro section, the biggest headline jumped out: "Mystery Witnesses Name Former DA's Nephew in Cop's Murder."

Before reading further, the headline alone nettled her. Something was not right. As far as she knew, the 911 caller, Carlos Rincón, had been alone and hadn't mentioned seeing anyone else. Or had he? Lina arrived after Rincón had left, and she was relying on the notes of the officer who interviewed him at the scene. How had these "mystery witnesses" surfaced weeks later, accusing Corey McBride of perpetrating this grisly murder? Crimes of passion between close friends are never out of the question, and Corey was known to have his problems, an occasional defensiveness and insecurity. But Lina did not believe that the boy was capable of thrusting a knife into the heart of his best friend. She'd seen them together too many times to think otherwise.

As she read, her fury grew. The two men voluntarily contacted the police and gave statements via Skype on Friday, April 3. The newspaper reporter shouldn't have said even that much. But the article went on at a level of detail that astounded her.

The witnesses claimed to have seen Stokes and the killer drinking together at The Book and Brew. Minutes later, on the Brooklyn Bridge, they saw the men in a tight grasp, the killer hugging the victim as he slumped to the ground, hanging on with an arm hooked around the killer's neck. The witnesses asked if everything was all right, and the man said his friend was only drunk. They kept walking, but several yards on, turned around to look. The victim was alone, lying in a fetal position on the ground. They didn't have a cell phone and asked someone on the bridge to call 911.

That someone must have been Rincón, Lina thought.

The article quoted one of the witnesses: "After I saw the news story about the murder, I realized that the tight hug was really that man stabbing the other!" The witnesses gave the police a description of the killer's height and complexion and crew cut, and his clothing, jeans and a navy-blue windbreaker or jacket, the edge of his white shirt showing above the jacket collar. And here was the kicker. Both witnesses identified the killer by photograph as Police Officer Corey McBride, nephew of former DA Patrick McBride.

"District Attorney Jared Browne was contacted and declined to comment," the article concluded.

Lina was beside herself. She got up from the kitchen table and paced the room, trying to walk off her outrage. Someone had leaked the full content of these witness statements. The only missing facts were the witnesses' names and other identifying information.

The investigation was irreparably compromised. There were details here that the killer would know. What he was wearing, how he was holding the victim, their exact location on the bridge, the time of night, what he said to the witnesses. If those men were wrong in identifying Corey, there was now no opportunity to test another suspect on these details. Not to mention the impossibility of giving Corey a fair trial, should it ever come to that. The trial was being held in the press.

Who leaked this story? She had to find out. The article referred to "a source close to the investigation." If Kyle had anything to do with this… What incompetence! She picked up her cell phone, put it down again. The emotion was strangling her. She was *not* in control. Her eyes welled and her nose dripped. Too much, too much. She gazed heavenward. *Mateo, where are you?*

Minutes passed. At the kitchen sink, she splashed water on her face and toweled it dry. Took several deep breaths. There. Concentrate. This had to be done.

Rodman could see who was calling and didn't mask his surprise. "Lina? H-how are you doing?" She thought she heard a tinge of guilt in his voice. One would think that Kyle Rodman, second most senior homicide detective, would have called her personally to convey his condolences. Maybe her brain was muddled by grief, but she didn't remember getting a call or a message from him. She did remember that he signed the card that went with the flowers sent from the precinct.

"Hanging in there," she said. "I just saw today's news about the Stokes case." An awkwardness hit as she realized she didn't know the time of day. A glance at the digital numbers on her microwave told her it was after five in the afternoon. Rather late to be reading the morning news.

Kyle chuckled uncomfortably. "Not a good story."

"How on earth did this get out?"

"Damned if I know. I warned the witnesses not to talk to the press."

Did she have to state the obvious? "It wasn't the witnesses. They didn't give their names."

"Now, Lina, you know it's still a possibility." His voice dripped with knowledge of her recent tragedy in a way that nauseated her. Patronizing, coddling her like a girl who lost her teddy bear. "It could've been them. Maybe they get off on the idea of being the 'mystery' witnesses."

"Highly unlikely. What's in it for them? If they want fame or a movie contract, they'd give their names. And if it *was* them, that's on you, Kyle, for not controlling your witnesses. You're the one who interviewed them, right?"

"Sure, but that's another thing. With the pandemic we're interviewing everyone on Skype. The tech geeks have access and maybe a hundred other people for all I know. They're still working out the glitches. Besides that, there could be hackers—"

"Find out who it is." She intended to be stern, but her voice cracked under the heavy weight in her chest, a kind of mortal fatigue. "The minute you know what happened, call me."

"Okay. Meanwhile, I'm working on DA Browne."

"Working on him how?"

"He actually took a call from me today. Personally. He hasn't assigned an ADA to this case. We talked about the new evidence, and I recommended arresting Corey McBride. He won't authorize it. He's talking to the chief of detectives."

That, right there, told Lina what she'd suspected. There was something wrong here. This new evidence was bullshit and DA Browne saw through it. Maybe these were honest eyewitnesses, but their identifications were unreliable. Maybe this was a setup, a political hack job on the McBrides. She didn't know yet what to believe, but she wanted, more than anything, to get her hands on this case again and find out for herself.

"Leave the charging decisions to the DA and the chief, Kyle. Just find out who leaked the story."

"Will do."

8 » *THESIS*

Tuesday, January 11, 2022

A WOMAN ALONE, dead of night, heels clicking pavement. She wants to get home. Most apartment dwellers on this residential city block are asleep. The woman moves swiftly through variable light, receding and growing under streetlamps every fifty yards. Gusting wind screams around edges and corners of buildings.

We follow, walking behind. The back of her trench coat flares and whips. She pulls up her collar, a hand on either side, and clamps it tight around her neck, hugging herself. A shoulder bag hangs loose, bouncing on her left hip, buffeted by her movement and the wind.

Our perspective shifts. We *are* the woman, seeing through her eyes, feeling the blast of autumn wind. Half a block ahead, a figure approaches. Probably male. He tilts his head down, showing the top of his hoodie. In baggy pants, pooled around the ankles, he lopes like a bow-legged cowpoke, hands shoved into front pants pockets.

Closer now. We hug the curb on the right. He stays center, keeping his head down. Oblivious? Impossible to tell.

Ten feet away, directly under a streetlamp, he lifts his head and stares directly into our eyes. Who is he? We can't see his hair under the hood, but we see his face clearly for a second or two before he drops his focus again. He takes two lunging steps and butts his head into our chest, yanking the shoulder strap. The sudden impact sends us backward and down, falling onto one hip.

An "oomph," all the air knocked out, and we imagine the pain.

On the ground, propped on an elbow, we twist around and see his baggy, bow-legged run, purse under an arm, broken shoulder strap flying out behind.

"Natalie!"

She starts and swivels around, away from the computer screen. Zachary Talmadge has cracked open the door to her tiny office and craned his neck in. He's smiling at her in that way she finds slightly annoying. She's also a little embarrassed to be caught watching her crime scene video for the thousandth time.

"Hey, Zach." He's harmless, she keeps telling herself. A nice guy, really. They've almost forgotten that awkwardness between them when she finally, firmly, told him she wasn't interested. She's able to maintain a certain distance because they're researching different aspects of the cognitive interview. But collegiality is mutually beneficial to their work and useful for other reasons. Ever since this weekend, she's been dying to ask him about the Corey McBride case. Maybe he can share his case files. She wants to understand why her mother was so bent out of shape at the mention of Dr. Louden.

Zach fidgets, betraying his butterflies. She suspects he's still holding out hope. In typical fashion, he communicates in disjointed fragments. "Uh, just wanted to tell you. The Prof. In case you need to see him. He's in today."

Completely unnecessary. Zach should know that she's capable of making her own arrangements with Professor Louden, as she has, today. But she gives Zach the benefit of the doubt. Classes don't start for a week, and the professor's schedule is less predictable during semester break. She gives him a big smile.

"Thanks, Zach. I do need to see him."

"About your lesson plan for small seminar?"

"Yes. I'm handing it in today."

"Cool. I just talked to him about mine." He hesitates in the doorway, at a loss for words.

She should just go for it, the thing that's been on her mind. "Are you around all day?"

His face brightens. "Yup."

"I want to ask you something about your data. Can I come by later?"

"S-sure! Cool." Zach's favorite word. "Uh, okay..." More fidgeting. "See you later." He backs up and pulls the door toward him, leaving it open a sliver.

This is the only way, she thinks as Zach retreats. Her curiosity is screaming, but so are her instincts about Dr. Louden. If she asks the professor about it, he'll assume she has a surreptitious motive. (Well, maybe she does.) He knows that her mother was a protégé of Patrick McBride, close to the late district attorney, and by extension, emotionally attached to his family and legacy.

Was it really so awful what the professor did? Natalie recalls a fleeting impression that his opinion was uncharacteristic. Other than that, she didn't pay much attention to it at the time. Now, she senses the depth of her mother's distaste for the professor, and it falls into line with Natalie's own diminishing respect for him. The last four years have changed her. When she was accepted to this graduate program, her thrill was boundless. Studying under the eminent Emmett Louden, the biggest name in cognitive psychology! Proud of her accomplishment, she was hopeful and excited at the chance to make a difference in the field.

Coursework that first year was challenging. Dr. Louden was an exciting lecturer, even if he seemed a bit priggish and pretentious. She figured he was entitled to those qualities, owing to his stature in the field. Gradually, Natalie's reverence for him started to sour. Dr. Louden is frequently unavailable, out on speaking engagements or testifying as an expert witness at criminal trials. He's curt with her whenever she seeks his advice on her research. He lives for the limelight and shines brightest when speaking to audiences of strangers on the fallibility of eyewitness identifications. Photographers love his patrician looks. The narrow face with the sculpted salt-and-pepper beard and theatrically gray temples is a familiar image online and in the pages of professional and mainstream publications.

So, it came as no surprise that the media sought his opinion on the grand jury's verdict regarding Corey McBride. *Just the professor spouting off again*, she thought when she saw the interview. She was absorbed in other, more pressing concerns, madly questioning her study volunteers. Fifty on screen, fifty in person, scripted, identical questions. She was obsessing over the problem of facemasks for the in-person interviews. Covering half her face would blow the whole point of the research. As it turned out, she had enough volunteers who agreed (waivers signed) to sit across a table from her, six feet between them, both mask free.

Now, she wants to catch up with what she missed, and Zach will be more than willing to tell her what he knows. Later. As he shuts her door, she sighs and swivels around to her computer screen. The robber's backside is frozen in a fuzzy image of flight, his feet inches above the pavement. Today, again, she's feeling discouraged by the imperfections in her study.

Sunny and optimistic by nature, Natalie is not without despairing moods at times like these, slammed against a granite wall. She's good at hiding the pain of her frustration. And where did she learn that? From Mommy, calm, cool, and collected. Case in point: Her mother changed the subject and lapsed into generalities when Natalie mentioned Dr. Louden's interest in the McBride case. She could see right through it. Maybe the people closest to Natalie can see through her too.

The source of her frustration is the same old story. Her goal is unattainable. She wants to distill the truth in every human interaction, to reconcile the myriad discrepancies in human perception and memory. Impossible. If pushed, everyone in the department would admit as much about their own research. Perhaps even Dr. Louden, privately, in his head.

The word "truth" itself is debatable, but perfectionism and drive are good traits to have in getting closer to it. Without that energy, she couldn't inch forward the way she does, chipping away at the granite. Progress is made in baby steps toward understanding the human mind, discovering factors that skew perception and cognition, developing techniques to circumvent the contaminations to memory, enhancing accuracy in recall. Chip, chip, chipping. Taking that knowledge and using it to improve investigative tools.

She doesn't doubt that progress has been made. Investigative techniques are more humane, more accurate. Fewer mistakes are made today than fifty, or even ten, years ago. But still mistakes. Along the imperfect road to justice, Natalie's passion might consume her. Why is it so much to ask? To devise a foolproof method prompting a witness to reinstate context, capture the original encoding of the event, distill the experience, and articulate it accurately?

Impossible.

Take her simulation, for example, the tool she's been given to achieve this objective. How can she possibly know whether her test subjects would answer the questions the same way if they'd experienced this crime in real life? She almost wishes she could orchestrate a hundred identical simulations on a city street, each participant in her study playing the role of the victim. Even if this were possible, she can't eliminate study bias. Her test subjects are volunteers, aware that they're taking part in a fiction. And the "investigator" is Natalie, a twenty-seven-year-old grad student with an angel food complexion, pillowy voice, and gentle demeanor. Would her "witnesses" feel as comfortable talking to a brusque, six foot tall, street savvy NYPD detective?

Oh well, this is the best she can do. Every variable she can imagine also occurs in everyday life.

Natalie's research is rooted in the exigencies of the pandemic. Investigations and court proceedings went virtual, witnesses and victims interviewed remotely on computer screens. A new type of distance was injected into the process, an interesting topic for cognitive psychologists. How do virtual setups affect outcomes in criminal cases? Politicians are interested too, wanting to be prepared in the event (or in the likelihood, some would say) that such measures are here to stay.

In crafting her study, Natalie had to restrain her boundless curiosity about corrupting influences. Detours on the road to accuracy are limitless. She'd like to test for everything, but variables must be limited, or the research is useless. She settled on the overarching essence of the problem. Does the virtual setup improve or undermine the accuracy of witness testimony?

The first step in an ECI, the Enhanced Cognitive Interview, is to establish rapport. A victim of crime is asked to relate the details of a traumatic event to a stranger in a police station or courtroom. The mind must be free of resistance, to mentally recreate the event and articulate it without understatement or omission. How to achieve this level of comfort? Would a witness feel more at ease in a small interview room, eye-to-eye with a detective, or miles away, talking to an image on a screen?

Natalie is aware that she entered this study with a bias of her own. Instinctively, she doesn't believe that on-screen interviews yield more accurate accounts. The extra distance may seem helpful in relaxing the witness, but there's something unreal about talking to someone on a screen. Would this aura of unreality transfer to the witness's memory of the crime itself? In person, the intensity of eye contact may be intimidating, but the interaction is real and immediate, a parallel to the corporal encounter the witness is asked to recall and convey.

The clock on Natalie's computer screen gives her fifteen minutes before her appointment with the professor. She'll be sure to arrive on the stroke. He's a stickler for punctuality.

She takes these minutes to pore over her data and rue the imperfections in her study. The volunteers. A hundred people, male and female, all ages, pretending to be that woman, mugged on a dark street. In questioning them, Natalie worked at uniformity in her tone and demeanor and even wore the same conservative business suit for each interview. But really. No. What about all those little subconscious reactions she may have conveyed? Little shifts in posture, a smile or lift of the eyebrow, wordless noises that sound approving or disapproving. And consistency is just as concerning as inconsistency! After a dozen interviews, trying to make them identical, she started to feel like a robot. Maybe she acted like one too.

On her computer, she pulls up one of the many spreadsheets she created for her data, recording witness responses to the identification procedure. Each witness was shown the same six photos and given the same neutral instruction that the suspect may or may not be depicted. Half the witnesses saw the photos on screen, half in person, on real paper, pushed across the table. Her results yield a slightly higher rate of correct and positive responses among the in-person interviews. Is it significant? Does study bias account for the difference? Perhaps gender, age, or background affects the level of certainty or doubt. She struggles to reconcile the disparities.

And, for the hundredth time, she wishes she had real cases to work with. But it's no use dwelling on that sore spot. Professor Louden chose Zach. Natalie remembers what Daddy said this past Sunday, and she wants to believe he's right. Louden gave that arm of the research to Zach because Natalie enjoys an advantage in real-life knowledge, having grown up in a house full of lawyers.

The time has come. She closes her computer files and picks up the paper copy of her lesson plan. She already sent Dr. Louden a copy by email, but he rarely bothers to open the email attachments she sends. He'd rather look over the paper in his hand, scribble on it, and return it right there.

Down the hall, at the very end, is the largest office for the department head, the renowned Professor Emmett Louden. She knocks, and a muffled voice calls out from inside. "Come in."

She opens the door, closes it behind her, and says, "Hello, Dr. Louden." Some of her grad student friends in other departments are on a first-name basis with their thesis advisors. But Natalie can't imagine Professor Louden ever suggesting that she call him "Emmett." She strides up to the desk and holds out her paper. "My lesson plan."

He still hasn't looked up at her. He's jotting notes on a typed page on the desk. With his focus down, he holds out his hand. An amazing sixth sense, developed from years of ignoring people. Natalie's lesson plan is sucked in and clamped like metal to magnet. He looks up and says, "Good."

She sits in a chair across from him. He puts her paper on top of the other and scans it as she glances everywhere but him. By now, the contents of his office are familiar to her. Professor Louden is meticulously organized, keeping his desktop empty except for the immediate task, other papers neatly stacked on a side credenza. Displayed on the wall behind his head are the diplomas, awards, and photographs of the professor with important people, the president of the university and various politicians.

On the corner of his desk opposite the computer screen is a single decoration, a small perpetual motion sculpture of three empty metal circles rotating inside each other. Natalie glances there and averts her gaze, wanting to avoid hypnosis. She wonders how the professor can keep that spinning thing in his peripheral vision without going mad. A bit of Louden apocrypha has him explaining the gadget to his rapt followers as a representation of the Id at core, Ego at center, and Superego circling the two. Jokesters like to change the story, making it a representation of the professor's brain, but switching the Id and Superego.

Speaking of jokes and threesomes, an odd item on his wall fills a category all its own. Her eyes dart to the small, framed poster:

<u>*A Cognitive Psychologist's Three-Stage Theory of Humor*</u>

Mentally represent the joke's structure

Detect incongruous schemas

Inhibit the literal, appreciate the implausible

An incredibly boring, unfunny theory of the funny. Does Dr. Louden hope to lighten the mood of his office visitors with this bit of insight into the human mind? It has the opposite effect, adding to the overall impression of emptiness in the life of this late middle-aged bachelor. No framed photos of family or friends. Is there really no one worthy of display?

He scribbles on her paper. "Pinkston is about to publish. Work it into the fifth week. I'll send you the link."

Seems she's always a step behind, no matter how hard she works to keep up. But Louden has an inside track on the main players in the field. If *he* falls a step behind, his reputation is on the line.

He returns her paper with his written notes, and then he does something she doesn't expect. He sits back in his chair, elbows on armrests, interlaces his fingers in his lap, and deliberately makes eye contact. Smiles even. "So, this is your last semester as a TA."

So, this is the "so" conversation. "Yes. I've enjoyed the teaching. Had some smart groups of freshmen."

He smiles bigger, more relaxed than usual. "But..." He intones the word in a singsong.

Her eyes widen in the moment of his pause.

He fills in the blank. "It's not your life's goal." A correct reading of her mind.

"No, it's not. I prefer to do research, as maddening as it is."

"Maddening?" He gives a little theatrical laugh.

She shifts in her seat. "Difficult, and sometimes frustrating, but always interesting."

"And you like the challenge."

"Yes. It's a puzzle. Patterns are starting to emerge in my data."

"So, your thesis is on track, deadline in sight?"

She nods, wondering if this is turning into a real conversation. "You'll have my outline by end of semester." Is the mood right for her to ask a question about the case that's on her mind?

But he abruptly changes the subject. "How's my old friend, Professor Goodhue?"

"Quite well, thank you." Should she say more? Natalie's father and Dr. Louden met once at an academic function. They might have said five words to each other, as far as she knows. "He's—"

"And Judge Hargrove?"

"Doing very well."

"In her lofty perch!" A strange grin. "Gazing down into the trenches of criminal law from her appellate pedestal."

What is *this*? Natalie can't think of anything to say before he slaps the desktop, cutting off his bit of poetic rumination and her opportunity to respond. "Good!" Conversation over.

She takes her cue. "Thanks, Professor. I'll look for Dr. Pinkston's article." She retreats.

Out in the hallway, closing the door behind her, she shakes her head at the enigma that is Dr. Emmett Louden.

* * *

An hour later, in Zach's tiny office, Natalie stands with arms crossed on her chest, shifting her weight from right foot to left and back again, working her way up to *the* question. This isn't a matter of stealth or dishonesty. She *does* have a genuine interest in catching up. The contours of Zach's research are vague to her because, well, they had that little problem when he misconstrued her friendliness as something else. She's been keeping her distance and hasn't asked him much about his work. With effort, she has also suppressed her jealousy about Professor Louden passing her over for the research on *real* data. An old wound, now healed into a scar.

How many criminal cases has Zach been following? "Seventy-two. Actually, six, depending..." Zach stumbles over his words and totters next to his desk, bracing himself with a hand on the surface. He closes his eyes briefly and taps the desktop with his fingertips a few times, as if counting to himself. "I mean, six with the professor, where we went together. The preliminary hearings. But seventy-two total. The Prof leaned on some people. Got me a pass, you know, to get in. For the rest of those."

"I guess that's what clout will do for you."

"Yeah." He straightens up and beams. Anyone who doesn't know Zach might think his face and posture reflect an inflated self-pride. But Natalie senses the true motivation, a childish desire to impress.

"Was it really so hard to get in?" she asks. "The process is supposed to be public. The courts are for the people."

"It wasn't easy at the time. Restrictions and distancing rules. Couldn't just go into the courtroom. Permission and all that. Don't know why. Practically empty in there. Just the judge and clerk, sometimes the lawyers. Usually they stayed in their office. The defense attorney got private time on Skype with his client before the hearing started. In a little room at Rikers. The defendants, I mean. That's where they sat. Wearing a tan jumpsuit."

"Seventy-two! That's a lot of hearings to watch." A shivering thrill passes through Natalie from the pleasure of imagining the research possibilities. Of course, some of those hearings had only police witnesses, but others had civilians, many of whom were interviewed virtually before they testified. So much could be learned by comparing the witnesses' interviews and testimony. And all those on-screen cases could be compared to in-person cases, pre-pandemic. Was there any difference in the rate of positive eyewitness ID? Did virtual techniques skew testimonial accuracy and affect case outcomes?

"Yeah, it was a lot," Zach agrees. "Tedious. It gets old."

"You don't *know* the meaning of old till you interview a hundred volunteers!"

Zach smiles and nods, a glitter of admiration in his eyes. He drops his gaze to the desktop, littered with papers. "But I only have my notes of the hearings. Handwritten. They didn't allow computers."

"Don't you have the recordings too?"

"No video. No recording except by special permission. Too hard to get."

"Why? It would have been so easy to record the hearings and preserve them. Just click a button on Skype."

"Yeah, but the rules. Administrative judge made them. No recordings. No preserving. They did the usual court reporting though. We got typed transcripts for some of them."

Useless, Natalie is thinking. How can you see the demeanor of the witnesses from a printed page? "Too bad. But at least you get to compare witness interviews to your notes and transcripts. How many of those cases have videos of witness statements?"

Zach's glow noticeably dims. "Well," he laughs nervously, "not too many. We came across, uh..."

"Roadblocks?"

"Yeah."

"Even for the cases that are finished?"

"For acquittals and dismissals, yeah. They seal the record. Convictions, it's still against NYPD policy."

Does this surprise her? Natalie should have guessed. She knows enough law and procedure to understand the obstacles. Agency policies and professional ethics protect witnesses. Didn't her mother remind her of this the other day? *I'd leave it alone, Natalie. The witnesses have a right to their privacy*.

But her mom wasn't talking about witness statements. She meant the grand jury, a secret body, protected by law, and even there, witnesses can petition the court to get their own testimony. If that's so, why can't the NYPD release witness interviews for research purposes, especially if the witness has no objection? Attorneys could be another source, but Natalie understands the problems there as well. The prosecutor has a duty to give the defense all pretrial statements but also has a policy to protect witnesses. The defense attorney owes a duty to the client. Disclosing inculpatory witness statements breaches that duty, even after the case is closed.

"But Dr. Louden had ways around some of the roadblocks, right?"

"We got a few Skype interviews." Zach looks down again and taps those fingertips. "Um, I think, four. We're trying to get more, though." Natalie is beginning to feel bad for him. Not much data to go on. He confesses, "Your simulation and volunteers put you in a better spot than me."

"But you have *some* recordings. How did you get those?"

"All the cases were convictions. The Prof leaned on the police, got a clearance, and the witnesses signed a waiver for research use. 'I won't sue anybody,' they promised."

"So, only in cases with convictions?"

"Right. Oh." A lightbulb switches on. "That case your mom

decided. You're interested in that one? I guess you know the Prof wrote an affidavit for that group asking for the grand jury evidence."

Natalie nods. Of course she knows.

"I went to the hearing with him. It was one of the first. But the defendant wasn't convicted. Harder to get the materials."

Now it's Natalie's turn to feel embarrassed. But why should she? She's curious, and there's nothing wrong with that, except… Why go to Zach instead of her own mother, who (Natalie believes) is authorized to see the entire McBride file despite the sealing order? Because, because…

The curtain parts over her cover story, the niceties masking her self-delusion. This isn't about wanting to catch up with Zach on his research. Not completely. Only a little. This is about her disappointment. Is Dr. Louden really an asshole? She doesn't want to believe it, needs to see the evidence that her mother hinted at. Everyone knows *what* Louden did. But why? And does it matter? Her mother strongly implied he stuck his nose where it didn't belong, spouting opinions like it's an academic exercise or a simulation instead of a real case involving real people.

But the Honorable Dana Hargrove can be perceived as harsh. Natalie knows this, has overheard people expressing that impression. Has heard her own parents joking about it. She has seen her mother in action, as an attorney and as a judge. Has observed the sage professional, austere and regal. That beautiful shell with its cool sheen protects the big heart inside, the compassionate core that doles out tough love from an unshakable belief in personal responsibility. Natalie loves and admires this woman and craves her approval.

Is Mommy right about this, the thing that Natalie only senses? Why not ask her about it? Because it would put the judge in a bad position, tempting her with an ethics violation. Mother cannot tell daughter about the evidence in a sealed case file. Hell,

Judge Hargrove wrote an opinion saying that the public has *no* right to examine the grand jury evidence!

But there lies the narrow avenue for Natalie's own inquiry into the facts, a way to do it without getting anyone in trouble. True, the grand jury evidence is confidential, but she's more interested in videos of the witnesses' statements to the police, and those weren't in the grand jury. That's Natalie's best guess, knowing what she knows about criminal procedure. The prosecutor uses live testimony, not recordings. Why can't the witnesses get copies of their own recorded statements? Maybe they've already asked the police and received them. Maybe they even figured out how to record them in real time on their own computers. What's wrong with using those videos for research? A limited use. Natalie sees no harm in asking for their permission.

She doesn't need to mention to Zach that her interest in his research includes her desire to analyze her thesis advisor's motivations and character.

"Yeah, I'm interested in that case," she says to Zach, trying to sound nonchalant. "But I know the file is sealed."

"If you want, I'll give you my notes. They aren't typed though. Maybe I'll…" He looks down at a mess of papers bearing his left-handed scrawl, perhaps indicating an enduring intent to type up his notes from 2020. "At the hearing, the witnesses IDed the defendant on screen, in his Riker's cell. They also said they IDed him from a photo on Skype, you know, with the detective."

"Do you have the hearing transcript?"

"We tried, but they ignored the request too long. Couldn't get it before they sealed the case. But you know about that other thing, right? About Judge Kaplan?"

Natalie scrunches her brow and shakes her head. What could he mean?

"The Prof and Kaplan are friends. Or, anyway, worked together. A lot. Kaplan used to hire him as an expert on his cases when he was a defense attorney."

"Hmm. Interesting. What does that have to do with this?"

"Well, after the hearing, the Prof told me to get lost while they had a private meeting. Kaplan played the witness statements for him."

"What?"

"Yeah, crazy. It wasn't kosher. The Prof must've leaned on Kaplan."

"This is *after* the judge made his ruling, holding the case for the grand jury?"

"Yeah. And set bail."

"You think Judge Kaplan wasn't so sure about his decision? Maybe he wanted some moral support from his buddy, the expert."

The gleam of admiration returns to Zach's eyes. "Good theory. Anyway, I only found out later when the Prof let it slip. He said, 'What a bombshell. Those witnesses nailed that cop in the videos.'"

"Does he have copies?"

"Sorry. Don't think so. He tried, but it was a big media case. The NYPD wouldn't go for it. But, hey, maybe he got them and doesn't want me to know."

"Why wouldn't he?"

Too late, she realizes he was attempting a joke. He gives a little laugh and says, "Course he would, but anyway, go ahead and ask the Prof about it if you want."

"Nope." No way is Natalie that much of a fool.

"Right. I wouldn't either." Zach knows the risks.

"That was a sensitive case." She thinks a moment. Why not? Zach *did* offer. "But I'd love to take a look at your notes, if that's okay." She'll hone her skills at deciphering hieroglyphics.

"Sure!" He starts shuffling through the papers on his desk. "But wait." Flustered, he swivels around to the file cabinet. "I'll have to look for my notebook."

"That's okay, Zach! Later. No rush." He seems confused, so she changes the subject to a lingering thought about an inconsistency. "There's one thing I don't get. You said Judge Kaplan hired Dr. Louden, back in the day, to testify for the defense."

"Yup. Even won a few for him. I think. Acquittals in eyewitness ID cases."

"That's what seems weird. Defense attorneys want to prove the ID is no good, or at least, raise a reasonable doubt. They hire experts to testify about conditions that distort perception or memory."

"Right. So, you're thinking… Uh-huh. Right. Strange." He seems surprised. "The things the Prof said to the press. Doesn't make total sense."

Natalie gives him a direct look and holds it. "What do you think? You saw those witnesses at the hearing. Was the professor right?"

Zach drops his gaze and shrugs. "I didn't see the videos. The photo IDs."

"But if you were the judge, watching them in court…"

"Well, you know how it is. Doing an ID on a computer screen. That's what we're researching. The problems with that. They weren't completely sure, but maybe because it's not the same as seeing someone in person. And they didn't see the stabbing. Not exactly anyway. So, I don't know how…"

Natalie nods. "How Dr. Louden could say it was a 'slam-dunk' case?"

"Is that what he said? Something like that."

Maybe "open-shut." No, Natalie remembers the basketball metaphor. "Thanks, Zach. I *am* curious about your notes, but don't worry. Whenever you find them." Maybe he wrote down the names and contact info for the detective and the witnesses. Too much to hope for? She doesn't dare ask.

"Just give me a minute." He turns to the file cabinet again. "I'll find—"

His voice is overwhelmed by Natalie's cell phone, loudly announcing a call with her default setting, an old-fashioned ringtone. She pulls it from her jeans pocket and looks at the screen. "Sorry, gotta take this." With a friendly wave goodbye and a toss of her thick, dark blonde hair, she touches the screen. "Hi, Max!" She steps into the hallway. "Yeah, dinner at six sounds good."

Her last impression before closing the door is a frozen image of Zach's fallen face.

Back in her own small box of an office, Natalie looks for her notes on the McBride case. She has a computer file with a list of URLs, and a physical file in her cabinet, so thin it might be empty. Inside the folder, she finds printouts of two articles, one from the *New York Times*, the other from the *New York Post*. Always worth it to compare those newspapers and ten others. Even then, it's hard to break through the spin and the slant to find the facts and the truth.

Another instance of: Where did she learn that? Again, from her mother.

The printed articles are from April 2020. *Two witnesses come forward... Why isn't Corey McBride behind bars?* The witnesses aren't identified, except to say that they work as security guards, but the articles lay out the details of their statements. There's so much here. Did the newspapers have access to the videos? That would be completely wrong, but it almost seems like the reporters watched the interviews. She finds URLS linking to op-ed articles that speculate about DA Browne's motives, concluding that his close relationship with former DA Patrick McBride indicates favoritism.

Professor Louden's public involvement surfaced months later, after the grand jury heard the case. News 7 reporter Tanya

Jordash got the exclusive. She did her homework and learned that the renowned cognitive psychologist Emmett Louden had watched the preliminary hearing in April 2020. She reached out to him and asked for an interview. He granted the request. Right there, that says something about his ego.

The interview with Tanya Jordash launched the professor more notably into the limelight. In the following months, Natalie saw his face and perfectly trimmed beard on many more public interest news programs, Zoomed from his university office. He loved to expound on pop psychology topics. She doesn't know how he remained so well-groomed throughout the pandemic when barbershops and salons were closed and people lapsed into shagginess.

With a bit of searching, Natalie finds the URL for the video of the News 7 report from August 2020. Index finger hovering over the link, Natalie looks over her shoulder to make sure her office door is closed. She gets up and punches the doorknob lock, returns to her seat, and puts on her earphones. Not good to have the professor's voice leaking out into the hallway if he happens to walk by.

It's a day after the grand jury's decision, and Emmett Louden is a special guest on Tanya Jordash's segment, "In the Courts." Some government restrictions were temporarily lifted in those days, and Tanya might have interviewed him in person, but she opted for the remote setup, mask free. The impeccably made-up newscaster sits in her TV studio, on a split screen next to Professor Louden. Erect and distinguished, he sits at his office desk, diplomas on the wall behind him.

Tanya establishes the preliminaries, Dr. Louden's reputation in the field of cognitive psychology, with a specialty in facial identification. After that, this is how it goes:

> "Professor, you saw the eyewitnesses testify in April when they identified Corey McBride as the man on the

bridge with Marlon Stokes. Were they credible?"

"Very much so. That's why Judge Kaplan held the case for the grand jury."

"In your expert opinion, why do you say their identifications of McBride are reliable?"

"One of the best indicators of accurate facial recognition is recent opportunity to see that face in a relaxed setting. These two men had just been at a pub where they stood very close to McBride and Stokes. Ten minutes later, a few blocks away, they saw them again on the bridge. McBride even spoke to them. This is not a case of mistaken ID."

"So, Professor, are you surprised that the grand jury exonerated McBride?"

"Very surprised. The jury had to reject the eyewitness testimony to get to that result. This is a slam-dunk case. How did the DA fail to get an indictment?"

There it is. Natalie remembered it right. The "slam-dunk." Dr. Louden seems to want to be more of a legal expert than a cognitive psychologist.

Is she convinced by his opinion? No way. Glaringly obvious are the factors that Dr. Louden omitted. Myriad circumstances impact perception and memory. After reading the news story about the witnesses' statements, Natalie can tell that many of these factors come into play here. Distractions at the pub, crowding, noise, dim lighting, and what many people are uncomfortable to say, differences in skin tone or social class between observer and the observed. On the bridge, same things. Lighting, distance, stress, and the real biggie, degree of intoxication. After the fact, add on the potential influences during the photo ID procedure with the detective. Phrasing and suggestion. Had the witnesses seen McBride's face in the newspapers or online before they answered the detective's questions?

And all this diverts attention from the real issue. Even if they accurately placed McBride on the bridge, does that mean he was the stabber? She doesn't hear the professor say that the witnesses observed the act itself.

Natalie can think of all these problems even without seeing the video recordings of their statements. There's so much going on here, it makes her head spin. She can't account for why she wasn't outraged a year and a half ago, when all this was going on. She knew that Zach attended the court hearing, but she was avoiding him in those days. She was also distracted and burdened by her own research project. And maybe, her blind reverence for the professor hadn't cooled completely. She was still enamored with his reputation and how it enhanced her own. Bottom line, she was in denial, refusing to wake up from her idea of the exalted expert.

Cut him some slack? Maybe his offense is forgivable. Blame his ego for accepting the invitation to appear on TV but forgive the unthinking moment when he stuck his foot in his mouth with a hasty opinion. Maybe he rued it later. But if he regretted what he said, why would he support COG's lawsuit with an affidavit that basically repeated what he said in the Tanya Jordash interview? Did COG pay him? Was it merely another expression of ego, the need to demonstrate loyalty to his own opinions?

After running this in circles through her mind, Natalie is left with one thought. She has to find out why Dr. Louden said the witnesses were so convincing.

9 » *THREADS*

Tuesday, January 11, 2022

THIS IS DELICATE. It always is.

After a year of getting to know her colleagues, has Associate Justice Hargrove learned anything? Reasonable judicial minds usually agree. A bit of compromise here, an analytical tweak there. The hotly debated appeals are few, but when they arise, Dana holds firm to her convictions, puts up a fight like the rest. Among the eighteen justices, degrees of push vary, techniques ranging from subtlety to bluster. Dana falls somewhere in the middle.

A year. In that time, she's chalked up one huge win, a victory of persuasion. Other clashes were lost. She handled those defeats by swallowing her minor misgivings or writing brief dissenting opinions. But she always tries. She makes the effort to convince, even with those colleagues who stand firm in wet cement, daring her to watch it dry as she talks herself blue in the face.

Today's challenge might be of that ilk, a tussle with Associate Justice Nathan Shields. She's on her way to see Nathan now. On a morning like this, the good old days float on a cloud of sweet nostalgia. Eight years a trial judge, queen of her courtroom, the world at her feet, heeding her word. She traded that in to become a member of the pack, a negotiator low on the totem pole. She's seen it all. The prodding and diplomacy, supplication and deference, grandstanding and rank pulling. Dana simply tries to remain true to herself.

This is the morning to start laying the groundwork, to make her views known in *Josefina M.* Briefs are due in two days, and oral argument is scheduled for Friday. Because the case is sensitive, a special panel of five will convene, headed by the presiding justice of the court. Five, not four, to ensure a quick turnaround. In case of disagreement, a majority of three will win the day.

The more Dana studies the case, the deeper she's pulled into the crisis of this young woman's life. How dare they rip her from the embrace of family at a time like this? The lower court's order should be reversed and Josefina sent home to her aunt. Immediately. Dana senses the fierce love and mutual support in this small family, two women pitted against a righteous and paternalistic monolith. The Administration for Children's Services should keep its hands off Josefina, mature and capable of making her own health decisions with Bianca's guidance.

Nathan Shields is the justice on the panel most likely to disagree. He denied the aunt's motion for a stay of the removal order pending appeal.

By now, Dana and Nathan have worked on many cases together, engaging in the usual friendly legal discussions and debate. She doesn't know him well but has a strong gut feeling about the sum of his character, gleaned from collected tidbits. His legal opinions. His questions to attorneys during oral argument. His offhand comments and non sequiturs during consultation. His energy. In his mid-fifties, Nathan smiles warmly and bounces with the kind of idealistic fervor usually seen in twenty-somethings. Is the world doomed? Yes, unless we, the smart people, tell everyone else what to do and make sure they do it.

Hands off. Save the saving for the helpless children, the truly abused and neglected.

But it's delicate. A blunt exhortation will backfire.

Nathan stands and bursts into a broad smile as she enters his spacious office of well-oiled mahogany and shelves of New York Reports. He's tall and wiry, the fingers long on the hand extended outward, palm up, indicating a seat for her. Although she's about five years older than Nathan, *he* is five years her senior in the hierarchy of the court, appointed in 2016. His office is, therefore, larger and nicer than hers. But like every room in this 120-year-old building, the majesty is tinged with hints of ambient mildew and ancient dust, the threat of rot, the unpleasant suggestion of impermanence and mortality.

"Dana! How are you? Please sit!" The hand.

A loud "clank-clank" drowns out her return greeting. The radiator. She smiles through her voiceless words and takes the seat offered. To be professional and polite, she's wearing a business suit with jacket. Would have been more comfortable in a sleeveless summer dress and flip-flops. Her nasal passages are dry, her underarms wet. In winter, the uneven heating system in the building keeps some rooms at 80 degrees, others a drafty 60. Dana eyes a window. If she were Nathan she'd open it, but he doesn't seem to mind. He's not worried about appearances and has stripped down to rolled up shirtsleeves and a loosened necktie.

After her inaudible greeting, he says, "So, you're here on the special Friday calendar." He shakes his head in a show of consternation. "What a case this is! So sad. A young life in the balance. We have to do what we can to save her."

There it is. A preview of his vote, feet settled into wet cement.

"Yes, very sad for this young adult." Persuasion Technique Number One. Find an area of agreement and build on it in terms supporting one's own views. Josefina is an adult. "And very sad for the parent." Dana shakes her head, mirroring Nathan. "As a parent of two young adults, I feel Bianca's pain. What a time to rip this family apart." A subtle reminder of her superior experience in raising children. On a bookshelf, Nathan displays a crystal-framed photograph of his wife Lisa, an attorney for the ACLU. The couple is childless.

Dana and Nathan once sat on a panel considering an appeal from a multimillion-dollar verdict in a toxic tort case, compensating the plaintiff for her child's disabling injuries. During consultation Nathan remarked, "Greedy corporations like this are polluting our dying planet." He gave his characteristic shake of the head. "This poor child was better off not being born. Money isn't enough, but it's the best we can do." Although Dana was not persuaded by Nathan's view of the case, she agreed with the panel to affirm the damages verdict because it was supported by the medical and financial evidence.

Children should not be brought into this dying world, so he believes. A decision he and his wife made many years ago. Or did he create this justification out of regret for a lost opportunity? Either way, Nathan seems to hold strong beliefs on what should and should not be done about children, despite having no experience raising them. Maybe he thinks Josefina would have been better off never being born, but since she exists, the court must step in and do its "best." Does that mean, in Nathan's view, that the court should mandate the medical treatment it thinks "best" for Josefina?

He says, "Sure, we can feel sorry for the aunt, but Josefina is the one suffering a life-threatening illness. I feel more for the child—"

"Then you must see how cruel it is, yanking her from the love and support of family. It's unconscionable. The emotional trauma itself causes more harm to her. And if she happens to die in the next six months before she's eighteen, ACS is denying her a mother's comfort on her death bed."

Nathan almost laughs. "You call that a mother's love and

comfort? I call it child abuse. Depriving a child of needed medical care is neglect under the law. ACS *must* step in. This woman shunned her duty. She doesn't understand the obligations of parenthood."

And you do, Nathan? Though her heart is pounding, Dana works at a façade of humble confidence, holding steady against her colleague's building fervor. "Maybe I've jumped the gun, but I already reviewed the entire file." She's taking a risk here. Nathan is also the type to be prepared in advance. "We can talk later, but I think you'll find that the appellant's affidavits establish the very *opposite* of neglect. There's been plenty of medical care. Bianca herself is a nurse and they've consulted top oncologists. So the issue *isn't* whether a parent withheld medical care. It's about *who* gets to choose among options with uncertain outcomes. I say it's the patient's choice. The doctors disagree on Josefina's prognosis and the efficacy of chemotherapy."

"They disagree, but *all* on the positive side. Fifty to seventy-five percent chance of extending her life for five years." So. Nathan has also read the entire file.

"A fifty-fifty chance of five years doesn't factor in the debilitating pain of treatment and damage from emotional trauma, forcing her to live in exile among strangers—"

"But it's her *only* chance!"

"You're forgetting the percentages on the other side, the chance of survival without that specific treatment."

"Vitamin C and green leafy vegetables? Chemo is her only chance. The aunt is enabling the child's fantasy, her so-called 'decision' to refuse life-saving therapy. ACS is giving the girl that chance—"

"Based on an abstract statistical percentage. You'd give that decision to an impersonal government agency over a mature young adult who bears the consequences. I just can't play God under those circumstances."

Nathan has a retort for that one.

She responds.

He comes back at her.

They go on a while longer, gradually losing steam, drifting into a vanilla cordiality, floating above the drying cement. Under the top layer, Dana contemplates his depth of feeling. The instinct to nurture is in everyone, Nathan included, though he never had the chance to satisfy that impulse by raising a child. A warmth for humankind, a sensed duty to protect the young and the helpless, is directed to the world at large.

Finally, Dana stands up to leave, and they exchange promises to seriously consider the other's arguments when the briefs come in.

Out in the drafty hallway, Dana feels the cool relief of unheated air. Any optimism she felt twenty minutes ago, making her way to Nathan's office, has shriveled in her retreat, replaced with a familiar frustration of recent times. *Greetings! Your government, the Nanny State, has arrived, ready to think and decide for you.*

Let it go for now. Save it for Friday, with the anticipation that the views of other justices on the panel will fall closer to hers.

In the anteroom to Dana's chambers, Nia sits at her computer. "How'd it go, Judge?"

"Just peachy!"

"I can tell. Speaking of food, I was about to order lunch. Can I get something for you and the detective?" Nia pushes a takeout menu across the desk toward her boss.

"That's really nice." Dana doesn't expect this kind of service from her law clerk and doesn't want Nia to think she expects it. But the offer is accepted. She chooses two club sandwiches and leaves Nia with her promise to pay when the delivery comes.

It will be good to see Aurelina. Dana has invited her friend to the courthouse for lunch. Very elegant. Deli sandwiches at the little round table in the corner of Dana's office. Lina expects nothing less.

Dana pushes her unsuccessful morning out of mind and logs into the court's e-file system. She wants to review the evidence in the McBride case before Lina gets here. *Citizens for Open Government v Jared Browne, District Attorney of New York County*. A year ago, she saw everything in this file, but she was reviewing it for a different purpose. COG's appeal. Now, she wants to focus on details in the eyewitness statements to see if they yield any clues or leads that should be followed up.

A message in red font warns her: "SEALED: unauthorized access prohibited pursuant to CPL 160.50." The sealing statute is meant to protect the wrongly accused. Corey McBride has the legal right to see his own case file and has given Lina open-ended permission for access. Has he offered the same to Dana? Not expressly, but he knows she's already seen it.

As her index finger hovers over the mouse, a voice whispers: *What are you doing?* A powerful impulse overwhelms that doubt. The heartbreak of this case just won't let her go. She could call Corey, reveal her mission to find Marlon's killer, and ask for his blessing, but she doesn't think it wise. Not yet. Why plant the seed of an unrealistic hope that something promising could come of her meddling? She'll do what she can, knowing that Corey won't mind having someone else on his side, a loyal friend of the McBride family. Becoming a judge didn't erase her decades of experience in criminal justice, working with cops, brainstorming with talented detectives like Aurelina Vargas. Corey would approve. She doesn't need to think twice.

Dana searches the records and brings up the transcript from the preliminary hearing. When she saw this a year ago, she didn't pay close attention. Her focus then was on the evidence COG sought to disclose: the testimony and exhibits in the grand jury. Now, she's curious. Did she miss anything that could reveal a new lead? Weaknesses in the witnesses' testimony or details in their observations that were overlooked?

The hearing witnesses are Wesley Guerrier, Janjak Bernard, Detective Kyle Rodman, and in his own defense, Corey McBride. She reads the transcript carefully, then watches the videos of Detective Rodman's initial interviews of Guerrier and Bernard, conducted a week before the hearing. The younger man, Bernard, says he was the first to contact the police. Other than that, their responses to Rodman's questions are similar.

And now something else strikes her. A thread of consistency. Their responses are not only similar to each other, but they also sound familiar. Dana plays each video again, listening to the way the witness responds to Rodman's questions, while she scans that witness's responses to the attorneys' questions at the preliminary hearing. Many answers in the interviews and at the hearing are nearly identical, down to the words and phrasing. Overall, the comparison exudes a flavor of rehearsal. Were they coached? If so, Dana wouldn't lay blame on ADA Ernest Chin, who represented the People at the hearing. Ricky, formerly Dana's deputy when she was a bureau chief, is a man of impeccable integrity.

The similarity could just be a function of repetition. Witnesses commonly use the same phrases when describing an incident more than once. Natalie would agree. Dana smiles to herself, remembering her daughter at age thirteen when she experienced the life-changing event that set her on a course to study perception and memory. Natalie was summoned to testify before a grand jury. Afterward, she questioned the accuracy of her own testimony and came to this realization: At a certain point, a witness may not be remembering the event but remembering her previous description of the event.

On further examination, Dana does find a notable difference between the interviews and the hearing testimony. Ricky covers a topic that Detective Rodman ignores. Alcohol consumption. In response to ADA Chin's questioning, Bernard says he was drinking beer. When asked how much, he says, "a couple." When asked if he could put a number on that, Bernard says, "I don't remember, but it was more than one." Reading the cold transcript, Dana senses his hesitancy. He seems to be downplaying the amount he drank. Guerrier, the older man, is very precise in his response. "I had two beers. They were green." Typical, right before St. Paddy's Day. He also says, "I usually don't drink at all, but it was a celebration."

And another thing. *Boy, wouldn't Natalie have something to say about this?* Rodman's photo identification is problematic. It was the start of the pandemic when the NYPD was transitioning to remote measures. Even taking that learning curve into account, Rodman's technique is laughable. He conducts a sequential photo "lineup," showing one photo after another, rather than a photo array with six on one page. The procedure itself isn't improper. Studies are inconclusive which technique yields more reliable results. But the *way* he shows the photos is from a comedy routine. Instead of screen sharing a computer file, he holds one printed photo after another up to his computer camera in a play of perpetual motion and experimentation. Fingers shift and obscure different corners and edges as he adjusts the distance and angle to the camera, making the image, at moments, fuzzy or crooked or distorted. Even so, Bernard and Guerrier seem to have no trouble at all immediately identifying Corey's photo, the third one shown. Rodman follows up with an incorrect, leading question: "So, this was the guy you saw on the bridge, hugging the victim tight?" "Yes."

Botched from the get-go.

Dana freezes the screen on Corey's photo. She could be wrong, but she thinks it's the same photo that was posted on many news sites before Bernard and Guerrier came forward. Did they see it online or in the newspapers in the days after the murder? You'd never know it from these videos. Rodman doesn't ask the question.

Another thought occurs. Dana searches every item in the file and doesn't find something she would expect Jared and Ricky to subpoena. Of course, it could be in the NYPD's or DA's files, never making it into the court file because it wasn't in evidence at the hearing or in the grand jury. She'll ask Lina when she comes in.

Neither woman has ever been a big eater, so the sandwiches on paper plates are more of a social pretense. A lunch date for a detective and a judge who run at top speed on the fuel of hard work and tough cases. They nibble.

"So good to see you, Lina."

"It's been too long."

They haven't met since before Mateo's death. If a funeral had been allowed, Dana would have been there. As it was, a sympathy card and phone call had to do. Since then, emails: "Just checking in to see how you're doing."

Their friendship dates back to 1992. Lina, then a ponytailed rookie, collared an armed robber Dana prosecuted for felony murder. Over the years they've kept in touch, fitting social occasions around the edges of their busy careers.

The judge towers eight inches over the five-foot detective, but their mutual respect and admiration stand at eye level. Petite Lina is grayer and physically tinier than the last time Dana saw her. She's lost some of the perkiness and sparkle, but her lovely smile still beams compassion, self-assurance, and proficiency. Although a homicide detective sees more than her fair share of death, the unexpected loss of a beloved husband is something else entirely. Lina's appearance and mien bear the weight of that experience.

Dana gently encourages Lina to open up, and she talks about

Mateo for several minutes, ending with, "A bad time. In a way, I still can't believe it." In sympathy, Dana briefly palms Lina's hand where it rests on the table. Lina goes on. "Insult to injury, the timing sucked. I had to leave Marlon's murder in Rodman's hands. When I got back, I was still distracted, and other things got in the way. The investigation is at a standstill for months now." She looks heavenward and says, "Not blaming you, *mi amor*." She levels her gaze at Dana. "It's Kyle. We overestimated his abilities."

"I looked at Detective Rodman's interviews of the witnesses. I wasn't impressed."

"To say the least. And then those interviews got leaked, starting that whole fiasco, the bad press. Compromised the investigation. Kyle never discovered how it got out, and for all I know, his sloppiness had something to do with it. Mateo was dead only a few days when I saw the article and called him about it. I was out of my mind..." She ends with a muttered expletive.

"Yeah. Not good." Dana is reminded of the evidence that wasn't in the court file, something Lina might have. "Another thing about those interviews, I'm wondering if you reviewed the NYPD Skype account records."

A look passes across Lina's face. She recognizes the significance of Dana's question. "You're thinking... Hmm. I haven't looked at the records, but I'm almost sure we have them. If not, I'll get them."

"Just in case there's anything there."

"Yeah, I don't like the look of Kyle's interviews. He's also the one who did most of the Q&As with the officers who were at The Book and Brew that night. Then, after the grand jury no-billed it, he worked the case a couple of months. That's it. Says he followed up on leads in the neighborhood Marlon was working and came up with nothing. I want to redo most of that. I'm taking it over."

"What'd he say when you told him?"

"Just looked at me like, 'Yeah. Okay.' That's his attitude. I can tell what he's thinking. Why waste the effort looking for another suspect? Corey did it. A friendly DA and a wacko grand jury got him off."

"He thinks Jared threw the case?" Dana asks. "What does he have against the DA?"

"You know how it is. Always been some anti-McBride bullshit at the precinct. Corey's name is two strikes against him. Petty stuff. Jokes behind his back. Uncle Patrick got McNephew into the academy. Uncle got Corey his badge and big boy gun, etcetera. Marlon was Corey's only real friend."

"And that gives Rodman enough reason to bury the case?"

"Part of it. He's said some things, hints, nothing too obvious. But I can tell he buys that garbage about McBride's influence over Browne. Rodman's also allergic to hard work. Add it together, and things don't get very far."

They pause for a bite. A few moments to think. Is Lina swayed by any of that media hype about favoritism? "What do you really think, Lina? Did the grand jury get it wrong?"

"Hell no, girl. Corey is innocent as a lamb. I'd stake my career on it. Those two were like brothers. I could see the love, and the family could too. That morning, I broke the news to Marlon's mother and fiancée. Half of their wailing was for Corey, how heartbroken he'd be. No hint of any suspicions against him."

"Even after the two witnesses identified Corey?"

"Don't know how they felt about that. I was on leave by then and didn't talk to the family a second time. But those witnesses don't cut it for me. Kyle botched the IDs..."

Dana rolls her eyes.

"And," Lina goes on, "the grand jury obviously had big doubts that the man they saw was Corey, even if a few things in their descriptions matched. You know. The descriptions they gave before their ID of Corey's picture. Height, build, haircut, clothing."

"Five ten, a hundred sixty. He's average. Could be anybody. A lot of men's clothing looks alike too. It was late. Dark."

"Right. Could be half the world. But a few other things cut against him. The argument in the bar. The timing. The killer had to be right there the minute Corey walked off. And the drinking isn't a good look…"

"How much?"

"Don't know. He still smelled like a brewery when we interviewed him at six-thirty. They'd been knocking 'em back until two thirty that morning. Toxicology on Marlon puts the number at about five drinks. Corey was drinking beer, probably the same number of glasses."

Dana has a thought about that but takes another bite of sandwich and chews to avoid voicing it. Lina reads her mind. "We had no reason to ask for a blood test. You gotta remember, a few hours after the murder, we didn't have anything. No witnesses. Corey wasn't a suspect. Why would he knife his best friend? Like that? But we could see he'd been drinking. A lot. He admitted it."

"How does Corey handle alcohol? Have you ever seen him drunk?" Dana plays devil's advocate by force of habit, even when she believes the opposite of what's implied. She, too, has faith in Corey's innocence, but faith isn't fact and has to be tested. "Friends and alcohol don't always mix. Even the closest friends may have a history of slights and grudges. Alcohol can stir up the bad feelings—"

"You're talking love and hate, like this?" Lina holds up a hand with index and middle fingers glued together. She tilts her head down and directs a skeptical gaze at Dana from under her brow. "Are you getting these ideas from our interview with Corey?"

"I didn't have time to watch the video this morning. I'll get to it."

"Take a look. You'll see. Me and Jared shocked him bigtime.

He had no idea why we called him in. He was crushed. Started beating himself up over his argument with Marlon."

"Must've regretted that argument. I understand that Marlon didn't say much. Just hinted at things. What's your take on it?"

"Corey's guess was that Marlon had crossed the wrong person. Either that, or 'Chug' had been made and Marlon was scared. But why all the secrecy? From his best friend? Corey wanted to help. He was pissed that night in more ways than one. Kept pushing for information and Marlon kept holding him back. It got heated, but they cooled it down before they got to the bridge and said goodnight."

"Did Corey give you any idea who we're looking for?"

"No more than what we all think. It has to do with the undercover work. Marlon had no enemies. Everyone loved him." Lina looks off into a near distance. "He was quite a guy."

"So, a vendetta, perhaps. Or someone mixed up in the synthetic Mary Jane ring. And a good opportunity. Victim dulled by drink, streets almost empty, people sheltering in before lock-down. But it's also a good setup for a random armed robbery."

"Not likely. Nothing was taken."

"The robber was scared off by those two men. Bernard and Guerrier."

"They walked away! Had their backs turned before they decided to go back. Plenty of time for a thief to find Marlon's wallet."

"An incompetent robber, then. Or a mentally ill homeless person."

Lina smiles. "Dressed neatly and speaking nicely? 'My friend here had a few too many.'"

Dana knows she's gone into overkill. She and Jared already talked through all this. But she wants Lina's thoughts on *every* possible angle. "Okay. Back to vendetta. Against a guy everybody loved."

"Yup."

"Or someone involved in the crime ring he was investigating. This bad guy had to be watching and following Marlon, either in the pub or outside."

"Most likely. That's why we called Corey later that day and told him to bring his clothes in. It was a longshot, but the perp could've been rubbing shoulders with them in that crowded bar. We did Marlon's clothing too. Forensics picked off a few hairs, only Corey's and Marlon's. No one else. The hair on Corey's jacket was inconclusive for a few weeks until we swabbed him in April after his arrest and matched it. But we could tell it was his. He has that short haircut, rusty color."

"Like Patrick."

"Strong family resemblance."

They smile at the memories and turn their attention to their huge club sandwiches. They each manage to get through one of the four quarters on the plate. Pickles ignored.

While chewing, Dana's been thinking, and this is where it leads. "We have no match for the DNA under Marlon's fingernails. It's not Corey's. That's one good thing for him, but not conclusive. If it's the killer's DNA, and if we think it's a bad guy Marlon was onto, he'd probably have a record, possibly with DNA in the databank. A killer like that wouldn't fit well in the bar scene at The Book and Brew. It's a cop bar. You're looking for a cop, Lina."

"Gee, how'd you guess?" The twinkle in Lina's eye says she's way ahead of Dana on this.

"Of course, anything's possible. A clean-cut assassin hired by the bad guys, no DNA in the system, following Marlon, lurking in the shadows, or even fitting into the bar scene. But more likely a cop. A cop who isn't Corey. A cop who, maybe, was on the take from that synthetic marijuana business. Marlon was getting too close to him."

Their eyes lock as they smile their agreement. After a moment, Lina says, "This sandwich is delicious, but I think I'm done."

"I am too." Dana eyes their plates, in turn. "Evan's dinner tonight and lunch tomorrow."

"You're such a homemaker, Judge."

"Leftovers are my specialty."

They talk a bit longer about the case, Lina's plans to re-interview people on the street, to check on the DA's GEDMatch subpoena, and ways to follow the money. Marlon had started to figure out the flow. Is anyone at the precinct looking flush? Lina has certain people in mind.

Personal topics, life and family, take over. When it's time to part, Dana opens her special drawer of odds and ends, everyday supplies, including household plastic wrap. Companionably, they enclose their delicious deli sandwiches in airtight layers, and on the way downstairs, deposit the leftovers in the little half fridge in Nia's anteroom.

In the court's lobby, Dana suppresses an impulse to hug Lina goodbye. Instead, she grabs her hand for a warm squeeze, then heads back upstairs.

Dana pulls out her ringing cell phone as she returns to her office and sits at the desk. She's pleased to see her son's name on the display. "Travis! How's everything?"

"Good, Mom, great."

"Ginger's okay?"

"Yeah, she's feeling well, better actually. No morning sickness and a lot of energy."

"That's great. And how are you? Been working hard?"

"Yup. This is a tough case I'm working on."

"Something in my court?"

"Um, yeah." A pause. "This is confusing."

"How so?"

"I've been so busy writing my section of the brief, I didn't even bother to check the calendar. Noriko just walked in here and told me I'd better call you and find out what's going on."

Why on earth is Travis's boss telling him to call his mother? "About what?" But the minute she says this, it dawns on her. "Oh, no. Hold on a minute."

Dana brings up the court tracking system on her computer screen and enters the case name as her son's voice floats into her ear, a gentle background to the nervous buzz in her head. He explains, "Noriko is sure she listed me as co-counsel for ACS, but you're still on the panel."

"Josefina M."

"Right."

Dana purses her lips into an angry line, disappointed in herself for not being more careful. "Our data entry clerk must have made a mistake. You're not listed as counsel in the system."

"Sorry, Mom."

"No problem. I'll recuse and they'll assign someone else."

She agrees with Travis that it's an interesting, important case, but doesn't express her views. He knows his mother well enough to guess what she thinks.

Dana changes the subject, and they chat a while longer as a persistent thread weaves through her thoughts. Just this morning she tried to persuade a judge on the panel to adopt a view contrary to the one her son is sure to argue in his brief. She smiles to herself at the irony. Her disqualification flips the reason for recusal on its head. Would this proud mother's impartiality and judgment fly out the window the moment her brilliant son steps up to the podium? Is she likely to change her ruling based on a family relationship with an attorney on the case? No way. The rules of judicial ethics were made for families of weaker character.

This mother-son relationship is not threatened by intellectual, or even emotional, disagreement on a court case.

But let's not get smug. Dana's principles aren't immune to the subtle push of subliminal forces. It's best that she begs off.

Too late now to undo what happened this morning. Perhaps Nathan will laugh when he finds out that the strident mother who believes in close family bonds wasn't aware that her own son would be arguing this case. Did she commit a professional indiscretion, arguing with Nathan about this case? Although her ignorance of the data entry clerk's error saves her from any ethics violation, she deeply regrets her hastiness. The conversation never should have happened.

But what does it really matter? Dana seriously doubts she convinced Nathan Shields of anything.

10 » BLAMELESS?

April to August, 2020

WHEN THE STORY of the two eyewitnesses made the news, Corey was sunk. Out of thin air, three weeks after Marlon's murder, two "concerned citizens" came forward. A setup? They claimed to have seen him on the bridge, in a death hug with Marlon. *Also* saw him at the bar. Reportedly. Who were these guys?

Breathing, thinking, existing had been unbearable since March 16. The void, the guilt, the remorse. Corey took a week of personal leave but couldn't delay his return any longer. Staffing was low, officers out sick or on leave to look after the sick and dying. When he returned to work, he was met with expressions of sympathy and fond reminiscences of Marlon. There were other reactions too, not so nice. Some of his colleagues greeted him tersely and eyed him warily. He tried to shrug it off, but every new slight added to the foreboding, his anticipation of a sledge-hammer about to fall.

Memories of that night came in segments. A spoken phrase, lyrics of a song playing in the background, Marlon turning to look him in the eye, desolate city streets as they walked to the bridge. Corey wasn't sure of everything between these images, and he kept to himself, didn't look for comfort or advice. Oh, there were plenty of people he could talk to. His sister and his brothers. Not his mother and father. Maybe his uncles. But he wasn't going to open up to them.

When it came to sensitive issues, Marlon was the person he'd come closest to confiding in. His absence brought that truth home. Why had they grown close? They were polar opposites in background and appearance, and sometimes, in point of view. From those differences, self-awareness and honesty grew, expressed in truth-laden, ironic comparisons, revealing who they were.

He didn't remember what he'd said to Detective Vargas. She treated him square, the day of the murder. The shock loosened whatever his mind held, letting thoughts and fragments of memory tumble out, perhaps incoherently, with gaps, blank spots, and uncertainties.

A shame about Vargas and her husband. Corey didn't trust the new lead, Rodman. The man never liked him, so why would he be expected to treat him fairly? A day or so after April Fool's, Corey accidently bumped into the detective coming out of the men's room. Rodman said nothing, just threw him a devious look that barely covered the knowledge under his glare. A few days later it came out. On April 7, the first news story broke.

What a royal fuckup, letting those witness statements slip out to the press. The precinct was in chaos, trying to figure out how to maintain physical distance from people while conducting investigations. Interviewing witnesses on Skype was a disaster waiting to happen. Digital connections between personal devices and the precinct, just waiting for hackers and leakers. Whether Rodman was negligent or not, he clearly didn't give a damn when the story broke.

What would the Stokes family think of Corey now? The two most important people to Marlon were his fiancée, Chantelle, and his mother, Destiny. Lockdown restrictions had precluded a proper funeral, but two days after the murder, Corey called Destiny to offer his condolences. Crazy with grief, she could barely talk except to beg, in a jumble of words, for an explanation. He said only that he'd left Marlon at the Brooklyn Bridge and never saw him again. He didn't mention what Marlon told him and how they'd argued. If he suggested that someone was after Marlon, she might take it the wrong way, imagining a continuing threat to the family. Corey left it out.

The news stories gradually progressed from suspicion to public crucifixion. Corey's fate was sealed by the media hype that he was getting away with murder. DA Browne couldn't ignore the heat. The blow was about to fall, certain as death and taxes. Uncle Patrick knew it before Corey did and called to prepare him.

Corey hadn't spoken with Patrick since the day after Marlon's death, when they talked of tragedy, loss, and grief. What could he say to his uncle now that two witnesses had nailed him as "the man on the bridge"? But when Corey's cell phone rang and he saw who was calling, he couldn't avoid it. Would not. He accepted the call but shrank inwardly, in shame, at the sound of that powerful, resonant voice.

"I've spoken with the DA," Patrick said. "He thinks, and I agree with him, that it's best for all concerned to face this directly."

"I…um…okay." Corey was tongue-tied. Couldn't deny it, couldn't defend himself, couldn't fight. Would he be able to fight in court?

"The grand jury is closed. A preliminary hearing is your only shot. You can waive the hearing, but I'd recommend against it."

"Otherwise…" Corey knew what was implied. He just couldn't say it.

"Otherwise, it's not clear how long you'd be sitting in Rikers, waiting for the grand jury to open. With a hearing, you have a chance for dismissal before it goes any further."

"Then, they're going to… There's no way to avoid…"

"I'm sorry, Corey." Was that a small catch in his voice? Uncle

Patrick wasn't happy to be the messenger. "A grand jury can indict or exonerate behind closed doors, without an arrest. But without the grand jury, Jared has to arrest you to get a hearing. He's agreed to do it discreetly. Nothing public. No perp walk for the cameras. A planned, voluntary surrender. I've gotten you the best lawyer I can find. Cynthia Pullman."

She was a good lawyer. Of course she was good, one of the best, but instead of thanking his uncle, Corey blubbered and whined. "I-I can't go to Rikers, I can't, God, I'll be a target, I won't get out alive—"

"Corey, no, listen," Patrick kept trying to cut in until Corey shut up. "We're talking two days, tops, even with all the processing involved. Jared's gone all out to move this through the system. Surrender on Monday morning. A hearing is already scheduled for Tuesday. You'll be protected, and with luck, you'll be back out by Tuesday evening."

Or not. Uncle Patrick didn't give an opinion on Corey's chances or say what he thought of the witnesses and the case against him. Nor did he declare faith in his nephew's innocence. Corey noticed the omissions, wouldn't beg for a statement of support or accuse his uncle of evasion. For the rest of the call, Patrick's instructions floated into his ear from afar, a low rumble of distant thunder.

Patrick ended the conversation with no questions asked, nothing said about innocence or guilt.

Judge Seth Kaplan stepped up to the bench in one of the preliminary hearing parts, PH2, trusting that the court techies had smoothed out the glitches. Yesterday, the "grand opening" of PH2 had been a disaster. Three hearings scheduled, commenced, screwed up, and rescheduled for another day. Internet connection to Rikers interrupted in number one, defense attorney inaudible in number two, screen-share function for documentary evidence bungled in number three.

A full day was scheduled for *People v McBride*. DA Browne had twisted some arms to reserve PH2 on the second day of this experiment in virtual justice, Tuesday, April 14. Understandable, given the public's fascination with the case and the gravity of a cop killing. But Kaplan had a problem with the DA's save-ass priorities. Hundreds of arrestees, presumed innocent under the law, were languishing in pretrial confinement indefinitely, their cases at a standstill by the governor's executive order suspending statutory time limits. Their wait got a little longer when the ex-DA's nephew cut the line.

Every player in the system was stressed by the unsettled, everchanging rules in pandemic control. A new executive order mandated facemasks, starting Friday the 17th. For today's online hearing, everyone would be mask-free: ADA Chin and witnesses in the DA's video room, defense attorney Cynthia Pullman in her downtown office, and Corey McBride, wearing a government-issued khaki jumpsuit, in a closet-sized video room at Rikers. Kaplan didn't look forward to the day he'd have to assess witness credibility from muffled testimony spoken by half-covered faces. Eyes: a window to the soul? He hoped for such insight but was having enough trouble trying to read people's expressions on a computer screen.

As DA Browne must have realized when Kaplan's name was pulled from the hopper, this judge would not be an apologist for the McBrides. He'd prepared for the hearing by reviewing the "*Rosario* material," the witness videos. From what he'd seen so far, dismissal wasn't a likely outcome in his courtroom, but he was ready and willing to listen.

A lonely sight. Judge Kaplan appreciated an audience, but the only bodies in the courtroom were the clerk, the court reporter, and two members of the public granted special permission to attend, Professor Emmett Louden and a gawkily enthusiastic graduate student. They stood up when the judge entered the courtroom. Louden's wry smirk and sparkling eyes mocked his own compliance with ceremony. Kaplan was happy to see his longtime friend, an expert who had helped him win a few acquittals back in the day. He swiped the air with a hand and said, "Sit, Professor. Welcome to our reality show."

"Thanks for letting us sit in, Your Honor." Louden and student resumed their seats at a table with computer monitor, some distance from the bench. Separate screens were provided for the judge and the clerk.

"Case of the century," Kaplan deadpanned with a wink at Louden. Off camera, off the record. Although the proceeding had already started, the first half hour was reserved for a private consultation between defendant and attorney. No one else allowed on screen. Silence fell over the courtroom for the remaining minutes until the clerk officially called the case and logged the others in.

ADA Ernest Chin opened with the People's case. His burden to prove reasonable cause was far lower than the trial standard of proof beyond a reasonable doubt. But this preliminary hearing would go longer than most. DA Browne had been accused of *not* wanting to prosecute Corey McBride. To counter the DA's critics, Chin had to show he was serious and diligent. The press was excluded, but word of the day's proceedings would eventually leak out. It was always that way.

First up, Detective Kyle Rodman. He set the scene: 911 call, location and condition of body, no weapon found, forensic tests, witnesses interviewed, McBride's voluntary surrender and submission to a DNA test.

Second, Chin introduced the autopsy and DNA analysis, admitted into evidence without objection by the defense. The clerk did better with the screen-share function and displayed the documents. Cause of death: a single, deep stab wound into the heart. No match found for the DNA under the victim's fingernails. In other words, no match to McBride.

Third, Janjak Bernard.

The witness briefly testified about his background, occupation, and reason for being at The Book and Brew with his older colleague, Wesley Guerrier. Chin asked, "How much did you drink that night?" After some back and forth, Bernard testified he had a "couple of beers." Eyeing his demeanor, Judge Kaplan guessed that he'd drunk considerably more than that.

ADA Chin asked a few questions about Bernard's observations of the two men in the bar and had him identify Marlon Stokes by photograph. Bernard described the second man as five-ten, one sixty, average build, pale skin, buzz cut, nothing remarkable about the face, wearing jeans and a white polo shirt, and later, on the bridge, in a dark blue windbreaker.

"Must've put the jacket on by the door before they left."

"Did you see that?"

"No. But there's a coat rack when you come in. It was the same man on the bridge. I'm sure of it."

Judge Kaplan was watching the witness closely, looking for subtext. No motive to lie, no agenda, but possibly something else. Bernard projected an air of self-importance and braggadocio that only the young possess. He was enjoying the limelight. Maybe needed this excitement in his life.

Chin slowed the witness down and took him through his route with Wesley, after they left the bar.

"We turned onto the sidewalk to the bridge. Right there, at the beginning. That's when we saw the two men again."

"Objection," Pullman said.

"Sustained." Judge Kaplan didn't need to hear the defense attorney's reasoning. "Mr. Bernard, tell us only what *you* saw, not what you think Wesley saw."

"Right, yes!" Very eager to please.

Chin went on. "What did you see when you turned onto the bridge?"

"The two men from the bar, the, the Marlon Stokes and the other, wearing a dark color jacket. He was holding Stokes tight," Bernard hugged the air with his arms, "trying to keep him from falling, but they were both slipping down. Wesley asked if everything was okay." Bernard hesitated. "May I say that?"

"If you heard Wesley ask that question," the judge instructed.

"I did."

"That's okay. Go on. What happened next?"

"The man turns like this," Bernard twisted his neck and tilted his head up briefly, "kind of laughed, and said, 'My friend had a few too many.' We just kept walking." A look crossed Bernard's face and he quickly corrected himself. "*I* just kept walking. Wesley was next to me of course."

The judge, with a mental eye-roll, said nothing. No use reassuring the witness again.

"How close were you when the man turned around to answer Wesley's question?" Chin asked.

"Close. A couple of feet. It was the same man from the bar."

"Take a look at the people on the computer screen. Do you see that man here today?"

Who would doubt that a man in prison garb, sitting in a cell in a fuzzy video, was "the one"? Oddly, though, this witness, who was so sure of himself a minute ago, seemed uncertain. He hesitated noticeably. Five seconds, ten, a bewildered look.

"Take your time, Mr. Bernard," ADA Chin said. "The man you saw that night may or may not be here on the screen—"

"Of course," the witness blurted with a laugh. "That's him in the tan shirt. His hair is longer, that's all." He patted the top of his head. "That reddish color. I didn't see it before."

Corey McBride's buzz cut had not seen a barber in the past month. Unlike his NYPD photo, the one that most news outlets had published, his hair had become a prominent feature, two inches of orange-rust thatch.

Judge Kaplan had never heard an in-court identification like this one, the witness describing the man sitting right there. Usually, the witness just nodded or pointed a finger and said, "That's him." Speaking to a computer screen may have given the witness a sense of distance and anonymity, releasing his private thoughts to the world.

But Bernard's uncertainty stayed with Kaplan as the hearing continued. ADA Chin finished direct examination, then Cynthia Pullman crossed, challenging Bernard's testimony about his drinking, his opportunity to see the men, and his delay in contacting the police. She avoided saying McBride's name and spoke only of "the man with Stokes." She finished with a tricky maneuver. Leading up to it, she repeated key phrases in the witness's direct testimony about coming within a couple of feet of the men on the bridge after having seen them in a heated argument at the pub.

"So, you walked right up to them. A couple of feet would be, what, two or three?"

"About that."

"And this was when Mr. Stokes was slipping down to the ground?"

"Yes."

"Mr. Bernard, please hold an arm straight out in front of you."

A puzzled look. Judge Kaplan said, "It's okay. Go ahead and do what Ms. Pullman asks." The witness chuckled softly, nervously, and complied.

"Thank you," the defense attorney said. "Assistant DA Chin, would you please walk up to the tips of Mr. Bernard's fingers and crouch down near the floor?"

In an open courtroom, Pullman would have walked right up to the witness's face to demonstrate physical proximity. Kaplan had to admire her technique here. It could have backfired, but she made the point flawlessly. Bernard was visibly appalled that he'd suggested coming so close to people he'd been wary of.

And ADA Chin cooperated, without hesitation. Although he'd been standing out of view, at a distance from the witness in the DA's video room, he walked right up to him for the demo. Apparently forgot, or simply didn't mind, the risk. Social distancing, incongruous to the crush of humanity in New York City, would take a while to become habit.

After cross-examination, the court called a lunch break, followed by Wesley Guerrier's testimony. He was a quieter, conservative and cautious man, his answers similar to Bernard's but shorter. The two security guards had, undoubtedly, discussed this case many times, giving them repeated opportunities to shape their stories. Now and again, Kaplan glanced away from his screen at Professor Louden, trying to read his reaction to Guerrier's testimony. What did the expert think about these witnesses, the accuracy of their memories and identification testimony? Kaplan would like to know.

The final witness of the day was McBride. Unusual for a defendant to testify at a preliminary hearing, but Judge Kaplan understood the stakes. McBride was probably out of his mind with worry, knowing he could be sitting in Rikers a long time before the grand jury opened again. He had to convince the judge to dismiss the case. *Now*.

Under sparse questioning by his attorney, McBride gave a long narrative. He concluded, "When we got to the Brooklyn Bridge, I said goodbye and walked to the subway. I didn't look back. I never saw my best friend again."

Predictable, either way you cut it: the fabrication of a guilty man, or the truth of an innocent one. He came across as gentle, humble, depressed. An easy target for blood-thirsty cop haters in lockup, Kaplan was thinking.

The attorneys gave closing arguments, and the court called a recess. Everyone waited as Judge Kaplan retreated to his office to consider his decision.

Bernard and Guerrier were key. They were right, or they were mistaken. If they were right, McBride was "hugging" Stokes, and that meant only one thing. He was in the act, or immediately after the act, of taking a life. Could the witnesses have missed the real killer? Maybe McBride returned to help a falling friend. Impossible. The timing didn't work.

Alternatively, the witnesses were mistaken. An honest mistake. They had no reason to utter mistruths, but they were misguided by alcohol and their impressions of the recent altercation at the bar.

Being true to his instincts and experience, Judge Kaplan tended to think the witnesses were mistaken. Another factfinder might disagree. Where a case hinges on witness credibility, the charging decision shouldn't be left to him. Twenty-three citizens on a grand jury should decide whether to indict Corey McBride for murder.

The judge called the clerk to say he was returning to the courtroom to announce his decision. But he paused at his office door, caught in the wake of his doubts. Visit not the sins of the father on the son...or something like that. Any lingering animosity against Patrick McBride had no place in his treatment of Corey McBride. The former DA, revered by many, was also disliked by many, including the once idealistic public defender Seth Kaplan, champion of the underdog. He disagreed with many of the DA's policies and charging decisions, his over-prosecution of lower-level crime and under-prosecution of white-collar crime.

But if today's defendant were someone else, not a cop, not a

McBride, Judge Kaplan wouldn't hesitate to do what he was thinking of doing right now. Yes, why not? He'd surprise them all. Deliver a tough blow, tempered by a palliative to make it go down easier. For them and for himself.

In the end, all went well. Judge Kaplan delighted in the astonished look on ADA Chin's face when, after finding reasonable cause to hold the case for the grand jury, he invited Pullman to make a bail application on behalf of her client. The judge granted the motion he'd encouraged, and Corey McBride, with the help of family assets, would soon be out on bail.

A tidy, well-balanced decision. Still, an unsettled edge lingered. Judge Kaplan prided himself on decisive action, true to his instincts and principles. Perhaps his doubts were unfounded. He wondered… What did the expert think? Emmett loved talking about stuff like this. The judge would be taking a risk, but the temptation to ask was too strong.

As the clerk erased the participants from the screen and powered down, Professor Louden stood and offered his thanks to the court.

Judge Kaplan said, "Emmett, do you have a minute?"

"Yes, certainly."

The overeager student at Emmett's side confusedly ping-ponged his focus between his elders. "Young man," the judge said, "would you mind waiting outside?"

"S-sure." The boy turned to go, then swiveled around again. "Th-thank you, Your Honor." Almost a little bow. Kaplan smiled at this extra bit of obsequiousness. To be sure, that kid would be back, wanting to collect more data for his research.

The judge stood and twitched two fingers, beckoning Professor Louden up to the bench. "Excuse me for not shaking hands, Emmett. It's good to see you again."

"Same here, Judge. I'm also good with skipping the elbow bump."

Kaplan laughed and said, "Let's go to my office." The professor followed him out the door behind the bench and down the hall to chambers. They sat on opposite sides of the desk.

"Just curious about your thoughts on this case."

"As far as I'm concerned, you made the right call, holding this for the grand jury."

Kaplan liked the sound of that, but he wanted to be sure it wasn't lip service from a man to whom he'd paid expert witness fees many times in the past. "So, you bought the identification testimony. In your expert opinion."

"We haven't studied courtroom identifications in this setting. A Skype hearing is a different animal altogether."

"True—"

"And any cognitive psychologist would want to review every iteration of the witness's narrative. You're asking my opinion without giving me everything you've seen."

The judge smiled. "And what do you suppose 'everything' might be?"

"Well, it's pretty clear from the testimony today that the witnesses gave statements to that detective."

"You're right. I *have* seen those. Hold on." The judge found the file on his computer and angled the screen so the professor could see it. "Here you go." They sat for several minutes, watching the recorded Q&As.

Afterward, Kaplan said, "Now what do you think? Middle of the night on a dimly lit street, and you've been drinking. You see two men acting strangely, so you give them wide berth and catch the briefest glimpse of a face as it turns toward you and away again."

The professor laughed theatrically. "Testing me, are you? That demonstration by Ms. Pullman was a clever little sleight of hand. But isn't that the game? To distract, to divert attention away from significant facts?"

Judge Kaplan understood the point, even as he felt somewhat offended by the professor's implication that a defense attorney's "game" was to obfuscate the truth. "So, tell me what's significant here."

"Facial Recognition One-Oh-One. If you've recently seen a person in close proximity for an appreciable amount of time, a mere glance is enough to recognize that person again."

Kaplan nodded. He'd predicted this answer.

"Your instincts were correct," Louden went on, "notwithstanding the prosecutor's failings. He should have done more to emphasize the barroom scene, don't you think?"

"Should have or didn't want to. DA Browne's 'game' might have been to put on a decent, but mediocre show. Nothing more."

"I see what you mean." The professor met the judge's eyes in silent acknowledgment of the scandal, the alleged favoritism. "I'm no lawyer, so correct me if I'm wrong, but that assistant DA should have asked for redirect examination to rebut Pullman's implications. He could have underscored the witnesses' observations in the bar—"

"Certainly."

"And maybe, he should have petitioned the court for a voice identification."

"You're reading my mind." An interesting test. Compel McBride to recite, in open court, "My friend had a few too many." Would Bernard recognize that voice? Perhaps ADA Chin wasn't up for a legal battle over whether the test would violate the defendant's right to remain silent. He could have argued it was admissible as non-testimonial evidence. Judge Kaplan didn't know how he would have ruled. Either way, the prosecutor just didn't try.

"So." The professor leaned back in his chair. "Have I answered your question?"

"Yes. More than answered it." They'd agreed on a critical

point. Ernest Chin, an experienced, skillful prosecutor, hadn't done his best. And why was that? Did he think the witnesses were unassailable? Hardly. The ADA was clever enough to see the problems. No, he'd held back because he was protecting a McBride. Whether the incentive was subliminal or intentional didn't matter. Judge Kaplan had convinced himself to see this undercurrent in the proceedings. His old friend, the esteemed Professor Emmett Louden, had helped him to reach this certainty. Chin's failure to fully develop the record on every fact supporting the reliability of the IDs gave Kaplan the luxury of supposing that such facts exist.

Beyond that, was Corey McBride a killer? Although the needle had angled closer to *Yes*, Judge Kaplan abandoned any further thought on that question. An old habit from his early career and the proscription against an attorney suborning perjury. Don't ask the client if he did it, and never be certain one way or another. Then, if the client insisted on spinning a creative story under oath, Kaplan could honestly say he didn't know it was a line of bullshit.

The question of McBride's guilt or innocence was for a jury, for another day. The case was out of his hands. What mattered to Kaplan now was his renewed confidence in the small part he'd played. Today's ruling was correct. Tonight, he'd eat a big dinner with a glass of wine and have a deep, untroubled sleep.

Corey was relieved to be out on bail, but his career was blown, suspended pending the outcome of the case. He toyed with resigning but couldn't seem to make a decision about anything important in his life. His thoughts were stalled on certain parts of the witnesses' testimony. *That reddish color. I didn't see it before.* More like they didn't see him. Period. And his own testimony. *I didn't look back.* His closing line rang in personal rebuke or accusation. He came across as nervous, not innocent enough to convince that judge. A murderer wouldn't look back. A murderer would keep going.

The months dragged on through idleness and isolation. He felt beholden to his family for bailing him out, too ashamed to face them until the case was over and their money returned to them. Marlon's absence was the biggest pain, the tarnish to Uncle Patrick's reputation the biggest regret. Days on end, holed up in his small apartment, hair and beard growing, Corey manufactured ways to keep busy. On his computer, he researched the law and fantasized about the alternative career path he could have taken. When his case went live again, he would be prepared to help his defense.

Summer arrived. Caveman Corey bunkered indoors, shunning the sunlight.

Edict from on high. Long Island reached Phase Four of the reopening plan. The governor allowed gatherings of up to twenty-five people. How fitting to celebrate that number on July 25. Corey's mother called to invite him to a family reunion at the home of her sister and brother-in-law. "Please send my regrets, Mom. I can't make it." They didn't mention his father, who hadn't spoken to Corey since the day after Marlon's death. Dad's silence could mean anger or shame. Or it could mean permanent estrangement. Corey didn't know and wasn't going to initiate contact. He wanted to dig his way out of the grave first.

After the family reunion, a few people called and left voicemails. His sister. His older brother. Uncle Patrick: "We missed you at the picnic, Corey. I want you to know that the family supports you. Give me a call and we'll talk. Take good care."

After hours of pacing and pushups on his living room floor, Corey roused the courage to return the call of the man who had done so much for him. The conversation hobbled out of the gate with superficial, stilted talk of cousins, aunts, and uncles.

Gradually, the suffocating heat in Corey's chest built to an intolerable level. He blurted, "But you haven't said a thing!"

"Said what, son?"

"No one admits what they think! They send emails and leave messages saying nothing about the case. They're not touching it, 'cause they know, yeah, they know what's what. It's going to the grand jury, and we all know what *that* means—"

"We support you, Corey."

"The family? The law-and-order McBrides?" The dam broke behind the pressure of self-hatred and frustration. Water streamed down his cheeks. "Yeah, we know you're guilty—"

"Hold on there—"

"You just won't say it!"

"Corey," Patrick rasped. He waited, perhaps unsure if his nephew would calm down enough to listen and comprehend.

After a moment, Corey sputtered, "I'm sorry."

Patrick regained his deep, reassuring voice. "I believe in you, Corey. You've got to trust in that. I'll do everything I can to help see you through this."

Corey heard his uncle's message and believed it, but the unspoken parts blasted louder. *I know you didn't do this. I know you're not a killer. There was nothing you could have done to prevent this.*

The call ended with none of that said. And what unfolded in the following days placed another load of guilt on Corey's head. Those days impressed a permanent calendar in his brain.

July 30, two days after the phone call, Patrick was admitted to the hospital.

August 8, Patrick died.

August 10, the grand jury heard the case and dismissed the charges.

And through it all, Corey replayed their final phone call, remembering the rasp in his uncle's voice, wondering if the stress of this legal mess contributed to his illness. Even worse, Patrick died not knowing of the exoneration. Perhaps it was best that he never knew what happened next.

August 11, renowned expert Dr. Emmett Louden stated on a local news show that he was puzzled by the grand jury's vote in this "slam-dunk" case, setting off another nasty news cycle against the present and former DAs.

The next day, Corey got two phone calls. The first was from Judge Dana Hargrove, a woman he didn't know well, except by stellar reputation. They'd spoken a few times at social events, and he knew how much Uncle Patrick loved her. She was heartbroken about his death, expressed her condolences, and congratulated Corey on his exoneration.

"Thank you, but did you hear that news report last night? The interview with Professor Louden?"

"Yes, I did. I'm outraged that he would make comments like that—"

"People are already saying the grand jury got it wrong. I've given my uncle a permanent stain—"

"No, you haven't. It's just one opinion. It'll blow over. And the investigation continues, doesn't it? When they find the killer, the doubters will be proven wrong."

"Still, it doesn't feel very good, not knowing if Uncle Patrick believed in my innocence before he died."

"What?" Dana seemed stunned. "Of course he did." She seemed very sure, and Corey had to take comfort in that.

The second call he received was from Marlon's mother, Destiny. They hadn't spoken since the day after Marlon's death. They recalled that conversation, affirming Corey's belief that she never suspected him of the murder.

"I have to admit, my doubts were raised when you were arrested. I always considered DA Browne to be an honest man. But now, the grand jury has spoken, and I believe in their decision."

"Marlon was my best friend."

"I know. I know you couldn't possibly have done this. But that means..." She choked and hesitated. When she spoke again, the pitch and intensity had grown higher. "Dear God! We have to find the killer. Who was it, Corey? Who was it?"

"I wish I knew."

"Help them find that man. Help them!"

He made a comforting, agreeable sound, but otherwise, didn't answer. He couldn't tell her that he had no help to give. If detectives came calling, of course, he'd cooperate with anything they asked. But he couldn't actively *do* anything. He'd decided, finally, to quit the force. He just couldn't go back.

"One other thing I have to tell you," Destiny went on. "Someone from a citizens' group called me. They're filing a lawsuit. They want to get the grand jury testimony and all the police files."

"Really. What did you say?"

"They want me to be a named party, but I'm not giving my permission for that."

"A citizens' group. Is that Citizens for Open Government?"

"Something like that, yes. I don't want to get involved as a party, but I have no objection to what they're doing. They said they want 'the real truth' to come out. Marlon used to say it could harm an investigation to put the details out in public, but I suppose it could also help them find the real killer. What do you think?"

Corey hesitated, wanting to pick the right words. COG's real motivation was political. Their platform to fight "corruption" was a cover for an attack on law enforcement. In this case, that meant an attack on District Attorney Browne and the former DA, Patrick McBride. What good would it do to share this dose of reality with Marlon's mother? He didn't want to add to her distress. There was nothing either of them could do to stop COG's mission.

"I suppose anything's possible," he said. "We'll just have to wait and see." And hope that a court would toss COG's lawsuit into a shredder.

11 » SECURITY

Wednesday, January 12, 2022

NO KIDDING, ZACH is lost without a keyboard. The scribbles in his bent and stained notebook are beyond frustrating.

With diligent effort and a few follow-up questions, Natalie gets what she hoped for, even if Zach isn't entirely sure of his own spellings. He noted all the basic personal information each witness gave at the beginning of their testimony. She understands why. Background, age, employment, and family status may explain differences in perception and the way that perception is communicated.

Natalie types the essential facts into a Word document. Names: the detective and his precinct, the two eyewitnesses, the security company that employs them, the investment bank on Broad Street where they work. The exact address isn't given but it's easy enough to look up.

Her attention is drawn to several bits of testimony punctuated with Zach's heavy-handed question marks. He presses so hard on the page that the ballpoint creates grooves and nearly breaks through. She feels the physicality of his curiosity. Some phrases are parenthetical. Zach says he uses parentheses to set off his own thoughts as distinct from the testimony, and he places question marks for unknowns, details he wishes they had provided.

"In bar (lighting?) two argue (how close, how long?) one pushes (which one?)"

"Jacket 'windbreaker' dark or navy?"

"Bridge (streetlights?) 'hugging' turned head (how fast?)"

"Cross-X 'sorry' not close???"

"(ID of D on screen HESITATES?) 'reddish' hair didn't see"

After a full review, Natalie finds more questions than answers in Zach's notes, omissions in the testimony and points of weakness in the identifications.

Why did Professor Louden get so involved in this case? Was it a pure, scholarly interest or did he have a personal agenda? And why was he so confident about his opinion of the witnesses? Was he impressed with their statements to the police? No way is she going to ask the professor. Nor is she going to press Zach any further about this. She's already had two long conversations with him and can't bear the thought of another. From his notes and everything he's said, she can tell that he isn't impressed with the identification evidence.

If only she could see those videos. Maybe she should call the detective. Play dumb. Give him the spiel about her research, ask for the videos and promise anonymity for everyone concerned. He'll refuse the request of course, but maybe he'll let something slip out during their conversation, a piece of useful, behind-the-scenes information about the investigation.

Would he know who she is? Her last name is Goodhue, not Hargrove. Still, many people in law enforcement know her parents. Too risky. He'll catch her with, "Why don't you ask your mother?"

Natalie will talk to her mother all right, but not until she has a better idea of what happened. In this hypothetical conversation to be held on a future date, should she defend her thesis advisor or disparage him? Has she made the mistake of her life, signing on with this man? If Mommy, the judge, thinks so, why hasn't she been direct about it? Why hasn't she come down harder? Judge Hargrove is always a force to reckon with, a pillar of strength, the most important woman in Natalie's life. A deeply buried, persistent longing for her mother's approval propels this personal investigation of Dr. Louden. Natalie wouldn't deny her motivation if she stopped to reflect on it. She places supreme importance on her mother's opinions and advice, to the point of forgetting that her mother can be wrong. But she's right most of the time, and anyone who wants to argue with her must support their position with facts, details, reasoning. Baseless emotion does not win the day.

So, the only course open to Natalie is to find those witnesses and talk to them. She might get nowhere, but what could it hurt? She starts by looking up the address of the investment bank where Janjak Bernard and Wesley Guerrier were security guards in April 2020. With luck, they'll still be there, or someone will know where to find them.

Midafternoon, Natalie enters the high-ceilinged lobby of gleaming marble and chrome. Wanting to fit in, or at least not stick out, she wears her one and only business suit, the same one she wore to interview her volunteers. Her hair is pulled back, knotted, and pinned into a bun.

She has picked the time well. Not lunch, not morning or afternoon rush hour when the place might be teeming. As she steps in from the street, a man briskly approaches, passes her, and exits the building through the same revolving door. Natalie pauses momentarily in the lobby, getting her bearings. A woman enters behind her and skirts the front desk with a perfunctory wave at the uniformed security guard. She taps a keycard on a reader at a waist-level gate, pushes through, and continues to the elevator bank. Clearly, she belongs here. For Natalie, and others like her, a prominently posted sign tells them: "All Visitors Must Sign In."

She walks up to the guard, smiles, and says, "Good afternoon."

"Good afternoon, Miss."

She likes the sound of his old-fashioned manners. He is a man in his forties, appropriately authoritative without forsaking his natural pleasantness. "I'm hoping you might help me."

"I will do my best, Miss." The edges of his mouth turn upward in a smile that reaches his warm brown eyes.

"I'm trying to find two men who work for your security firm. Janjak Bernard and Wesley Guerrier."

In the same instant, his features scrunch in bafflement and a flash of gold catches her eye. Her focus drops. Distracted by his welcoming face, she has missed it, the brass nametag on his chest: "Wesley Guerrier."

The awkward moment is eased by another person walking up behind her. Guerrier says, "Excuse me," and takes a step to the side, meeting the man at the desk. A FedEx driver. The business of logging in the afternoon deliveries takes a few minutes while Natalie glances around the lobby, uneasily shifting her weight from one foot to another in the high heels she rarely wears.

When he's done, he turns back to her. "Miss, you said you want to talk to me?"

"Yes. I'm a doctoral candidate researching criminal investigations and courtroom procedures. I understand that you and Mr. Bernard testified at a hearing conducted on Skype—"

"That was a long time ago," he interrupts in a voice barely above a whisper. His mouth cranks into a forced smile and his eyes dart here and there.

"Anything you remember would be a big help to my research."

"I don't think..." His reluctance is clear enough.

"My work is confidential. Anonymous. I don't publish names. I'm only interested in the way investigations are conducted, the procedures." She gestures with an open hand at the desk. "I know you're busy here. Can we schedule a time away from your work when you might be able to talk?"

"I'm sorry, Miss. I don't remember much about it. That was a long time ago. You can talk to the detective maybe."

"Unfortunately, that isn't an option. Maybe we can sit down over coffee, or how about tomorrow, on your lunch break? My treat."

"Uh…" He hesitates, sees another employee approaching the keycard reader, smiles and waves. He turns back to Natalie, his face brighter with the innate friendliness he showed minutes ago. "I know what would help you. Janjak remembers more about this than I do. Mr. Bernard. He was the first one to call the police. He's younger than me." Guerrier laughs and taps his forehead with an index finger. "Better memory."

"Okay, good idea. Is he here today?"

"No, no. He works the midnight shift."

"Oh my! Don't know if I can come back that late."

"And he's away for another week, visiting family in Haiti. You know, with the long weekend coming up, it adds a day to his vacation time."

Next week, after MLK Day, Natalie's semester will start, adding her TA duties to the seemingly never-ending work of compiling her data and writing her dissertation. "I see." She tries to hide her disappointment. "I'll call him when he gets back. Do you have his number?"

"Yes." He grabs a pen and notepad, then seems to think better of it. "But you should give me your number. I'll tell him to call you when he gets back."

The words are almost out of her mouth, another attempt to get Bernard's number, but she holds back. *Don't press your luck.*

This man has shown in more ways than one that he's cautious and respectful. Obviously, he doesn't want to hand out his colleague's phone number without his permission. The decision to contact her should be left to Bernard.

Natalie leaves her cell phone number with instructions to call her "any time, day or night." "You, too, Mr. Guerrier, if you change your mind. Any little bit you remember would be helpful to my research. We're trying to streamline the procedures, make them more effective and accurate for future cases."

She hopes she's made a favorable impression. With a big smile and a thank you, she walks away, not feeling optimistic that anything will come of this.

12 » MINOR

Friday, January 14, 2022

FIFTEEN MINUTES BEFORE the call of the calendar, Dana paces the five-by-eight floral area rug in her office. Butterflies flutter and tumble high in her chest, as active as the first day she appeared in this court, a young woman representing the People of the State of New York.

What's to be nervous about?

This is what it means to be a mother. After a certain number of years, you think you've moved on, but your children are always your children, whether three or thirty years old. *Josefina M.* is the biggest case Travis has ever argued. Vicariously through him, Dana is stepping up to the podium today.

She knows what's underneath the calm, even-keeled manner Travis projects. Is it learned or inherited, in the genes? Friends and colleagues have noted the similarities in the way Dana and Travis advocate. Measured and thorough, reasoned, strong, and full voiced. Inside, a battle rages. Forces are at war. Emotion and self-control, nagging doubts and jolts of confidence, the lure of resignation and tenacity of an indomitable will. Stagecraft? Oral argument is a performance, aided by an objective eye on the self, attuned to the impressions conveyed and reactions evoked. Language and voice, music and instrument. To captivate and convince, the orator's music achieves a rhythm and cadence, fluctuates in subtlety and brashness, hush and roar. Flexibility is needed. This isn't a place for a politician's tricks, dodging the questions. The judges can't be ignored or misdirected. It doesn't work.

"Just be yourself," Patrick told her once before she walked into court to deliver a closing argument. Off-the-cuff maybe. A casual remark. But that advice, in his voice, resides in her heart. She has carried it with her daily in her professional life as an attorney and judge, and still she wonders if that's all she has ever been. The endless analyzing and fretting over strategy, content, and performance have added up to just that: being herself.

Travis has the advantage of being a man. Do people still live by that bias? Dana would never suggest this out loud. Her entire career has been a silent campaign against chauvinism, never a word of complaint at the slights, condescension, and paternalism she has encountered. There've been plenty of instances, but her response is to work harder, to show strength in doing and achieving, not whining. Bitterness and rage can entrench division. Integrity and ability make a more lasting impression and can change minds.

Travis might change a few minds today, just being himself. She loves that boy, her firstborn, now a persuasive, talented advocate. But she doubts he will change her mind about this case. What does it matter? She's no longer on the panel.

"Judge." Nia speaks from the open doorway. Dana turns. How long has her law clerk been standing there? "Want to borrow my Fitbit?" Long enough, apparently.

Dana smiles. "No need. Finished my laps for the day."

"What am I getting into here?" Nia glances down at her hand, resting on her rounded belly. In her other hand, she clutches a slender stack of papers.

"Motherhood is pure joy, Nia, if you're wondering what this is." Dana gestures toward herself and shrugs. "Whatcha got there?"

"My draft of the memorandum decision in *COG v AG.*" She steps in and hands it to her boss. "Short and sweet, as requested. Citing to last year's case."

"Good. Hopefully everyone will go along and we'll be done with it. If Judge Morgenstern circulates a dissent, we'll have to revisit the case."

"Great. I'll go back to reviewing the reports for next week's calendar. Maybe I can multitask, put on my earphones, and listen to the argument while I work. You want to talk about it later?"

"Sure. I'd love to hear what you think."

With a nod, Nia retreats, then puts a hand on the doorknob and says, "Want this closed?"

"Yup. That way, I won't have to be self-conscious when I start talking to the screen."

Their eyes meet in a smiling connection before Nia closes the door.

Five minutes remain. Dana forces herself to sit at her desk and click on the livestream from the courtroom. No way can she go downstairs to watch in person. It wouldn't look good for her to be in the audience. Not only might her presence make Travis nervous, it also could silently convey an improper message to the panel that she supports her son—even though she doesn't agree with his client's position.

The judges haven't entered the courtroom. The audience is filling up. On one side of her split screen is the bench, five empty high-backed chairs, swiveled sideways, awaiting the backsides of the judges. The other side of her split screen, from the judges' viewpoint, shows the attorneys' tables and podium with a few rows of the audience behind them.

She cannot see her son, but there, in the first row of spectators… That must be Bianca Merced! How to be sure? She's exactly like Dana imagined her. Even more telling are the people flanking Bianca. On one side sits a dour, middle-aged woman who often appears in court for child protective cases. Amy Shapiro, a social worker for ACS. On the other side of Bianca sits a teenager, bundled in a puffy down coat to her knees. Josefina. Her face, though pale and emaciated, radiates an ethereal glow. She's half here, half there, a foot in the entrance to the lighted tunnel. But maybe the halo is mere imagination, encouraged by the fuzzy, pixilated image on Dana's screen.

Thank God they've allowed this much. Despite the removal order, ACS has given Bianca the opportunity for courtroom "visitation" under the watchful eyes of the social worker. Dana's heart goes out to the family of two. Bianca clutches her niece's hand, and Josefina leans toward her as if wanting to rest her head on her aunt's shoulder. The strength of their love, and the gravity of Josefina's illness, are projected in their body language. Motivated by the chance to be with her aunt, to sit next to her and hold her hand, the weak young woman has managed to make it to the courtroom today, driven by sheer will and determination.

"All rise!"

Bianca wraps an arm around Josefina's waist and helps her up.

The five black-robed justices file in. Everyone sits down again and listens to the opening spiel. When the case is called, two women sitting in Josefina's row walk up to the appellants' table: Bianca's attorney and the "attorney for the child," a legal term Dana finds incongruous as applied to Josefina. From offscreen, two other attorneys walk up to the respondent's table, Noriko Takeda and Travis Goodhue. They'll be splitting the oral argument today. Noriko first, then Travis, arguing against adopting the "mature minor doctrine."

Dana's heart pounds.

After the argument, Nia and Dana do a postmortem.

"Bianca's attorney was thrown when Judge Navarro asked if she had a religious reason for refusing treatment," Nia says.

"I saw that too. She knows it would strengthen their argument, but her client isn't going for it. Bianca and Josefina are Catholic, not Christian Scientists. Their rejection of chemo isn't based on a religious taboo."

"Her other argument was strong. Making a healthcare decision isn't child abuse or 'imminent danger to the child' justifying removal from the home. The experts don't even agree on how effective the treatment is."

"What did you think of the response to that?" The lead attorney for ACS, Takeda, came on strong. Her tone expressed outrage on behalf of every decent person who believes in saving a young life. She likened Bianca's parenting to cruelty, almost homicidal, as if her "healthcare decision" steals Josefina's last remaining chance at life.

How difficult that must have been for Bianca, sitting twenty feet away from Takeda as she delivered that scathing indictment.

"Noriko is awesome," Nia says. "A powerful advocate." Dana isn't surprised by Nia's answer, knowing that she holds Takeda in high esteem. The ACS attorney is an adjunct professor at Nia's alma mater, where she teaches family law. "And so is Travis," Nia goes on. "They're both very persuasive. Doesn't mean we buy their arguments, does it?"

"No, it doesn't. But I detect evasion here."

"Guilty." Nia gives a sheepish look. "Not good to evade a judge's question, I know. But I'm divided on this. Is it possible to agree with both sides? I want to save this girl's life, but ACS is stretching the law. They went too far, removing her from the home."

"I don't see that you're divided on the main legal issue. You didn't buy Noriko's argument under the child protective statute. Your emotional reaction is another matter entirely."

"You're saying my opinion is based on emotion, not the law?"

"No, not exactly. You've already shown that you're applying the law when you say removal wasn't warranted. But that issue is tied up with the question of who has the legal right to make the medical decisions, the aunt, the niece, or the state. Whichever way the law leads us on that issue, we still have no guarantee for Josefina's health. That's the emotional part. It's our human desire to control fate, but we can't conquer the unknowable."

"Three parties to choose from, but it feels more like two. The aunt and the niece are of one mind, don't you think? So it's interesting that Josefina's attorney argued it doesn't matter what Bianca thinks. She stressed Josefina's independence and maturity, her right to make her own medical decisions."

"My feeling exactly."

Nia smiles and lifts an eyebrow. "Your son was pretty convincing on the opposing view."

Dana's face turns dreamy, a proud smile gracing her lips. "He was, wasn't he?" Then she gets serious. "But he's wrong."

"On all three points?"

Knock down one pin and Travis had another one standing. He argued, first, that New York has never recognized the mature minor doctrine and should not adopt it now. Second, the age of majority is set by statute at eighteen, a bright line that leaves no room for doubt. And third, even if the court adopts the mature minor standard, Josefina has not shown sufficient maturity.

Judge Shields loved Dana's son. Lapped up every word, even as he purported to "question" Travis vigorously. But his questions merely reiterated the strongest points, a ploy meant to bowl over the other four judges on the panel.

"Yes," Dana says. "Wrong on all three points. In my view."

Nia laughs. "I see now what you were up against when you visited Judge Shields the other day!"

Dana rolls her eyes and shakes her head. But before she can say anything about the tiff with her colleague, her desk phone rings. "Lobby" shows on the caller ID. Dana holds up a finger to Nia and answers. "Hi, Gary. What's up?"

"Cheryl Hargrove here to see you, Your Honor." Dana can hear the little thrill in the court officer's voice, although he's making every attempt to sound businesslike. It's not every day that a popular actress of stage and screen visits the courthouse, and Dana is well aware of Gary's fascination with her sister. He's apt to quote from his favorite scenes in *Swamp Wars* or recount memorable episodes of *Plain Justice*, a long-running series in which Cheryl played a prosecutor.

"Thanks. Send her up."

"I need to stay on the desk, but I can find another officer to escort her."

"Gary. She knows how to use an elevator." And she's been here before. No need to hold her hand.

"Right." His voice trails off, and he seems to forget that Associate Justice Dana Hargrove is still on the line. Imperfectly covering the mouthpiece with his hand, his voice comes over muffled as he gives unnecessary directions to Cheryl. Dana can almost sense his beating heart at the vision of her gentle sway and the waft of her delicate fragrance. He comes back on. "Judge, she's on her way up."

"Great. Thank you."

Nia returns to the anteroom, and a minute later, Dana hears, "Oh my goodness, you look so beautiful! What a lucky baby to be growing inside of you! She'll have brains *and* beauty." Dana comes to the doorway. Cheryl turns to her. "Hello, mother of the most magnificent son! Travis blew that whole panel of judges away. Gale force winds. They staggered from the bench, in awe!" Arms dramatically thrown into the air.

"That impressive, eh?"

"Why weren't you in the courtroom?"

"You know I couldn't go down there. I watched it on the computer. I'll call him later."

"Of course. All that protocol!" She winks at Nia, and with a little wave, walks past Dana into the office. Grabbing the doorhandle, Dana returns Nia's amused look before disappearing inside with her sister.

"Natalie was here to watch her brother," Cheryl says. "She asked me to send her regrets. Had to get back to that important work she's doing." Cheryl slides out of a fur-collared designer winter coat and deposits it on a chair. "Actually, this is what she really said. 'You can have my mother *all* to yourself.' It was just her way of saying—"

"Take my mother, *please*."

"Not quite. She was deferring to our greater need for sister time."

"Right. There hasn't been much of that lately. And today—"

"Oh, I know you're busy. We'll catch up for real another time. I won't stay long. Look, I'm not even going to sit down, and I already picked up my coat from the cloakroom. Just had to come up here and gush over your genius of a son."

"He *is* a genius, isn't he? What did Troy think? Is he downstairs?"

"No, sorry, he wanted to come, but the service called him. A toddler with a hundred and four temperature takes priority over a dashing nephew-in-law saving a seventeen-year-old."

Dana likes to see Cheryl this way. Vibrant, glowing, excited about life. At fifty-three, Cheryl's natural beauty is enhanced by the full-blown happiness that has taken hold of her. The trajectory of her love life, from youth to middle age, has been this: Too many men in her twenties and thirties, followed by an improvident choice of mate for a belated motherhood at age forty-one. The father disappeared, only to resurface four years later, penniless, purporting to want a relationship with his daughter. But fatherly love wasn't the driving force. Greed and envy of Cheryl's success were his motivators. Litigation, disentanglement, and finally, personal happiness. Three years ago, Cheryl married her daughter's pediatrician, Dr. Troy Belson.

"It's been a morning of law and medicine, hasn't it?" Dana says. "All about a government agency dictating medical decisions under the pretext of following the law."

"My goodness! That sounds familiar. Big bad government. But I seem to remember you complaining, not so long ago, about 'the pretext of following the science' not the law."

Familiar, indeed. The parallel jumps out at Dana. Why hasn't she seen it until now? During the pandemic, the sisters had more than one disagreement over the proper role of government. Josefina's case brings back a similar source of frustration and indignation. Forced medical treatment. Hands off.

"Yes, well, this is a bit different," Dana says, trying to steer away from past unpleasantness. "ACS is taking a broad view of the law to separate a family at a critical time for them." She turns her back and walks behind the desk, creating some distance. Hard to avoid the intermingling of law and science in this case. The law permits removal of an abused child from the home. Medical science predicts an outcome for a particular treatment. Layered on top of both: a government agency. Bureaucrats, not lawyers, not scientists, not doctors.

Dana doesn't want to get into this. She adores her sister, every ounce of Cheryl, the artist, the extrovert and bohemian, the lover of life, the believer in the core goodness of people. The sisters' hearts beat to the same drum, and they both possess a sharp intelligence. But Cheryl tends to stop at the surface, taking lofty language at face value without questioning the underlying motives, the logical progression, the consequences.

"Just a minute ago you agreed that your son is a genius."

"How could I not?"

"But it's clear you don't agree with his argument."

"He's articulate and very persuasive, but he's obligated to argue for a certain position, and I don't agree with his client. They've caused this family of two horrible, unnecessary pain."

"They're trying to save her life! I saw them there in the courtroom, holding hands. The aunt and the niece. My heart goes out to them. But if no one steps in, that girl won't be around in six months for the aunt to hold her hand."

"Death in six months isn't inevitable. Nothing is certain. Imagine if it was you and Kaitlin. Five years from now, she's seventeen and has cancer..."

"Dana!"

"...very ill, weak and suffering. She needs your comfort and care more than ever and a couple of strangers come up to you, all high and mighty, and say they're taking her away. You're a bad mother. You made the wrong choice of treatment. *They* will decide what that is."

"That would *never* happen to us. I'm not like that woman. I'd always give Kaitlin what's recommended. Only the best."

"But this family *did* decide what was best for them. A government agency doesn't know what that is. Doesn't know these people or what's important to them. It's a blind exercise of power, inflicting a huge emotional toll!" Dana has lost herself in her convictions.

Cheryl's eyes go wide. "Listen to you! What about *this* government institution?" Cheryl gestures and glances around the office. "What do *you* do here every day? What about *your* power? I'd say a million-dollar judgment or a prison sentence can inflict some emotional pain."

They fall silent. Cheryl's buoyancy and vivacity have turned sour. Dana sorely regrets it. "You're right," she says quietly, because Cheryl *is* right. A useful reminder. Has Dana forgotten where she is, become complacent and entitled? She thinks not. She hopes not. She's mindful of the impact her decisions have on the lives of others, every time she picks up a case and maps out the consequences. Every conflict has two or more sides. Only rarely does a clear answer emerge.

"I'm sorry," Cheryl says. Also quieter now. Dear Cheryl.

"No, *I'm* sorry. I shouldn't have mentioned Kaitlin…"

"You didn't mean it like that. You were using an example to make a point."

"This case has touched me. It brings out a lot of emotion."

"And everyone just wants to help that sick girl. Everyone wants to do the right thing by her, don't they?"

"That's the crux of it." No big bad government. No big bad court. Just people with different ways of looking at things, everyone trying their best. That's the way the sisters will leave it, for now.

Dana gazes into a near distance at the law books on her shelf, caught in a moment of retreat from self-importance. But before she can refocus, Cheryl has flown around the desk and pulled her into a strong, loving embrace. Dana feels her beautiful soul. And she smells good too.

13 » *INVESTIGATION*

Tuesday, January 18, 2022

A SINGLE NAME on the list of nine stands out. Aurelina doesn't recall seeing it in the case file. "You gave this list to Kyle when I was on leave? The whole list?"

"Affirmative," says the young officer, Hakeem Farah. He sits opposite Aurelina at her desk, the investigative file spread out between them. Hakeem worked closely with Marlon on the undercover operation in Sector B of the Fifth. He wasn't undercover but supported the operation at a distance, backup and surveillance. Hakeem is closer than anyone to knowing everything and everyone that Marlon knew and didn't know on the streets. "I gave Detective Rodman all these names and he followed up on them, as far as I know. I wanted to catch the bastard more than anyone. It still gets to me, what happened to Marlon."

"I know that, Hakeem. Kyle told me how you helped the investigation. I just don't see your original list in the file. I've gone through all of Kyle's notes on every suspect he followed up on. 'XT' doesn't seem to be one of them. This is the first I've heard that name."

"Good old XT. Took us a little while to figure out his given name, Dexter Jackson. Older guy, a steerer. Low level. Marlon wanted to flip him, but we weren't sure how many higher-ups he knew. Then, of course, we had to abandon the whole op." It went nowhere after Marlon's identity was spread all over the news.

"Did 'Chug' cross XT in any way, or did he figure out Marlon's identity?"

"Nah. I doubt it seriously. If he's not in Rodman's notes, could be because the dude is absolutely no threat. But check him out. I hear that he turned his life around. Found religion and runs a neighborhood mission, all on donations. I doubt it's a front, but I could be wrong. He doesn't go by XT anymore, takes in a few homeless people, whatever he has room for, and runs a food pantry. Helped a lot of unemployed people during the pandemic."

"Sounds like my kind of guy."

"Oh, you'll love him, Detective!"

On her way to Dexter's mission, Detective Vargas wonders if she's wasting her time. When she confronted Detective Rodman about XT, his answer was plausible but typical of his usual attitude. Kyle is always quick to explain and slow to demonstrate an adequate level of professionalism about anything he does.

"Sure, I checked him out. Dexter Jackson. A nobody. He picked up a few dollars steering customers in the right direction. Didn't know anyone in the organization. He isn't a hitman, that's for sure."

"But someone Marlon frequently ran into. Hakeem said Chug and XT got friendly."

"Sure, XT was friendly, but not friendly like this." He clasped his hands together tightly and grunted. "Not like the bromance with the buddy who got drunk and lost it."

"Corey didn't kill his best friend."

"Who found him innocent? Just not indicted. There's a difference. I can't help it if the DA botched the case." Lina shook her head and almost got into it with Kyle but held back. Angry words would serve no purpose. She already relieved him of this assignment, knowing his bias and complacency. Though he never says it in so many words, he firmly believes that Corey got away with murder. For this reason, the case needs a fresh set of eyes. A review of every angle. If Lina's investigation ultimately leads her to the same conclusion, well then, she'll accept it and move on.

"I'm not interested in the DA's performance," she says. "I'm interested in ours, what *we* did. This XT sounds like someone who knows everything going down in the neighborhood. He should be in the file. Where's the write-up?"

"Thought it was in there. Look, I know I wrote it up, but anyway, trust me on this. The guy isn't our guy. Go talk to him, you'll see."

So that's where she's headed now, to an address on the Lower East Side. Along the way, her mind is stuck on the reasons she's compelled to review and redo every scrap of Kyle's work. Lina's dislike for him has steadily grown in the fifteen years of their association. She's tired of his defensive justifications, the smugness and inflated ego. When Kyle was considered for promotion to detective second grade, she handed up a lukewarm appraisal of his work. The CO didn't ignore it but was more impressed with Kyle's results on a couple of cold cases.

Yes, he's had successes, but Lina isn't impressed with his work on *this* case. A shame that she wasn't able to oversee the first months of the investigation. Just thinking about it saddens her. The events of that horrible time converge, proof that terrible things can happen in threes: the pandemic, Mateo's death, and Marlon's murder.

Kyle claims to have investigated every person on Hakeem's list and to have followed all leads flowing from it, eliminating each potential suspect for reasons that go beyond the mere lack of a DNA match. On that subject, Kyle laughed and said, "Go swab Marlon's fiancée! He could have dropped his pants before work and dug into some skin!"

Despite Kyle's irreverent vulgarity, Lina does not reject the possibility that the skin cells under Marlon's fingernails belong to someone other than the killer. But no way is she going to bother the family for something like that. It would get them nowhere. She works from the assumption that the DNA is the killer's as she awaits a return on DA Browne's latest subpoena to GEDMatch—one more chance to find a link to someone whose genetic material isn't in the databank for convicted felons.

Vargas has dressed down for this occasion, shield on her waistband, service Glock in a shoulder holster under a puffy down jacket. It's cold. She exhales frosty puffs of mist. Up the block she sees it, the crudely hand-painted sign over a door: *FRIENDSHIP MISSION*. The cedar-shingled storefront is narrow, ten or twelve feet, with a single, small window displaying another handmade sign: "Do you *need* food, clothing, or shelter? Do you *have* food, clothing, or shelter to give? Come in and share your burden or bounty with your neighbors."

Lina enters, setting off an electronic chime. Directly ahead in the small room, a countertop stretches the length of the farthest wall. A door behind the counter presumably leads to a back room. Homes for a few homeless? Hakeem says that the mission gives needy people shelter, as room permits.

A woman stands at the counter, talking to a man on the other side. High on the wall behind him, Jesus sags on a cross. The walls on either side of the room are cheaply constructed with faux wood paneling and furnished with dented metal shelving that holds a hodgepodge of canned and dry goods, household items, heaps of clothing, and used paperbacks. Oddly, the temperature in here feels almost as cold as outside. The two occupants of the room are wearing their coats. The detective will happily keep her own down parka zipped up to the chin.

Lina's intuition, helped by her sense of smell, tells her that the charitable business of the Friendship Mission, and its facilities, do not comply with applicable licensing laws and health codes. She doesn't care. She likes the whole idea of this place and isn't here to bust chops. Her own mission is foremost on her mind.

The woman steps away from the counter, her matted hair and dirty winter coat giving off a ripe odor. She carries a cloth bag, heavy with canned food. Lina walks up to the counter and receives a welcoming smile from the man. He's slight and underfed himself, although his clothing and wiry Afro are clean, and his bright eyes and taut skin are healthy. He could be forty, fifty, or sixty. Whatever his age, he's a man who has lived a lot. She likes him immediately.

"Good morning, sister. How may I help you?"

"Are you Dexter Jackson?"

"Indeed, I am. Brother Jackson here to help my neighbors, a bridge between the needy and the philanthropic." His smile grows larger as he regards the detective without judgment. Does he understand who she is, just by the look of her? Most likely he does, but his tone doesn't imply it. "Are you a sister down on your luck or up on your luck? Let me know how I can help."

She almost wishes she'd brought a can of soup or beans. "I'm afraid I haven't brought a donation, but perhaps you can help me on something else. My name is Aurelina Vargas. I'm a homicide detective, working out of the Fifth Precinct." She lifts the bottom of her jacket and steps backward, away from the counter, to show her shield.

"Lord help us. Has there been a homicide in our neighborhood? I haven't heard of anything lately."

"Actually, I'm here on a cold case that happened almost two years ago." She takes a photo of Marlon out of her jacket pocket and puts it on the counter. "This man, as you may have heard, was murdered in March of 2020."

Dexter fingers the edges of the photo and lifts it, regarding the face for a long time. The cheeriness slowly fades into a look of warm memories. "My friend Chug. He was a good man. We'd see him on the corner, knocking back bottles of that light green stuff."

Dexter screws up his mouth and nose.

"Green tea."

"Yeah. Organic, he said. Didn't drink anything hard. Smoked, oh yeah! Homegrown, all-natural weed. Or so he said. Smelled like it, but I never caught him at it." Dexter chuckles and hands the photo back. "He was curious about the nasty stuff but wouldn't smoke it." Dexter's eyes flit sideways. Guilty thoughts about his role in the synthetic market? "And no alcohol. Against his Rasta religion."

"But you know that—"

"Oh, sure, we know all that. Surprised a lot of folks 'round here to find out he was a cop. Me?" Dexter shakes his head. "A little surprised, but it made sense. He was on a righteous path, or so it seemed. Funny though. His death was my awakening, my exodus from the grip of evil. Made me toe a straight line and never look back."

"If that's true, one good thing came of it."

Dexter's cheer seems to return, then quickly hardens, showing a glimpse of his old ways and the wariness that went along with it. "You're not here for that other thing, are you? Because that's long behind me, and I don't know *anyone* in that life. Don't ask, don't tell. This is my bag now." He holds his hands palms up and swivels right and left. "What you see is what you get."

"My only interest is following up on Officer Stokes' murder. Nothing else. The wrong man was accused and charges were dropped. The killer hasn't been found."

"I've been waiting a long time for y'all to come around. To come ask me about this. Wasn't gonna walk into a police station and start talking, you understand. Not in those days. The devil still had me under his thumb."

"Understood. So you're saying *no* one came looking for you to talk about this? No cops or detectives?"

"Was one guy, two or three months after. Didn't say who he was, but he looked like a cop to me. Sure didn't look like anyone my friend would hang with, but he came asking, 'Where do I find Chug?' I said, 'Where you been? Chug's dead. Come to find out he's an undercover cop.' 'Oh, really?' the man said. 'Who do you suppose killed him?' Right then I knew it was a cop, 'cause I didn't say Chug was murdered."

Lina guesses he's talking about Detective Rodman. She wishes she'd brought a photo of him. She'll ask Kyle later if this conversation sounds familiar. "Did you give the man any information or ideas who might've done this? Were there people who didn't like Chug or suspected he was a cop looking into their business?"

"No, now, like I said, those people… I can only guess myself, who they might be. Never did know nothin' about them. Don't know who or where they are." Dexter's tone is solid. *Don't go there.* "If Chug was onto someone, that was his job, right? He must've told y'all who that was. But I can give you names of other people who hung out with him. Just friends. They're friends of mine too, so they're good folks."

"I'd appreciate that."

From under the counter, Dexter pulls out a square of used brown packing paper, as if he saves these kinds of scraps for his writing needs. With a stubby pencil, he laboriously writes five names in block letters.

Lina recognizes them as people she already interviewed. All except one. "This one: Rihanna. Do you have a last name?"

"No, I don't. That one-track girl is livin' the life of Rihanna. Wants to be her. Skimpy clothes, the makeup and hair. A young thing, star struck. That's what I got out of it anyway when she told me she went by that single name instead of her given name."

"How did she know Chug?"

"I found that out a day or two after he passed, the day I met

Rihanna. It was in the park, across the street." Dexter nods in the direction of his front door. The park he refers to is no more than a widened strip between the north- and south-running sides of the avenue, a littered installation of stressed lawn, park benches, and a basketball court at center. It's also a popular spot for drug deals. "I walk by this girl, couldn't be more than sixteen or seventeen, sitting on the bench, crying, staring at her phone. You couldn't ignore her. Like the world had ended. Makeup streaming down her face. I look down at her phone and it's Chug's picture. She's crying over Chug. I stop and talk to her."

Dexter told Rihanna he knew the man in the photo and asked if she knew him too. As Dexter relates the girl's story to Lina, she's filled with awe and respect for Marlon all over again. Yet another example of his compassion and caring.

"It took me a good while to get anything out of her," Dexter says. His mouth turns up in a little smile of self-pride. "But people give me their trust, you know? I'm blessed with this gift. Meeting Rihanna was just one more thing to get me turned around onto the right path back then. Know what I mean? I was meant to reach out and help people. By the time we finished talking about Chug, she was smiling again."

Dexter's "gift," however, wasn't enough to get the full story out of Rihanna, only a taste. As he tells it, in the dead of night about a week before the murder, Marlon came across Rihanna, propped against a building in an alley, sobbing uncontrollably. Chug asked if he could help. She was in a dark and terrible place in her life and something horrible had just happened to her.

"What was it?" Lina asks.

"So bad she couldn't even repeat it to me. Things happen on these streets. I can only guess. But she said Chug was a real friend to her. She cried on his shoulder for at least an hour, she said. He comforted her like a father. Really helped to soothe her, to calm her. He offered to get help for her."

"What kind of help?"

"She wouldn't say exactly. I got the idea she needed services of some kind, medical help or a shelter. Maybe she was homeless. Whatever he offered, she refused. He asked her to call him if she changed her mind. They walked out under a streetlight so he could write down his number. He used the name Chug, but when she saw the news report about the officer's murder, she remembered his face and was sure he was one and the same."

"Do you have any way to get in touch with her? Does she still hang out in the park?"

"I've seen her a few times on the street. We stop and say 'hello' and sometimes talk about Chug. She's doing better, what I can see. But I don't know where she lives. Back when I first met her, I thought she could be a runaway or on her own, grown up before her time. I didn't have the mission back then, but it got me to thinking…"

"If you see her again, ask her to call me?"

"Sure thing."

Lina heads back to the precinct, heartened by the story about Marlon and Rihanna, but otherwise not feeling any closer to the truth. What did she get out of today's episode? A new acquaintance, a likeable, garrulous man who will get a contribution of canned goods from her the next time she visits. A list of four names, people she's already spoken to and has no reason to contact again. And a new name, a person who can attest to Marlon's stellar character. Lina has no expectation that, even if Rihanna surfaces, she will offer any clues as to Marlon's killer.

She passes Kyle's desk, unoccupied. No problem. She has no burning desire to confront him about the incognito interview technique he used with Dexter. At her own desk, she reviews her notes and dead-end theories for the tenth time, looking for what she's missed.

Was Marlon getting too close to a cop on the take from the crime ring? She already looked into the financials of two colleagues who seem inexplicably flush with cash. The results are interesting but have nothing to do with Marlon. A detective third grade bought a Ferrari with a legacy from his grandma who died of Covid. A sergeant moved into a multimillion-dollar condo with her husband, a high-level Pfizer exec, making a killing from vax dollars. The theory is still plausible, but Lina has no leads on suspects.

She gets a call from ADA Ernest Chin. "Brace yourself. I've got something for you in the Stokes case." It's the break they've been hoping for. The return on the GEDMatch subpoena came in, and they have a hit. He asks her to follow up.

Lina considers her approach. Should she handle this covertly, set up surveillance? She has only a name, Veronica Littleton, an age, sixty-eight, and an address in Queens. A search of online sources and criminal justice databases yields nothing else. In a way, the lack of information on Littleton is a good sign. She's a normal, law-abiding citizen, even if one of her relatives, distant or not, is a murderer. Or could be.

Considering the woman's generation, her neighborhood and likely economic class, Lina's instincts tell her that a direct approach will work. And it will be faster.

Let's hope I'm right.

Veronica Littleton examines the petite gray-haired "detective" through the peephole before opening the door a crack. She keeps the chain on. Can't be too careful. Without unhooking the chain, Roni asks, "Detective Barges? Did I get that right? How do I know you're a detective?"

The woman holds a shield with ID card in the sliver of space between the door and doorjamb. "Aurelina Vargas, Detective First Grade, NYPD Homicide. May I come in and ask a few questions?"

Homicide! Roni goes for the chain but hesitates on a palpitation of fear and excitement. Is she supposed to ask for a warrant? No, that's just TV, a question asked by criminals with something to hide. Roni lives alone, but it *is* broad daylight, three in the afternoon, and she's shivering from that knife-sharp draft blowing through the opening. The little detective, half Roni's size, doesn't look threatening. *I wish*. How nice, to be that petite. Of course, a six-foot bruiser could be right behind her, out of sight. Just to be sure, Roni asks, "What is this all about?"

"I'd like to talk to you about the genealogy search you signed up for. There's a slim chance you could help us develop a clue in a cold case."

Roni's palpitations deepen to a thumping beat. Cold cases and DNA! It's like she's in the middle of a real-life CSI episode. Roni didn't expect anything so exciting when she gave her consent to law enforcement use of her genetic profile. Just think, a couple of cells from strands in her hairbrush led to this! The buzz in her head makes her forget the disappointment of her failed genealogy search. The service hasn't given her any names of potential relatives. She knows it isn't their fault. A connection can't be made unless a member of her family tree also submits their DNA. Still, it's been a disappointment, one that completely slips her mind as she removes the chain and says, "Come in."

The detective steps into the tiny foyer and Roni quickly closes the door behind her, blocking the cold air. "We can go into the living room. It's warmer there. Excuse the mess." If she'd known about this visitor she would have prepared. Maybe the detective intentionally caught her off guard in the hope of flustering her into revealing all her terrible secrets. Ha ha! Soon enough, she'll know there's nothing criminally interesting to find. Roni is clueless as to the identity of anyone on her mother's side of the family, and if the detective is looking for her father, well, Roni will be more than happy to give him up. The man disappeared sixty-seven years ago, but who's counting? Seems unlikely that law enforcement would want him. If he's alive, he'd be in his early nineties by now. Maybe the cold case under investigation is an ancient one.

"Please sit," she tells the detective, swooping up the dog-eared Agatha Christie novel from the seat of the easy chair and depositing it on the cluttered coffee table. Once the detective is seated, Roni scooches around the table, careful not to knock off the newspaper sticking out over the edge. She sidles in and plops onto the couch. A loveseat, really. Whenever she has a visitor, she's doubly aware of her cramped quarters, this tiny living room in her aging row house. She's lived here since childhood. One and a half baths, three bedrooms not much bigger than closets, the second smallest formerly Mama's, now used for sewing and crafts.

"Now, how can I help you? Oh, my goodness. I'm sorry. Can I get you anything?"

"No, thank you."

"Won't take but a few minutes to make coffee or tea."

The detective unzips her jacket but doesn't take it off, giving Roni a glimpse of a shoulder holster. "Really, I'm fine, thanks. Just a few questions, if I may. Do you mind if I take notes?" She takes a little pad and pen from her jacket pocket.

"No, ma'am. Go right ahead." Roni likes the detective's pretty smile, but there's a bit of sadness in it. Must affect a person, being around all that death. "But I don't know how I can help you with a cold case. You mean a homicide, right?"

"Yes. It happened in March of 2020. A DNA sample recovered from the victim bears some link to your genetic profile." A smidge of shock splashes onto Roni's face. The detective seems to notice it and hurries ahead in a soothing voice, as if trying to calm her. "This means only that a relative of yours *could* have left that DNA, and if so, it may very well be a distant relative, someone you don't even know. We just aren't sure, so I'd like to ask you a few questions about your family and your reasons for doing the genealogy search."

"Sure, of course."

"It could help us tremendously."

"I'd like to help." Roni's excitement surges anew and unleashes a gush of information. "I know absolutely nothing and no one on my mother's side of the family. Blood relatives, that is. She was adopted as a child and never tracked down her biological parents. Never wanted to. Absolutely forbade me from asking! I respected her wishes while she was alive." Roni raises a hand, gesturing, her eyes sweeping the room. "This was her house, our family home. I've lived here most of my life, decades of it alone with Mama. Never had a husband or kids of my own, and she was very clear about never trying to find her biological family. She figured they abandoned her, so she abandoned them right back, in her mind. But she died last year—"

"I'm sorry for your loss," the detective cuts in, glancing up from her notepad with one of her pretty, but sad, smiles.

"Thank you. She lived a long life, but it *is* a bit strange, being alone in the house this past year. Don't get me wrong! I have my friends, even a few from high school days, and my book group." She points to the Christie paperback, splayed on the table. "We read a lot of mysteries." Does that make Roni an expert of sorts?

"I imagine your mother's death might have renewed some of your questions about your ancestry?"

Roni laughs, feeling a bit ashamed. "I admit, my curiosity got the better of me. I've been pushing down these questions my whole life. So I contacted that ancestry site. Unfortunately, they haven't found anyone in my family tree. So far anyway. They keep your genetic profile on record as long as you want, and someone from my family could come in with their comb or hairbrush, couldn't they?"

"Very possible. So, you say you have no children?"

She shakes her head. "Missed that boat."

"How about your father's side of the family?"

"Aha, yes, my father." Roni's excitement grows, because if anyone in her family could be linked to a homicide, wouldn't that be someone related to her father? That no-good deadbeat who left her mother with two babies to care for. "Let me show you a picture I have." She bends forward, puffing a little from the strain on her arthritic hip, and pulls out a photo album from the shelf built into the coffee table, under the tabletop. The album is stuffed with photos and quite heavy.

"Can I help you?"

"No, no, I've got it, thanks!" She hoists the book onto her lap and opens it. Everything chronological, so it's easy to find what she's looking for on the first page with her baby photos. There. The only photo she has of her father from 1955. A black and white Kodak, poor quality, but Roni has always had a good idea of his features from that fuzzy image. All her life, she's faced a bit of him in the mirror, in her own eyes and shape of her chin.

Roni turns the album around and places it on the coffee table, opened to that page. She points. "That's him. He left us not long after that picture. I was less than a year old. Never knew him. Robert Littleton. Maybe he had some crooked relatives. Mama said he had a brother in Wyoming. I never met my uncle."

The detective leans forward and looks. "This is you and a sibling?"

"Yes."

"Are you the older or younger child?"

"I'm the baby in my mother's lap, and that's my sister Candace, at age three." Roni squirms uncomfortably on the loveseat. "We used to call her Candy, but we don't anymore."

"Is your sister still with us?"

"Oh, yes, very much so. I just don't see her very often. She lives here in Queens, not that far away. You could talk to her too if you think it would help your investigation. I'll give you her address and all that. I'd just rather not be the go-between is all. I haven't seen her since the funeral." A single-syllable, bitter laugh bursts from her throat. "Lou actually allowed her to come to her own mother's funeral."

Detective Vargas has been writing in her little pad again, but she looks up and focuses hard, apparently sensing Roni's anger. Can't very well hide it, the bane of her life. But the detective says nothing, just waits the second or two it takes Roni to spill her guts. "Maybe you can tell I don't like her husband very much. He's a contractor with a home improvement company, nothing very big, but he walks around like he's Man of the World. Ever since he married my sister, he's done everything he can to cut her off from us. Always glossed it over with excuses, but I've heard plenty behind my back, all his criticisms of me and Mama, how we're boring or beneath him or not worth visiting. Candance has to sneak behind his back to see me. Forty-five years of this. And you can bet, neither one of them or their kids ever lifted a finger to help me with Mama in her final years when I really needed a hand. How do you like *that* for a family?"

"Doesn't sound like an easy situation—"

"Not easy at all and… Hey, that's a thought! What if *Lou* is somehow wrapped up in this homicide of yours? There's your bad blood, right there. A petty, selfish man. Wouldn't surprise me if he has a criminal record, or someone in his family tree." Roni shakes her head, but a moment later it comes to her, the logical gap. "But that couldn't be, could it? He's no blood relation of mine."

"But your sister…"

Roni dazedly meets the questioning eyes and murmurs, "My

sister?" not quite getting it.

"You say she has children. Could they be in their thirties or forties by now? Maybe they have children of their own?"

"My niece, Karly, she's, I think, thirty-nine. Her married name is Springfield. They have a couple of teenagers in high school. Heavens! You think kids that young could have murdered someone? In 2020, they were no more than thirteen or fourteen. I'll give you their names if you really want them. I suppose anything's possible. Karly pretty much ignores her kids, goes to work every day in Manhattan. Her brother, my nephew, he's about forty-two or -three, still not married as far as I know. But you wouldn't need to investigate him. He's a police officer in Manhattan." Roni brightens. "That's right! Maybe you know him! Where's your precinct?"

"Lower Manhattan, but the police force is very large."

"Well, maybe you recognize the name. Kyle Rodman. The whole family is Louis Rodman, Candace, and their children Karly and Kyle. I don't know Kyle well at all. Haven't seen him for years, not since he graduated from the police academy. After the ceremony, Mama and I congratulated him, but he barely said two words to us. You see how it is? It's like Lou infected his whole family with his bad feelings for us. *That's* what I've been putting up with for years…"

But Detective Vargas is looking down at her notes, silently scribbling, and Roni can't tell if anything she's saying is any help at all.

14 » RECORDINGS

Wednesday, January 19, 2022

A WEEK HAS gone by since Natalie left her cell phone number with Wesley Guerrier. Nothing has come of it, but what did she expect? She's resigned to the likelihood of never hearing from either of the two witnesses.

But then, she gets a call at the oddest time. Eleven o'clock at night.

In winter PJs, snuggled up next to Max in bed, eyelids drooping, Natalie is rereading a paragraph for the third time. Max gently turns a page of his script for an upcoming screen test, muttering the lines under his breath, a habit she finds oddly comforting. Sometimes, if he needs to get into it, he goes into the living room to project in full voice. But in bed, he's considerate of her in all things, including these sessions with his craft.

His deep-voiced murmurings lull her. She closes her novel, puts it on the bedside table, and reaches for the lamp switch when her cell phone rings. She looks. *Bernard, J.* Could this possibly be…? "Hello?"

"Hello! This is Janjak Bernard! Is this the lady who talked to Wesley?"

She sits upright, suddenly awake. Max turns to stare at her, curious. "Yes, this is Natalie Goodhue. Thank you for calling. Did Mr. Guerrier—?"

"I got back from Haiti this morning. Sorry I took so long to call." *Not long at all, if he just returned stateside today!* "But I've been sleeping. I work at night, you know."

"Yes, he told me—"

"And I only heard his message a minute ago when I woke up. It's not too late, is it?"

"Not at all." She doesn't know if "too late" means the time of night or a missed chance to participate in her study.

"He said you're doing some research about that case. The murder! I can tell you everything that happened."

"That would be helpful."

"It was strange they didn't have a trial against that man they arrested. I'm not sure why they let him go. I told everyone I saw him do it. Looked like it anyway."

"We can talk about it."

"But I can't right now. I'm going to work. Is tomorrow okay? I'm off at eight."

Natalie is impressed. This man is ready to jump right in. She suggests a Starbucks near his building, and they agree to meet in the morning.

"What was that all about?" Max asks.

"A new volunteer for my study. A real life case."

"Cool." He turns back to his script. But now, even as he resumes his soothing drone, she's all wound up, unable to sleep. She opens her book again and tries to bore herself into drowsiness.

At eight fifteen, they've selected their coffees, and Mr. Bernard seems relieved when Natalie says, "It's on me." The tab is more than ten bucks. They find a corner table and she starts right in, addressing him formally as Mr. Bernard, but he insists that she call him Janjak. "Or even Jan, if you like!"

As she summarizes her research, Janjak's face lights up with interest. "Don't mind Wesley," he apologizes. "He doesn't like to get involved. He's always like that." Are the two men close or merely friendly compatriots? Guerrier is quite a bit older than Bernard. Soon enough, Natalie understands their relationship. Janjak is forthcoming with every detail.

He's easy to talk to, energized and keen to help. Witnessing a crime and testifying about it could be the most exciting events of his life. He tells her all about the night of March 15 to 16, 2020. The celebration, the pub, the green beer, the two men arguing next to them, what they looked like, and what they were doing a few minutes later, on the bridge.

She listens carefully without interrupting, as she's trained, avoiding questions for now. Anything she says poses a risk of suggesting ideas that tamper with memory. Asking him to parse his observations into detailed segments can reinforce selective images and descriptive words. She's leery of cultivating distortions, a habit she's developed over time in her work, even as she chides herself for an overabundance of caution in this particular situation. The event Janjak describes happened almost two years ago. In that time, he's reviewed what he saw thousands of times in his head and in conversations with friends, the police, and attorneys. The corrupting influences are so plentiful that what he's telling her now is no better than a fictional crime drama on TV.

The difficulty in drawing the line between fact and fiction reminds her why she's gone to the trouble of meeting Janjak. What is it about this man and his friend that convinced Professor Louden they identified the killer correctly? Made the Prof so sure of it that he broadcast his opinion to the world? Louden threw his reputation behind damaging insinuations. The grand jury got it wrong. The district attorney failed in his job or was guided by favoritism. The real killer, Corey McBride, got away with it. No justice for Marlon Stokes.

Natalie understands very well why her mother is upset about this. She just wants to know why it happened. Why her professor said what he said and whether she can morally stay in his research group. She's ignored these unpleasant questions for more than a year while continuing to work by his side—a tacit indication of her support. Should she feel proud of her association with the professor or ashamed or something in between?

So far, Natalie isn't impressed with Janjak's exposition. Oh, she likes both men, Guerrier and Bernard. She believes they're sincere and came forward out of a sense of responsibility, wanting to do the right thing, to tell the truth as they remember it. But the witnesses themselves and their good intentions are not what concern her. She sees the many details that potentially skewed their perception.

An undergraduate freshman in cognitive psychology could point out the problems. A dimly lit bar, so crowded that people were bumping shoulders. The celebratory mood, the drinking. The brevity of the encounter, a few angry words overheard, an elbow in Wesley's ribs, a quick apology, no big deal, no reason to study their faces. Outside in the night, intermittent LED street-lamps, location unknown. The "hug" on the bridge, the quick turn of a head, the vague description: pale skin, crew cut, medium build, dark jacket. "He was the same man from the bar," is Janjak's conclusion, shaky at best.

In response, Natalie merely nods.

"We said all this at the hearing and again, a few months later. It was a big room full of people, the grand jury. The judge believed us the first time and charged him with murder, but the jury didn't believe us. They threw out the case."

"Could be any number of reasons for that. Not that they didn't believe you." This seems to reassure him, which is all she wants, just to keep the conversation flowing. She won't correct Janjak's mistake about the procedure. The judge didn't charge

McBride with murder but made a finding of reasonable cause to hold the case for the grand jury. It was the jury's decision whether to file an indictment. She quickly changes the subject to an area she wants to explore. "Tell me about the virtual hearing with the judge. Where were you when you testified?"

"In that building that looks like a big pyramid. The district attorney's office. Man's name was Chin."

"Who else was in the room?"

"Just me and him. Wesley had to stay out in the hallway. He went in after I left."

"What could you see on your computer screen?"

"Mm," Janjak searches the ceiling for his answer. "The judge and a lady. She was the lawyer for the man we saw on the bridge. He was on the screen too."

"Anyone else?"

"Maybe a court employee."

Apparently, he couldn't see the professor and Zach, who were somewhere in the courtroom with the judge, as she understands it. "Did Mr. Chin ask you to identify anyone?"

"Oh, yes!" Janjak's face brightens. "He asked me if I saw anyone on the screen who could be the man on the bridge. I said yes. I had to think for a minute. He looked a little different."

"How so?"

"His hair was longer. I suppose he didn't cut it. Maybe he was trying to change the way he looked, to confuse me and Wesley and get away with it!" Janjak smiles proudly. "But I could tell it was him. He was wearing those dull color clothes they give you in jail."

Red flag. "How about your interview with the police *before* the hearing. You were on Skype, right?"

"Yes! I don't have a computer, so I went to Wesley's house to use his."

"Did the detective ask you to identify anyone? How did he

handle that?"

"He showed me some photos. He held them up to his computer camera."

"Do you remember what he said when he was holding them up?"

"The first time or the second time?"

Natalie is taken aback. "There was more than one time?"

Janjak chuckles, casts his eyes down and back at her. "I was a little nervous about being on a video. It took me so long to convince Wesley we had to call the police. So, when I was finally talking to the detective, I got a little clammy. I told him I don't want to screw it up, you know? He said, 'Relax, man, relax! I'll go through all the questions with you before I turn on the camera.' He was nice about it. We did the whole thing first, just for practice."

"This was on Skype?"

"Yes, on Skype, but he didn't turn the recorder on right away. He asked all the questions, then he showed me a few photos and said, 'Does this look like the guy?' When he got to the right one, I said, 'Yeah, could be him.' It really did look like him. So, the detective told me what to do when the recorder is on. He'll show each photo and say, 'This could be the man you saw hugging the other one on the bridge, or maybe not.' He told me to be brief, just say, 'Yes, that's him' on the right one. After we practiced, he turned on the video and we did the whole interview."

Natalie is momentarily speechless. The detective was putting words in his mouth!

Janjak seems to notice the astonishment she's trying to hide. "Do you want the recording?"

She gulps to keep her jaw from dropping. "You have a copy of your interview?"

"Not exactly!" He laughs with a little devious twinkle in his eyes. "The detective said I couldn't get a copy of the video, but I had my phone there, next to the computer, recording it. He didn't see! I wanted to be sure I remembered everything I said, in case I had to go to court."

"You have an audio recording?"

"Yeah, I do."

"Of the whole thing? Before and after he turned on the video?"

"Yes, ma'am!" Janjak bobs his head, very pleased. "It might help your research about the procedures. That's what you're studying, right?"

15 » POWER BLIND

Thursday, January 20, 2022

CAREFUL CAREFUL CAREFUL has been Aurelina's mantra since Tuesday. Seething, dizzy with grief and anguish about Marlon, she mustered every ounce of strength to hold herself together after Veronica Littleton uttered the name "Rodman." That name triggered a powerful call to action. Hunt the man down, shackle him, remove that piece of filth from "public service," dump him in the hold, never to see the light of day again.

But when she stepped out of that little row house in Queens, the frigid air smacked her in the face, jolting her into clarity. She took a huge gulp of oxygen and counted to ten. Then counted to ten again. Not wise to go off jacked and hasty. Sloppy. Everything has to be done right. It's been this long. Another week won't matter. When she hands the case to the DA, it better be airtight.

That is, if Kyle is the one. Could there be a mistake, a lab error, a switched sample, a botched DNA analysis, a tenuous connection that means nothing? Impossible, or near to it. If not a mistake, an innocent explanation? That night, at the stationhouse, did the men have a little friendly physical contact? Marlon digging into a bare patch of Kyle's skin? Ridiculous to imagine. Those two never got within ten feet of each other, even on a good day.

Of course he's the one. What else could it mean? Lina is

convinced. She just doesn't know the "why" of it. Not yet.

Which brings her to this: Dislike is no motive for murder. Maybe for psychopaths, but not for relatively normal, unpleasant human beings like Kyle. He has said a few nasty things to Marlon over the years, but then, Kyle says nasty things to a lot of people a lot of the time.

Motive will be revealed. First things first. Absolute confirmation. Funny how it might seem easy to collect a DNA sample. People shed their biological fluids and cells all over the place. But it's almost as if Kyle senses she's looking. He keeps all extraneous articles of clothing, his dress uniform and cap, in his locker, the combination to himself. Leaves no coffee cups or soda cans or writing implements on his desk. No used tissues in his trash can. No cigarette butts outside the back door. He doesn't smoke.

As lead investigator, before Lina took the case back, Kyle knows that DA Browne subpoenaed GEDMatch previously, twice. He must have heaved a huge sigh of relief each time those searches turned up nothing. He doesn't know that Lina and Jared have renewed that search, but his habits have kicked in. He's cautious. She understands that now.

Lina finally has a bit of luck. From her office window, she sees Kyle come into the communal office and go to his desk, the other desks empty. He doesn't seem to notice she's in. He drapes his winter jacket on the chairback and goes to the men's room. Quickly, she slips out, under pretense of just passing through, if caught. Her sharp eye spots a big find. The man is getting to the age of shedding on top. She plucks two short hairs from his jacket collar, pinches them tightly, returns to her office, and drops them into an evidence envelope. In the nick. As she closes the drawer on her prize and looks up, she catches his eye and receives his phony expression of respect, a grimace and a nod acknowledging her, his superior.

Lina's poker face is legend, but unspoken tension often

resonates at palpable frequencies. The energy of antipathy has the power to cut through space, veil, and substance.

She waits until he's gone, again, before making a special delivery of the sample to a trusted messenger, with orders to the lab to expedite.

Meanwhile, Lina reviews the records she ordered. Precinct phone and Skype account data from April 2020. Her fingertip traces down the page to the dates of Kyle's interviews with Janjak Bernard and Wesley Guerrier. She compares the time stamps with notes in the file and the length of the videos—the Q&As that flow a little too smoothly. Kyle has been dismissive of her questions about those interviews. She can imagine how it went. What better way to frame an innocent man than to suggest his guilt to well-meaning witnesses, grooming and coaching them? Easy to shape their testimony after the passage of time when memories are fading. Easy to wield that power with the flash of a badge and the patina of superior knowledge. *I know something about this case you don't know.* Under the thumb of subtle manipulation, witnesses and the wrongly accused often cave, crumble, and submit.

As the "why" remains out of reach, Lina concentrates on the "how." How to explain the witnesses' mistaken ID. Skin color, height, and build are roughly similar. Corey's face has a boyish softness while Kyle's is harder, with a clifflike forehead over deep set eyes. Clean haircuts, different hair color, but Corey's was so short that the orange-rust hue might not have been visible at night. Nearly everyone on the force has one of those dark blue PBA windbreakers, the one Corey was wearing. And, of course, Kyle has said nothing to deny what many witnesses can confirm. He was at the precinct that night before the troops left for the bar. Opportunity and feasibility.

Lina plans to meet with Bernard and Guerrier, to confirm the backstory behind the time entries for their Skype meetings with Detective Rodman. But for now, it's important to bring the DA up to speed. This case will snowball quickly. They should be ready.

Finger hovering over keypad, she looks out her window. Kyle has returned to his desk and is slouched back in his chair, holding the phone receiver to his ear, the other hand waving in the air. With his back to her, he gesticulates and talks loudly on his phone, exhibiting that familiar air of smugness. No way can he hear her. She punches in the numbers.

"ADA Ernest Chin."

"Hi, Ricky. It's Lina. I'd like to come over and give you an update on the Stokes investigation. Is now a good time?"

"For the Stokes case I'm always available. Is this something the DA should hear?"

"Yes." She glances at Kyle's back, the square hand that jammed a knife into Marlon's heart now stroking the nape of his own neck. "I'm very close to something."

"Good. I just saw Jared. He's in his office. Come up to the eighth floor when you get here."

Vargas scoots past Kyle's desk while he's still on the phone, making him lose his train of thought. The forensic investigator on the other end continues to spout her theories about the blood spatter in a gangland homicide. What does Rodman care? Let those animals kill each other. He cuts the call short.

Vargas has been too interested in him these days. He can feel it in the way she shuffles by, slower than usual, hesitating and hovering near his desk. Calls him into her office with those questions. Last week it was about Dexter, a man he hopes never to see again. XT was all eyes and ears in that neighborhood but doesn't have a thing on Rodman. He's convinced himself of that after checking up on it. Not a flicker of recognition in Dexter's eyes when Kyle went to ask him about Chug. And on the night that matters to Kyle, XT was nowhere to be seen. Still, there's always a possibility of eyes behind a curtain, in a dark doorway, or around a corner of crumbling façade. Rats everywhere, watching. There was one in particular he had to take care of.

Vargas. This week her curiosity switched from XT to the eyewitnesses. Is the file complete? Does he have any other notes? Are these the correct phone numbers for Bernard and Guerrier? "It's all in there," he told her, nodding to the file in her hand. "You have the videos. You even have an expert who watched the hearing and said they were reliable. What more do you need?"

Exactly. What more did anyone need to bring down that brown noser, Corey McBride? That pretty-faced soft touch would have climbed the ladder in the NYPD through no merit of his own, banking on the family connections: his uncle, the former four-term DA, and another uncle, a captain uptown. Well, DA Browne needed more, that's clear enough, the way his assistant gaslighted the twenty-three grand jurors into doubting the evidence and dropping the charges.

Rodman is royally pissed to be second-guessed. Didn't Vargas make him lead investigator when her husband came down with Corona? Trusted him with months of work while she was on leave. Now, out of the blue, she pulls a power play, yanks the case from him for a full re-do. Where did this come from? At forty-three, not getting any younger, and with twenty years on the force, Rodman should have been promoted to detective first grade by now instead of getting cut down by that little woman. His status seems to mean nothing to her. He knows more about the streets and the minds of criminals than Vargas ever could. Murderers, thugs, and drug kingpins step aside when they see him coming. *I own the streets, little Boricua*. It's a status that has its benefits, a power he enjoys. And it's the thing that got him into this spot in the first place.

* * *

As the workday draws to a close and Dana looks forward to a quiet dinner at home, Nia delivers the latest opinions circulated to chambers, one in draft form, the other published to the world. A respite from conflict is a rare find for Judge Hargrove. The papers in Nia's hand guarantee that Dana's thoughts will not be tranquil this evening.

"Judge," Nia starts, standing at her boss's desk, "I'm sorry to say, Justice Morgenstern wasn't convinced by the memo in *COG v AG*, citing your earlier opinion." Nia's draft, with Dana's edits, was circulated last Friday. Since then, Dana has entertained a slim hope that all three of the other judges would sign off on the memorandum decision. Nice and easy. Deny COG's request based on well-established principles, keep the grand jury evidence in the Lonnie Douglas shooting under seal. Dana feels she can still count on Justices Khouri and Navarro, but they've been quiet this week, waiting to see what Morgenstern would do.

"Short and sweet to affirm doesn't do it for him, eh?" Dana holds out her hand for the dissent. "I had my hopes, but we knew it would likely come to this." She looks down at the fat set of stapled papers and turns the pages quickly, one at a time, without reading. "Has nothing to do with your draft, of course. Let me decide how to beef up the order to affirm, and we'll talk tomorrow about writing a longer draft." Fingers crossed that Navarro and Khouri aren't swayed to join Morgenstern.

"Okay. And this..." Nia purses her lips and glances down at the other papers in her hand.

"Let me guess. *Josefina M.*"

Nia hands it over with an affirmative nod. "Handed down today. Three-to-two, not the way you would like. Judge Shields wrote the majority, Navarro wrote the dissent."

Dana eyes the caption page, the lineup of judges in opposing camps. She's been anxiously awaiting this decision. With Josefina's life hanging in the balance, the panel should have ruled immediately, but it's been nearly a week. Rumors have been flying about hot and heavy debates in the conference room and private, one-on-one meetings of shifting alliances in chambers. The outcome fits one of Dana's predictions. The judges on either side of the three-two divide voted the way she guessed, even if all five understood the value of unanimity, were it possible to achieve.

"Thanks, Nia. This outcome highlights everything we've talked about. The issues in this case provoke sharp division."

"It's a tough one."

"So maybe I'm just as glad I didn't end up on this panel." Not.

Nia looks at her boss, piercing the transparent veil of disclaimer. "Could have been three-to-two or four-to-one the *other* way if you'd been there to convince them."

"Could have, but not much use speculating at this point." Dana notices the fatigue in Nia's face and feels a protective surge. That baby in her belly is more important than anything. "For now, we've done what we can. It's time to pack up and go home. Don't stay late."

"I won't, Judge. Have a good night."

"Good night, Nia."

Alone with Justice Shields' opinion, Dana takes a few minutes to read, to understand the rationale. He writes that imminent danger to Josefina's life justified the emergency removal from her home. The legal guardian's withholding of life-saving treatment constitutes "neglect" under state law, and government has a sacred duty to protect young life. He actually used the word "sacred." His opinion expressly avoids adopting the mature minor doctrine but includes an "even if" analysis. Even if that doctrine applies, Josefina hasn't demonstrated sufficient maturity to appreciate the consequences of her decision. Just like Travis argued.

In dissent, Justice Navarro doesn't go into the mature minor doctrine at all. She would hold that Bianca did not commit "neglect" as defined. The state improperly removed Josefina from her home and has no other legal basis to forcefully impose any specific kind of medical treatment.

"Imminent danger to life," Shields writes. Danger to the law, Dana is thinking, a bad precedent that could affect many cases to come, forcing parents and mature teens to relinquish their freedom of choice and submit to the paternalism of government officials against their will. Institutional entitlement. We, the intelligentsia, know better. Power blind.

And how is it different if Dana had been on the panel and the decision had gone for Bianca? Isn't that also an official mandate? Cheryl's words have been haunting her. *What about* this *government institution? What about* your *power?* Dana's court is the final arbiter of most cases, only a small percentage reviewed by the Court of Appeals in Albany. Is Dana blind to the way her decisions affect people? Three-two the other way and Josefina goes home, free to make her own choices. Free to make stupid decisions? Free to choose death? Government sanctioned suicide?

Stop. That's going too far. The health outcomes are unknown, subject to intelligent guesswork only. Three-two the other way is not the same as *we know better*. That's the difference. It's *you know what's best for you*.

Dana weighs Josefina's case in her hands and sets it aside, exposing the other opinion underneath. How she would decide *Josefina M.* is an abstract question, but that's not the case in *COG v AG*. She scans Morgenstern's dissent. He's swayed by the public outcry, the demand for transparency in this and every case involving a police shooting. He's also swayed by the attorney general's compromise position—a disingenuous CYA in Dana's view, not to mention a disregard of the correct legal standard. Witnesses came forward at personal risk to testify. Disclosing the transcript with their names redacted will not be enough to protect them and will renege on a promise of confidentiality. Dana will not back down from solid principle on this one.

But the problems of the world won't be solved sitting here at her desk, lost in thought. She picks up her cell phone and checks the time. Almost six o'clock. With a "ping," the display announces a text from Evan: *Got something yummy ready for you! And a surprise.*

Time to get out of here. Pack up and go home to Evan.

16 » *HEART*

A HEAVENLY AROMA greets Dana as she walks in the front door. Familiar. Evan is cooking his specialty, prime rib.

"Hello," she calls out and drops her briefcase on the way to the kitchen. She finds him bent at the waist, leaning into a hot blast from the open oven door. "You're making my mouth water."

He lets the door bang shut and straightens up. She likes what she sees: Evan in an apron, potholder in hand. "Prime rib!" He's looking proud of himself.

"I can tell. And it's only Thursday, not even the weekend. Special occasion?"

"I have some news."

She comes close and plants a wet kiss on his cheek. "I can't wait."

"Don't distract the chef!" He swivels to the hiss and sizzle on the stovetop. A pot is boiling over. Undoubtedly the potatoes for garlic mash, his go-with for the specialty.

While Evan averts near disaster, Dana goes to the bedroom to change out of her business attire. What a wonderful man she has. What a wonderful life she has. Everything she needs to tear her mind away from the cares of the day, lurking in the recesses of consciousness. Go away. The Lonnie Douglas shooting. The murder of Marlon Stokes. The family torn apart, Bianca and Josefina, sleeping under separate roofs tonight. Appellate judges, wise women and men who can't agree. A disquiet simmering under a permeable barrier, percolating up.

She'll do her best to forget. Shall she dress up for the special dinner? She chooses a jersey pullover and sweatpants, loose and liberating. Under that apron, Evan is already comfortable in his sloppy plaid shirt and soft baggy cords. It's an evening to feel young and excited and oblivious to anything but the moment they're in. They'll tuck into the meat and potatoes heartily, with abandon. She'll erupt in joyous surprise at Evan's big reveal, although she already knows what it is.

There's been no public announcement as yet. That will come, probably tomorrow, in the *Law Journal*. But she knows. She knows.

And how does she feel about it as she hangs up her skirt and blouse? Unchanged from last week when they discussed it. She's proud of him, wants this for him, even as she recognizes how it would change their lives. Dana and Evan. A solid couple. Together almost thirty-five years. A team, but individuals too, with unique talents to share with the world. She's happy about this. Really? No question about it.

But after his proud reveal and her hugs and praise, after they've basked in good feelings throughout the dinner hour, the discussion still isn't laid to rest. As they sop up the last savory juices on their plates with crusts of baguette, Evan says, "Just wanna make sure you know the reason I bought the prime rib. Why tonight?"

"Because we have something to celebrate."

"Yes. And because I have no illusions. The short list is the plum, farther than I thought I'd get. So we might as well celebrate now or forever lose the chance."

Dana frowns at him under a lowered brow.

"Don't look at me like that," Evan says. "I *did* buy an apple pie for dessert."

"I'm not worried about pie. That's not what you meant."

"Well, anyone can see what I meant. There's no way. Look at these names again." He picks up the paper he so proudly placed on the table in front of her when he made his big reveal. The short list for the opening on the Court of Appeals. Seven names, his included, were sent to the governor by the nominating committee. The governor's pick will undergo a confirmation hearing in the state senate. He slaps the page. "Garrison! Delgado! Fres—"

"Wait, wait a minute! Are you *serious*? You're the standout candidate here. No one even comes close."

"Your fealty is duly noted, dear wife, but your bias is showing." A gleam in his eye.

Back to the comedy routine? She tests him with a bit of doublespeak: "You've got that backwards, darling. To reveal my *true* bias, I'd lie and say you don't have a chance, you're at the bottom of the pack."

A pause, eyes leveled on each other with straight faces. Five seconds. The corners of their mouths start to twitch involuntarily. A second later, big smiles burst into belly laughs. She gets up, circles the table, and hugs his shoulders from behind. Squeezing, she whispers in his ear, "You can't get out of it that easy. I already planned a party for when you're confirmed."

"Thanks for the warning. I don't like surprises."

"Aw. I told everyone to hide and jump out when you walk in." She picks up the dirty dishes and says, "Let's have dessert."

The piece of pie in front of her awakens the flood of cares at the back of her mind. Odd that a wedge of Grandma's apple pie would do that. This grandma isn't a relation but a bakery by that name, which happens to make the best apple pie in New York. The kids' favorite. Dana latches onto a memory of their family of four, sitting around the dining room table relishing this treat down to the last crumbs. The kids lick their plates while the parents laugh delightedly, overlooking any lessons in table manners. Travis and Natalie, the brightest, funniest, most loving and uniquely interesting human beings in existence, Dana would say. Talk about biases.

Cinnamon and apple, buttery crust. Dana swallows the first bite, surprised at the swell of emotion in her chest. Is she going to cry?

Evan sees it. "What's up?"

It all spills out then, the details of the opinion handed down today in Josefina's case.

"You're really upset about this, I can see."

She merely nods.

Gently, he suggests, "It may be for the best. They might have many years together if Josefina's life is saved."

"Let's hope." She says nothing more, ready to change the subject. They've already been through every aspect of this case. Dana has discussed it endlessly with Evan and Nia and her colleagues. Not so much with Travis.

And that's it, the source of her emotion, the hidden, uncomfortable part of her distress. The personal part. Naturally, she feels the anguish of Josefina and Bianca, as much as anyone would feel for strangers. But the plight of the Merced family reaches beyond them, into her own. Travis. And another wrenching case does the same. Naturally, Dana has strong feelings for the McBrides, but in the end, they aren't family either. Natalie is. No matter how fervently Dana believes in respecting and considering divergent opinions, to be standing on the opposite side of the fence from her children doesn't feel good. It just doesn't.

Natalie, working for that unethical "expert." Travis, representing the agency that ripped Josefina from her home. Her children, doing their jobs so well. They're so damn smart, dedicated, and skilled at what they do.

Stunned by her realization, Dana searches for words and considers evading the subject altogether with another bite of pie. But then, a sound saves her. "Is that your cell or mine?" she asks.

"Yours, I think."

"I'll just go see…" Dana gets up and heads for the repeated ringing where she laid her cell phone, on a side table. Looking at the display, she surrenders to a second of hesitation, no more. She'll take this call. She's not one to run.

"Hello, Travis." She settles into another seat at the dining table, farther away from Evan, pie out of reach. He looks up at her, attentive.

"Hi, Mom. Am I interrupting dinner?"

"Nope. It's dessert time. We're having Grandma's apple pie."

He laughs. Nervously? The Josefina case is at the back of his mind too. "We just had Grandma's pie too! A couple of weeks ago when Natalie and Max came over."

"Nice."

"Is it a special occasion?"

"Your father just got the word. He's shortlisted for the Court of Appeals."

"Awesome! Give him my congratulations."

Dana glances up at Evan and smiles. "I will." Still, she selfishly keeps Travis for herself, doesn't put the call on speaker-phone. They last spoke the night of his argument, when she called to let him know she'd been watching on her office computer. Kept it brief, told him she was proud. No details. No legal discussion. No personal views. But he knows. "And *you're* entitled to hearty congratulations on your win today in *Josefina M.*"

"Thank you." An awkward silence. "Now that it's over, I want to talk to you about the case. I…um… I had mixed feelings about my client. It was difficult for me to get a hundred percent behind our position."

"And you're worried that it showed? It didn't."

"Maybe not worried about *that*—"

"You were very on track, organized, forceful, and I believe your argument helped persuade the majority."

"But I had my doubts—"

"We all have them. But this is our system of justice. You're an advocate. You're duty bound to make the strongest argument for your client, just as your adversaries make their strongest arguments. Truth and justice arise from this clash of opposing views and lead the way to the fairest outcome." And something else "arises" from the sound of her own voice—a ball of emotion, clogging her throat. Why is she reciting this…pablum? Is she speaking tongue in cheek? Does she really believe her lofty principles as Josefina languishes in a stranger's house tonight, longing to go home to her aunt? "And all the judges, including yours truly, are duty bound to hear every opposing viewpoint with an open mind, to apply the law as written to the facts."

"The law as written. 'Neglect.' Come on, Mom. I'm only glad I didn't have to take Noriko's part of the argument. I didn't believe the aunt committed neglect under the law. As written. My part of the argument was hard enough, but at least I could see some sense and logic in the idea that a definite number is easy to follow. A bright line. Eighteen. That's the law of majority, as written."

He makes a strong point, of course. But… "A definite cutoff never takes individual circumstances into account, does it? It goes both ways. An immature twenty-year-old. And a very mature seventeen-year-old, who understands the stakes, willing to take responsibility and accept the consequences of her decisions."

A long pause. Finally, Travis says, "And eighteen doesn't take into account parents who respect their children's intelligence and train them to take personal responsibility. Because that's what we learned. That's what I got from you, my mom and dad."

Now there's nothing she can do to control it. The moisture in her eyes wells up, shimmers at the brink, and spills over the edge, making warm lines down her cheeks that drip off at the chin.

The room is quiet. Their connection falls silent.

Evan focuses on Dana, frozen in a watery, stunned silence. He gets up and comes to her side, puts a hand on her shoulder and another on the hand that holds the phone. In the distance, Travis is speaking. "Mom? Mom, are you there?" Evan guides the phone down to the table and presses the speaker button. "Dad here, Travis."

"Hi, Dad. That's great news about the short list. Congratulations."

"Thank you."

"I'm sure you'll get it."

"We'll see. There's a lotta competition."

"It'll be a big change from being a law professor."

"A transition from molding young minds to moldy old minds."

"Hah!"

"Sorry, I couldn't help it."

"You'll be a great judge. Listen, I wanted to let you guys know… I'm also going to be making a change in my career. I'm asking for a transfer to another bureau of the Corporation Counsel. Can you tell Mom?"

"I'm right here, Travis."

"Oh."

"A wise decision," Evan says. "You've put your time in, helping abused and neglected kids. It must be wearing on you."

"I feel good about most of the work, but it's tough, you know. Heart wrenching, and now, with the baby coming—"

"We love you, Travis," Dana cuts in, tears still flowing. "We love you so very much."

17 » *BROTHERS*

Friday, January 21, 2022

RODMAN'S CELL PHONE is buzzing in his pocket when he walks into the precinct, a few minutes after eight. One look at the display and his heart jumps. A coincidence, or is Vargas talking to this guy too? Maybe he's calling to ask why another detective reopened the case.

"Detective Rodman, Homicide."

"Hello, Detective. I don't know if you remember me, but—"

"Sure, I remember you, Janjak." The kid sounds as enthusiastic as ever. Hasn't changed a bit. Let's hope he's just as easy to control.

"Sorry I didn't use the station number. I still had this number you gave me. Thought it would be faster."

"No problem." Kyle doesn't mention he's glad that Bernard *didn't* call his desk phone. He thinks that Vargas has been monitoring his calls. "What's up?"

"I know the case is over," Bernard says, "but this young lady came to see me about it yesterday. She's doing some research. Sounds interesting. I want to help her out, but I only have the audio—"

"Audio?"

Janjak stutters and backtracks. "I-I mean, I can only tell her what I remember saying to you, so I'm wondering, can I get a copy of that video we did?"

Maybe the kid doesn't understand the word "audio." Rodman smooths over his alarm with a diplomatic rejection. "Well, now, Janjak, you know I don't give out videos like that. We talked about this. The investigation stays under wraps. You shouldn't be talking to anyone about it. Even what you *remember* about our conversations."

"I know, I know, but it would be for a worthwhile cause. It's an official study, she said. She's trying to improve interview tactics for investigations, especially when you use computers. Our video could really help, right?"

Official study. Who could be doing an official study? "Did you get the name of this person?"

"Yes, oh yes! Really good-looking young lady." Bernard chuckles uneasily at revealing his attraction. "She's a little older than me, a graduate student. Her name is Natalie Goodhue."

Rodman needs only a second to make the connection. He's been in law enforcement long enough to know the important names, the alliances, the loyalties. Good chance this "official" researcher is the offspring of that renowned couple, Goodhue-Hargrove, cronies of the former and current DA. Is Judge Hargrove using her own kid as a work around? Did Hargrove and Browne come up with this idea to reopen the case? Is this what's lighting a fire under Vargas? The three of them go way back.

He'll check it out. "Did she give you a phone number? I'll deal with her directly. If it seems like the right thing to do, I'll give her the video."

This makes Janjak very happy. He recites Natalie Goodhue's cell phone number, and this makes Detective Rodman very happy. He'll just see what this Goodhue kid is up to.

"Thank you, Detective. I think her research is important, and she's real smart."

"I bet she is. No problem. But," the word "audio" floats at

the back of his mind, "before I call her, let's meet so you can tell me more about her research. Where are you?"

"Downtown. Just got off work. About to get breakfast."

Rodman offers to buy him breakfast and they decide on a diner. "Get a booth. I'll be there in twenty minutes."

"Okay!" He sounds excited beyond words. This will be easy.

"Just be sure you have your phone with you. I'll call or text if I'm late."

Natalie loves morning coffee with Max in the breakfast nook of his apartment. There's a reason she's (almost) living here. His place on the Upper East Side is twice the size of hers, a recent upgrade in his lifestyle thanks to the extra income he made from *Swamp Wars*. The apartment faces the back of the building and overlooks a courtyard, no street noise, southern exposure, bright. A king size bed. A shiny machine in the kitchen makes Barista quality coffee.

Still, she isn't really living here. Neither one of them is pretending, although Max is closer to that fantasy than she is. Geez, they've only known each other five months. Her own apartment, a modest studio, is closer to the university. Now that winter break is over and the semester has started, she can tell him (if she wants) that his apartment is inconvenient. The escape hatch is there if Max ever displays evidence of the doubts that Travis has been pushing.

A few things her brother said the other day were not so subtle. "What if he's only interested in you as the niece of Cheryl Hargrove?"

"Thanks for reminding me I'm such a loser."

"You know what I mean. Max is really into his career, and Cheryl is a powerful name in the business." Protective older brother speaking from the height of his important self-imposed role.

It can be nice, sometimes, to have a brother looking out for her—but come on! Travis is so wrong! "Max knew Cheryl before he knew me. They were in a *movie* together, duh."

"He had a small part compared to hers."

"But they're *friends*, Trav. Why do you think she invited him to her party?"

Her brother backed off then, but he left a small doubt in her mind. Max is still struggling in his career, working hard at it. He attends auditions and takes screen tests. Connections and networking can advance a career. Not too shabby if a star like Cheryl Hargrove suggests "Maximilian Hastings" to a casting director. But how can Travis miss the genuine side? The part of Max that puts Natalie first?

At the moment, the "you-first" side isn't so visible, but that's understandable too. Max sits across from her, oblivious to her presence, his focus alternating between his coffee cup and the script in his lap. He's prepping in his head, getting psyched for his screen test this morning.

Natalie takes the last sip of her coffee. It's almost nine, time to get going. Another day with her data, broken up by an hour in the afternoon to fulfill her TA responsibilities, teaching a small seminar of freshmen undergrads.

As she sets her cup down, the table vibrates with a buzz from her cell phone, close at hand. A quick look, something odd. The preview on the screen shows a phone number with the name "Bernard, T." and the first line of the text message: "This is Janjak Bernard's brother."

What? She taps the message and opens it.

"This is Janjak Bernard's brother telling you to get lost. This case is over. Janjak had enough of this shit. Bad enough he saw a man get killed. Does the right thing, goes to court, and the killer walks! The murderer could come after him. Janjak lives with that threat every day. Enough. Fuck off, or else."

Or else what? She's alarmed and puzzled at the same time. Yesterday in Starbucks, Mr. Bernard was gregarious and open, eager to help in any way possible. Friendly. Big smiles. Unafraid. A week ago, his colleague Guerrier was different. Wary and stand-offish. But not Janjak. Why would he complain to his brother? Another protective brother, it seems, one who might use more than words to get his point across.

The air around them pulsates with Natalie's tense energy. Max feels it, looks up, stares hard. "What's going on?"

Her heart is pounding, forehead and underarms damp. Max is tuned into her. *Doesn't that prove something, Travis?* But she can't answer him with all these thoughts rushing through her head, her eyes wide and blank.

He says, "You look like a deer caught in the headlights."

She takes a deep breath and pushes the phone across the table. "Look at this."

He reads. "Holy shit! Who is that? Who's Janjak Bernard?"

"A subject in my study. He was a witness to a real crime." She gives Max all the essentials as the consternation on his face deepens.

"Natalie! I don't get it. Why didn't you ask the professor or Zach to come with you when you saw this witness? It's their case."

"It isn't *their* case. It's just *a* case. And I didn't tell them I was going to see the witness. I had to find out for myself what happened, without their input. Kind of a blind study."

"So, tell them now. Maybe they know this brother. Your professor has a lot of influence. He can help."

"I…I can't, Max. It would look bad for me in the program, in the department. Maybe I screwed up, but I can't tell the professor any of this. I don't trust him. Or Zach either. He lives his life under Louden's thumb. He needs to stay on the Prof's good side to keep his own research on track. If I tell Zach about this, he could tell the Prof." Notwithstanding Zach's crush on her. She doesn't tell Max that part of it.

"This gets worse by the minute. You're working with people you can't trust?" Max is getting theatrical now.

She tells him. Tells him all. Her mother's emotional investment in the McBride-Stokes case. Her fears that her mother disrespects her for working with Dr. Louden. Natalie is embarrassed that she stuck her nose where it doesn't belong, but she has to find out *who* she's working for. Louden compromised a criminal investigation and the integrity of his own research by saying those things in his interview on the news program. If Judge Kaplan showed him the witness videos, as Zach claims, why didn't he pick up the irregularity in the ID procedures? After the detective coached them, the witnesses would have been too smooth, their identifications of McBride too pat. An expert like Louden should have noticed it. Natalie still hasn't figured out his reasons, but she does know one thing: Professor Louden is often guided by his oversized ego.

"I understand all that," Max says, "but we're back where we started. What'll we do about this threat from Bernard's brother? I'm worried about you. Maybe he followed you and knows where to find you."

"No, he wouldn't have. Whatever Janjak told his brother, there's nothing specific. He doesn't know anything about me, just my name and mobile number. And you should see him, Max. He's a really sweet guy, happy to talk to me, not afraid of anything. I can't believe his brother would be much different. I'm not afraid of this." She points to her cell phone. Does Max believe her? Does she believe herself?

"You have a lot of confidence in the Bernard family genes. Janjak could be sweet as sugar because his brother got the bad seed."

"He just wants me to go away. If I back off, there's no reason for him to do anything. I'll text Janjak and say I'm finished with my research. I won't be needing his help anymore. He'll tell his brother, and it'll be like this never happened." Except, Natalie is happy to recall, she got a valuable audio recording out of this! Janjak AirDropped it to her phone yesterday. The full interview on Skype, before and after the video recording was made.

Max reaches across the table and caresses her hand. With a gentle look under lifted brow, he adopts a paternal tone. "No wonder I'm crazy about you. Always see the good in people. But Natalie, this dude doesn't sound reasonable. He's angry. He could do anything. I think we should call the police."

"No way."

"They can identify Janjak's brother in a minute. What if the guy has a criminal record? You need some muscle on your side."

"They wouldn't do anything about a text message. People get scary anonymous messages all the time. The police are stretched thin. They have more important things to spend their time on. I know from experience, cases my parents were involved in." Like that awful time, seven years ago, when everyone in her family was getting those anonymous cryptic messages and veiled threats. The police didn't get too excited about it. Did next to nothing, as she remembers. Well, that's beside the point. She'll tell Max the whole story another time, if he doesn't already know about it from the news coverage years ago. For now, they've already spent too much time on this topic, and she's beginning to feel guilty, distracting Max from his important screen test today.

"But you have people in your family, legal experts with connections to law enforcement."

"Yeah, well..."

"Go talk to your mom. Get her advice."

"I, uh, do you know how hard that will be?" This is where it all started for Natalie. This is all about her and Mommy.

"You have to. You know you do. You said a minute ago your mom is the reason you wanted to talk to this Janjak Bernard in the first place. Isn't that right?"

Of course he's right.

A minute later, Natalie calls her mother and they arrange to meet in the judge's chambers. She has an hour to think about how she's going to break the news.

"I'll go with you and drop you off," Max says.

"No you won't. I've taken enough of your time."

"My screen test isn't until eleven, and the court is on my way."

Natalie doesn't quite believe him, but he insists. He's worried about her.

And truth be told, she's relieved to have him sitting next to her on the subway and walking with her to the courthouse. In her dazed state, a creepy, frosty mist outlines the frigid morning air. Street noises are muffled. Absently, compulsively, she glances right and left and over her shoulder, behind them. Max squeezes her hand every time she does this.

At ten fifteen, on the courthouse steps, Max kisses her goodbye. His face registers relief that she's safe before he leaves for his audition. She hopes she hasn't blown his chances for the part.

Strange to be here two Fridays in a row, Travis's court appearance last week, and now this, the moment she's been avoiding. But Max is right, face it head on, confess everything (well, not *everything*). Beneath the calm, unshakable persona, Natalie's mother isn't immune to intense emotion. She's apt to lose it if she believes her kids are in danger. Threaten their health or safety and she turns all Mama Bear. Natalie must tread lightly.

But she can't hide this or sugarcoat it too much. Ten times

worse if her mother finds out what she's been up to before having a chance to confess. And after listening to Janjak's recording yesterday, Natalie also feels the call of civic duty, a pressing obligation to turn this evidence over to someone in the NYPD. Who? She doesn't know. Certainly not the detective who was interviewing Janjak. He's the problem. Incompetent. Ruined any chance of finding the facts. His interview technique is so bad, he mangled any remaining untainted corner of Janjak's memory. If that detective is still assigned to this cold case, they're in trouble. She hopes they've assigned someone else. Her mother will know who that might be. This is a case near and dear to her. She's probably looking for the killer herself!

Natalie's butterflies flutter as she steps into the ornate lobby. This courthouse really does impress her with a sense of awe. Surrounded by fine art and lofty principles, she stands in the center of reason, law, and justice, a place of wisdom, civilization, and brotherhood. Everything will turn out all right. She'll talk it out with the smartest woman she knows. They'll find an answer, together.

She could have come earlier this morning, gotten this over with by now, but her mother suggested waiting until ten fifteen. Makes sense. Easier to get into the building. Only a few people remain in the lobby. Attorneys and spectators for the ten o'clock oral argument calendar have already been screened and are in the courtroom. Fortunately for Natalie, Associate Justice Dana Hargrove is not on the bench today. She's in her office, fully available to hear the revelations of a wayward daughter.

Turn and run! How did this become such a difficult day? She'd much prefer the mundane comfort of poring over data in her office computer.

But she resists the flight urge and places her shoulder bag in the plastic bin. With a smile at the young court officer manning the metal detector, she walks through without a beep. The X-ray of her shoulder bag reveals nothing dangerous inside, unless you count certain information on her cell phone related to a horrific murder. A threatening text message from a stranger. An audio recording of a detective manipulating an eyewitness.

Also on her cell phone, her outgoing text message to Janjak: "Thanks for taking the time to meet me yesterday. Just to assure you again, I'm keeping our meeting and everything you said entirely confidential! Your name will not appear in my study. I appreciate your help, and this concludes your participation in my research. I won't be contacting you again."

Max insisted on adding the last line because "this concludes your participation" didn't seem strong enough. Together, they went through many drafts before settling on the wording and sending the message. She asked Max, "Do you think I should forward a copy to the brother or answer him directly?" He was dead set against making any contact. "No. You never know what might provoke someone like that. It's best to ignore him." Natalie supposed that Janjak would update his brother, just like he told his brother about her in the first place. Her text to Janjak will have to be enough to get the Bernard brothers out of her hair.

At the lobby desk, Natalie's favorite guard is on duty. She eyes his nametag: Gary Overmeyer. The lobby desk seems to be Gary's usual assignment, a good spot for an amiable man who enjoys talking to people but also knows when to enforce the rules. There was a day she witnessed his amazing transformation when faced with a troublesome visitor to the court. Gary's big smile instantly disappeared under a stern show of authority, backed by a suggestion of force.

Gary is older than Natalie's parents. Maybe getting close to retirement? Gray and loose-jowled, but not unfit. He perks up when he sees her and doesn't need a reminder of her identity. "Miss Goodhue. Your mother is expecting you."

"Thank you." She glances down at the visitor log on his desk.

"Shall I sign in?"

"Already got you down. Just do me a favor and wear this." He hands her a paper nametag that says "Visitor." She peels off the backing and sticks it onto a shoulder of her winter coat.

Gary seems to approve. "Go on up. You know the way?"

She nods and hesitates as if a few more lines of small talk might save her. But she can think of nothing to say and heads for the elevator. No turning back now. This is really happening.

Upstairs, Nia welcomes her, cheerful as always. Soon enough, the judge appears and whisks Natalie into her office, closing the door behind them. Natalie dumps her shoulder bag and coat on the little round table in the corner. "Sorry to bother you at work, Mommy."

"Anytime. Never a bother. How is everything? You said this was something important. What's going on? Is it something I can help with?" As she says all these things, she walks toward her desk and around it, settling into the big leather swivel chair.

The office is small, an appropriate size for one of the newer judges on the court, as Natalie understands the hierarchy. Even so, Judge Hargrove looks regal here, framed in mahogany, law books and diplomas lining the walls. Not like Mommy with messy hair, in a bathrobe, drinking coffee on a Sunday morning, the last time Natalie saw her almost two weeks ago. That was the day she was awakened to the displeasure in her mother's voice when speaking of Professor Louden. No doubt that displeasure was evident on other occasions, but Natalie just didn't notice. She was tuned out, foolishly in the stars about working alongside a world-renowned expert in cognitive science. How juvenile.

"You know how I've been wanting to work on data from real cases, not just my simulation? Well, this is about that. I have to… I need to tell you… I guess I'll just go right for it." Natalie has been standing, glancing around the room without looking her mother in the eye. She sits down and their eyes meet across the desk. "I tried to get the data from Zach in the Stokes murder case, but he didn't have much. No recordings of the witness statements or the hearing he attended. So I contacted the witnesses myself."

The judge's eyes widen almost imperceptibly, a reaction Natalie doesn't miss. "You mean, the witnesses who were on the Brooklyn Bridge the night of the murder?"

"Yes. Those witnesses. One of them didn't want to talk to me. Wesley Guerrier. But the other one was very friendly. Janjak Bernard. We met for coffee and talked about the case."

"When did you see him?"

"Yesterday morning." The disapproval on the judge's face deepens, and Natalie makes a desperate attempt to lighten the mood. "Ugh! Really early, right after he got off his midnight shift."

A pause. "You know this is an open case, don't you? They're still trying to find the killer." An edge to her voice.

"I'm sorry, Mommy!" The words come out shaky and tears threaten. "I was worried about the way Dr. Louden butted into the case. I could tell you didn't like what he said on that news program. I had to find out if he was right or wrong. I had to find out *why* he did it!" Her voice breaks and the tears spill.

Her mother jumps up and comes around the desk, pulls Natalie up, and hugs her close. "If I sounded harsh just now, I didn't mean it. I just want to understand what happened." She pulls away and holds Natalie by the shoulders, giving her a warm look. "And whatever I may or may not think of Professor Louden, I'm sorry I didn't address it with you directly."

Natalie drops her head. "I should have…"

"No, *I* should have! And I'll say it now. You're right. I'm not pleased with that interview he gave or the affidavit he signed. I think it damaged the investigation and the reputations of good people. But that has nothing to do with you and your research." She guides Natalie back to the chair. "Come, sit." She takes the other chair on this side of the desk. They face each other.

Natalie grabs a tissue from a box on the desk and wipes her eyes and nose. "The problem is, now that I know more about the case, I think everything he said on that news program was wrong. I don't understand how he could be so wrong after watching the court hearing and seeing the police videos. It's so obvious to me that the witness IDs aren't reliable."

"You're saying the professor watched the witness Q&As with Detective Rodman?"

"Yes."

"I had no idea."

"He admitted it to Zach. Not right away. Kind of recently. At first, Zach only knew that Judge Kaplan invited his good buddy Dr. Louden into his office after the hearing."

"So, they're good buddies. I imagined as much. Your professor won a number of big cases for Seth when he was a defense attorney."

"Is that any reason to show him the witness statements in *this* case? I don't know why he did that."

"It's irregular, but maybe it's no more than two friends talking about something they're interested in. Seth was indulging a friend who's crazy about interview techniques. It's even possible Seth was fishing for a little moral support from an old pal to make him feel okay about his ruling in a tough case."

"Yeah, but what about later? Judge Kaplan had nothing to do with this case after it went to the grand jury. Why did Dr. Louden have to say on the news that the grand jury was wrong? Did he think he still had to stick up for his good buddy? Now that I know more about Janjak's testimony—"

"'Janjak'! Sounds like *you two* are good buddies."

"He was very nice to me. Easy to talk to. Interested in my research and excited about being a witness and testifying in court. He told me everything he saw the night of the murder. So now, I can't believe *any* cognitive expert would say that Janjak's identification of Corey McBride is airtight."

"Any expert, much less your professor."

Natalie nods and drops her head. "I don't know how he could be so wrong. Or if he knew he was wrong, why would he say those things?" She looks up at her mother, searching her face for an answer. "I've really lost respect for him. How can I keep working for him?"

Her mother leans forward and places a hand on her knee briefly, delivering a healing touch. "Your work isn't exactly for him. It's for you and for the world at large. Your research is valuable. Have faith in it. Is the professor conducting *your* survey and analyzing *your* data? No. You are, and you deserve credit for your contributions to the field."

"But my name will be associated with his."

"I don't see a downside. We're talking about a single unsupported opinion in one criminal case. Maybe you like him less, but Dr. Louden is a big name in the field. His work has been successfully implemented all over the country, to great benefit. Maybe we'll learn one day why he did what he did in this case, but I don't think it undermines the value of his research or yours. It certainly doesn't undercut your own scientific integrity, does it? The questions you're asking right now prove to me that integrity is foremost on your mind. It's engrained in who you are."

Mommy just has this way about her, doesn't she? Natalie almost starts crying again, not from despair, but from euphoric weightlessness, a huge burden lifted. "Thank you. You made me feel better."

"Well, you should feel better. You should feel proud of your daily work, even if," she smiles wryly, "I don't approve of what you did, meeting those witnesses."

"I know…"

"I understand why you did it, and I'm glad you told me, but

it was wrong. One of us will have to tell the investigating detective."

"Who's that?"

"Aurelina Vargas. You remember her, don't you?"

"Sure. She's good. She'll be much better than that Detective Rodman."

"Have you arranged any other meetings with Mr. Bernard?"

"No, and actually, Janjak's brother texted me—"

"His brother?"

"Yes, only because—this is what he said anyway—Janjak went through a lot with this case and he doesn't want me seeing him again, it would cause too much emotional trauma. I didn't quite believe it because Janjak was so happy to talk to me."

"What did the brother say exactly?"

"That it's best we don't meet again." She rushes on. "So I texted Janjak today and said I didn't need his help anymore. Thank you very much, but my research is complete, and everything we talked about remains confidential and anonymous." Natalie hopes her mother doesn't notice how she hasn't answered her question. She absolutely cannot show her that text message!

"Well, that's a wise thing you did. I'm glad you've cut it off—"

"But there's something else, Mommy. Something really important!"

Her mother perks up. "You *are* full of surprises today."

"Sorry. But this is the last surprise. I actually know way more than the professor about this case. I came across something he never saw. Only one other person knows about it." And Natalie launches into a description of Janjak's audio recording, the circumstances under which he made it, and her analysis of Detective Rodman's improper leading questions that shaped Janjak's testimony, ensuring his identification of Corey McBride.

"This is important," the judge says. "Makes me doubly glad that his coaching didn't get Corey indicted. The grand jury made the right credibility finding based on the witnesses' live testimony in the jury room."

"That detective is *so* incompetent! There should be consequences, don't you think?"

"Definitely. We have to get this recording to Lina."

"I have it on my cell phone."

"Can you AirDrop it to me now?"

Natalie gets up, retrieves her shoulder bag, and pulls out her phone. With a glance at her inbox, she sees that Janjak hasn't replied. Maybe he's sleeping after a long night at work. His brother's message glares back at her. She almost changes her mind about withholding it but realizes how badly her mother would freak if she saw it. And for what? That man can't possibly bother her after Janjak assures him there will be no further visits from that nosy grad student. She has backed off. *I won't be contacting you again.*

As Natalie looks for the audio recording, her mother backtracks. "Never mind. Don't send it to me. I shouldn't be in the middle of this. I'll have Lina contact you today so she can get it directly from you. She'll want to get the original from Mr. Bernard as well."

Natalie puts her phone away and gives her mother a big hug. "Thank you so much for everything, Mommy."

"Sweetie," she strokes Natalie's blonde head. "Please don't be afraid, ever, to talk to me. About anything, anytime. I love you. I'm always here for you."

Natalie knows this, has always known it. But when you set unattainable standards for yourself, and when you're blessed with a mother who exemplifies unattainable standards, confessions and cries for help don't come easily.

18 » LINK

WHAT DOES THIS mean? Questions race through Dana's mind as Natalie describes the "rehearsal" she heard on the audio recording. Rodman carefully instructed Bernard how to answer the questions and what to say when Corey's photo was shown. According to Bernard, Rodman also gave Wesley Guerrier the benefit of a "practice" session.

Was the detective so insecure that he felt the need to lock in the witnesses' testimony before recording it? Maybe he found *these* witnesses unusually nervous and worried that they would equivocate under pressure. Or, more likely, he suspected that they *wouldn't* be able to ID the photo of McBride and he needed to make it happen.

As Natalie frets about police ineptitude tainting the witnesses' testimony, Dana is focused on a problem far worse than mere incompetence. Kyle Rodman's behavior indicates more than a need for schooling in better interview techniques. He's an experienced detective, competent enough when he wants to be.

He was deliberately coaching the witnesses, doing his best to railroad Corey McBride.

Was it professional ambition that drove Rodman to "solve" the case at all costs? Does he harbor animus toward the McBrides? These possibilities don't fully explain his actions. If something in his relationship with Corey triggered a desire for payback, Dana isn't aware of it. She can reach only one inference from what she knows. Rodman picked a convenient scapegoat to divert attention away from the real killer.

She's eager to hear the recording, but before Natalie can AirDrop it to her phone, she blurts, "Never mind." She shouldn't get in the middle of this. The original recording and Natalie's copy should go directly to the lead investigator. Lina will compare them, analyze them, look for edits or alterations, and arrive at her own conclusions.

Having settled on a plan of action, Dana's thoughts return to family. Feeling a mix of tenderness and regret, she hugs her daughter tight, says "I love you," and sends her on her way. Her internal self-critic has emerged from hiding, a reminder that motherhood is forever. Although her children have become wise young adults of twenty-seven and thirty, Dana still flogs herself for her own mistakes and lost opportunities.

Natalie was reluctant to come to her. Why? The anticipated heat of her mother's judgment. A stern expression, a harsh tone, a hint of intolerance for anything less than perfection and virtue. Dana catches herself in these behaviors at times, wanting to scream, too late, *I didn't mean it*. She doesn't want to raise walls or cut off communication. She listens, doesn't she? Shows softness and love. She's seen a lot in her life, and her children know it. For them, she wants to be a fount of experience and perspective, open to talking, sharing, working things out, advising. Teaching, not lecturing, and learning at the same time. It goes both ways.

She has much to learn from her smart, accomplished, beautiful daughter. How brave was that? So courageous to contact the witnesses directly and embark on her own investigation! As wrong as it was, Dana gives Natalie high marks for chutzpah, wanting to find out for herself what motivates Dr. Louden to act the way he does. To be who he is. A jerk. Stronger terms come to mind, but Dana holds her tongue around Natalie. Tones it down because she understands her own bias, her strong attachment to the people he hurt with his baseless "opinion." The renowned expert did a bad thing, but it was only one thing and Dana doesn't have evidence of much else to hold against him, other than his arrogant personality.

Natalie was brave, but foolish. *Should I have been harder on her?* Caught up in regrets and self-analysis, Dana is forgetting the seriousness of Natalie's infraction. But the girl knows she was wrong, and that's what brought her here today, to come clean with her mother. Of all people, a budding expert in cognitive science understands the consequences of contacting witnesses in an unsolved murder case. Her involvement adds another layer of taint. Natalie knows better. A mother's rebuke wouldn't have been all that constructive.

And what was that about Bernard's brother? Another source of rebuke. He was angry at Natalie for dredging up the murder case, causing more "emotional trauma." With regret, again, Dana wishes she'd pressed harder to see that text message. She recalls the way Natalie rushed ahead (nervously?), failing to quote from it or give any details other than her surprise at having received it. Janjak Bernard wasn't emotionally distraught. He was excited to talk to her about the case. Well, we all know about protective brothers. Maybe this one should get credit for driving Natalie to the point of coming to see her mother today. A wakeup call, reminding her of the gravity of what she was doing.

After Natalie's departure, Dana spends no more than a minute with these thoughts before taking action. Her hand is on the receiver of her desk phone when it rings. Eyeing the caller ID, she recognizes the string of numbers with no name, a personal, non-official cell phone number given out to a select few. She picks up and says, "Well, what do you know? I was about to call you. Natalie was just here, and she's been looking into Professor Louden's involvement in the Stokes case. Long story short—"

"We've got our killer, Judge," Aurelina cuts in. "I have a DNA match. Jared asked me to put you in the loop."

This surprising news takes Dana's breath away. "You arrested someone?"

"Not yet. He came in this morning and left again before I had the lab results…"

"Came in…?"

"…but we've got a team looking for him now. I had to be careful who we picked. Jared gave me a few men from the DA Squad. You'll be pleased. Anyway, they're out looking for Kyle now."

"Kyle Rodman?"

Lina sighs, and her disgust comes through loud and clear in the single syllable of her response: "Yes."

With a quick apology for her daughter, Dana sums up Natalie's conversation with Bernard and the contents of his audio recording. "I haven't heard it, but the way Natalie describes it, Rodman was coaching the witnesses."

"Makes perfect sense," Lina says. "I've been looking at the Skype records and suspected he did a number on the witnesses."

"But… Kyle Rodman? Why?"

"We haven't figured out the motive. But the evidence nails him, so we'll find out in time. The DA wants him arrested and asked me to give you a heads-up before it hits the news."

"Thanks, Lina. Natalie still has a copy of that recording. Can you call her?" She gives Lina the number.

"I'll call her later, but for now I have to keep tabs on the team in the field. It shouldn't take them long to find him. Gotta go."

Dana replaces the receiver and realizes she's been standing for the entire conversation. Her heart races, palms sweat, muscles tense. That was good news, wasn't it? She should feel relieved and she does, in a way, but the angst remains. Random facts drift aimlessly, seeking a link. Something tells her this isn't over…

And then it hits, the horrifying possibility that clicks into place. The sunny face comes to mind, Natalie's positive outlook blinding her to evil under the surface. Instead of a criminal, she sees a detective guilty of atrocious interview techniques. And Bernard was so happy to be of help that it puzzled her to get a text message from… Janjak's *brother*? *He doesn't want me seeing him again; it would cause too much emotional trauma…*

Detective Rodman needs to cover his tracks. But how could he know about Natalie? Through Bernard. Is it a stretch to imagine the eager witness calling the detective to get his "okay" to participate in a research study? Not a stretch at all. And Dana said nothing to Lina about that text message from the "brother."

Quick. She finds the last number on the incoming call list of her desk set and hits dial. It rings in her ear as she rushes to the door, getting only halfway before she's yanked to a halt by the curly cord of her landline. She goes back, puts the receiver down, and hits the speaker button as it rings a second time, strides to the door on the third ring, and… Where does she think she's going? Trying to do two things at once. Tell Lina! Find Natalie! On the desk, her own mobile phone sits in silent rebuke next to this clunker as voice mail comes on. "Lina, Natalie got a text message telling her to back off. I think it was Rodman. He could be after her for that recording. She was just here. Send someone. Please! I'm going to look for her now."

She hangs up, grabs her cell phone, and runs for the door, through the anteroom into the hallway, passing a startled Nia on the way out.

Natalie is happier leaving the courthouse than she was when she arrived. The relief of having accomplished her mission puts her in the right mood when Gary engages her in a bit of inane chit-chat in the lobby.

He can't help it, of course. He's a diehard fan of Natalie's aunt.

The minute she steps out of the elevator, he snags her. All his duties are on hold for the moment. The lobby is empty except for Gary and a fellow court officer, the one who was manning the metal detector when she passed under it almost an hour ago.

"Natalie Goodhue!"

"Officer Overmeyer!"

"Please, call me Gary."

She walks up to him. "All right." She looks at the men one at a time, both standing behind Gary's desk with big grins on their faces.

"You're just the person we need to solve an argument," Gary says. "You got a minute to talk about my favorite actress?"

"Sure! Let me guess who that is." She gives him a sly smile.

"Gary told me I screened Cheryl Hargrove's niece this morning," the other officer says. "I didn't realize, but now I see the resemblance. Just as pretty."

"No way is anyone as pretty as Aunt Cheryl," she says, watching the color rise in the young officer's cheeks. He's embarrassed that he's gone too far with his comment in this day and age of sexual harassment training. Natalie doesn't mind what he said and appreciates his show of self-awareness.

Gary cuts in quickly, protectively. "We were just talking about the series *Plain Justice*."

"That's my favorite character she ever played," Natalie says. "Prosecutor Blaire Kendall."

"Reminds you of your mom?"

"Maybe a little."

"We were debating the best episode. Todd here says it's the finale of season two, and I say it's the finale of season three by a longshot. What do you say?"

"Hmm, tough choice." Natalie's head is so full of what she

19 » *PURSUIT*

COLDER THAN SIBERIA out here on the corner of 25th and Madison. A bright, sub-freezing day, tolerable in direct sunlight, away from the buildings. But Kyle Rodman shuns the light, seeks the shadows.

He doesn't have a plan. Hasn't even deleted the audio recording on Janjak Bernard's phone. He's not sure what to do with it. Maybe there's something there to help him. Solid proof that Corey McBride really is the killer and Detective Second Grade Kyle Rodman was right all along, grand jury be damned. Realistically, he knows that's a hard sell. Listening to the recording, he hears the manipulation in his own voice. But if he tries to delete it, there's no room for mistake. Can't leave a copy in the cloud, and not sure he could find one if it's there. Besides the original, he'll have to delete the copy on the Goodhue kid's phone. And now she's gone to her mother! He'll have to shake it out of her whether she gave Judge Hargrove a copy. If not, well, then, there's only *one* witness to scare off. Or get rid of.

His thoughts ricochet without settling on an answer. Maybe it's best to do nothing at all. Explain his interview methodology if confronted.

One thing no longer worries him. He's taken care of Bernard. This morning at the diner was the second time they'd met eye to eye, but Bernard was clueless. Good. No sudden awareness of a just told her mother that the season finales of *Plain Justice* arer foremost in her mind, notwithstanding her unofficial status a trivia expert in all things Cheryl Hargrove. She fakes it. "I'm wit you on this one, Gary. Finale of season three."

Gary elbows Todd in the ribs. "What did I say? Her last lines are classic! You know the scene. After she says, 'Take him!' like that." Gary impersonates, straightening up and sticking out his chest. "The agents are slapping cuffs on her ex while he's blubbering, 'But Blaire! I-I'm sorry!' She looks at him like this," Gary cocks his head, "and says, '*No* one is more disappointed than I am, Jed.'"

Natalie smiles at Gary's rendering. "Yeah, assistant DA Jed Markham was her ex-lover who turned out to be crooked. Tampered with the evidence in a big case."

'"No one,'" Gary repeats, enjoying Natalie's attention.

"What a good memory you have!"

"Pathetic," says Todd, eyeing Gary's profile. But then he glances at Natalie and stutters, "I-I meant Gary's acting, not your aunt! She was *great* in that scene."

Todd is embarrassed again, and Natalie thinks she'd better head out before this gets any worse. They exchange another bit of cheery banter and then she takes her leave.

subconscious recognition of his face or voice from their encounter on the bridge. "Nice to finally meet you," Bernard said. As far as he knew, their contacts have always been on the phone or virtual, on screen. Kyle's status as a detective, an authority figure, had a sleight-of-hand effect from the start. When reporting information about a murder, a witness would hardly expect he'd reached the killer when he called the police tip line.

Facing each other in the cramped booth of the noisy diner, Kyle reminded him about his slip of the tongue. *I only have the audio.* Got Bernard to admit that he'd made a recording of their Q&A. Kyle laid into him then. Got him good and scared, as he should be. "It's an unauthorized recording. You know that's illegal, don't you?" Not exactly, but Kyle didn't go into details.

"I...but you said there would be a hearing, so I wanted to remember everything—"

"That's no reason to record it behind my back. This isn't about memorizing your testimony! The court strictly forbids it. Contempt of court, on top of the charge for illegal recording."

Bernard was trembling by then. Kyle can have that effect on people, and he uses it when he needs to, whenever he wants something. Like that night almost two years ago, on the Lower East Side, when he saw what he wanted and took it. But where did *that* lead him? A week later, to the Brooklyn Bridge in the dead of night. After that, a bogus investigation, and now this—backed into a corner looking for a way out.

"You're facing some serious shit here," Kyle said. "Tell me everyone and every device that has a copy."

"Just my phone. And the researcher's phone. That's all. I didn't send it to anyone else. I didn't tell anyone else. I swear."

Kyle held out his hand. "I have no choice. I'll have to confiscate your phone."

"Okay." The surface was slick with sweat when he handed it over. "But I need it. I don't have money for another."

"We'll do forensics and give it back. This recording belongs to the investigation. You have no right to it."

"And, what about…" His eyes actually filled with tears! "Are you going to arrest me?"

Complete control over the subject was far easier than Kyle had imagined. "That's yet to be seen. If you cooperate fully and keep this to yourself, I can cut you a break."

"I'll cooperate."

"Not a word to anyone. Don't talk to that graduate student—"

"Not again! Never, I swear."

"And if anyone asks, keep our conversation to yourself. You never made a recording and you never saw me today."

Bernard nodded vigorously, sending a tear down his cheek. He swiped it away.

Now, hand in pocket, Kyle fingers the edges of the little iPhone, an older model with a cracked screen. In his other jacket pocket, he clutches the cell phone that "Janjak's brother" used to text Natalie Goodhue, telling her to fuck off. An hour later, on Bernard's phone, Kyle received her text to Janjak: "This concludes your participation in my research. I won't be contacting you again." All good, he thought, but still, he debated what to do about her copy of Bernard's recording. He decided to track her for a while and see what comes to mind. After removing the SIM card and battery from Bernard's phone, he used the tracking app on his other phone to find her.

No one has followed him today, downtown to the diner or here, to the courthouse. He's sure of it. After getting Bernard's call at eight this morning, he brushed shoulders with Vargas on his way out of the station—a reminder to take extra precautions. She knows his personal cell number, the one Bernard called, and she's able to track his city-issued unmarked vehicle, a '19 Chevy Caprice. Before taking the subway downtown, he put his cell phone in the glovebox of the Caprice and pulled out another, the phone he keeps in a hidden cavity under the passenger seat, available for his special needs. The number is registered in his mother's name. Some years ago she "lost" this phone and he persuaded her to get another with a different number. Today he programmed it to show the name "Bernard, T." on the outgoing caller ID.

At ten fifteen, fighting his mounting panic, Kyle sees the young blonde kiss her boyfriend goodbye on the courthouse steps. What has she told him? What will she tell her mother, the judge? He's antsy with the need to act. Catch her unawares, somewhere hidden from view. Will he get the chance? Maybe he'll have to "arrest" her. His handcuffs are attached to his belt next to his shield, and he carries his service weapon in a shoulder holster. That's the way to do it. Arrest her for obstruction of justice, interference with a murder investigation. It's even plausible. The girl is messing around with a murder witness in an open case. After the arrest, there will be an unfortunate mistake with the evidence. Somehow, the recording will be erased, inadvertently of course.

She's been inside now for half an hour, long enough to freeze his butt off. His nose and ears are ice. He considers ducking into a coffee shop while keeping an eye on the GPS, but he doesn't want to miss anything, the sliver of a moment that will reveal his chance. How much longer can this take? Doesn't the judge have work to do?

He'll stick it out. Kyle is no stranger to waiting and watching. Opportunities arise, ripe for the taking. Like that night before lockdown, March 2020, an opportunity too convenient to pass up. Revelry, everyone drunk and distracted. The bar was so packed, no one seemed to notice when Kyle slipped inside for a minute, spotted Marlon, and slipped out again. He wasn't going to join a crowd where people knew him. On the street, a pint of Kentucky bourbon kept him company while he loitered in the shadows, ducking into an alley whenever a fellow cop walked by.

It was early spring, chilly but bearable, not icy like today. He told himself to go slow, but small sips tend to add up over a period of two hours. By the time he was on the move again, half the pint was warming his belly down to the handle of the sharpened knife in his belt. No guns, registered or unregistered, service, or personal. He'd calculated the difficulties: noise, darkness, aim and proximity, shells, traces. He knew how to kill without a sound if he got the chance.

During his long wait outside the pub, he was having thoughts like the ones he's having right now, outside the courthouse. *It can't be much longer. Will I get a chance…?*

But there was one thought he *didn't* have while waiting for McBride and Stokes to emerge. It didn't occur to him to frame Corey. Not then. That's the irony of it. Kyle has no love for Brown-Noser McBride, but he didn't need to shove him under the bus until those two witnesses showed up. Out of nowhere. Shattering the perfection.

At about two thirty, McBride and Stokes pushed out the door, staggering from drink, embroiled in a heated exchange. It was easy to follow them, no one around. By the looks of it, the bromance had gone sour, Corey bitching and nagging, Marlon holding him off, eventually cooling him down when they got close to the bridge. Then, how sweet. An embrace with manly pats on the back before they parted.

Desolate, quiet, empty. Kyle made sure with a quick scan, two seconds. He saw McBride's backside as he sloppily trotted away toward the subway station. In the far distance, a few tiny, dark figures rushed here and there, near City Hall Park and the Municipal Building. No one close enough to see what he was about to do. Repeat that. No one nearby.

How did he miss those two?

And so the plan had to change. He became McBride. And it wasn't implausible. They're about the same height and weight. Similar skin tone and short haircut. Kyle is fifteen years older, but who would notice in the dim lighting? And was it luck or subconscious design that they were similarly dressed? Kyle *did* see what Corey was wearing before he left the stationhouse for The Book and Brew. From the choices in his locker, Kyle put on a light-colored polo shirt and his navy-blue jacket, the one that half the force wears, thanks to the PBA fundraiser for the Widows' and Children's Fund.

The knife and jacket, bloodstains and all, have long since been crushed into the bed of a NYC Sanitation truck and sent to a landfill. He recalls his long jog home in the middle of the night, carrying the jacket inside-out and balled up around the knife. He was sweating too much to notice the brisk air.

Stokes. Kyle's nose fills with the memory of his stench. The booze, the apricot-scented pomade, the sweat of shock and fear mixed with blood. Eyes popped wide in surprise, no sound, Kyle's "hug" perfectly placed, one arm above his shoulders and wrapped around the neck, hand over the mouth, the other finding that hollow under the ribs, the place to thrust upward, at the exact angle to do the job.

Too late, Kyle felt the fingernails digging into his neck as Marlon crumpled to the ground. He would have taken care of those fingers, but then, out of nowhere he heard, "Everything okay?" A glance upward, a fleeting connection. What rotten luck. And rotten luck again that an overeager graduate student is nosing around where she doesn't belong.

A few minutes after eleven, the GPS indicates that Natalie Goodhue is on the move. He sees her descend the front steps of the courthouse on 25th Street. Will she go east to Park Avenue, or west, to Madison?

Dana is dialing Gary in the lobby as she runs for the elevator. The first ring sounds in her ear as she punches the "L" button hard, again and again, *come on*, her emotions battling the pull of reason.

Doors close, boxing her inside with her overreaction. False assumptions? Rodman didn't send the text. It really was the "brother." Whoever it was could be bluffing. Just enough to get Natalie to back off. But if it was Rodman, and if he tries to harm her and fails, he will only expose himself. That means if he tries, he *has* to succeed. That means Dana isn't going to worry about looking ridiculous until she finds her daughter, safe and sound.

Come on, come on, come on. "Lobby," he answers as the doors open.

"Gary!" Her voice is in both his ears, the phone receiver and from twenty feet away. Their eyes meet. "Judge Hargrove." They abandon their phone connection.

"Did you see Natalie? Is she still here?" Dana sounds frantic but can't help it. So angry at herself for wasting precious minutes. How long was she lost in thought about her relationship with Natalie? Then there was Lina's phone call, more ruminations, her awakening, her attempt to call back when the detective is busy and has no reason to answer. *Just spoke to Dana, told her what was going on, no need to pick up…*

"She left maybe two minutes ago," Gary says. "We were debating the best episodes of *Plain Justice*—"

"I need your help, Gary. We have to find her! She can't be far." Dana's mind stalls on a way to explain. *Threatening text message. Killer on the loose. Possible stalker.* Histrionics. The level-headed judge going bonkers. What comes out is this: "I'm worried someone's following her."

Gary doesn't need more of an explanation. He sees mother love and panic. This is critical. "Todd, come with me. No, wait. We need coverage." Todd is manning the screening area, people coming in the door now.

While Gary radios for assistance on his two-way, Dana is already headed out the front door, dialing Natalie's number.

Another two minutes wasted. Why didn't she call Natalie from the get-go? Could have caught her in the lobby when she was chatting about Cheryl's damn TV show!

Behind her, Gary is calling out, "Judge, hold on!"

Not wise to go outside without a coat, but she doesn't feel the cold. In her skirt suit and low heels, she clunks down the stone steps, oblivious to how she looks and the breach of protocol. A court officer always escorts a judge to her mode of transportation, providing a layer of protection against a public that isn't always friendly.

Pick up, pick up, pick up! Dana has never tracked her kids by phone. She wishes she'd figured out how to do it. Too late now. Natalie, where are you? *Pick up.*

After the fourth ring she answers. "Hi, Mommy!" Sunny as ever.

The young voice jolts Dana out of her buzzing electric field into a crystal moment of calm. Let's do this carefully, without raising undue alarm. Keep our heads. Stirring up panic won't help the situation.

Detective Vargas is on the line with Gilbert Herrera when Judge Hargrove's call comes in. She lets it roll to voice mail. Important details are being discussed.

They've already lost so much time. The team has been on the case, but it was too slim to make an arrest without a DNA match. Word from the lab came in at ten thirty, almost two and a half hours after Lina bumped into Kyle leaving the precinct.

They exchanged their usual tight smiles and tense good mornings. Kyle is keeping up appearances, still invested in his charade of being on the clock. Just another ordinary day in the field, working his cases. He'll be back. Maybe. Recently, he's been hard to find, failing to produce results on his assigned cases. She believes he's out doing whatever he thinks he needs to do today to cover his tracks. Either that, or this is it. He's already fled.

The new information from Dana gives her pause. Janjak Bernard secretly recorded Kyle's manipulative tactics. Is there any way Kyle knows about that recording? Natalie told her mother that Janjak confided in her alone, no one else.

Lina tells Gil about it now. "She just left the courthouse, on her way to the university."

"Why'd the kid have to get in the middle of this? Not good."

"She says Bernard told no one else about the recording."

"Doesn't mean I like it."

With a smile, Lina imagines Gil's face as he says this. He's the master of telling it like it is. Dana will be pleased he's on the case. A longtime friend and colleague, Gil first earned his reputation working undercover, his rough looks an asset. A wiry, crooked body, craggy, pock-marked skin and asymmetrical features. He's cleaned up nicely in his advancing years, gray and groomed, distinguished, and highly regarded as head of the DA's Squad. Pushing seventy and still going strong, thriving on tough cases.

Gil and Lina are behind the scenes on this one, in their respective offices and on the phone. Veterans of a certain age are not the best candidates for chasing and tackling young fugitives. They each assigned two members for the takedown team. Lina chose men she can trust, officers who worked closely with Marlon and are loyal to him, Hakeem Farah and Donnell Robertson. Gil's investigators, Luis Sandoval and Dylan Pierce, have been nosing around uptown in Kyle's neighborhood, his apartment building and places he frequents. A neighbor saw him leave for work at seven thirty this morning and he hasn't been back.

Hakeem and Donnell have been poking into Kyle's work areas at the station. Broke into his locker, rifled through his desk, read his emails on the NYPD system which, by employee agreement, are open to inspection. Searched his unmarked detective ride and found his personal cell phone in the glovebox. So, no way to track him by car or by phone, and nothing else lends a clue as to his current whereabouts.

Meanwhile, Lina has been checking on the witnesses. Even before speaking to Dana, she suspected that Kyle had coached them and might now be reasserting his influence in a bad way. She called Wesley Guerrier at work, identified herself, and set up a meeting for next week. He told her Janjak Bernard is still working the night shift. Lina kept the call short, just enough to confirm Guerrier was safe. Kyle wouldn't do anything rash in a public building downtown, now, would he? Next, she called Bernard, but his phone was dead.

"I've asked Hakeem and Donnell to check on Janjak Bernard," she tells Gil. "Just in case Kyle had the same idea this morning. They left for Brooklyn maybe three minutes ago. They'll find out if he sent that audio recording to anyone else. What are Sandoval and Pierce up to?"

"Left Rodman's hood twenty minutes ago. On their way to talk to the sister." Karly Springfield works for a dentist on West 23rd Street in Chelsea. "Almost there now."

"Worth a shot, I guess."

"But you're thinking…"

"…that Kyle isn't close to his sister."

"So, no reason she knows where he is."

"It's unlikely."

A pause. Then Gil voices the concern at the back of both their minds. "This thing with the Dane's kid… I don't like it. Give me the girl's number."

Lina reads it to him and says, "Hold the line a second. Dana just left me a voice mail. Maybe there's something new."

A minute later, she comes back on. "Gil! Change of plans."

"We're sending the team to Madison Square Park?"

"Affirmative."

"I already have a bead on the girl."

Natalie turns right at the bottom of the courthouse stairs. The slap of cold on her face feels good after the stress and emotional release in that overheated building. No rush to get back. She'll just take a few minutes to walk and forget everything before she starts her workday.

She crosses the avenue and heads into Madison Square Park. Bare trees, empty benches, and patches of old, dirty snow line the pathways. People, not many, hurry on their way. A few talk into the air for their ear pods to pick up, others tilt their hat-covered heads down, intent on the path ahead.

Natalie's hat is in her pocket and will stay there until she cools down. She's grateful anew for her mother's understanding. *Why do I always build these things up in my mind?* She should have known it wouldn't be as bad as she'd imagined.

Her phone rings in her pocket and she puts it to her ear. "Hi, Mommy! Thanks so much for talking to me. I feel better about everything."

"Good! But I just thought of something else. Are you still close to the courthouse?"

"Not super close. In the park. You sound out of breath."

"I ran downstairs to try and catch you."

"Why?"

"I forgot to give you that book you wanted to borrow."

"What book? Oh, yeah." Wanted to borrow? Not really, Natalie thinks. It's not important. A comparative law study of criminal cases in the U.S. and France resulting in miscarriages of justice based on mistaken identity. "I can come get it another time. I'm on the other side of the park."

"I'll walk toward you then. I'm already outside. You won't

have to come the whole way."

What an important book this is! "Thanks, Mommy, but go back inside and get warm. I can see you this weekend." Her phone beeps. The screen shows "Accept" in green and "Decline" in red under the name "Bernard." Janjak must have gotten her text. "I've got another call. Can I call you back?"

"Don't hang up! Put me on hold."

Geez. "Okay. This'll only take a minute." She has to catch it before it rolls to voice mail. Convince him she *really* meant what she said. "Hello, Janjak. Did you get my text?"

"Yeah," says a low voice in a slow drawl. "He got it. This is Janjak's brother."

She stops short, pulls the phone away from her ear and looks. Missed the "T" after "Bernard." But the brother sounds different than she imagined. Something familiar about his voice, but nothing at all like Janjak's. Shouldn't he have the same kind of Haitian Creole accent?

She starts walking again, slower, measuring her words. "So, if he got my text, he knows I'm not going to contact him anymore. I don't need him for the study. Isn't that what you want?"

"I know that I told you to fuck off. But you went running to your mother instead."

She jerks to a stop, all the air squeezed out of her lungs. Pivots madly in a circle. On the path opposite, a man is talking on his phone, but he turns his back to her and walks away. Other people don't seem to notice her. Where? Where is he?

"Yeah, I can see you," the man says. "Calm down and we'll have a talk."

"You're not his brother. Who are you?" Natalie keeps searching. She doesn't know which way to go to get away from him.

"Smart girl. No, I'm *not* his brother. But you'll want to talk to me about this. I know you have that recording."

The last word triggers a connection. It's the voice she heard on Janjak's recording. Detective Kyle Rodman. Where is he? How can she get away? She picks a direction and starts walking, fast.

"Slow down. Stop right there. Sit down on that bench."

She's looking everywhere but where she's going and bumps right into it, hitting her shin hard. She buckles, rubs her leg, straightens up again, and feels a powerful hand grabbing her arm, pulling it into the small of her back. The shock makes her drop the phone in her other hand. She can't see his face, and now he's yanking her free hand into her back too.

"I'm a police officer. You're under arrest!"

"What for?" He pushes her forward, past her phone, and stomps on it before shoving her down onto the park bench. She sits sideways on one thigh, her back to him.

"Obstruction of justice. Illegal recording. Interference with a murder investigation."

Natalie hears the metallic whir of handcuffs opening and feels the hard metal on her wrists as he clamps them shut.

This can't be! She's trembling violently but tries to reason with him. "My mother is a judge. She didn't say I did anything illegal."

"Why would she? You're her little angel." His voice drips with sarcasm. "I bet she's trying to fix this case for you right now." He bends over and picks up her cracked phone. For the first time, she sees part of his face in profile. A cheekbone sharp as an arrowhead. A clifflike brow over a dark eye that shines with arrogance, battling his desperation.

The line goes dead when Natalie takes the incoming call. Is Dana still connected? She's been standing on the east side of Madison Avenue waiting for traffic to clear. She crosses now and enters the park at a fast clip. *Other side of the park*. It's not a big park, but "other side" could mean a couple of directions. She scans forward, left, and right. People walking, none of them Natalie, but then she spots an ominous figure in the distance.

More than a city block away, a man leans into a tree trunk, peaking around the side. His back is to Dana, but she sees enough of his posture and stealth to know who he is. On the phone? Elbow bent, hand to ear. She follows the direction of his gaze and finds Natalie, fifty feet away from him, spinning around in place, trying to find the person who speaks into her ear. Dana starts toward them just as Natalie darts away, not minding where she's going and bumps into a bench. The blow halts her, and please, no! Rodman is fast behind.

Dana breaks into a run, takes three long strides, and… She's on the ground.

How? In a blink. Up one second, down the next, kissing asphalt.

"Judge!" Gary is behind her.

Sprawled out long, Dana lifts her head and sees her phone on the path where it slid out of reach.

"A patch of ice here." Gary is on her left, bending over, maybe wondering if he'll be able to stand up again if he squats down to help her. Todd says, "Let me, Gary." The younger man comes up on the other side, drops into a crouch, and gently grasps her right upper arm. "Are you okay, Judge?"

"No, yes, I'm okay!" But she isn't okay. She's trying to ignore the pain in her left forearm as she pushes up to sitting.

"That's a slick patch there," Gary says. "We saw you go down."

"I don't think you hit hard enough to break anything," Todd says.

Oh, why are these men wasting their efforts on her? "My daughter! Over there!" She tosses her head. "A man is chasing her. Call for backup!"

"Where?" Gary scans the near distance and gets on his two-way radio.

"To the left, closer to Fifth Avenue!" She tosses her head again, the only thing she can use to indicate. Todd holds her right arm, and every movement of her left sends shooting pains from wrist to elbow. "Go! Run! Don't you see her?"

Gary moves haltingly forward and to the left, right and left again, searching, apparently not seeing what she describes.

Dana cradles her left arm in her right. Todd holds her good elbow and says, "You hurt your arm, didn't you?"

Gary walks further away from them but seems uncertain, not hurrying toward anything, talking to someone on the two-way. To Todd she says, "I'm okay, really. Go with Gary." But he's helping her up now, hand under her elbow, his other arm around her back.

By the time she's up, Natalie and Rodman are nowhere to be seen.

Sandoval and Pierce get word from Gil and abandon their trip to the dentist. Bad luck for Rodman that his sister Karly happens to work in a dental office on West 23rd Street, mere blocks from Madison Square Park.

Farah and Robertson aren't as close. Lina caught them before they started over the bridge into Brooklyn. "They've turned around, but they're still ten minutes out," she tells Gil. "Your two will have to take him down. If he's there." She still holds out the hope they'll find Natalie alone, her victimhood a figment of Dana's imagination.

"Better that way," Gil says. Not boasting. Just a fact. Rodman knows Lina's men, but he's never met Gil's. "They can get right up on him."

"Careful, now. Dana's daughter—"

"Like my own."

Gil is multitasking, tracking Natalie's phone, monitoring NYPD frequencies, and keeping lines open to Lina and his two men. On his screen, the pin shakes and jerks within the southwest quadrant of the park. Sandoval and Pierce are nearing 23rd and Fifth when an alert comes over the NYPD band. Can't be a coincidence, must be Natalie and her pursuer.

"D'you get that?" Gil asks his men. Someone in the area called it in. Who? Gil's betting on the Dane. She must've pulled her court officers from their sanctuary of noble principles, marble, and fine art! Out of the clouds, down to earth, feet on the ground.

"Got it," Pierce says. He's riding radio and Sandoval's at the wheel. "Possible 1 - 3 - 5 in progress, southwest park." New York Penal Code for kidnapping and unlawful imprisonment.

"This fool's grabbing Natalie out in the open?" A desperate move, but nothing surprises Gil. He's seen everything.

"We're on foot," Pierce says. "Going in now, Broadway and 23rd."

With the girl in cuffs and her broken phone in his pocket, Rodman snaps alert to the implications of his improvised plan. This'll work. He'll make it work. He's an officer of the law acting on probable cause for a valid arrest. That doesn't change even if the recording eventually disappears "by accident." With one hand on her cuffed wrists, he unzips his jacket and tucks an end into the back of his belt, revealing his shield and maybe a flash of shoulder holster to any passerby who gets too curious.

But the girl won't shut up. "I didn't make that recording. You can have it! I wasn't going to use it."

It's too open here. People around. He looks for cover, sees a clump of trees and bushes that will give partial camouflage. It's the best he can do. He grabs her elbow, tells her to shut up, and pushes her off the path, behind the bench, into the bushes.

They stand inside a circle of tree trunks. Fuck! From a certain angle, anyone can see them, but he'll be quick. She's weak and scared, won't take long to convince. He even recites a shortened version of *Miranda*. Something for the girl to tell mom when describing her brief brush with the law.

Gil's men have seen what they need to see, take cover, and discuss a plan.

"Holster, left armpit. Does he carry anywhere else?"

"Vargas says no, but not a hundred percent."

"Sick move, cuffing her in public."

"Making like an arrest."

"Legit?"

"Yeah."

"So we'll play along with him."

"Not both of us at once. He'll turn and run."

"Take him front and back?"

"Yeah, eleven and five."

"But if he sees only one, more chance he'll draw."

"Then we wait for backup."

Pierce sneaks a look over his partner's shoulder. Rodman is oblivious to the world, getting rough with his prisoner. "We can't wait."

They'll split up. They know their strengths and weaknesses. Sandoval is better with words; Pierce has the muscle. Wrist to chin, Pierce tells Gil, "Moving in now."

Tears stream down her face, and she won't quit her manic defense through dripping snot and quivering lips. "I said, zip it!" Her eyes go wide as Kyle tightens the vise, maximum pressure around her skinny arm. He gives her a good shake. "Didn't you hear your rights?"

She nods repeatedly.

"Shut up then."

But the hiccups and choking sobs won't stop, pathetic and sickening.

"You want these cuffs off? You're looking for a break?"

She shudders and looks down. Her weakness rankles him. The privileged A-student know-it-all thinks she can tell a detective with twenty years on the streets how to police. Scaring her off is too easy, won't extinguish the fire inside him. She deserves worse.

"If you want this arrest to go away, you'll do what I tell you."

She's whimpering now, not even a nod. Kyle shakes her again and she gasps.

"You hear me? You'll do what I say!" He two-hands her shoulders and shoves her hard, snapping the back of her head into a tree trunk.

The judge's daughter is on the ground when Investigator Luis Sandoval casually walks up to Detective Kyle Rodman and gives him a big smile. Luis is a good-looking man with a sparkle in his eye, a smooth storyteller. He knows where he's at and what's likely to be believed.

Sandoval's shield flops on his chest from a chain around his neck. He holds it up, knowing that Rodman is too far away to see the details. "How's it going, Officer? Luis Sandoval from the 13th."

Rodman quickly bends and pulls his captive up from the ground, gentler with her now that he has company, a fast mood change from a minute ago. Luis is steadily approaching and notices the cringe of revulsion on the young woman's face as

Rodman takes her arm.

"Need any help with that arrest?"

"Nah. All good. Got it covered. Obstruction charge."

Luis keeps smiling as he walks closer. "Looked like she might've been resisting too." But Natalie Goodhue is the picture of docility, shackled and limp, face wet with tears. Despite her apparent revulsion, she obediently endures the aggressor's hand on her arm.

Luis flashes her a look full of empathy, but the sparkle is fleeting. She'll have to pick up the message quickly. He doesn't dare do anything to reveal his plan to the target. For now, Rodman seems to believe Sandoval's allegiance to his brother officer.

"No problem," Rodman says. "Everything under control." To prove it, maybe, he drops his hand from the subject's arm and sneers at her. "She ain't going nowhere."

His brief shift of attention gives Luis an opportunity to flick his eyes past Rodman's shoulder to Dylan Pierce, who stealthily approaches from behind. A signal.

Luis continues to distract with questions—"You got backup coming? Where's your ride?"—as they move in and pounce, overpowering their prey! Rodman is immobilized, panini pressed, the stuffing inside a muscle sandwich. Luis two-hands Rodman's left, bending and squeezing it up between their chests, and Dylan two-hands the right arm, yanks it back, twisting it at the elbow, pulling the hand up between his shoulder blades. Rodman grunts in pain. He won't be reaching for his gun. In another sudden move, Luis twists and yanks the left arm behind to meet the other. As they cuff and disarm him, Dylan says, "You're under arrest for the murder of Marlon Stokes."

But what of the other prisoner? Somewhere in the middle of the excitement, Natalie lets out a cry and drops to her knees. Crumpled and sobbing, arms pinned behind her back, she's still a captive, awaiting her freedom. Luis and Dylan are patting down the detective, pulling all pockets inside out and emptying them in a search for other weapons or dangerous objects. Finally, Luis pulls out a pants pocket and the keys fall to the ground. With an arm around her shoulder, Luis helps Natalie to her feet and unlocks the cuffs.

Rubbing her wrists, Natalie looks up to see her mother awkwardly rushing toward her, cradling her left arm as a court officer escorts her by the elbow. Not minding their pain, mother and daughter fall into a tight embrace. For a long while they hold each other close, feeling the air enter their lungs, the release of tension, the glorious relief. Minutes pass in cascading emotion, their fears calmed and mistakes forgotten. Dana pulls back and holds Natalie at arms' length. Their eyes catch and hold with a twinkle through the tears. Nothing need be said as they gradually awaken to the noise and hubbub of the gathering crowd.

Kyle Rodman now has more company than he bargained for. Within a few minutes, it has turned into a regular party with Kyle the center of attention. In order of appearance: Luis and Dylan, Gary and Todd, two units of two each from the 13th Precinct responding to the radio call, and last but not least, Lina's men, Hakeem and Donnell.

And back in their respective offices, Gil and Lina heave huge sighs of relief.

20 » *MOTIVES*

DANA CONVINCES EVAN they're fine, no need to cancel his afternoon lecture at the law school. "We'll be out of here soon." She holds the phone to ear with her right hand, looking away from her left forearm where it rests on a little side table.

"You sure?"

"Positive."

Unlike Evan, the younger teacher in their family has canceled her small seminar with the undergrads. Natalie sits in a corner of the procedure room watching the orthopedist apply a cast to her mother's forearm and wrist. Dana suffered a hairline fracture when she caught her weight on the left hand to break her fall. Natalie has been seen and released with a few minor injuries: a bump on the back of her head, bruises on her knees, and friction burns on her wrists.

Any emotional or psychological damage? They'll take stock when the excitement of the day ebbs into the quiet reflections of evening. For now, the banter has remained superficial, with plenty of laughter about Dana's failure to deliver that book Natalie wanted to borrow.

"I'll head home right after my lecture," Evan says.

"Good. We'll see you there. Natalie will be joining us for dinner." Dana shoots a look with raised eyebrows at her daughter. "Maybe Max too, right?"

"Wait a minute!" Natalie waves at the doctor who's on the verge of wrapping the cast with layers of white fiberglass material. "Don't you have pink?"

"White is fine," Dana says.

"So boring!"

The doctor points to a rack of supplies. "A lot of choices here! Blue, gray, orange, seafoam, yellow…"

"Seafoam! That's so pretty, Mommy!"

"What's going on there?" Evan says in Dana's ear.

"Nothing much." She turns to the doctor. "I'm fine with any color my daughter wants." Natalie sits up taller, smiles brightly, and silently applauds in approval.

"Did I hear color choices? Are you two on a shopping spree?"

"Kind of. Tonight, I'll model what I picked out. A private show, just for you."

"Sounds exciting. Can't wait."

"It'll be fun. We have reason to celebrate. It's Friday night, a killer is behind bars, and Max did well on his screen test today. We'll all be hungry. What are you fixing for dinner?"

"What am I fixing…?"

"I'm afraid you're on cooking duty tonight."

"Is that so?"

"I'll make it easy on you. That leftover prime rib goes great in sandwiches. For tomorrow, you'll have to come up with something else."

"So, I'm on cooking duty tomorrow too."

"Yes, and the day after tomorrow, and…"

"And what?"

Dana whispers to the doctor, "How long will this be on?"

"About six weeks."

To Evan: "Six weeks, darling."

"A mere six weeks, she says, all honey and sweetness."

"You know how I *love* your cooking."

* * *

Dexter Jackson hears the electronic chime on the front door of the Friendship Mission, followed by three footsteps in the tiny room. He stands up from his crouch behind the counter and faces a young woman on the other side, luminous eyes finding his. Her emotional energy radiates and grips him hard. She's sad, conflicted, a little scared and hopeful, anticipating a connection.

"Rihanna," he says. "How are you?" It's a Saturday, the busiest day at the Mission, but they're alone at the moment.

"Hey, XT. I need someone to talk to."

He cringes a bit from the sound of his former moniker, remembering that he identified himself that way the first time they met. But he puts on a cheery voice and says, "You came to the right place!" This morning, he saw a news article that suggests the reason for her visit. "Should I close up shop while we talk?"

She looks around nervously. "That'd be cool."

"Okay, then." He grabs his little cardboard clock with the moving hands, positions them for a half hour hence under the words "RETURNING AT," and puts it in his front window before locking the door. When he comes back to the counter, Rihanna is looking down at her phone, touching and scrolling. "You remember that first time you saw me? The day we met?" She looks up at him.

"Sure do." He compares his mental picture of her from that day nearly two years ago to the Rihanna he sees today. Maybe sixteen then, eighteen now, with a hard-knocks maturity trying to toughen that youthful face. She's bundled up for the cold weather, but he guesses that her clothing under the winter coat is more conservative now, less self-consciously screaming a teenage desire to be noticed. She wears no makeup and has abandoned the fashionable braiding with extensions, her natural hair slicked back in a small ponytail. "That was right after Chug died," Dexter says.

She nods and shows him the screen on her phone. "Did you

see this? They caught the killer." The culprit's face fills half the screen. An official NYPD photo of the detective who came to the Mission incognito, pretending to be looking for Chug. Would've been a couple of months after he stabbed Officer Stokes to death.

"Yes, I saw the news. Hallelujah. Justice will be served."

"Justice for sure." She lowers her hand to the counter, phone resting in her open palm. With a glance of disgust at the screen, she jerks away like it's a hot coal. The phone clatters onto the counter. Her beautiful brown eyes fill with tears. "But, but I… It's all my…" She might crumple and collapse.

Dexter runs for a folding chair and sets it up behind her. "Sit!" He manages to guide her down into the seat, and she buries her head in her hands.

He spies boxes of tissues on the shelf of donated household goods. Odd things find their way into his Mission. When he accepted these tissues, he was skeptical of the donor's definition of "essential." Today, that definition is realized. He rips open a box and gives a handful to Rihanna, then grabs another folding chair and sits next to her.

In a brotherly gesture, Dexter pats her shoulder and murmurs soothing words. She allows him to comfort her, seems to need it. He wonders, not for the first time, who her people are, where she lives, whether she has a mother or father, sister or brother. But if she has someone to talk to, someone she trusts, she wouldn't be here with him, right now.

Through her sobs, she blurts bits and pieces of her story: "Went to a party… I was stoned… no one around… I was walking home and that sick fucker… Said he's a detective, he's been watching me, gonna arrest me for hooking. But I'm not—"

"Of course, you're not!"

"Grabbed my arm, threw me in the back seat. Drove me around, somewhere, I don't know, nowhere near any police station. Got in the back seat, stuck a gun in my ribs, did his thing…

Nothing I could do! I can still smell him." Her nose wrinkles again. The disgust. "Drove back, stopped where he found me. Said he's giving me a break, letting me go. Some break! Said keep quiet or he'll arrest me or kill me. Pushed me out on the street… And there's Chug, my angel. He was right there! Must've seen him." She stops. The tears and mucus flow. She blows her nose and says, "It's all my fault."

"That's the *last* thing you should think. None of this is your fault."

"Chug must've seen him throw me out the car. He was right there a second later."

"Nothing for you to feel bad about. No way you could've known who they were."

"After he did all that to me… I thought he was lying about being a detective. But now I know. In the news, they said he *is* a detective. So they must've known each other. I told Chug everything. He was gonna help me. Wanted me to turn him in and said he knew a way to do it. But I was scared. I should've done it. They could've locked him up before he killed Chug."

"Nothing's on you. This isn't on you. The man is an animal."

Her eyes widen with new fear. "They'll let him out. Like they did with the last one."

"Ain't gonna happen. The last one was a mistake. They won't let this man out. They got the right one this time, and cop killers stay locked up. You're safe."

"But how do they really know he's the one? They have to prove it, right? He could beat the case."

"Won't happen." Dexter pats her shoulder again and gives her a warm look meant to convey "trust me." But a worm of doubt wriggles inside him. What guarantees do they have? The news reports say nothing about the evidence against this detective, Kyle Rodman. How strong is their case? Are they trying to figure out *why* he did it? No one in the police department could possibly know Rihanna's story. The one person she told is dead.

As they sit together in silence, he senses they're both thinking the same thing. He's about to suggest it, but she speaks first, rejecting the idea. "I can't go to the police."

"You're strong enough for this. I feel it. You can tell them why this man killed Chug. Make sure he never sees the light of day again."

She shakes her head. "Uh-uh. This detective will have a story." On the word "detective," she squinches her nose against his bad smell. "He knows how to get his way. Made sure he showed me."

"You mean those threats he made? That's just a sick, guilty man trying to scare a young girl. Words with nothing behind them. He's got no fire power left. He's locked up, facing a murder rap. From inside...a *cop* on the inside? Nothing he can do to you."

"But no one will believe me. It's too long ago."

"I believe you. The rest of the world will too. Why would you be saying this if it wasn't true?"

She drops her head and they lapse into another silence. He feels the gears turning in her mind, searching for an objection. This is the reason she came here. To set up every possible objection and get his reaction, get him to help her knock down the barricades, one at a time. Here's the next one: "You're saying I should talk to a cop about another cop. Those men stick together. They cover for each other."

"Not all of them. Think of Chug. He was gonna help you turn him in."

She gazes off into a dream. "Yeah. He wanted to help me. But he wouldn't have done it. How could he? He was working undercover. He was 'Chug' and he had to stay that way. It was all on me."

"I think he would've gone all out for you, and his killer knew it too—" Dexter stops himself, not wanting to reignite her self-blame. Without skipping a beat, he says, "But I know a good person in the police department you can talk to."

"XT! You're the only man I would ever talk to about this."

"She's a she, not a he. The woman working this case is real good people. A fine woman detective, easy to talk to. I saw her not so long ago. She'll do right by you, I'm sure of it. You'll see."

Rihanna gives him a pleading look. "I'm scared."

"You're not alone, sister. We'll go together."

Dana wants the answers to questions left open after the arrest of Kyle Rodman. But it's up to Lina and Gil whether they'll let her in on their discoveries about the murderer's motive. Meanwhile, Dana will search for answers to other lingering questions. Nothing can stop her from doing a little investigating on a matter of family importance. It couldn't hurt and might help.

Natalie has gone through so much, she deserves peace of mind. Over the weekend, in the days following Friday's excitement, mother and daughter exchanged ideas about Professor Louden. Natalie's conflict about her thesis advisor has only worsened. Now that the error of his public opinion is confirmed beyond all doubt, she wonders how he could have made such a mistake.

Should Natalie raise the issue with him? There's no way she can avoid that conversation. By now he knows of the arrest. Journalists didn't mention Natalie's name or the details of Rodman stalking her, but the professor will put two and two together. When she canceled her afternoon seminar, she mentioned her trip to urgent care after being assaulted in Madison Square Park. It would be disingenuous to hold back the rest of the story, given his involvement in the case.

Monday afternoon, Dana calls Natalie to check up on her. "How's your workday going?" Subtext: *Have you seen Dr. Louden yet?*

"Fine. All good." The quaver in her daughter's voice tells Dana otherwise. "But…," Natalie starts.

Dana waits, and when the sentence isn't finished, she says, "Anything I can help with?"

"He isn't in today."

"Maybe tomorrow or another day. Everything will sort out in time."

"But I'm constantly thinking about it!"

"Try to get your mind on other things. Your lesson plan and your research. That'll be the best outlet." Dana doesn't mention that, with everything that's happened, she's *also* having a problem trying to concentrate on her work. They end the call with promises to talk again later tonight.

Maybe Professor Louden will open up to Natalie next time he sees her. Maybe not. Dana would love to confront him herself, but it isn't her place to get in the middle. She has another idea. Her former nemesis, a man who's now a good friend, might shed some light. If so, it's a way she can help her daughter reach an explanation.

When Dana calls Judge Kaplan, she offers to meet him downtown, in his chambers in the Criminal Courts building. But Seth declines. "No, I'll come to you. I'm in the mood for a change of scenery."

At the end of their workdays, six o'clock, Seth takes a seat across from Dana at her desk. He glances around her office. "So, this is upward mobility?" His mouth turns up in a wry smile. He still has those deep not-exactly-dimples, the attractive lines that carve into his cheeks like quote marks when he smiles. "Thank you, no, Judge Hargrove. My office is bigger than yours."

"Not only that, you also remain king of your own courtroom."

"Suits me fine." He nods at her injured arm. "Does the cast

come with the job?"

Dana laughs and relates the short version of the story behind her hairline fracture.

"They didn't mention your rescue attempts in the news articles I read about the arrest."

"A small concession to my dignity."

"Really? I didn't know journalists were so generous."

"Actually, I successfully evaded them."

"Clever woman that you are."

Something in his tone and choice of words sends her back in time to their rookie days when they bantered in night court, trying to stay awake. She had a little crush on him that disappeared after a single, disastrous date that ended in an argument. The eighties. Those two young adults are not the same people who sit here today. Wiser, deeper, experienced, more nuanced. Although they don't always see eye-to-eye, Seth has proven his friendship on many occasions. She respects his compassion and commitment to humanity, felt deepest for the underdog. But the powerless often exist on both sides: the victim, the perpetrator. While Seth and Dana judge criminal cases within a framework influenced by their respective experiences, the extremes have inched inward. These days, the outcomes they reach are likely to match or hit close to the same mark, driven by the core sense of justice they share.

She pulls herself back from the edge of reverie. "If you don't mind, this clever woman will get straight to the point."

"Go for it."

"I'm aware that you showed Emmett Louden the Q&A videos after the McBride hearing. I want to get your take on why the professor expressed the opinion he did, even after he saw those interviews."

"You want to know because of your daughter." Seth *also* gets straight to the point!

"Yes."

"You're aware of my friendship with Emmett, and I'm aware that your daughter works with him. He's her thesis advisor, right?"

Dana nods. "And she's trying to make sense of his blundering opinion in that television interview. She's questioning his expertise and his ethics."

"But this isn't *all* about her, is it, Dana?"

The question sets off a swell of emotion. She takes a deep, calming breath. This is about her daughter, but from the start, it was mostly about Patrick and Jared. "No, it isn't all about her. Louden's comments hurt the reputations of people I care about. But much of that is water under the bridge. Now, the most pressing concern I have is for Natalie. That man has a lot of influence over her academic career."

"Fair enough. You want to know why I showed him those videos?"

"I can guess why, and I'm not saying—"

"I hear you," he cuts in. "You're not criticizing *me* per se." The eyes twinkle, the quote marks deepen.

"Not at all!"

"Emmett and I go way back, as you know. He was my go-to expert witness. Helped me get acquittals for the wrongly accused, back in the day. Single eyewitness cases with a defense of mistaken ID."

"Potential miscarriages of justice. Averted," Dana agrees, while keeping her disagreement on *some* of those cases to herself. Cases with such strong circumstantial evidence of guilt that the questionable reliability of an eyewitness who saw a fraction of what happened did *not* mean the defendant was innocent. Reasonable doubt is just that, a weighing of the unknowns. Each case is unique, and Dana isn't about to argue with Seth over a handful of cases from the past. But she can't ignore that the same thought goes both ways. Isn't this exactly what happened in

Corey's case? Strong circumstantial evidence against him but faulty eyewitness testimony from people who saw only a small part of what happened. This combination ended in the wrong person being accused.

"Emmett's work on faulty identification is important. So, I showed him the Q&As. He has a burning interest in this stuff. He's studying the impact of virtual interview procedures on criminal justice. We should all be concerned about this after everything we've been through in the pandemic."

"Indeed, we should, and we are."

"Showing him the videos was an academic exercise. I'd already made my ruling from the bench, and nothing he could say would change that. I held the case for the grand jury. Impossible to do otherwise. It's a threshold standard and we had two eyewitnesses who claimed they saw McBride in a compromising position, along with other evidence. Credibility issues were up to the grand jury. You would have ruled the same way, Dana, your personal relationships notwithstanding."

She nods. Being true to her principles, she knows he's right.

"I had no misgivings about my ruling. But I saw problems in the eyewitness testimony, and that's why I couldn't, in good conscience, let Corey McBride have fun and games in Rikers for the months it might take before the grand jury opened. Emmett, by the way, saw the same problems in the testimony and told me so while we were watching the videos."

"Adding further mystery to his public opinion. Did he give you a heads-up before he appeared on Tanya Jordash's program?"

"He called and asked if I was okay with it before he accepted the invitation. The grand jury had just declined to indict McBride, so I assumed he was worried he might make me look bad if he told the world about weaknesses in the evidence. But I wasn't worried about that. My ruling stands. I said, 'Sure, go ahead. I can't stop you from expressing your opinion.' Emmett has always placed a high value on scientific integrity. I assumed he was going to say the witnesses were unreliable, if he said anything at all."

"So, you were just as surprised *then* as we are *now*."

"I was astounded. But I have my thoughts on why he did it."

"Please elaborate."

Seth hesitates and gives her a direct look. "Out of respect for you, Dana, I will. But you didn't hear this from me."

"Understood."

He thinks a moment, shifts his weight in his chair, and continues. "As much as I admire Emmett's work, the man has a side to him I find hard to stomach. In my office, after the McBride hearing, he said a few things that later led me to believe he was guided by pure self-interest. In other words, he made a calculated decision that a bit of sensationalism would help him more than a commitment to integrity. In this instance anyway. Have you noticed that he lives a rather lavish lifestyle?"

"I don't know the details, but I remember how he dresses for court. I could swear those are thousand-dollar suits."

"You have an eye for fashion." Their gaze locks in a smile, and Dana wonders if she hears irony in his tone. Her own wardrobe could be called classic, conservative, and tasteful. Not exactly high fashion. Seth goes on, "He lives in a penthouse apartment and drives a late model BMW. Monthly garage fees for that car rival the rental of a one-bedroom apartment. You don't get those things on a professor's salary. He makes most of his money in expert witness fees and speaking engagements. At the time of the McBride case, I think he was beginning to feel the pinch. All of his extras were drying up due to the pandemic."

Seth goes on to describe Louden's offhand comments, enough to indicate he was concerned about his tanking sources of income. "Got to keep my name out there," he told Seth. Didn't want the world to forget about him during the shutdown and preoccupation with illness and death. When things got back to normal, the money would flow his way again. And what better way to remain in the public eye than grab an offer of free publicity to expound on a media case, taking a stance consistent with the political climate. 2020. Anti-police, anti-prosecutor, anti-grand jury. Louden felt secure in expressing his "opinion" that the eyewitnesses were reliable, knowing that the grand jury proceedings weren't public and his insinuations about Corey McBride's guilt and DA Browne's corruption couldn't be checked. Dirt and scandal draw more attention than a good weather story about upstanding public servants.

"This case was all about law enforcement on every level," Seth says. "The victim, the accused, and the two district attorneys, current and former. What kind of splash would Emmett make if he said, very vanilla-like, 'So wonderful that the DA did the right thing, bringing this case to the grand jury, and so wonderful that the grand jury came in with the correct vote.' People would scroll to another story. The way he spun it, his interview clip was shown repeatedly on every social media platform, drumming up a demand for DA Browne's response."

"Jared wasn't going to dignify it with a response."

Seth looks away, nods, turns back to her. "I can't blame him. But you know, I also can't say that Emmett acted out of ill will against Browne. That was his only interview about the McBride case, and he couldn't have predicted it would go viral. After that, he grabbed every opportunity for free publicity, but he said nothing more about *this* case."

"He signed an affidavit for COG's petition to release the evidence."

"Well, yeah. He couldn't very well contradict what he'd already said. But he didn't mention the case again in any of his TV and internet appearances. He wanted people to remember his expertise as a cognitive psychologist, to keep his business prospects alive. His interviews and articles centered on his research and the general topic of wrongful incarceration based on mistaken eyewitness ID."

"And that's another appealing topic in the political climate of recent years."

Seth hardens. "Not just appealing and popular but *critical*."

"I don't disagree. You know I don't, Seth. Enlightenment and necessary change go hand in hand." A moment of silence. "And I have a daughter working very hard to build on our knowledge of why things can go wrong in criminal investigation. Her research can contribute to finding solutions."

"Admirable. I respect her work."

"If not mine."

He laughs. "Oh, you usually get things right these days!"

"Thank you so much."

"Including what you're doing here today."

"What's that?"

"Trying to find a diplomatic way, without mentioning my name, to convince your daughter she should continue her very important work with the professor."

"There's nothing higher on my list."

Tuesday. Regular office hours. A knock on the door. Emmett can't very well deny entry to his first visitor of the morning. Natalie left a voice mail warning him she'd be coming around on the stroke of ten "to talk about the arrest of Detective Rodman."

To be fair, the word "warning" is too harsh and says more about his own perception in the given circumstances. Natalie isn't the type to warn. She's sweet and lovely and inquiring. Smart and outspoken but respectful, a girl who knows her place. Diligent, a worker bee. If Emmett had any kind of "warning" it came from the obsequious Zach, who timidly mentioned Natalie's interest in the McBride case some days ago. "Just thought you'd like to know." Came as no surprise to Emmett, knowing of her mother's relationships with the people involved. Precisely why he didn't want her to gather data on this case.

In Natalie's message, her voice wavered enough to tell him she's nervous. Skipped a beat after saying "Detective Rodman" before adding, "I was there," in a softer voice he didn't hear at first. Had to replay her message. Of course she's nervous. Outrageous what she did! He imagines the ways she could have gotten herself mixed up in this sordid affair to the point of witnessing the man's arrest. Not just witnessing it, getting assaulted (by him?) in the park. What else did it mean when she called from urgent care to cancel her seminar?

Let her be nervous, as she should be. Emmett won't surrender to his own nerves, a palpitation in his chest and a little voice at the back of his mind that says, *Who's crime is worse?* An intelligent graduate student, a girl who knows better, has been mucking around in an open police investigation. Did she contact the witnesses? For a cognitive psychologist, tampering with witness memories is tantamount to academic insurrection. He'll dig it out of her and find out if she spoke to them. If so, the answer to *Who's crime is worse?* will be simple. On the scale of integrity, her misdeed weighs heavier than his single lapse, a brief abandonment of scientific method, warranted by the unique circumstances that befell him: The specter of ebbing significance and tanking wealth. He appeared on TV and uttered an opinion he didn't believe in. Knowingly. He did it for the sheer entertainment value, a way to get noticed. So what? Now, after everything, this comes down to *so what?*

And when Citizens for Open Government contacted him, what else could he do? He hadn't earned any expert witness fees for a very long time, and once he accepted their offer, he couldn't disagree with himself, could he? His affidavit was couched in general language, avoiding any inconsistency with what he'd said on TV.

Still, he lives under the threat of being called out, having his opinion slammed in his face as evidence of "incompetence." So far so good. No one has been interested enough in his 2020 interview with Tanya Jordash to revive it in the news cycle. No one is reminded of what he said. Why should they care? They've got the killer, a new face, and it's still a cop-on-cop murder to whet the appetite, everything else forgotten.

He's ready for her. Immediately after hearing the knock, he yells, "Come in." As Natalie enters, a small reality touches his mind and floats off into the ether. The differentials in age, experience, and authority. It hits him briefly when he sees her young face, but he quickly moves past the discomfort and ignores it. He draws her in with a stern, "Take a seat." She looks scared. All of this will be easier if he keeps her trembling and biting her lip.

But she doesn't hesitate. Launches right in. "I should have come to you sooner. I have a lot to tell you."

Emmett's instinct to deflect kicks in. "I'll say you do! Getting mixed up in a murder investigation!"

His muted rage has the desired effect. Momentarily. She quivers and shrinks, says, "Not good, I know," before straightening up again. She clears her throat and starts to explain everything she did, holding nothing back. He needn't confront her to pull out the truth. She fully admits she contacted Janjak Bernard, describes his audio recording, Rodman's threats, her meeting with Judge Hargrove, and her encounter with Rodman in Madison Square Park. It all makes perfect sense. In the Q&As, Emmett saw how Rodman led the witnesses to the testimony he desired. Manipulated them with suggestion.

When Natalie comes to the end of her revelations, she levels an accusation: "How could you possibly say those witness IDs were reliable?"

Her pluck and resolve surprise him. He didn't anticipate

such a formidable challenge. He freezes up and stammers the only valid tidbit in his favor. A dodge. "The, the factor I relied on is correct. You know that." He can hear his own defensiveness. "A recent opportunity to see a person in a relaxed setting is one of the best indicators of accurate facial recognition."

"But then you said this isn't a case of mistaken ID. That's wrong, and I think you knew it was wrong."

"Not technically. I was speaking generally. Most people define a mistaken ID case as one that hinges entirely on eyewitness identification. The McBride case involved many pieces of evidence on the question of guilt, not just the ID testimony."

She lets out a quiet sigh of disgust and shakes her head almost imperceptibly. Emmett can tell she's summoning all her strength to hold herself back. Because now (*my God, did she memorize my entire interview?*), in an acerbic tone, she delivers the kicker. "But then you said it was a 'slam-dunk' and the DA should have gotten an indictment. You made it sound like the DA's fault. It was a personal attack."

Emmett can't look into those prying eyes. He wriggles in his seat and directs his gaze at the hypnotic three-sphere perpetual motion sculpture on his desk. The Id, the Ego, and the Superego. His "attack" on the DA wasn't personal, he could say, but professional. No, not an "attack" at all but a legal opinion (though he isn't a lawyer) that the grand jury's vote was wrong and the DA had a role in that, because… How does the saying go? A prosecutor can convince a grand jury to indict anyone and anything, even a ham sandwich. DA Browne had gone that far, he *should* have been able to get an indictment. Wouldn't have mattered to the outcome of the case. McBride would have gotten off eventually, wouldn't he? They couldn't have met the higher standard of proof at trial.

Emmett knows he's mentally going off the rails on a line of BS. Natalie has backed him into a need to explain. So, he *will* explain. To an extent. "There are a few things you've overlooked, Natalie. Context and purpose. This wasn't my testimony as an expert witness in court. It wasn't a lecture to students or colleagues at a professional conference. It wasn't part of a scientific paper or study. If it were any of those things, then, yes, I would have been more careful with my comments. But it was entertainment, nothing more. A superficial interview with that fluff of a journalist, Tanya Jordash, about a popular topic that was making the rounds."

Will she notice the small inaccuracy in his explanation? He *did* sign an affidavit in support of the petition to unseal the evidence. Statements under penalty of perjury are the same as testifying in court. But, as he recalls, he stuck to generalities in that affidavit, harping on the fact (established) that these witnesses had just seen Corey McBride at the pub minutes before they (claimed) to have seen him again. The concluding statement of his "opinion" was not perjury. Mere professional dishonesty.

Natalie lifts her eyebrows in subdued astonishment. Or does that look on her face say, *I know* exactly *why you said those things!* He won't go there. This is a girl who's been a student most of her life, hasn't yet embarked on her profession, doesn't know the stress of shaping her career and building a reputation, supporting herself in a lifestyle she desires. Is it his place to teach her these realities of life? Certainly not.

"There's one thing I haven't overlooked," she says. "Words are important. We work with words, don't we? Part of our research is about the way people convert their perception and memories into language." She stops, and their eyes meet. He knows where she's going. "And the wrong words can be a problem," she continues. "They can get you to the wrong result and hurt people."

There's nothing he can say to refute her point. He accepts its theoretical validity. But he isn't willing to admit the implication that he hurt people—a supposition without proof.

She stands up and turns to go, this girl who waltzed right in here to challenge him. Is she merely leaving this meeting or leaving for good? Inured to the usual sycophants, Emmett has been startled into an odd admiration of Natalie's strength, the purity of her integrity. A reminder, an echo of himself, in his youth. Suddenly, he knows he doesn't want to lose her, wants to keep her here in the department. He needs to repair this as best he can. A small concession might be enough to put this matter behind them.

"Just one more thing, Natalie."

She swivels around and isn't afraid to meet his eyes.

"I do have some regrets about this. Since then, I haven't given an unfounded opinion in public on an issue of witness credibility. Won't do it again. The risk of bad consequences is unacceptable." Consequences for *himself*, primarily.

"Good," she says, and her face lightens a little. "Because that's what I expected from the first day I started working with you." They exchange lukewarm smiles, she turns, and walks out.

Jared Browne takes the seat at the head of his intimate conference table in his enormous ceremonial chambers on the eighth floor of the Manhattan DA's Office. To his right are Dana and Ricky Chin, the man who served as her deputy when she was chief of Trial Bureau 90 many years ago. Across from them sit the two lead investigators in the Rodman case, Gil and Lina.

Dana is surrounded by her closest colleagues from days past. Smart people she admires and respects. True public servants. Good friends.

She glances around the room. The awards, diplomas, photography, and artwork on the walls reflect Jared's achievements and personality. The furniture is arranged differently than it was in the McBride era when Dana served as an ADA, but Patrick still commands a presence. The most prominent photo on the wall is an image of the former DA shaking Jared's hand upon appointing him Executive Assistant District Attorney.

Many significant moments in Dana's career are tied to this office. Triumphs and losses, justice served or not, lessons learned from mistakes, discovery of the straight path, and resolve, always, to do what's right. Sitting here now, she's pulled into a heart swell of sensation from the energy that lives in this space. Memories of meetings with DA McBride. They talked strategy and debated ethics. She soaked up his advice and spilled her regrets. Even cried on his shoulder a few times.

"How's it feel to be back home?" Jared wants to know.

Dana's eyes glisten and a beatific smile graces her lips. With her good hand, she touches her heart. That brief response says it all.

With his trademark irreverence, Gil scolds Jared in a way that only the veteran investigator could get away with. "'Back home,' my ass, Mr. DA. Better watch the influence peddling. The lady here is a neutral."

"Judge Hargrove has proven she cannot be bought," Jared says.

"But there's no way to erase my history," Dana says.

"We all have one," Ricky adds. "A past full of life's lessons."

"Well, the Dane here forgot her lesson about keeping her kids away from dangerous felons. Seems this happened to her more than once."

Dana laughs. "You crack me up, Gil. You should've been a comedian."

"Yeah, and you should give up high heel ice skating. I'm worried about that grandkid on the way. Winter sports with grandma."

"I do tend to lose my head just a *little* when my kids are

involved. You know."

"Tiger Mom on the loose. We've seen it before."

Dana nods sheepishly.

"She just wanted that designer cast," Lina says. "I hear that Natalie picked out that lovely green color."

"Seafoam," Dana corrects her.

"Seafoam," Gil repeats prissily.

When they finish laughing, Dana says, "I appreciate you inviting me here."

"We knew you'd be hounding us for details if we didn't," the DA says.

"You're right about that. But rest assured that I'll recuse if Kyle Rodman ever takes an appeal to my court. A judge who saw the arrest and has a child for a witness can't sit on the case."

"Damn," Ricky says, tongue-in-cheek. "Thought I had a free ride to play fast and loose! Was counting on you to excuse my mistakes and affirm the conviction."

"There will be no mistakes," Lina says dryly, giving him a withering look. They break into toothy smiles. There's not much chance Ricky could screw this up even if he tried.

Rodman has been indicted for murder and remanded without bail. He sits in protective custody until plea or trial. A guilty plea is doubtful, no deals on the table. If he pleads, it'll have to be to the charge, with the DA's recommendation that the court impose the maximum sentence of 25 to life. Jared and Ricky assume he'll opt for a trial. What does Rodman have to lose? It's his only chance to get lucky. Maybe he can get off on a series of mistrials for technical mistakes or whacky holdouts on the jury. It's been known to happen. But no chance he'll be able to chip away at the rock-solid evidence against him. And although the prosecutor isn't required to establish a motive for the killing, that loose end has been tied up too. Dana has been curious to learn what that evidence is, and she hears it now, the full story Rihanna told Lina.

"How awful," Dana says. "Very brave of her to come forward. Clears everything up, what Marlon meant when he told Corey, 'Don't be surprised if you hear something about me.' He was going to turn Rodman in."

"And Rodman knew it," Lina says.

"Has he admitted any of this?"

"Nah," Gil says. "Lawyered up immediately. We don't need the scumbag's confession. He's cooked. Not a leg to stand on, even if the girl doesn't testify."

"Then you can avoid putting her on the witness stand?"

"That's the hope," Ricky says. "She's reluctant. We already have him on murder, so we didn't indict him for rape. Her testimony is purely about motive, and you know how tricky that is. Juries want to know why he did what he did even though we don't have to prove it."

"I don't want her to have to testify either," Jared says. "Worst case scenario, we call her on rebuttal if Rodman goes off on a defense of no motive. I don't think he'll touch that because he knows she came forward. We have an overwhelming case."

Besides the DNA evidence, details about Rodman's coverup are adding up, beyond what they already know about his manipulation of the eyewitnesses. As lead investigator, he interviewed everyone at the precinct who went to The Book and Brew that night. A fellow officer, during his interview, happened to mention seeing Kyle on the street, outside the pub. All very friendly and not suspicious, but Rodman made sure to exclude that officer's name from the case file. After Rodman's arrest, the officer contacted Lina about it. And an examination of records from Rodman's two cell phones led to an interesting discovery: a phone call he made in April 2020 to the reporter who broke the story of two eyewitnesses on the Brooklyn Bridge. Kyle Rodman was the anonymous police source that leaked the details of Corey

McBride embracing Marlon Stokes in a "death hug," setting off the media frenzy.

"I was still on leave when that story broke," Lina says. "I was pissed as hell. Thought Rodman might have been sloppy with the evidence but didn't blame him directly." She looks down and shakes her head. "How the hell did I end up assigning this case to—"

She breaks off, emotion clogging her throat. Her colleagues around the table fidget uncomfortably, feeling her pain.

"It's what I woulda done," Gil says in his gruff voice, oddly comforting. "I'd've assigned it to him. He was second in command. Nothing to kick yourself for."

Keeping her head low, Lina sighs and mutters, "God, I miss Mateo! Every minute of every day."

A shroud of silence falls over their gathering, an invisible embrace of unity and feeling. Lina sniffs and wipes an eye. In a moment, she lifts her head resolutely, and they're off and running again, discussing the evidence.

But few tears are shed, a week later, when Kyle Rodman's body is found in his cell, empty of blood, his thin mattress soaking up most of it. Not much sadness, but some people express regret, opining that the authorities erred in failing to place him on suicide watch. There was no indication, the experts determined. He passed a psych eval and was acting his usual cocky self. Other half-hearted accusations are leveled at prison authorities for their sloppiness. After shaving under guard in the shower room, Rodman somehow managed to take that razor with him into his cell.

A month later, after a full investigation, no correction officers will be facing charges.

LIFE

Tuesday, May 3, 2022

LET HER SLEEP. Peaceful, dreamless, deep. No fear, no pain.

Stillness. A spectrum of whites: machinery, pillow, bloodless face. Wrung out and empty, Josefina's shell remains, her essence released to the heavens.

Bianca stares dazedly, no sense of time. The nurse has left the room, giving her "a moment" at bedside. Tubes and IVs have been removed, poles wheeled away. Bianca gently touches the flesh as it begins to grow cold. Forehead, bald crown, earlobe, cheek, chin, arm and hand resting atop the sheet. Without Josefina's voice and breath, Bianca cannot grasp the meaning of this physical remainder, the housing for personhood. A warmer remnant rests in Bianca's other hand in her lap. A foot-long clump of lustrous black hair, saved from her niece's fallen tresses.

Before speech was lost a day ago, Josefina said this: "Don't cry, Auntie. I'm glad now that I tried the treatment. We tried everything. I love you." Remembering that voice, those words, Bianca allows the tears to spill from her eyes. The water flows down her cheeks and drips onto the strands of Josefina's hair.

She's thankful, at least, for the time they've had together these last few months. After the court decision, they yielded to the powers against them. They felt helpless to resist. Another appeal to the highest state court would have taken too long and was unlikely to succeed. Time was ticking, their separation growing unbearable.

So they surrendered. But the defeat also brought some relief. The Family Court approved a settlement agreement between the Merced family and the Administration for Children's Services. In exchange for relinquishing any further objections to chemotherapy, Josefina was allowed to return home. They've had five months of closeness, highs and lows, in and out of the hospital. Bianca will never know how Josefina would have fared without the treatments and their debilitating side effects. Will never know whether she would have died sooner—or later—than this, two weeks before her eighteenth birthday.

What good did it do them or the world to fight their case in court? To bring all that attention down on them? Bianca doesn't know, but she's proud they did it. And she's even prouder of her niece, who faced every challenge bravely and optimistically while suffering unimaginable physical pain. Through it all, Josefina found the strength to enjoy the brighter moments in her last days.

The lovely, youthful voice lives in memory, speaking words of love and reassurance. *I'm glad now that I tried.* A strong message, entirely for Bianca's benefit. Josefina wasn't thinking of herself, so close to death. She was concerned for her grieving aunt, doing her best to comfort her. What would those attorneys and judges in that court say now if they knew? The behavior and words demonstrate admirable maturity, adult maturity.

But Bianca doesn't dwell on that episode from the deepest, coldest days of winter. It's a beautiful spring afternoon, and Josefina has been released from pain. *I'm glad now that I tried.* Bianca hopes to God that Josefina meant what she said. She has every reason to believe it.

The glass doors at the entrance slide open, and a small, grief-stricken woman shuffles out. Without a glance, Dana and Evan rush past her, into the hospital lobby.

Dana stops at the information desk. "Maternity wing. Which floor?" She gave birth to both her babies in this hospital, but it's been almost three decades. The birthing center is in a separate, secluded wing, but how could anyone expect her to recall exactly *where*?

"Fifth floor, follow the yellow arrows to the skyway."

She grabs Evan's hand and gives it a tug, stepping out lively.

"Slow down, Grandma! They aren't going anywhere." He's enjoying the warmth of her hand in his. Dana's renewed enthusiasm for spontaneous displays of affection is part of the new closeness that has magically blossomed between them since his appointment to the Court of Appeals. They've already survived three long separations, two weeks each time, when he traveled to Albany for court sessions. Is it true what they say? Dana and Evan seem to be living proof that absence does make the heart grow fonder. Either that, or the fondness that has always existed bursts more readily into demonstration.

In the elevator, Dana and Evan are pushed to the back by a half dozen people squeezing in, each one eyeing the excited new grandmother talking on her cell phone. She's giving Travis a heads-up. "Just got on the elevator. We're on the way up!"

On the fifth floor, Travis is waiting at the elevator door to show them the way. He looks tired but the happiest Dana has ever seen him. It's that special look that takes possession of every recent witness to the magic, wonder, and mystery of new life.

"Congratulations, son," Evan says.

"Thanks, Dad, but I think Ginger gets all the kudos."

"They don't call it labor for nothing," Dana says. "How are mother and baby doing?"

"Perfect. All good. Troy is coming by soon for the first well visit." Of course. Dana didn't know their choice of pediatrician, but it makes perfect sense. Cheryl's husband, Dr. Troy Belson, is one of the best in his field.

Travis leads them through the skyway and into a broad corridor. "Our room is at the end. Ginger's mom is already here," he adds with an oblique look at his mother. Does he think it wise to give her advance notice? After all this time, Travis couldn't possibly believe that Dana needs mental preparation for a meeting with Vesma. In a distant past, the two women faced off against each other in court. Early nineties. In the most notable case, a homicide prosecution against a late term abortionist, the opposing attorneys were in advanced stages of pregnancy, Ginger and Travis kicking their respective bellies. Interesting how life throws unexpected curveballs. Now, related by marriage, the mothers-in-law cordially enjoy each other's company.

"Hernando too?" Dana asks. Ginger's stepfather.

"In court. He'll be here later. He's in the middle of a trial."

At the threshold, a nurse stops them for handwashing and PPE. Facemasks, hair coverings, paper gowns, booties over shoes. The sight of everyone papered up is familiar, something seen too frequently in recent times.

Ginger, the only maskless adult, sits up in bed, cradling the sleeping baby. Travis goes right up to her and stands alongside, stroking her crown of thick auburn hair. From a chair in the corner, Vesma gives Dana and Evan a silent "hello" with a nod and shining eyes between facemask and hair covering. Ginger greets them with a glorious smile lighting up her face. Flushed and happy, she beams an enviably healthy glow. "Meet Lilija," she says. "All seven pounds, three ounces of her." The baby has delicate porcelain skin and wisps of orange-brown hair poking out from the blanket that covers part of her head.

"How lovely," Dana says in a whisper.

"A beautiful baby," Evan agrees.

They tiptoe closer. The room is bathed in ethereal radiance.

A month ago, Dana stepped into a similar atmosphere when she visited Nia and her newborn. But the feeling today is more intense. Dana is fully connected and utterly euphoric, enclosed in a floating, blissful bubble of family. She squeezes Evan's hand. He squeezes back. *We started this, way back when,* their touch seems to say.

"Hello, Lilija." Her granddaughter. "So lovely."

Travis spells out the name and adds, "It's Latvian," with a glance at his mother-in-law. Maybe *this* is the source of slight uneasiness Dana senses in her son. She certainly doesn't mind. Not at all! She thinks it's wonderful to honor Vesma's Latvian heritage this way. Her parents were "displaced persons" who fled Latvia when the Germans and Soviets invaded their homeland during World War II. After a few years in a DP camp, they settled in America.

"I love the name!" Dana assures him. "So, you don't pronounce the 'j' at all?"

Vesma explains. "It sounds a bit like a 'y.' In Latvian, the country name also has a 'j' like Lilija's name." Latvija.

"Travis and I spent forever going over names," Ginger says, "and this one just kept coming back to us."

"As you can see, I had nothing to do with it," Vesma says dryly. "But, of course, I'm happy!"

Just then, Natalie and Cheryl walk into the room, and a few minutes later, Ginger's older brother Sean arrives. The baby sleeps through the hubbub, the voices now well above a whisper. After ten minutes of a growing party mood, Doctor Belson steps in. Good-naturedly, he exclaims, "Quite a congregation! You know, you're in violation of every rule. How did you get away with this?"

"We were just leaving, Doc," Evan says.

"Good! I'm going to take a look at that baby."

Travis stays while the rest of them file out and shed their

gowns. Happy chatter continues in the waiting room. Cheryl offers to hold a party in her Westchester home when everyone is up for it. The new grandparents excitedly arrange babysitting schedules with the hope that the "kids" will let them take turns with Lilija. Finally, with hugs and goodbyes all around, Dana and Evan break away.

Outside, they walk into a soft spring evening in the city. Pedestrians and traffic noises are noticed less than the fragrance of flowers in sidewalk tree wells and the delicious touch of a gentle breeze on their cheeks.

Holding hands, swinging their arms playfully, they stroll in silence and delight. Three blocks from the hospital, they wake up to realize they don't know where they're going.

"Where to, Madam? I think we're entitled to a celebratory dinner."

"We definitely deserve it after working so hard to have that baby."

"Years of solid effort."

"A labor of love."

"Let me offer the fruits of my labor and treat you to a fine meal. Something expensive for a change."

"You're such a gentleman. How about that French bistro we used to go to? In the old neighborhood."

"Would be nice, but I'm afraid it might have been one of the casualties of 2020."

"A shame. I really don't care where we go, as long as there's wine."

"Done deal," Evan agrees.

"And, as long as you let me daydream now and then about the baby."

"Ditto."

"I can't wait to hold the little one. It's been so long since I've held a baby."

Evan stops dead on the pavement, bringing her to a halt. Pedestrians nearly bump into them and dodge to avoid the obstacle they create. "I'm offended," he says with a hurt look.

"How so?"

"It hasn't been so long. You forgot about *this* baby."

"How could I forget you, darling?"

Evan takes Dana in his arms and throws her back in a kiss to rival Eisenstaedt's iconic "V-J Day in Times Square" photo. Alas, no one stops to snap a picture, but a few people, as they pass, dart embarrassed glances at the old folks shamelessly pressed against each other, oblivious to the world around them.

« »

ACKNOWLEDGMENTS

TO THE Honorable Daniel D. Angiolillo, special thanks for contributing your insight and experience during the writing of *Power Blind*. I'm grateful for our friendship and the years of our working relationship, a highlight of my legal career and intellectually rewarding.

To my sisters Annette Swackhamer Drohan and Aina Louise Kemanis, thank you for supporting my writing endeavors from the very start. Your comments, critiques, and suggestions for all the Dana Hargrove novels have been invaluable.

To C.W.P. Jones, many thanks for reading an earlier draft and contributing your legal expertise and stellar editing skills.

To my husband Kevin Stamey, my biggest fan and discerning beta reader, I couldn't have written all these novels without you! Thank you for your love and unfailing support.

And thank you, dear readers! My message to you is on the next page...

DEAR READER,

This has been an exciting decade for me, 2012 to 2022, bringing you six Dana Hargrove novels. I'm calling *Power Blind* my last, without excluding the possibility that, one day, I might get the urge to write another: A prequel or sequel or an in-between-quel.

I introduced Dana Hargrove to the world when she was twenty-six, and I leave her, for now, at the age of sixty. Each novel is a standalone, taking place in the year indicated:

Thursday's List (1988)
Homicide Chart (1994)
Forsaken Oath (2001)
Deep Zero (2009)
Seven Shadows (2015)
Power Blind (2022)

Dana has ridden the wave of change in criminal justice and law enforcement from the eighties to the current day. Some of the misdemeanor cases Dana handled in *Thursday's List* would not be prosecuted today, and there've been other significant changes in criminal procedure and alternatives to incarceration. Over the years, Dana's views have evolved with societal trends and changes in the law while she continues to hold fast to her core values. I hope you've enjoyed these stories and discovered food for thought in the dilemmas she has faced.

If *Power Blind* is your first Dana Hargrove novel, let me whet your appetite for the others with the brief references to earlier stories woven into these pages. For young Dana's disastrous date with Seth Kaplan and the investigation that brought Dana and Evan together, read *Thursday's List*. Natalie's reference to Travis's nanny when he was two years old is at the center of *Homicide Chart*. The murder case that pitted Dana and Vesma against each other when they were pregnant with Travis and Ginger is described in *Forsaken Oath*. Vesma plays a more prominent role in *Deep Zero*, along with the grand jury investigation that set thirteen-year-old Natalie on her obsession with witness perception and memory. And Gil's and Natalie's comments about previous threats to the Goodhue-Hargrove family come into play in *Seven Shadows*. Also in *Seven Shadows*, you can enjoy Evan's law class lecture incorporating Elvis's "Jailhouse Rock"!

Let me know what you think! Now's the time to return to the page for *Power Blind* at your online bookseller and leave a reader review of any length. You can also send me a direct message through the contact page on my website, vskemanis.com. While you're there, subscribe to my blog and take advantage of the free e-book offer for one of my award-winning story collections.

To keep up with the latest on my books and life, look for "V.S. Kemanis" on BookBub, Facebook, Twitter, Goodreads, YouTube, and Instagram.

Thank you for reading!

V.S.K.

January 2022

P.S. For insights into legal issues explored in *Power Blind*, go to the next page for a special afterword…

AFTERWORD FOR LAW BUFFS

YOU DON'T NEED to be a law buff or lawyer to enjoy the Dana Hargrove novels, but if you like legal stuff, here is some info with a few citations for further reading.

In my legal career in criminal justice, I've worked on both sides of the aisle and at center, for the courts. My experience includes law clerk to appellate judges, assistant district attorney for the Manhattan DA, assistant deputy attorney general for the New York State Organized Crime Task Force, court-appointed appellate counsel for criminal defense, and principal court attorney and supervisor for the Appellate Division of New York State Supreme Court. So, while the cases in the Dana Hargrove novels are born in my imagination, they always incorporate real legal principles, New York statutes, and caselaw.

The cases in *Power Blind* take place during a time of sweeping change in New York criminal procedure. Public demand for transparency and accountability in policing and prosecution led to a shift in prosecutorial authority from local district attorneys to the New York State Attorney General in cases involving deaths allegedly caused by law enforcement officers.

In July 2015, by Executive Order No. 147, New York's governor appointed the state attorney general as the special prosecutor "to investigate, and if warranted, prosecute certain matters involving the death of an unarmed civilian, whether in custody or not, caused by a law enforcement officer." In *Power Blind,* the fictional Manhattan District Attorney Jared Browne investigated the fictional Marlon Stokes murder that occurred on March 16, 2020. The state AG declined to take the case because Police Officer Corey McBride was not initially a suspect and Police Officer Stokes did not clearly fall within the definition of "civilian."

Had the Stokes murder occurred a few months later, the AG might have handled the case. On June 12, 2020, legislation was enacted broadening the scope of the 2015 executive order beyond cases involving "unarmed civilians." New York Executive Law Section 70-b authorizes the AG to:

> "investigate and, if warranted, prosecute any alleged criminal offense or offenses committed by a person, whether or not formally on duty, who is a police officer…concerning any incident in which the death of a person, whether in custody or not, is caused by an act or omission of such police officer…or in which the attorney general determines there is a question as to whether the death was in fact caused by an act or omission of such police officer…"

In *Power Blind,* the fictional case against Officer Michael Welton for the July 2021 death of Lonnie Douglas in the Bronx was handled by the state AG, not the Bronx DA, pursuant to this authority.

Also mentioned briefly in *Power Blind,* New York attorneys and courts were acclimating to new criminal procedure statutes on pretrial release and pretrial discovery, effective January 1, 2020. New York Criminal Procedure Law Section 510.10 ("Securing order; when required; alternatives available") abolished cash bail for most misdemeanors and non-violent felonies. New York Criminal Procedure Law Section 245.10 ("Timing of discovery") provides an accelerated timeline for the prosecutor's disclosure duties, and Section 245.20 ("Automatic discovery") provides an expanded list of items the prosecutor must disclose to the defense, even absent a request.

During this same period, a movement to amend the statute governing grand jury secrecy has been underway. In *Power Blind*, the fictional organization Citizens for Open Government filed two petitions for disclosure in the midst of this limbo, when legislation was proposed but not yet enacted. Accordingly, Dana's court applied the traditional legal analysis to COG's petitions.

At the time of this writing, a bill which passed the New York State Assembly in June 2021 died in the New York State Senate in January 2022 and was returned to the Assembly. While some version of this legislation may eventually pass, it is too early to tell. Here, below, is a summary of the longstanding statute and caselaw, with comparison to the proposed law.

New York Criminal Procedure Law Section 190.25(4)(a) provides:

> "Grand jury proceedings are secret, and no grand juror, or other person...may, except in the lawful discharge of his duties or upon written order of the court, disclose the nature or substance of any grand jury testimony, evidence, or any decision, result or other matter attending a grand jury proceeding... Nothing contained herein shall prohibit a witness from disclosing his own testimony."

Caselaw under this statute has required applicants for the release of grand jury materials to surmount a prohibitively high hurdle. Under the traditional analysis, an applicant must establish a "compelling and particularized need" strong enough to overcome the presumption of confidentiality. Only if that threshold is passed will the court balance the public interest in disclosure against the public interest favoring secrecy (*see e.g. Matter of District Attorney of Suffolk County*, 58 NY2d 436, 444 [1983]). For an application of the traditional legal analysis (in a case I argued in the Appellate Division courthouse described in *Power Blind!*) read *Melendez v City of New York*, 109 AD2d 13 (1985). In that case, the victim of a police shooting wanted to use grand jury evidence in his civil lawsuit against the city. Release of materials was denied despite the liberal discovery rules for civil cases.

Courts have rejected the argument that curbing public unrest and restoring confidence in the grand jury system and the prosecutor are enough to establish the threshold "compelling and particularized need" for disclosure. Noteworthy cases denying release of grand jury materials include *Matter of Hynes, District Attorney of Kings County*, 179 AD2d 760 (1992) (grand jury declined to indict motorist responsible for fatal accident that triggered race riots in Crown Heights Brooklyn), and *Matter of James v Donovan*, 130 AD3d 1032 (2015) (grand jury declined to indict police officer for the death of Eric Garner during his arrest).

By contrast, the proposed law, in effect, undercuts the traditional approach by making "significant public interest" in the investigation a key factor favoring disclosure. The bill (A05845) which passed the New York State Assembly in June 2021 provides that a court may order disclosure upon making three findings:

> "(i) a significant number of members of the general public in the county in which the grand jury was drawn and impaneled are likely aware that a criminal investigation had been conducted in connection with the subject matter of the grand jury proceeding; and
>
> "(ii) a significant number of members of the general public in such county are likely aware of the identity of the subject against whom the criminal charge…was submitted to a grand jury, or such subject has consented to such disclosure; and
>
> "(iii) there is significant public interest in

disclosure."

In addition to all these changes in law and policy, New Yorkers were dealing with lockdown measures of the pandemic in 2020-2021, some of which are key to the plot of *Power Blind*. By executive order effective March 16, 2020, the governor closed all nonessential businesses (Executive Order No. 202.3). Also on March 16, 2020, New York City's mayor closed all schools with an order to transition to remote learning, and the state's chief administrative judge suspended all nonessential functions in the court system, transitioning essential functions (*e.g.* criminal arraignments) to video remote proceedings. Since then, up to the time of this writing, lockdown measures and other government mandates have gone through several permutations, either extended or modified or terminated and reinstituted.

By Executive Order 202.8, dated March 20, 2020, the governor "tolled" all limitations periods, civil and criminal. Subsequent extensions of the executive order, however, used a combination of terms, "tolled" and "suspension" (*e.g.* Executive Order 202.67). With respect to the time limits for commencing civil lawsuits, this ambiguity led to the debate Evan had with a member of the Commission on Judicial Nomination during his interview in *Power Blind*. On the criminal side, the closing of the grand jury and suspension of time limits had serious implications for defendants' statutory and constitutional rights. Prosecutors have a six-day time limit from arrest to indictment to avoid pretrial release of a person held on a felony complaint. With the grand jury closed, emergency measures for virtual preliminary hearings were instituted (*see* New York Criminal Procedure Law Sections 180.65 and 180.80).

As for Josefina's story in *Power Blind*, the inspiration came from a news story about a Connecticut seventeen-year-old who experienced a similar ordeal of court-imposed treatment against her wishes (*see In re Cassandra C.* [Connecticut Supreme Court 2015]). Some states have adopted the "mature minor doctrine" by statute or caselaw. New York is not one of them. New York Public Health Law Section 2504 establishes eighteen as the age of consent for medical treatment, with certain exceptions. Policy Statement No. 99-09 of the New York State Department of Health asserts that "an individual who is legally a minor cannot give effective legal/informed consent to treatment and therefore, conversely, cannot legally refuse treatment."

The New York Civil Liberties Union has published a comprehensive *Guide to Minors' Rights in New York* which includes the topic of refusal and consent to medical treatment. Where New York trial courts have considered the issue, they have ordered minors to undergo medical treatments against their wishes. In *Matter of Thomas B.* (152 Misc 2d 96 [NY Fam Ct 1991]), the court ordered a fifteen-year-old diagnosed with a tumor to undergo a surgical biopsy despite his vehement objections. In *Matter of Long Island Jewish Medical Center* (147 Misc 2d 724 [NY Sup Ct Queens Co 1990]), the court found merit to the mature minor doctrine, encouraged appellate courts and the state legislature to adopt it, but found that the child in that case, a few weeks shy of eighteen, was not mature enough to understand the consequences of his refusal, for religious reasons, to undergo blood transfusions. Other commentators have advocated for adopting the mature minor doctrine in New York (*see* "A Child's Right to Consent to Medical Treatment," *NYSBA Health Law Journal*, Winter 2020, Vol. 25, No. 1; "The Mature Minor Doctrine: Should a Mature Minor Have the Right to Refuse Life-Sustaining Treatment in New York?" *Albany Gov't Law Review Blog*, Feb. 1, 2010).

« »

OPUS NINE BOOKS

All works published by Opus Nine Books are dedicated to the nine members of the family headed by John and Kate Swackhamer at 3 South Trail, Orinda, California — a large world under one small roof.